A NEW HOPE IN THE HIGHLANDS

Rachel Debrave writes contemporary and fantasy romance with an often twisty, dark sense of humour and a taste for the emotionally charged. Expect quickfire chemistry, emotional depth, swoon-worthy MMCs, and heroines who don't just survive – they set the pace.

When she's not writing, Rachel can be found wandering the Scottish countryside with her dog, Daisy, reading, or playing the piano (rarely very well!) with dramatic flair.

You can find her on Instagram @racheldebrave and in all the other usual corners of the internet.

A New Hope in the Highlands is the first book in *The Haddon House* Series.

A NEW  IN THE HIGHLANDS

A Haddon House Book

RACHEL DEBRAVE

First published in 2025 by Rachel Debrave

Copyright © 2025 Rachel Debrave
Paperback Edition

Rachel Debrave has asserted her right to be identified as the author of this Work in accordance with the Copyright, Designs and Patents Act 1988.

This novel is a work of fiction. Names and characters are the product of the author's imagination and any resemblance to actual persons, living or dead, is entirely coincidental.

All rights reserved. No part of this publication may be reproduced, stored in a retrieval system, or transmitted in any form or by any means, electronic, mechanical, photocopying, recording or otherwise, without the prior permission of the copyright owner.

A CIEP catalogue record of this title is available from the British Library

ISBN: 978-1-0684703-1-8

ACKNOWLEDGMENTS

Huge thanks to

Kat Howes, Nicola Davidson, Jackie O'Neil, and Willeke Schouten – thank you for being my fabulous and encouraging beta readers, back when I'd barely figured out what a beta reader even was.

Susan Buchanan – the most generous author, who gave me so much of her time and wisdom on this (sometimes terrifying!) indie journey. Forever grateful.

The Procrastination Begone WhatsApp group – my incredible, inspiring, and supportive bunch of writer friends. I feel so blessed to have found my way to you all. 🖤

The Scottish Chapter of the Romantic Novelists' Association.

The Romantic Novelists' Association.

– The NWS scheme and the 2024 Conference were the catalysts I'd been needing and waiting for. Thank you so much to all the volunteers who make the magic happen.

My amazing ARC Team – your early reviews and willingness to shout about my books on social media mean the world. Thank you.

Rachel from Rachel's Random Resources – thank you for filling up my blog tour calendar and to all the fantastic bloggers taking part.

Sue Baker from the *Riveting Reads and Vintage Vibes* Facebook group – for your launch day celebration and the daily posts that always bring a smile. Thank you for your kindness and support!

To all of my super-supportive fellow authors – your support is much appreciated.

Thank you to the catnip to my wildcat for inspiring me, and to my friend, Ed, for the loan of his name – *and no, Ed, this book isn't about you!*

Of course, not forgetting my family – your unwavering love, encouragement, and general cheerleading make all of this possible. Love you lot immensely!

And to *you*, my lovely readers – thank you for investing in my stories and in this author journey. There's so much more to come, so strap in for the ride. 😊

If you'd like to connect with me about my books, feel free to email me at rachel@racheldebrave.com.

A very special thank you to:

Claire at *Jaboof Design Studio* – for my gorgeous cover, and her endless patience with my obsession with a *certain* actor in bringing Edward to life!

Julia King – for her superb copyediting and proofreading: www.reedsy.com.

Paul Salvette and his team at *BB eBooks* – for expert formatting: www.bbebooksthailand.com.

AUTHOR'S NOTE

This is an adult novel featuring open-door romance, steamy scenes, and moments of tension involving consent. It contains explicit sexual content and adult themes, and is therefore intended for mature readers (18+).

While the tone of the story is largely light-hearted, humorous, and heartwarming, it does explore some sensitive themes, including historical family trauma, medical topics and terminology, and instances of unwanted advances.

Just a quick heads-up for my lovely American and Canadian readers: this book is written from a British perspective, so you'll notice British spelling and a few UK-specific expressions sprinkled throughout.

Happy reading – enjoy the ride, and may your coffee be strong and your snacks plentiful!

With love,
RDB x

DEDICATION

For anyone who's ever hit reset on their life.

May you find hope in the endings, courage in the unknown, and strength in every new beginning.

CHAPTER 1

SCARLETT LEANED AGAINST the far corner wall, sipping her negroni as she observed the mingling guests, her eyes drifting around the room as she soaked in the atmosphere.

Not bad.

She nodded to herself, feeling satisfied with the outcome of her weeks of planning. The opulence of the venue was exactly what her mother-in-law, Tara, had requested – luxurious Georgian architecture blended seamlessly with just the right touch of modern, bold glitz. The presence of a resident French Michelin-star chef was an added triumph, with polite servers gliding through the crowd, offering beautifully presented platters of gourmet delights. Scarlett noted people's eyes widening as they sampled the truffle arancini, mini lobster tacos, and stuffed Peppadew peppers, and smiled.

Her gaze travelled across to the far side of the room, where a pretentious jazz band played on a small stage, exuding the haughty air she knew the guests enjoyed. For a birthday party, it wasn't a bad effort at all.

"Happy birthday, Scarlett!" A small balding man approached her, and pulling her towards him, his hands settling on the small of her back, a millimetre away from being inappropriate, he kissed her on both cheeks. "What a delightful evening."

Scarlett smiled politely, struggling to remember the

man's name.

"Thank you very much," she said, trying to take a step back, but he filled the gap to speak closer to her ear.

"And the food! Mon Dieu!" His eyes scanned their immediate vicinity, and he lowered his voice even further. "Better than sex!"

He began laughing loudly and nudged Scarlett, who smiled again and proceeded to drain her glass in one gulp, quickly raising it to show it was empty. "So glad you're enjoying it. Time for a refill."

"Don't enjoy yourself too much now, dear." He winked at her, and spotting someone across the room, he moved away. "Gerald! My God, it's been an age!"

"Grand party, Mrs Shrewsbury!" Another random person touched Scarlett's shoulder and kissed her. Smiling and nodding her thanks, she continued to move through the room, searching for Jason.

"Happy birthday, dear," an older woman greeted her.

"Thanks. Lovely to see you."

Then another.

"Great that you could make it."

And another.

"Thank you, much appreciated."

By the time she reached the bar, she felt exhausted. The girl serving smiled at her.

"Same again?" she asked.

"Please," Scarlett responded, handing over her empty glass whilst still scanning the room for Jason.

It wasn't that Scarlett didn't appreciate the compliments or well wishes, but large social events had always pushed her out of her comfort zone – especially if it placed her at the centre of attention.

Organising gatherings like this was second nature to her; she regularly handled Jason's book launches and the openings of the family's hotels – over the years it had literally become her full-time job. But when it came to her own party, she preferred something quieter, more intimate.

Despite her pleas to Jason for a more low-key celebration – perhaps a weekend in the Lakes or even an escape abroad, just the two of them – she had still ended up planning this monster event, most of it by herself. Jason's schedule was packed, and her thirty-fifth birthday had conveniently aligned with the completion of his most recent novel – the grand finale to his six-book series, with film rights now in negotiation.

It was an exciting time for him, and she understood his desire to celebrate, so when he suggested a party, Scarlett had reluctantly agreed, even though everyone knew she hated them – but, as Jason told her, it had the bonus of being a great PR opportunity. Tara, of course, wasted no time in vocalising her expectations of the event either.

As Scarlett glanced towards the entrance, she finally spotted Jason tucked in the corner near the coatroom, deep in conversation with their young lodger, Angelica – the daughter of one of Jason's old school friends.

At first, nothing seemed unusual. Jason had always made an effort to ensure Angelica felt at home, helping her avoid the pangs of homesickness. Her parents had moved to France the previous year while she was still in her second year studying Modern Languages at the university in Bath. Scarlett had suggested she stay with them until she graduated, and Jason had agreed with little fuss. Angelica was a sweet girl, after all.

Scarlett was about to turn her attention elsewhere when something in their body language shifted and caught her eye. Something felt *off*.

That's when she saw it – Jason placed a hand on

Angelica's abdomen, and in turn, she gripped his belt. He leaned in closer, his expression serious, mirroring Angelica's intense gaze. They continued speaking in hushed, loaded tones – words Scarlett couldn't hear but didn't need to. The silent exchange between them said it all.

They're fucking.

SCARLETT WASN'T SURE if it was the negronis she'd downed the night before or the shock of what had apparently unfolded right under her own roof, but when she woke the following morning, it took her a long moment to piece together what had happened.

She knew she was alone in their bed and her head was pounding, her mouth bone-dry. She felt sick. Forcing her eyes open, she squinted against the autumnal sun that blasted through the window like an assault. Groaning, she draped an arm over her face and slowly fragments of the previous night came back to her – coming home in a haze, angrily packing a bag.

She peeked out from under her arm, hoping it had all been a terrible dream, but the small case sitting by the window confirmed it was all *very* real. The nausea surged again as she sat up.

Holy mother of shit.

She swung her legs over the edge of the bed and reached for the clothes she had tossed aside the day before, when she'd been rushing around to shower and dress for the party. Tugging on the crumpled t-shirt and jeans, she was at least relieved to find she'd had the presence of mind to charge her phone. She tapped the screen, bringing it to life. One word flashed back at her: *June.*

Scarlett blinked in confusion.

Then it all hit her.

After flying into a rage and humiliating herself in front of all their guests, she'd stormed out, flagged down a taxi, come home, packed a bag, and sent a message to her mother, June – the woman who had disappeared almost fourteen years ago, leaving nothing but a nonsensical note, and who she had barely spoken to in over six years. Not since Maggie's funeral, when her mother had insisted Scarlett take her number, *just in case*.

Apparently, *just in case* just happened.

Scarlett scanned through the messages, impressed by the weirdly formal but well-written texts she had sent to her mother – especially given her alcohol-fuelled rage at the point she'd written them.

> **Scarlett:** Hi Mum. It's Scarlett. Thanks for the birthday card and flower seeds. Very thoughtful. So, to cut to the chase. Turns out Jason has been shagging our lodger who is very young. Very pretty. Also very pregnant with his baby. I can't stay here. I have nowhere to go. Can I stay with you until I sort myself out. Please. Thanks, Scarlett.
>
> **June:** Oh, Scarlett. I am so sorry! And on your birthday?! Are you ok? Of course you're not ok. Sorry. You do remember I am in Scotland?
>
> **Scarlett:** Yes. That's perfect.
>
> **June:** Do you maybe want to think on it?
>
> **Scarlett:** Not really, no. Unless you don't want me to come?
>
> **June:** I didn't say that. It's just all very sudden.
>
> **Scarlett:** Are you saying I should stay?
>
> **June:** No. I've told you before, you're always welcome here with me.
>
> **Scarlett:** Yeah, you said.

June: *Do you still have the address? Are you driving?*

Scarlett: *Yes. To both.*

June: *Ok. I'll speak to the laird, but I'm sure he won't mind – I have a spare room. When are you coming?*

Scarlett: *I'll leave in the morning. Probably stop over somewhere ... I'll let you know.*

June: *Ok, text me when you're on your way.*

Scarlett: 👍

Scarlett: *Are there any jobs going? I'd like to stay busy.*

June: *Not sure, I can ask him when I speak to him about you staying ... There won't be anything very glamorous. Maybe some cleaning? Gardening? Appreciate that's not really your thing. Don't worry about that for now though. We'll figure it all out.*

Scarlett: *Great, thanks.*

June: *Are you sure about this?*

Scarlett: *Yes.*

June: *ok.*

What a shit show.

Leaving her case by the front door, Scarlett had no desire to see or speak to Jason, but she needed to grab her handbag from the sunroom, and she could hear him rustling around in the kitchen.

"Scarlett—"

"Save it!" Scarlett walked past him to look for her handbag. "Have you seen my bag?"

"We need to talk about this." Jason was following her around the room like a retriever as she moved cushions around, carelessly discarding them on the floor in her search.

The quick movements made her feel dizzy to the point she needed to sit down for a minute, and feeling something uncomfortable underneath her, she realised she was sitting on it.

Jason took this to mean she was open to talking and sat across from her whilst Scarlett fidgeted around, removing the bag from under her. She was feeling increasingly crappy and leaned her head back, closing her eyes.

"It just happened, Scarlett," he said, taking hold of her hand. She noticed how hot and clammy his skin felt. She didn't like it.

Jason continued, "If I could go back and change it, I would, in an instant."

Scarlett couldn't move, let alone speak. Her chest felt tight and heavy, as if her heart was sinking deep into her stomach with the weight of his words. Even breathing felt like a monumental effort. And she felt sick.

I may actually just die here.

The idea seemed more appealing each time he spoke.

"Scarlett, it was a moment of madness. What can I say? I was a fool."

"Is this why we haven't had sex in months?" Scarlett straightened and opened her eyes. "I mean, it's not been very good for a long time. Did you get bored?" She paused for a moment and her eyes widened. "Have there been others?"

"Oh God, I, no, I – Scarlett, I'm so sorry." He shook his head, running his hands through his blonde hair.

Scarlett watched him, wondering if he'd been doing that all night, as it looked like it needed a good wash.

"I actually have no more words right now."

"I'm so sorry." He stroked the back of her hand with his thumb.

She sighed. "So am I."

A silence descended, heavy with pain and regret, as if they both realised there were no magical words to fix the damage done. To be honest, she hadn't been *happy* for a while, but she didn't think you were supposed to be after being married this long. She thought it was more a matter of being content at this stage. Although now she thought about it, she wasn't sure if she'd even been that.

"I can't ask her to leave. She's carrying my child."

Scarlett stilled – stunned by the barefaced truth of it all.

Just wow.

There it was. The real sting. Angelica was having his baby.

Holy fuck.

She already knew this from the previous night. But hearing it again, sober, was like having it speared through her heart a second time.

The child they had spoken at great lengths about not having. After all, his career had to be the focus, their marriage and relationship a priority. A child didn't fit into that. Or at least it hadn't until now, with their twenty-one-year-old tenant carrying her husband's baby.

She looked at the hot, clammy hand holding hers, attached to what she could only describe as a stranger.

Who was this man in front of her?

She genuinely wasn't sure. Looking into his dark brown eyes, she recognised nothing of the man she thought she knew. He looked tired and lacked the sparkle she was so used to seeing; years seemed to have piled onto him in a matter of days, and not in a complimentary way. Scarlett pulled her hand away. It didn't feel safe anymore. He wasn't safe.

"Angelica doesn't need to leave," she finally said, her voice steadier than she expected. "I'm the one who's leaving."

Jason looked taken aback, almost making her laugh out loud. Was he actually expecting her to stay?

"Scarlett, be reasonable." He shook his head. "Where on earth would you go?" His words stung her further. He was right.

There wasn't anywhere for her to go. She had no relatives. Her aunt Maggie, who wasn't even a real aunt, had passed away six years ago, and the only living family remaining was her mother, who she barely spoke to, and who now lived and worked on some crumbling old estate in Scotland.

"We can make this work," Jason said with such sincerity she did actually laugh.

"How do we make this work, Jason?" Her voice cracked as she tried her hardest not to let her emotions show, but she was genuinely curious about what he was thinking at this point.

"We, I – I'm not sure, but we'll find a way." He looked down at Scarlett's hand, as if weighing up whether she would allow him to take hold of it again.

"There is no more *we*. You saw to that when you put your penis inside our lodger!" Scarlett's vision blurred, and it took a few seconds for her to realise it was because she was crying.

That was the last thing she needed. She felt humiliated enough.

"Jason!" a voice called from the hallway. Scarlett and Jason looked at each other, panic etched across both their faces. "Jason, darling, it's Mummy. Are you home?"

"Scarlett," he said, almost in a whisper, "please don't go." At least he had the decency to appear sheepish.

"Jason!" shrilled his mother's voice again.

"In the conservatory, Mother." His eyes continued

to plead, but they left Scarlett feeling cold.

Mummy Dearest swept into the room like the potent perfumed force of nature she was, something Scarlett was not ready for.

"Oh, I see." Tara did not hide her contempt at the fact Scarlett was there. Anyone would think she was the one who had impregnated the lodger.

Tara ceremoniously sat herself down, smoothing the skirt of her light blue dress, whilst Scarlett's thoughts paused on Angelica, the sweet, funny, and quite literally full of life girl they'd taken in as a favour to Jason's old school friend. A smile played on Scarlett's lips as she imagined how that nugget of news would go down.

"Happy to see you still find humour in entirely inappropriate situations, dear." Tara's voice was thick with sarcasm.

Nothing new there.

Of course, Tara had been there last night when Scarlett had furiously confronted Angelica and Jason at the party, making Scarlett cringe.

To block it out, she brought her attention back to the room, her beautiful, lovingly decorated sunroom. It was comfortable and welcoming, with its soft pastels and cream, the light oak furniture she'd restored herself, and her indoor clematis climbing up and around the windows and double-door frame, bringing it all together.

She drank in the pleasing aesthetics – the situation was telling her it wouldn't be hers anymore, especially if Tara had anything to do with it. Even that being the case, she still didn't like that her mother-in-law was filling it with her toxic energy.

"Well, that was suitably childish and humiliating for all concerned." Tara took a dramatic pause to observe the two *non-adults* sitting across from her. "Do

A NEW *Hope* IN THE HIGHLANDS

neither of you have anything to say? And where is the girl now?"

Jason cleared his throat, as if readying to deliver a speech. "Angelica is out. She wanted to give me and Scarlett some time and space to talk." His words were barely audible. He was becoming less attractive each time he spoke, and Scarlett wondered if he'd always been this spineless.

"How on earth could you ever let this happen?" Tara aimed the question at Scarlett, who felt her face redden.

"Mother," Jason said, although any follow-up words seemed to evaporate in his throat.

"A woman should keep her husband satisfied enough to avoid this type of thing happening, or if you'd perhaps provided a child yourself, we wouldn't be in this predicament."

She registered the glint of amused malice in Tara's green eyes, which swept over Scarlett with indifference. Despite her age, Tara was still beautiful – tall, dark, and elegant – but Scarlett always thought her bitter personality detracted from her beauty, making her wholly ugly in her eyes.

"A woman has duties, after all." Tara was now openly goading her.

Bitch.

But Scarlett was too shocked to breathe, let alone speak. The room felt as if the air was being sucked out of it. Surely she was watching some insane reality show on Netflix, and this wasn't her own life playing out in front of her in three-dimensional, telenovela-style drama.

It all felt surreal – to the point she lost the use of speech or even the will to fight back. She had no desire to stand up for herself or slap that smug and sarcastic look off her mother-in-law's face, something she'd often fantasised about.

She had nothing. Her fight was gone. The inclination to say what was and wasn't fair had dissipated.

"That's enough, Mother, you're being unfair," Jason finally said.

Maybe he did still have a spine, but it wasn't enough to stop Tara's tirade.

"Hardly. A man has needs that must be attended to, including the production of a child to carry on our legacy." Tara examined her manicure. "At least this girl has provided that."

Jason could not make eye contact with anything other than the floor.

Scarlett suddenly stood up, surprising them all, herself included, and for a moment she was mute and bewildered. She was painfully aware of how she looked, especially in contrast to Tara's impeccably polished appearance. Her own hair was erratic and unwashed, much like yesterday's clothes that she'd absentmindedly put back on this morning, and she was now outwardly shaking.

As if things couldn't get any worse, Angelica chose that moment to materialise in the doorway, her tight blonde curls and fresh, dewy complexion exuding even more of a youthful glow than usual.

God, their baby is going to be sickeningly beautiful.

Scarlett shook her head to rid herself of the image of their family Christmas photo, instead – and also unhelpfully – noticing how full and bouncy Angelica's breasts were under the tight white t-shirt that hugged and accentuated every feminine curve, including her still tiny waist, where there was nothing but a hint of a bump showing, which somehow made her even more attractive.

Scarlett wanted to vomit.

Everything was suddenly too bright. Too beautiful.

The textures and colours of the plants, flowers, and soft furnishings were too colourful. It was *all* just too much.

In a vague attempt to embody the calmness of that one yoga class she went to a year ago, Scarlett closed her eyes and took a deep breath in through her nose, slowly opening them again as she blew out through her mouth.

"Hello, Angelica, you're looking well," Scarlett finally said, even managing a forced smile.

"Err, thanks." Angelica looked at Jason, her eyes wide and slightly panicked.

Scarlett turned to face Tara. "Have you ever considered the idea that you're not qualified to talk about keeping a husband satisfied when you literally drove yours into an early grave?"

The three other people in the room simultaneously gasped and Scarlett took a moment to enjoy the shock on Tara's face.

Feeling encouraged, she continued, "And it was your son's decision not to have children, a decision that until now he has adamantly stood by for the entirety of our," Scarlett paused for a moment to do the mental arithmetic, "thirteen-year marriage."

"That's a long time," Angelica mused out loud, immediately looking sheepish as everyone's eyes fell upon her with evident exasperation.

Angelica attempted a smile as an apology, which was ignored as they brought their attention back to Scarlett.

"Yes, it is," Scarlett said to no one in particular.

"Scarlett, darling," Jason began, promptly silenced by Scarlett's raised hand.

"I'm going now," she said, getting up and walking towards the doorway where Angelica stepped aside to let her pass.

She stopped and turned back to look at Jason.

"And I'm taking the car."

Scarlett briefly glanced at each of their faces, and, feeling confident in her decision, she left the room. She placed her handbag over her shoulder and grabbed her phone and the car keys from the ornate Indonesian-wood side table in the hallway, her fingers lingering on its smooth cool surface for a moment, before picking up her case by the front door. Then, she left the house, not looking back, and not bothering to close the front door behind her.

CHAPTER 2

EDWARD'S DAUGHTER, LILY, was like many girls her age, shaking off the remnants of her teenage years – garish polished fingernails and all – while hurtling blindly into adulthood. The transition terrified him.

She rarely spoke to him these days, and when she did, it was in a clipped and unpleasant manner, especially if he tried to pry her attention away from her phone. And whilst Edward was usually content to sit in silence during the drive back to her mother's house, today he felt compelled to fill the space with conversation.

"Do you have a busy week ahead?" He stole a glance at Lily.

"Not really."

Keeping his focus on the road, he tried again. "How's school? Anything new?"

"Nope. Just the usual." She began typing out a message at a furious speed.

Despite feeling it was another aimless attempt at a connection, he continued pushing. "And your brother and sister, are they—"

"Dad, we don't have to do this." She finally stopped typing and looked across at him, annoyance etched across her face.

He furrowed his brow. "Do what? Have a conversation?"

"Talk about shite neither of us cares about." She

shrugged and returned her focus to her phone.

"Watch your language!" he snapped, frustration bubbling to the surface.

"Apologies, *laird*." Lily rolled her eyes and huffed. She shifted in her seat and went back to typing on her phone, signalling their exchange was over.

Edward rolled his own eyes at her use of his title – something she only did to goad him into an argument.

This time, he wouldn't bite, but the silence that followed felt heavier than before.

He sighed, more at himself than at her. The distance between them seemed insurmountable, and no matter how hard he tried, he could never quite seem to find the right words to bridge the gap. When they eventually pulled up outside his ex-wife's house – a modest detached townhouse on the outskirts of Perth – he sighed again.

He turned to Lily, hoping for a last attempt at something more civil, perhaps even a few forgiving words. But without even a last glance his way, she tossed her long blonde hair over her shoulder, grabbed her overnight bag from the footwell, and stepped out of the car.

"Bye, Dad," she said, barely audible, before slamming the door behind her.

With a small wave, she bounded up the steps, opened the front door, and disappeared inside.

Edward stared at the closed door, feeling a familiar pang of regret.

He often wondered how things might have been different. If they'd stayed a family – *together* – would Lily still have grown so distant? Or was this always their inevitable dynamic?

It was a futile train of thought. They were where they were: Lily living with her mother and her new family in comfortable suburbia, and Edward alone in his oversized, draughty ancestral home.

They all seemed happy enough, and maybe that was the best he could hope for. He did his best to be a good father – he had Lily every weekend, attended every parents' evening, recital, birthday – but since her early teens, Lily's disinterest in his efforts had become the norm and her time at Haddon an inconvenience.

Noticing the front door opening, he saw Natasha appear, an older version of their daughter – taller than average with her blonde hair still long. She made her way to his car, and he lowered the window.

"Edward," she said in her usual cold way of greeting him.

"Natasha."

"It's just her age." She shrugged and picked at an invisible piece of thread on her jumper.

"You've been saying that since she was twelve." Edward glanced back at the front door where Frankie, her husband, appeared.

Frankie stood firmly with his thick, gym-toned arms crossed over his chest, watching their exchange with interest.

Amused at Frankie's transparent and feeble attempt at intimidation, Edward's top lip curled into a half-smile.

Natasha knew Edward well enough to read his thoughts.

"Stop it," she snapped at him. "And stop taking it all so personally. She just wants to hang out with her friends for her birthday this year. It's really no big deal." Natasha rolled her big blue eyes, her exasperation evident.

"You only don't see it as a big issue because you'll be seeing her on her birthday." Edward returned his focus back to her, suddenly surprised at how immune he now was to her good looks and childish petulance.

"Honestly, I don't know why you're making such a fuss. Just pop over the day before or after or do something special when you have her next weekend."

"She never *wants* to do anything. That's half the problem," he grumbled.

"If you're going to be negative about everything I say, then there's no point talking. It's always the same." She narrowed her eyes at him and shook her head.

"Oh, here we go." His turn to roll his eyes.

"No, actually, we're not going anywhere with this. Goodbye, Edward." She turned and walked away from him.

He watched her as she marched back to the house, storming past Frankie.

Edward offered him a sarcastic smile, to which Frankie responded with a disapproving shake of the head, disappearing after Natasha and closing the door behind him.

Prick.

With a final glance at the house, Edward released another resigned sigh.

He started the ignition of his Land Rover and pulled away, his thoughts reluctantly shifting to more immediate matters.

His younger brother Leonard was visiting from the States soon – not something Edward was looking forward to. Not in the slightest.

Although they were near replicas in appearance, both standing at around six foot two with brown hair that curled at the nape if left unchecked and deep blue eyes that could be warm or piercing depending on their mood, or so he'd been told, the similarities ended there. People had always compared them, even as children, though the truth was they never really liked each other.

And now Leonard was coming back.

Edward suspected it had something to do with the

house and the estate. His brother had been trying to convince him to sell to some eager American investors for years, but Edward had refused to even entertain the idea.

Their last encounter had been tense, and Edward wasn't keen on a repeat performance.

As if on cue, his phone rang, and the word **MUM** appeared on the screen.

Bloody woman is psychic.

He sighed before accepting the call.

"Hello."

"Finally, I've tried you four times this weekend! I was beginning to think you were ignoring me!" The car filled with the sound of her Southern Louisiana drawl, each word dripping with feigned innocence.

"I was going to call when I got back to the estate. I was just dropping Lily home."

"Aww, how is my angel? I'm sorry to have missed her. I'll call her after I speak with you." Her voice always softened at the mention of her granddaughter, whom Edward knew she sorely missed. He would need to take Lily across the pond for a visit soon.

"Not so angelic, but she's fine. Has her head down for her last year at school."

"And Natasha and the kids?" she asked.

Edward grimaced. "All fine too."

"Informative as ever, darlin'." Verity laughed, to which Edward grumbled an inaudible response – something between a growl and an *aye*.

"Right, well, the reason for my call. Your brother will be arriving soon. Have you prepared his rooms?"

"No."

"Now, Edward, play nice! Your brother hasn't been home in years."

"This isn't his home anymore. He lives with you." Edward bristled at the idea of Leonard, the literal manchild, being in *his* home once again.

"You're getting more like your father every year. He was a grump, too!"

"Grump is relative." Edward shrugged.

"Oh, Edward. You always get so prickly." Verity's sigh hung heavily between them.

"When is he coming?" Edward finally asked, sensing Verity's frustration and not wanting to upset her by being a dick.

"Next Saturday," she replied, clearly delighting in the news.

"Great."

"That's all that sorted then. Fantastic. You're a good boy. I love you," she said, ignoring his sarcastic tone.

"Sure." He rolled his eyes. "And in case you missed the memo, I'm a thirty-eight-year-old *man* at this point."

Verity laughed. "Just as well I know you love me too. Speak soon, sweet *boy* of mine."

"Goodbye, Mother."

The line went dead, and he knew his mood would be ruined for the rest of the day.

He hoped the visit would be over as quickly and painlessly as possible, which got him thinking about another visitor who was soon to arrive.

According to the conversation with his gardener, June Hope, early that morning, her daughter, who he didn't even know existed until then, was coming to stay – and he'd agreed to find her some work on the estate.

Just fucking great.

Edward groaned. He knew he was being unkind and miserable.

June was visibly nervous when she'd approached him in the courtyard. "Are you sure it's okay?" she had asked. Her voice had trembled slightly as she wrung her hands.

It really made no difference to him, especially since Mrs Wilson could always do with a bit of help around the house, and it might actually save some money on the increased fees the cleaning agency recently started charging, but he sensed this was important to June.

"Of course. My brother is coming soon, and Mrs Wilson will be glad for the help."

"I appreciate you may want to speak to her before she arrives, if she's going to be working for you."

From what little he'd gathered, June's daughter was fleeing some kind of domestic upheaval. Edward really wasn't interested in the specifics – and despite his quiet fondness for June, he wasn't particularly in the mood for carrying out a phone interview.

How bad can she be?

"I'll send you her number, just in case. She won't be arriving until tomorrow."

"Aye, that's fine." Edward had offered a tight smile and nodded. "I'll call her, but I'm sure it will be no problem at all," he reassured her.

June was an asset and a longstanding employee, which he appreciated. Not to mention a self-contained woman who never stirred up drama, never indulged in gossip, and was comfortable keeping conversation to a minimum.

Those were qualities Edward valued more than anything.

Like most of the staff employed by his late father, June had worked on the estate for a while and was indispensable to his groundskeeper. Together, she and Andrzej kept the sprawling acres in pristine condition, upholding the high standards Edward's father had always demanded. The house itself needed far more attention than Edward had time to give, but at least the gardens were immaculate, which gave him some comfort.

He briefly wondered how old the daughter was, as he wasn't entirely sure of June's age. He found it strange to think she was someone's mother, especially one old enough to be married and divorced, although for no reason he could put his finger on.

The older woman's energy radiated a kind of wholesome vitality, likely because of her outdoor lifestyle, but she didn't seem very maternal. Still, what did he really know and, more importantly, it was none of his business – she and Andrzej had formed a partnership that pleased Edward, which was all he really needed to know or care about.

SWITCHING ON THE light in the hallway, Edward shrugged off his coat and hung it over the easy chair as he entered the lounge of the apartment, which he used whenever he stayed in Edinburgh for business.

It wasn't as pretty or luxurious as the house in Dean Village, which was currently being rented to some family friends visiting from mainland Europe, but it was functional, comfortable, and perfectly located overlooking St Andrew Square. A spoilt kid's party pad, basically – lots of sleek steel and glass surfaces with scattered leather seats and sofas. Leonard used to spend a lot of time partying here when he still lived at home.

None of it was Edward's style – he preferred the aesthetics of his own home. Haddon House might be ancient and draughty, but it at least had some soul; this place simply served a purpose. He'd recently considered selling or renting it out, but it was convenient – for several reasons – so he'd thought better of it.

Edward groaned, stretching out the stiffness in his back after his long drive, and then sighed. He just wanted to go to bed, but he needed to get this call out of the way first. Finding the number June sent earlier, he tapped on it and pressed the call option.

It only rang once before the call connected and he could immediately hear the faint hum of tyres on a wet road and intermittent cars whooshing by; she was obviously still driving. The relentless rain had started soon after Perth and he wondered how far up she was already.

"Hello?" The female voice in his ear sounded tired.

"Hi, Scarlett?"

It was always worth checking.

"Yes, hello?"

He kicked off his shoes and sat on the sofa, leaning his head back and closing his eyes.

Fuck, I'm knackered.

"Edward Cameron-Reid. Your mother gave me your number. Hope that's okay?"

"Oh," she said, pausing briefly. "Her boss?"

"That's the one," he replied. "I understand you're coming to stay and are looking for work."

"Err, yes. Yes, please."

"Have you worked on an estate or done any housekeeping work before?" He pinched the bridge of his nose. He hated interviews.

There was a long pause.

"Hello? You still there?" he asked.

"I'm going to be honest, Edward, shit – sorry."

He let out a soft laugh.

"I'm sorry. Can I call you Edward? Am I supposed to call you a lord or something?"

"Edward is fine." He rubbed his forehead and temple with his free hand.

"I've not worked for anyone for a long time." She paused again.

"Right ..."

"I've obviously worked, though. Shit, sorry – none of this is coming out right. I'm exhausted. I've been driving a while. But yes, I mean – I've always worked."

"Well, that's something."

"God, I'm sorry. I can clean, though – of course I can clean. I've spent a lifetime *cleaning*."

Edward opened his eyes and shook his head.

Who is this woman?

"Please don't think I'll be any trouble – I can do whatever you need me to do. I'm honest and reliable, and I just really, really need to be occupied."

"I think you may need to pull over at the next services and have a coffee and a nap first."

"Err, yeah – that's not a terrible idea." Scarlett let out an exasperated groan. "Do I still have a job?"

Edward let out a small laugh. "Aye, I'm sure we'll work it out. Mrs Wilson, my housekeeper, will get you sorted after you settle in."

"Oh my God, thank you – I promise you won't regret it." Scarlett's voice cracked.

Fuck's sake – is she crying?

"I'm not usually emotional, I'm just a bit—"

"Tired. I know, me too. Let's catch up when you get here."

"Okay. Thank you again." She sniffed.

"No problem – and Scarlett?" Edward felt a sudden sense of responsibility for her, and the idea of her driving through the night made him uncomfortable.

"Yes?"

"Please pull over and get a room somewhere, so you get here in one piece."

It was her turn to laugh. "Yes, boss."

"See you soon."

"See you soon."

Edward ended the call and continued to sit a while longer, looking up at the ceiling, wondering what on earth he'd let himself in for.

―❦―

THE NEXT DAY, after hours of meetings, Edward returned to Haddon House, eager to get on with the rest of the jobs he needed to close off. But he slowed as he spotted June climbing into an SUV parked outside the house.

She made it then.

He slowed down even further, hoping to delay his arrival long enough for the two women to leave and drive to the back of the house where the stables were located.

June was pleasant but never imposed herself – another reason he appreciated her – but the idea of meeting her daughter felt like an intrusion he wasn't ready to deal with.

Safe in the knowledge the women didn't see him, Edward eventually parked up and, noticing Andrzej working on some shrubbery at the far bottom side of the front lawn, he walked down to meet him.

"Afternoon, sir." Andrzej stabbed his spade into the soil and shielded his eyes with his hand from the low setting sun.

"Afternoon. I see the daughter has arrived." Edward looked at the shrubs going in. "Bit late in the day to be planting, isn't it?"

"The heat's been turning up again, so I don't want the roots drying out, and June has been busy getting ready for the new arrival." Andrzej removed his handkerchief from his back pocket and wiped the sweat from his thick neck, deeply tanned from the summer months spent outside. "She's been feeling a bit nervous, I think."

"Not like her. She's usually quite composed." Edward looked back up in the direction they'd disappeared in.

"Yes, she is." Andrzej shrugged and smiled. "The wonderful mystery of women, they're always surprising us."

Edward nodded, lacking the humour that came so easily to Andrzej, whose wide grin disarmed many of Edward's more irritable moods.

"June tells me she will help Mrs Wilson with housekeeping, yes?"

Edward nodded again, his eyes focused on the shrubs. "Aye. They all seem happy about it, and it makes sense rather than paying the agency to come in. I'll redirect the work for them to something else for the time being. They're an unreliable lot, anyway."

The two men remained silent for a moment.

"June was telling me she doesn't particularly share her affection for the outdoors. Hay fever or allergies, so that should be interesting." Edward looked back at Andrzej's work. "Are these the blackthorns we discussed?"

"Yes, they should be in the ground in good time, so they'll flower in early spring." Andrzej inspected the plants by his feet. "Mrs Wilson will be glad of the help, no doubt."

Edward shrugged and placed his hands in his pockets. "We'll see how much help she'll be – I got the impression she's had quite a privileged lifestyle. But she's keen to get started, so who knows, it may work out."

Andrzej continued to observe the plants and the soil, apparently deep in thought.

"Privilege is relative, sir," he said eventually and then shrugged, returning his attention to his employer. "We are all privileged to live in this part of the country, wherever we come from, and maybe this lady will feel the same."

Edward scoffed. "We've yet to see if she's any kind of lady, Andrzej." Edward patted the groundsman's shoulder. "Keep up the good work and don't stay out too late. No doubt you'll have the extra workload whilst June helps her daughter learn the ropes around here."

Andrzej nodded and smiled in agreement. "Goodnight to you, sir."

"Goodnight, Andrzej." Edward walked away with a backwards wave.

CHAPTER 3

SEEING HER MUM standing there peering in at her had rendered Scarlett speechless. Loss of words seemed to be becoming a regular occurrence.

She'd refused to think about her strained relationship with her mother at any point during the drive up, not ready to unlock that part of her brain or heart. There was enough for her to be dealing with, such as the fact she'd started crying on the phone to her new employer.

Shitting fuck.

Scarlett had groaned loudly in frustration after she'd hung up on Edward the previous night.

Great fucking start.

But she had to push it aside. All of it. Especially the brazen fact her husband was a cheating rat. The man she thought she was spending the rest of her life with, who she'd been with since she herself was the same age as Angelica.

Thoughts and feelings were running wild in her mind, but words felt too difficult to grasp.

Thankfully, her mother wasn't suffering from the same affliction.

"Scarlett," her mother said, smiling as Scarlett lowered the window. "You found us then."

"Hi, Mum." Scarlett forced a smile in return.

"Shall I jump in and show you where to park?"

"Yes, of course – please get in."

June opened the door and sat down, bringing the

smell of the outdoors with her. They didn't hug; they rarely did. And if June felt any awkwardness, she was hiding it well. Instead, she fiddled around, trying to pull her seatbelt on.

Scarlett hadn't seen her mother in a few years, and while she knew June was approaching her fifty-third birthday, Scarlett couldn't believe how her mother didn't seem to have aged a single year.

Over the years, various friends had commented on Scarlett in the same way, but she never paid much attention to it. But her mother's youthfulness always irritated her, though she could never pinpoint the reason. Scarlett pushed the thought away – analysing her relationship with her mother had never been an appealing idea, and she didn't intend to start now.

"Lovely stuff." June smiled again and finally clipped herself in. "Just head around the left of the building and you'll spot the courtyard and stables. You can park behind there."

Scarlett stopped herself from wincing at the thought of the *stables*. Hay fever and allergies had plagued her since she was a child, but it clearly wasn't something June remembered. Not saying anything about it, she followed her mother's instructions.

Scarlett glanced at the back of the house and rear gardens, which were as impressive as the front. The property sat on an incline and beyond the woodland on each side of the lawn, she could see a lake shimmering in the distance.

"You're lucky. The sun is out today," June said, following Scarlett's gaze. "It's been miserable and grey until a couple of weeks ago, although it's still pretty stunning even then. But the autumn sun makes it all come alive somehow." June sighed, content. Happy, even. "I'm very lucky to work here."

Scarlett nodded, turning her attention back to the

approaching courtyard and stables, following a tight lane to the left, where she pulled into a parking space next to a small Ford Fiesta.

"I've still got her. She must be approaching twenty-two years now." June smiled again, this time her affections aimed at the car.

"Still running okay then?" Scarlett asked, not sure what else to say, and pondering the fact that even the car was older than Angelica.

"Oh yes, Andrzej, the head groundsman, my boss – lovely man. He looks after it and keeps it running for me."

Scarlett raised an eyebrow, but either June didn't notice or she chose to ignore her daughter's insinuation.

June continued, barely pausing for breath. "He's Polish, not much older than you, difficult family history, but his father worked the grounds for Edward's father and did so many impressive things all over the estate, which after the war had fallen into complete disrepair. He immigrated to Britain after the war, and there's an entire story of how he ended all the way up here. Lived here until his death. All very sad, but come on, love, let's get you settled. You must be shattered." She finally took a break from her incessant chatter, stepping out of the car to make her way around to the boot to help with the bags, of which there was only one. "Where are all your things, Scarlett?" June asked, her concern evident.

Scarlett cringed. "This is all I have."

"What do you mean?" June walked back around to peer in at Scarlett, who felt herself squirm.

Her mother's long dark hair framed her face, and her brown eyes, the same shade, were squinting at her. The women looked so different from each other. *Always* so different.

"The case, my phone, what I'm wearing ... it's all I

have." Scarlett couldn't hold her mother's gaze.

"He didn't even let you pack all your bags?" June's tone was clipped, hinting at anger, which was unusual for her mother.

"It's not that. It was just all very heated. Angelica was there, his mum was there …"

"Oh. I see," was all June responded with.

Scarlett had obviously given her mother a quick summary of the main events, but she had failed to mention the debacle of her ill-thought-out exit plan, which comprised leaving with a small case and her handbag and nothing more.

Although to Scarlett's credit, she'd executed that part perfectly.

"Did he at least give you money?" June scowled.

"I have some cash, my cards, and Apple Wallet."

"Apple what?"

"I have some of my cards on my phone. We'll sort that side of things out. I wasn't thinking; I just needed to get out. I couldn't stay. I didn't know what to do – I still don't know what I'm doing, to be honest."

The two women stared at each other for a long moment until June relaxed.

"Right, we are where we are. You have a home, you have food, you have work – we've seen to that – and, well, you have me."

The last part of that sentence felt odd, but there was an element of warmth that neither instantly rebuked, which could only be a good sign.

"Come on, let's get you upstairs. I've made some soup and sandwiches, and then you can have a bath. I've got some pyjamas if you haven't brought any with you." June paused for a moment, as though fully processing her daughter's predicament. "We can drive into town tomorrow and pick up some more essentials you might need. Plan?"

Scarlett fought back the tears and nodded.

"Right, then, out you come." June closed the passenger door and waited for Scarlett to join her at the bottom of some stone steps leading up to the apartment above the stables. "I've made up the spare room so you can get to bed as soon as you've cleaned up and had something to eat," June said.

Scarlett simply nodded again and followed her mother upstairs.

The whole situation had rendered her incapable of making anything but the most basic decisions, and even those felt overwhelming. A small part at the back of her mind recognised the oddity of her mother taking charge, especially over anything related to Scarlett, but she was too tired to explore those types of thoughts and quickly shut them down.

As she reached the top of the stairs, she entered through a bright red doorway that led into the apartment. Scarlett stopped in awe, not expecting the beautiful interior that opened beyond the small threshold. Two large roof lanterns dominated the high ceiling above her, the expansive blue sky, dotted with small cotton ball clouds, leisurely passing over, which opened the space like a breath of fresh air.

The stark white walls between the five doorways leading off to various rooms housed oversized Gustav Klimt prints, one she recognised from her younger years: *Judith and the Head of Holofernes*, a sensual depiction of a half-naked woman's torso that Scarlett remembered cringing over every time she passed the more modest-sized print in her childhood home. No furniture cluttered the hallway, giving the impression of an art gallery, and Scarlett stood planted to the spot, admiring its simple yet evocative impact.

She didn't recall her mother being all that interested in the aesthetics of their home. It was always clean and comfortable, but nothing like this.

Scarlett had no training, but over time she had assumed the role of decorating her marital home and the other properties dotted in and around Bath, including the small hotels Jason's family bought and renovated over the years – something she'd always enjoyed. She wondered if there was some common ground between her and her mother, after all.

"I'm putting the kettle on. Have a look around and make yourself at home," June called to Scarlett, who could hear her rustling around in the kitchen.

Scarlett didn't respond but closed the front door behind her and, noticing the polished herringbone flooring beneath her feet, she kicked off her trainers.

An open doorway piqued her interest, and she wandered over to peer in. It was clearly her mother's bedroom, which made her feel like she was trespassing. It felt too intimate.

The bed was half made, a dressing gown hung lazily over the top, and some clothes lay folded on a chair. Scarlett noticed a pair of reading glasses perched precariously on top of a small mound of books on the bedside table, along with the Tiffany-style lamp she remembered her mother having when she was a child.

The familiarity made her stomach contract, so instead she focused on the bare walls painted a delicate pale blue and the two arched floor-to-ceiling windows, with shutters dressed in cream voiles, that overlooked the lawn at the back of the main house, where she could see a path leading towards the woods and loch beyond.

The whole place, the estate, was something straight out of a nineteenth-century novel and she could see how this set-up would appeal to her mother. Scarlett's two dominant memories of June whilst growing up was her either being at work or engrossed in a book.

Scarlett bristled and moved away, walking past what she could see was a small toilet before pushing open another door to what she assumed was the spare room. It was like her mother's bedroom, although smaller, with only one arched window, yet it shared the same impressive view.

She walked in and sat on the antique brass bed, drinking in her new surroundings. Her new *home*.

The realisation of that truth didn't feel right, so instead she focused on her odd-socked toes sinking into the thick pile of the cream carpet beneath her feet.

Looking around, she noticed the room was sparse, with only a chest of drawers, a wardrobe, and a velvet vintage-style chair by the window, but it didn't feel cold.

She glanced over at a doorway that led to what she could see was an ensuite, but she'd lost interest in exploring further; the mattress felt so welcoming that Scarlett couldn't help but lie down on the pillow, which engulfed her heavy head, encouraging her to close her eyes. She didn't fight it.

CHAPTER 4

THE NEXT MORNING held the promise of another sunny day, still uncharacteristically warm for this time of year. It wasn't unusual for the first couple of weeks of October to be prone to spells of mild weather, but it felt like a summer's day, which, to be fair, said little about the Scottish climate. The summer months were just as erratic and changeable as the autumn months.

Edward could feel the warmth permeating through his blinds and he stretched out in bed, glad he hadn't yet upgraded his top sheet to a duvet. In this heat, a duvet would leave him sweating in the night, making him crabbit the following morning – even more so than usual.

It also wasn't like him to sleep in. He was usually up before the sun, but this morning he felt like the world could wait. His thoughts drifted to the day ahead and curiosity about June's daughter crept in. His hands lay across his chest, one absentmindedly playing with the small patch of hair nestled there.

Swatting away thoughts about what she looked like, he focused on the room instead. He needed to paint the ceiling – he couldn't recall when anyone last decorated the room, although, admittedly, it wasn't particularly high on his agenda. So much needed to be done in the house. It made him tired just thinking about it.

Feeling lazy and lacking motivation to take on any

of the day's endless tasks, he wondered when he'd last stayed in bed this long. Probably around the same time the room had last seen fresh paint.

He readjusted his covers with his foot, and the way the fabric stretched across his lower body created a slight friction that made him stir beneath the sheet. He looked down and sighed. It would be a while longer before he'd be getting out of bed then.

Torn between waiting for the situation to resolve itself or giving it a hand, Edward was too distracted to hear the voices of the two women approaching who, without warning and deep in conversation, entered the room.

They fell into immediate silence when they saw him, each momentarily too shocked to speak or move as they took in the sight of Edward and his tented sheet.

Incoherent words and hands frantically covering eyes and body parts ensued, nobody making any sense for several seconds.

"Mrs Wilson!" Edward finally said.

"Sir, I am so, so sorry, you're usually well out of bed by now and—"

"I understand that, but—"

"Obviously if I'd known, I would never—" Mrs Wilson's voice was high-pitched and verging on hysterical.

Edward cut in, doing his best to remain calm. "Mrs Wilson—"

"I was just showing Scarlett the house. As you know, she'll be—"

"Mrs Wilson," Edward said again, attempting to stop her nervous waffling. "I understand that, but if you wouldn't mind, if you'd give me some privacy to—"

"Aye, of course. Again, my sincere apologies. Come now." Mrs Wilson, a short and solid type of woman in her late fifties, who no doubt had seen it all, just not this particular version, regained her professional composure and ushered Scarlett out of the door.

Edward glanced at the younger woman, inexplicably annoyed by her attractiveness and the poorly hidden mirth in her eyes, which she quickly lowered when he caught her gaze, but not before she took a final glimpse at the area he was desperately trying to cover and tame, to no avail. If anything, it remained angrily rigid.

Once the women left the room, he groaned loudly. He could hear Scarlett's chuckle following her as they hurried away down the landing.

"Enough of that," Mrs Wilson chastised her.

He cringed and covered his face with his hands.

"Fucking hell!" Edward rolled onto his side, placing a pillow over his head.

He wasn't the most extroverted person at the best of times, but knowing he'd have to face the women again made him feel like never leaving this room.

Edward especially didn't want to see the fresh addition to his staff. Mrs Wilson would be the professional she always was, but he didn't know about June's daughter.

His thoughts drifted back to the smile in her eyes as they landed upon him, unsure if they'd been green or blue, and her messy mane of long wavy auburn hair.

She wasn't like the usual women he went for. Most of his girlfriends over the years had been tall, slender, horse-loving types, and honestly, he rarely paid much attention to his *type*, anyway. They were women he met in his, albeit now very small, social circle. Sisters of friends, so and so's cousin, daughters of family friends, and a couple of women he'd encountered through the running of the estate, but *never* an employee.

And he shouldn't even be going down that train of thought.

It seemed wrong to him. He felt it would be taking advantage of his position, something more expected of his brother, Leonard, but not him.

She was different, though. He'd never been so instantly attracted to anyone like that before.

He shook his head. How could he be attracted to someone he'd spent less than thirty seconds with? She was just a surprise, that was all.

The problem was, he didn't know what he'd been expecting; a more high-maintenance city type, perhaps. Someone with designer clothes, manicured nails, and highlighted hair – not the fresh-faced, curvy, hippy-type mess in jeans and a white shirt that appeared in his bedroom doorway.

"Fucking hell!" he groaned into his pillow again.

CHAPTER 5

SCARLETT DID NOT need the distraction of a man, but the image of the incident earlier that morning remained imprinted in her thoughts. The master of the estate was not some old decrepit gentleman, ageing and crumbling like some of the rooms Mrs Wilson had let her look in during their tour. Instead, Laird Edward Cameron-Reid was a bit of a dish, and she found herself captivated by more than just what he hid beneath the sheets.

She guessed he was in his late thirties and despite his dishevelled appearance and ever so slightly receding hairline, there was a boyish and vulnerable charm to his face – the blend of deep blue eyes, thin yet still alluring lips, all set off by a strong roman nose.

He appeared tall and athletic, with toned arms she imagined came from days spent taking care of the estate. He wasn't *poster-boy* handsome, but his features combined made him decidedly appealing.

Scarlett gave herself a mental shake.

Taking her mind off her train wreck of a marriage was one thing, but focusing on another man was not a healthy alternative, especially considering he was her new boss.

"Just no," she said aloud.

"What's that?" Mrs Wilson turned to look at her.

"Nothing, just a fly buzzing around my face," Scarlett lied, swatting away the invisible insect.

Mrs Wilson looked about her, squinting her already

small grey eyes hidden behind thin round glasses. She appeared ready for a similar fly attack, reminding Scarlett – not unkindly – a little of Moley from *The Wind in the Willows*.

Once satisfied it was gone, Mrs Wilson continued walking ahead, pointing to paintings and decor of particular interest and historical significance.

Scarlett only half listened; dates and names of people long dead were of no interest to her. She enjoyed and appreciated the beautiful aesthetics of the building and its contents, but how the late Laird George Cameron-Reid was the twenty-third generation of the family to reside at the house, extended over the years by different lairds in situ, having survived various clan feuds, Anglo-Scottish civil wars, and, apparently, if one was interested, whose lineage could be traced all the way back to Alexander II of Scotland, all did very little to excite her.

However, the building itself and the various rooms, some filled with all manner of interesting artefacts and furniture, left her in awe.

Over the years Jason and Scarlett had visited plenty of stately homes, taking gentle strolls through sections of houses no longer inhabited by rich earls, dukes, and duchesses who now preferred sunning themselves in more appealing climates across Europe and the rest of the world. Although impressive, Scarlett had never had the privilege of looking behind the scenes – not like this.

It was like entering a long-forgotten world, literally, with some rooms in the east wing having been closed off for decades. According to Mrs Wilson, she would do a weekly walk-through, and a company would come in every six months to do a surface clean and maintenance check to avoid the closed-off parts of the building falling into complete disrepair.

"I'm surprised he hasn't had the building listed and opened some parts to the public. I imagine it would bring in a decent income." Scarlett inspected an antique dressing table in one of the unused rooms. The smell of stale polish and dust pinched at her nose. "Seems a waste to have it all locked away," she added.

"Edward, you'll soon learn, is a very private man. He would baulk at the idea." Mrs Wilson bent towards Scarlett and lowered her voice. "Besides, money really isn't an issue. His mother has taken good care of that."

Scarlett wondered why they were now whispering, as there was nobody around except the potential ghosts lurking in the walls.

"Trust fund, by any chance?" Scarlett asked.

"Let's just say his American side of the family will never go hungry." Mrs Wilson straightened herself back up. "But let's not talk of such things. It's not polite."

"Of course, I completely agree." Scarlett looked around her, suddenly feeling a little self-conscious, wondering how one *should* conduct themselves in polite Scottish society.

She didn't imagine it differed massively from the south of the border, everything appearing shimmering and golden on the surface, all nicely contained. But Scarlett was of the opinion it was usually a facade concealing thinly veiled family dramas, lies, and other seedy and questionable goings-on.

Although, she realised, she may be projecting – *just* a little.

It may be her own personal dealings with Bath's self-nominated society darlings – aka Jason and his mother who undoubtedly behaved in that way – but she couldn't imagine it was that much different north of the border.

Money and power seemed to breed these dynamics.

Scarlett stopped herself, unhappy with her bitter train of thought.

Money wasn't the issue.

It was the actions and behaviour of those who thought that consequences were something that happened to other people, leading grown men to think it was entirely plausible to live in a house with their wife and young pregnant mistress.

Although not quite a trust fund baby, Jason's family's wealth had also blessed him. His father invested wisely whilst he was alive and his property portfolio across Bath, on top of his sizeable life insurance policy, meant that Tara would never be short of anything.

Scarlett also had to give credit to Jason, who was himself a respected author, which offered a generous standard of living.

But their lives, including the beautiful townhouse they moved into after their secret wedding abroad – much to his mother's disdain – were owned solely by Tara. Livid and disgruntled that Scarlett hadn't signed a prenuptial agreement, she refused to give her son the gift.

Still, Tara was always generous to her son, and in return, Scarlett helped look after the maintenance of the properties and boutique hotels scattered across the city. The arrangement satisfied everyone, meeting all their needs, and Scarlett, though grateful, had worked hard and requested little.

The realisation suddenly dawned on her that this was clearly her downfall, as now she didn't own anything.

She didn't even think they had a pension. The properties had been their safety plan, as Jason was the sole heir to his mother's estate. But as she was quickly realising, it was a solid plan by Tara to make sure Scarlett wouldn't receive a penny if she ever left.

A fresh wave of nausea flooded her.

Things just keep getting better.

"Are you alright?" Mrs Wilson's voice pulled Scarlett out of her reverie.

"Yes, I'm fine, thanks." Scarlett pasted a smile on her face. "Tired from the travelling, but nothing to worry about. So, how long have you been working for the family?"

Mrs Wilson seemed pleased with this question. "Well now, let's see. Must be coming up to forty years now. My family are from Aberdeen, see, and a job for a kitchen hand came up when I was just fifteen. Good God, doesn't even seem that long ago if I'm honest with you." Mrs Wilson chuckled to herself and continued walking on, her memories leaving a trace of a smile for the rest of their walk around the house.

Scarlett looked forward to hearing stories about Mrs Wilson's time with the Cameron-Reids. Over forty years, there couldn't be much she hadn't seen or heard, but she'd bide her time. She felt hesitant to ask more until she got to know Mrs Wilson a little better.

The tour took almost two hours, after which Mrs Wilson tasked Scarlett with polishing the oak balustrades on the wide carpeted staircase that snaked up to the first floor from the enormous entrance hall of the house.

Scarlett marvelled at the craftsmanship of the carved wood as she followed Mrs Wilson's very precise instructions.

"He had this all restored, you know, using the original staircase and other wood derived from the estate, with the help of a local carpenter, mind. So, it's important we look after it."

Mrs Wilson laid out her paraphernalia of cleaning items, ranging from a homemade vinegar and lemon solution to various cloths for different purposes and beeswax made from the estate's beehives.

Scarlett felt as if she were on an episode of *Countryfile* as Mrs Wilson rattled off a list of everything that was derived from the estate's apparently plentiful land and surroundings. Instead of commenting, she listened, nodding and taking mental notes of everything she was told.

"So, all very easy, really." Mrs Wilson looked at Scarlett to check she was taking it all in. "I'd best be getting on with lunch prep. Edward likes to have his dinner at lunchtime and a light supper in the evening – come find me when you're done, and if you're up to it, we'll get you started on something else."

Smiling, Scarlett said, "No problem, and thank you," hoping to convince her that she could be trusted not to damage the laird's pride and joy.

"You're very welcome. I shall see you soon." The older woman smiled and nodded, taking herself off towards the kitchen.

Scarlett took out her earbuds and phone, looking for an upbeat playlist to keep her company – steering well away from the sleepier ballads she usually sang along to whilst doing the chores at home. Crying into the beeswax would probably ruin the carefully balanced ingredients, which wouldn't please Mrs Wilson at all.

She decided on Muse's cover of "Feeling Good" and got to work, losing herself in the task at hand. She'd not listened to the band for ages, remembering how, despite the track no longer being popular, she went through a phase of playing it full blast in her room and requested it at every party one Christmas period, driving all her friends at the time mad.

With a smile and thoughts of happier times, she put the song on repeat, shaking her head and shoulders along to the beat each time the song hit its crescendo.

After what she realised must be its eighth or ninth repetition, a large pair of Barbour boots appeared in front of her. She pulled out her earbuds and hurried to her feet, using the banister as support whilst taking in the full length of the man standing on the staircase before her. She couldn't help noticing he looked as good dressed as he did half naked. Scarlett blinked the inappropriate thoughts away.

"Sorry, was a bit lost in the moment."

"I can see that."

There was little emotion in his thick Scottish accent, but Scarlett was certain there was a hint of a smile at the corner of his mouth.

CHAPTER 6

EDWARD REALISED THEY'D been standing there looking at each other and saying nothing for much longer than was socially acceptable.

"Settling in then?" he finally said.

Scarlett nodded and looked down at the balustrade.

"Yes, thanks. Mrs Wilson has been showing me the ropes." A blush spread from her neckline up to her cheeks.

"You'll be a big help for her." Edward followed Scarlett's gaze down the stairway. "Appreciate this isn't what you usually do for work."

She shrugged, and some curls sprang loose and hung over one of her eyes – giving him the overwhelming urge to brush them away and tuck them behind her ear.

Get it together, man.

"To be honest, I really appreciate you letting me just rock up and giving me some work." Scarlett absentmindedly tucked the loose strands behind her ear.

"Your mum has been here a long time – I was happy to help. And Mrs Wilson can always do with an extra pair of hands."

They continued to hold each other's gaze.

"Is your mother well?" he asked, scratching his thumb across his eyebrow, which wasn't actually itchy.

Stupid fucking question.

Scarlett narrowed her eyes at him, and he swore a

flicker of curiosity crossed her face, a smile tugging at her lips. "Yes, seems to be. Although she was keen to get back to her plants and harvesting this morning."

Edward nodded and looked away from her penetrating eyes, still unsure of their actual colour.

"And the apartment is comfortable?" he asked, taking a sudden interest in something else. *Anything else.* An invisible mark on the step between them – that would do.

"Extremely. It's beautiful. Amazingly renovated. Was it done recently?"

The way she cocked her head when she asked a question was distracting, and he took a moment to register the question before answering.

"No. It used to be my mother's art studio. She found the main house ..." He looked up and raised his hand, using two fingers to feign speech marks. "Stifling to her creativity." Seeing the sympathy in Scarlett's eyes, he quickly added, "She's still with us. She went back to the States not long after my younger brother started boarding school alongside me. She didn't get on with the Scottish climate. It's not for everyone."

"It's been lovely since I arrived. I'm assuming it's not always like this, though?"

"No, not really." He shrugged.

And now we're discussing the weather.

Edward cringed.

"I see." Scarlett shrugged in response. "A bit of cold doesn't bother me. I quite like the cosiness of being indoors when it's freezing outside."

"Great." Edward put his hands in his jean pockets, nodding. "The studio is fine, but this place is trickier to heat."

Someone below them cleared their throat, breaking the moment and making the pair turn in unison towards the foyer.

"Mrs Wilson, there you are." Edward nodded again, half smiled at Scarlett, and made his way down the stairs towards his housekeeper. "I wanted to speak to you about preparing a couple of rooms in the east wing. My brother will grace us with his presence on Saturday, and I'd like to keep him out of my way as much as possible. Could you make arrangements for that, please?"

"Of course. Should I open up your mother's quarters?" Mrs Wilson smiled politely, probably trying to erase disturbing thoughts of him in his own quarters that morning.

Fuck's sake – what a shitshow of a day!

Edward paused on the bottom stair and winced.

"If that's not appropriate, I can—"

"No, of course, that seems like the best idea. Be less work for you and Mrs …?" Edward turned to look at Scarlett.

He waited for her to respond as she paused for a long moment.

"It's just Scarlett. No need for formalities."

He watched her with interest as her eyes shifted from him to Mrs Wilson and then to the cleaning products in her hands.

Her face suddenly paled. "Just Scarlett will be fine."

"You look unwell. Are you okay?" Edward asked, his voice mirroring the concern etched on Mrs Wilson's face.

"I'm fine, thank you, just had a bit of a dizzy spell. It's passed now." Scarlett looked back at them with a dazzling smile that made his breath hitch. But he was unconvinced as he watched her.

This time, his awkwardness didn't force his eyes away as it had just moments before.

She said she was fine.

He tried to shake off the weird feeling he had

around her and wasn't entirely sure why he was so concerned – Mrs Wilson clearly had a handle on everything.

"I'll be in my office if you need me for anything." Edward glanced at Mrs Wilson before focusing back on Scarlett. "I suggest, Mrs – sorry, *Scarlett*." The word seemed uncomfortable on his lips. "I suggest you take an early lunch and maybe rest for an hour or so."

Edward didn't wait for a response and walked away from the two women.

He would not do this – he would not start something with the new employee!

No matter how attractive she was – or how those light blue jeans she was wearing accentuated every one of her curves.

Those curves but ...

He shook his head. He would disregard how those eyes of hers penetrated his, and how that deep auburn hair sprang free at every opportunity, as if it refused confinement.

After Natasha left with Lily, he'd sworn he'd never put himself or the estate at risk again. His mother, of all people, had to bail him out of that one – Edward had been too broken to be able to think straight and Natasha was going for the whole lot.

Nope.

He wouldn't and couldn't.

Fuck's sake.

His inner dialogue went in circles around his head, tormenting him until he finally reached the sanctuary of his office, and with the door firmly closed behind him, he let out a long sigh.

Edward shook his head again. He was a full-grown adult and would control and neutralise his ridiculous reaction to the woman – after all, he wasn't a hormonal teenager with an insatiable hard-on.

But Edward groaned loudly as his body instantly reacted to the contrary.
He really was fucked.
Shit. Shit. Shit.

CHAPTER 7

SCARLETT'S EYES FOLLOWED Edward as he walked down the hall until he was out of sight. She turned to find Mrs Wilson looking at her with narrowed eyes.

"Sorry," Scarlett said with a shrug. "I guess I'm tired and dazed after ... everything."

"I imagine it's been a long couple of days for you." Mrs Wilson still seemed to be sizing Scarlett up.

"I'm guessing there's not much love for the younger brother?" Scarlett wanted to change the subject and collected the cleaning products, wiping her oily hands on her jeans.

"They're like chalk and cheese, those two!" Mrs Wilson was soon beside her. "Let me take those down for you." She examined Scarlett's handiwork so far. "You've done a great job. We'll get the rest done later this afternoon, and then we'll look at Lady Cameron-Reid's quarters. Should be interesting – it's not been in use since the laird's ex-wife was still here."

"Ex-wife?" An estranged American mother, a strained relationship with his brother, and an ex-wife? Scarlett was intrigued.

"Aye, she left about twelve years ago, took their daughter and now's married with another two children." Mrs Wilson walked back down the staircase, inspecting the polish on the spindles at the same time. "Lily is here, well, used to be here, every weekend without fail. He's always trying to be a good father, but she's eighteen now, and you know what it's like with younger ones. They want to be busy with their friends." Satisfied with Scarlett's effort, Mrs Wilson veered off to the right. "I think it hurts him, though."

Scarlett trailed behind her through to the kitchen, hanging on to every word.

She wasn't sure why, but she hadn't pictured him to be a family man and imagined he was more of a solitary figure, obsessed with his ancestral home and work, leaving little room for much else, including romance.

Scarlett immediately realised she was being ridiculous. Of course he had a love interest. A family. She wouldn't be the only red-blooded woman who saw what she did.

She silently reprimanded herself for the creeping feeling of hope rising in her that *perhaps* it wasn't the case at the moment. What on earth was she thinking? Of course she wasn't going to end up with a hot laird in the Scottish Highlands – she wasn't living in some parallel universe where everyone ended up with their very own happy ending.

Scarlett wasn't a hopeless romantic like her mother, who, Scarlett was certain, would still be engrossed in some classic or historical romance novel when not working.

No, Scarlett lived in the real world. And in that world, women closer to middle age than their twenties – *especially working-class women* – enjoyed a comfortable and content existence for a few years until their husbands cheated on them, leaving them back where they started, probably cleaning houses for others.

She winced. She knew she was being dramatic. Scarlett rarely wallowed in self-pity or played the victim; she was stronger than that. And there was nothing wrong with cleaning and this wasn't a terrible situation to be in. This would all work out and was the perfect solution until she could form a more long-term plan.

Life wasn't over – it was just temporarily and completely fucked. But developing a crush on another man was definitely not the answer.

Everything would be just fine.

She *was* tired though and starting work only a day after arriving, having been through a traumatic break-up and a long drive north, perhaps wasn't the best idea, despite her desire to keep busy and occupied.

Scarlett admitted defeat. Following the laird's advice to rest up for a couple of hours wasn't a terrible idea. Her eyes felt heavy, and her joints were aching.

Sleep would be good.

―⁂―

A LIGHT TAP on the door woke Scarlett.

"Scarlett, I've brought you some tea and toast." June came in and set a tray on the dresser beside the window.

"Thanks." Scarlett's eyelids felt heavy with sleep. "What time is it? I was only going to rest for an hour or so."

"You've been asleep since yesterday lunchtime. It's just gone seven. I'm just heading out to work."

"As in seven am?" Scarlett sat up with a jolt.

June nodded.

"I've slept a whole day and night?" She couldn't remember ever sleeping that long.

"Take it easy. You'll make yourself dizzy again." June opened the window behind the closed curtains. "Edward suggested you start work on Friday. Give yourself another couple of days to get some rest and find your feet. What with all the travelling and, well, everything else."

June looked at Scarlett, her concern apparent.

She continued, "I agree with him. And you mustn't worry – it will still leave plenty of time for you to help Mrs Wilson with the east wing."

"His brother is arriving on Saturday." Scarlett plumped her pillow behind her before leaning back against the headboard, the smell of tea and toast rousing her out of her sleepiness. She reached over and brought the tray to the bed.

"Yes, seems to be causing quite a stir." June wiped her hands down the front of her green work trousers. She nodded towards the toast. "Mrs Wilson's homemade jam. I remember strawberry was your favourite."

"Thank you." Scarlett suddenly felt famished and took a large bite, melted butter and warm jam spilling onto her chin. She couldn't remember toast ever tasting this good.

"Glad you've got your appetite back." June smiled. "Right, I'd best get on. Make yourself at home, maybe take a stroll through the grounds if you feel up to it. Fresh air will do you the world of good. I'll see you around dinnertime. I've put chilli in the slow cooker for later."

Having taken another large bite, Scarlett just nodded and waved goodbye with her free hand, watching the back of her mother as she left.

She didn't want to make a fuss, but two days of not doing anything apart from being lost in her own thoughts didn't seem that appealing, even with what she imagined were good intentions.

But she didn't hate the idea either.

Her body seemed to be telling her the same as the laird, so she softened to his instructions. Perhaps he wasn't so surly after all, not that it made any actual difference to her. She wasn't likely to spend a significant amount of time with him.

Scarlett mused over their last meeting on the stairs whilst she polished off the remaining toast and drank her tea. She thought of the way he put his hands in his jean pockets, nodding, whilst his eyes widened and lips squeezed together – Scarlett wasn't sure if it was a grimace or a smile, but his awkward disposition made him even more endearing to her.

He must think me a complete liability.

She shook her head at the thought – in fact, she needed to stop thinking about him altogether.

To distract herself, she pulled a curtain aside and looked out the window. The sky was clear, and there was a certain crispness to the scene outside. She liked autumn and a walk in the woods felt like a great idea. She was getting agitated by the crumbs nestling between her breasts, and the idea of lying in the same clothes for almost two days made her grimace.

Scarlett moved the tray from her lap to the bottom of the bed and swung her feet onto the floor. The tiredness plaguing her for days seemed to have finally lifted and the debilitating feeling of dread no longer sat on her chest like an anvil.

At least that was something.

In less than an hour, Scarlett had showered, dressed, and was standing in the courtyard, unsure where to go for a walk. She didn't much feel like running into Edward after their last awkward exchange, which had culminated in his pity and an extended duvet day.

Way to impress the new boss.

She cringed.

Equally, despite her kind nature, Mrs Wilson wasn't someone she wanted to see either. In fact, she didn't want to see *anyone*, so she followed the small path she could see leading towards the woods; trees and the odd bit of wildlife seemed like a much safer bet.

The path snaked alongside the main rear lawn with tall hedges that kept her from view from the ground level of the house and gardens. A short walk down brought her to an opening that formed a natural T-junction, where a solid wooden bench, with a detailed owl carved into its high back, greeted all who approached. Scarlett ran her fingers over the owl's face and smiled at its realistic features.

She looked both ways.

One way led into the dense woodland and the other she guessed headed towards the loch she'd glimpsed from the upper floors.

Scarlett opted for the protection of the woods.

The damp, heady smell of pine mingled with decaying leaves, moss, and fern drew her in. It reminded her of a recent article she'd read about the benefits of forest bathing instead of traditional medication, and although she was no scientist or medical expert, the sense of peace she experienced as she took in the sights and sounds around her made her see why there might be some truth to it.

A modest stone bridge that looked as old as the house itself stretched across a stream a couple of metres below her. She stopped to watch for a few moments before continuing up a small hill.

Ahead, she spotted another bench, similar to the one close to the entrance of the woods. Two otters, their faces showing bright curiosity, were carved into the armrests.

Scarlett smiled again.

Whoever had commissioned these to be distributed throughout the woods clearly had a keen sense of fun and love for wildlife.

She wondered if it had been Edward's mother when the boys were younger, or perhaps even his wife, and

A NEW *Hope* IN THE HIGHLANDS

Scarlett tried to imagine a childhood where she would've had this kind of freedom to roam. It was so far removed from her own, which had comprised being in their tiny flat or playing in the small back garden of her aunt's compact terraced house.

Looking around, she thought of Edward running around these woods, making up games with his brother and perhaps even their parents. With such memories and surroundings, it was no wonder Edward never left, or that her own mother would never want to – just the idea that the day would come when Scarlett would need to leave briefly filled her with a pang of sadness. She wasn't sure why.

"Stop feeling so sorry for yourself," she groaned, shaking her head.

"In some places, they call you crazy for talking to yourself," a voice spoke from behind her.

Scarlett spun around to see who it was. Judging from the gardening clothes and Polish accent, she guessed immediately.

"Andrzej, right?" Scarlett cocked her head to the side.

"Correct, and you must be Scarlett." A huge welcoming smile stretched across his face.

She nodded in response. "I didn't hear you coming, sorry."

"No need to apologise, and no need to worry. I also talk to myself. The trees are old and good listeners."

Scarlett flushed, feeling awkward. It was a sensation she was quickly becoming accustomed to around the various inhabitants of Haddon House.

"A fence has come down near the river. I'm just off to investigate." He nodded towards where he was heading.

"Sounds exciting." Scarlett smiled back at him, his own being contagious.

"You wish to join me?"

"Sure." She shrugged. "I didn't realise there was also a river."

"Yes, through the top of the woods and down the hill." He pointed up ahead. "Not far, lots of trout and salmon. You will like it. It's very beautiful."

"Sounds great." Scarlett put her hands deep into her pockets as they fell into step with each other.

"Plus, I'm also good at listening if you feel like talking to someone other than the trees." Andrzej gave a good-natured chuckle.

Scarlett laughed. "Thanks, they're not bad listeners but terrible conversationists."

Andrzej nodded. "Yes, although the same has been said about me also."

Scarlett smiled at his easy company. "So, a fence has fallen?"

"Yes, nothing too dramatic, but the neighbours can become a little upset when it falls on their side, you know. So, I must look and maybe pull it back onto our side until we repair."

"You mean you and my mother?"

Andrzej let out a gentle laugh. "Your mother is a strong woman and wonderful gardener, but myself and the boss do the heavy lifting."

"Edward does manual work too?" Scarlett asked, looking across at him.

Andrzej was a pleasant man to look at, and to talk to – she could see why her mother liked him so much.

"You seem surprised." He raised his eyebrows at the question.

"Do I?"

Andrzej nodded, glancing at her before returning his focus to the path. "Yes, you do."

"I suppose I just thought considering his rank, he'd leave the hard work to his staff."

Again, Andrzej laughed. "I don't think he would appreciate that thought."

"Good job he's not around to hear it then." Scarlett shrugged, smiling.

"Best keep your voice down. It's no longer only us and the trees. I think I see him up there."

Scarlett looked up ahead and saw his unmistakable silhouette waiting for them. "Great."

Andrzej gave her a questioning look, which she ignored, taking a keen interest in the boots she'd borrowed from her mother instead.

CHAPTER 8

IT WASN'T HIS intention to orchestrate another meeting with her, but after spotting Scarlett wandering into the woods, and Andrzej unknowingly following shortly after, Edward felt compelled to meet Andrzej at the crest of the woods to help him with the fence.

Quickly changing out of his chinos and shoes, swapping them for jeans and boots, he headed out to drive up to the top field so he could meet Andrzej there, meaning they could walk down together. Of course, he knew Scarlett would likely be there too, and the feeling of anticipation winding tightly in his stomach irritated him.

She's not for me.

He knew she had recently separated from a long marriage, and although he didn't know the details, he sensed the situation was messy and complicated.

Edward didn't do complicated.

He liked things simple, without drama, and definitely no emotional mess – all reasons he'd never remarried after his split from Natasha.

The estate was enough, and he had access to *company* when he felt the urge. He knew he wasn't unattractive and there were enough unattached women, or those with certain marital understandings, in his circle of acquaintances who were happy to meet for the odd drink and dinner when it suited both parties.

These types of meetings had recently become less

common, and he wasn't sure if it was him or his companions who'd become tired of them; perhaps it was both. He winced, suddenly remembering there were a couple of WhatsApp messages he still hadn't replied to.

They were the usual innocuous but loaded type, such as: *Hey, how's things with you?*

He knew engaging with them would lead to agreeing to a meeting, which rarely meant anything other than a night of banal conversation, too much alcohol, followed by mediocre sex – none of which seemed all that appealing, so he'd simply left them on read.

He wasn't proud of his often distant and insensitive approach to these things, but in his mind, he was always upfront about his intentions. Conventional dating and relationships weren't amongst them. But Edward couldn't help wondering if he found himself in a similar situation with Scarlett, would it be that easy to leave *her* on read?

The day before, despite his best intentions to block her out, he kept catching himself thinking about her. His thoughts would rest on simple things, like how loose strands of her auburn hair appeared amber in the light when they escaped her ponytail. Or how she'd absentmindedly move stray curls behind her ear when she spoke, despite them springing loose again moments later in their bid for freedom. He'd felt like a fool and kept pushing the thoughts away for the rest of the day, eventually falling into a fitful sleep.

But apparently sanity was not prevailing and this morning there was clearly no stopping him as he parked one of the small 4x4s they used for driving across the estate. He pocketed the keys and began walking up towards the entrance to the woods. He crossed the stile in a single stride and inhaled the familiar smells as he waited, the faint voices drawing nearer.

Mild annoyance prickled at him when he heard their laughter.

Andrzej was the first to wave, and Scarlett reluctantly did the same. Edward wondered if he'd interrupted something.

Had Andrzej already charmed her with his easy and kind manner?

He couldn't blame her. Despite the men being of similar age, compared to his own prickly and awkward ways, his Polish employee must seem like a warm hug in lionesque form with his thick mane of blonde hair and broad physique. He looked like a Danish Viking despite his Eastern European heritage, and even as a comfortably heterosexual man, Edward could see the appeal from a woman's point of view.

Although hesitant to admit it, he was particularly interested in Scarlett's thoughts on this.

"Good morning." Andrzej smiled brightly.

"Morning." Edward managed a tight smile. "I thought you might need a hand with this fence."

"We were just discussing this." Andrzej threw Scarlett a subtle conspiratorial wink.

"William's assistant said it was just a couple of panels, but we'll see once we walk down." Edward turned his attention to Scarlett. "You look better."

"I appreciate the couple of days to get some rest. Thank you for that."

Edward nodded. "You'll be no use to anyone if you're constantly fainting on the stairwell."

"I mean, I wasn't quite that bad. I think all that travel tired me out." She narrowed her eyes at him.

"Yes, I'm sure." Edward turned away, signalling their conversation was over, and headed back towards the field. "If you follow the path to the left, it will take you further up the hill. You'll then come to the waterfall. It's a pleasant walk up there, not too taxing."

"I was going to come down and see the river," Scarlett told him, a hint of annoyance now in her voice.

Edward turned, noticing Andrzej's mildly amused expression as he watched the exchange. It hardened Edward's resolve further. "No need to bother yourself. Best to stay out of the way." He turned again and jumped over the fence into the field. "Watch your footing if you walk to the pool below the falls."

"Right," Scarlett huffed.

"Enjoy your walk," Edward heard Andrzej say just as he was about to offer a similar comment, but he fell silent when he saw Andrzej gently touch Scarlett's shoulder before leaving her to meet Edward in the field.

Scarlett's face hardened when she looked at Edward, and huffing again, she headed off in the suggested direction. He internally scolded himself for being so harsh. She didn't deserve it, and he didn't understand why he had such a bizarre reaction to her.

"We go?" Andrzej asked, pulling Edward from his thoughts as he watched Scarlett walk away.

He avoided meeting Andrzej's curious gaze. "Yes, let's see what the damage is."

"I hear your brother arrives on Saturday – it's been a while."

Edward nodded. "Indeed."

"Is your mother visiting with him this time?"

"No, she's planning a visit late spring. She's hoping the midges won't be out in full force by then."

"But of course she knows they will?"

"Andrzej, as you well know, you can tell my mother the sky is blue, but if she wishes to believe it's purple, no mere mortal or God himself can convince her otherwise."

This made Andrzej let out a hearty laugh, making

Edward smile.

The two continued to walk down to the river in companionable silence. The surrounding beauty of the fields, with their now wilting wildflowers and colouring leaves on the trees, always filled him with pride.

He loved his ancestral home, but it was the woodlands, the fields, and the river below that provided him with a soft sense of unharnessed joy. It brought him peace, no matter how much turmoil the world around him was in – another reason he would never let his brother sell it, certainly not as long as he was alive.

"Ah, I see where it has fallen." Andrzej pointed to the four broken panels that were lying flat on Sir William's land.

His English neighbour, who he saw infrequently but had a good understanding with, took immense pleasure in taking his friends river fishing, and Edward liked to keep the peace as much as possible.

Andrzej continued, "The wood has split, but I have some spare panels in the storage which I can mend this easily with. It will be done today. I can do this alone, if you have other business."

"Think I'd rather be doing this." Edward needed something physical to do to work off this overwhelming restlessness he was struggling to shift.

Andrzej threw him a warm smile and shrugged. "Okay."

The pair began lifting and dragging the broken wood.

"The daughter seems to be settling in okay, then." The words were out before he could stop them.

"You tell me this or ask as a question?" Andrzej looked across at Edward.

"I saw you talking, that's all. She seemed like she was." Edward shrugged before yanking part of the fence free from a stubborn branch and continued,

A NEW Hope IN THE HIGHLANDS

slightly breathless, "It's better I give you a hand with this, then it's done quicker."

"I appreciate it." Andrzej lifted the other end of a larger panel of wood that Edward was dragging out of the way of the boundary. "I only spoke with her briefly. She is very easy to talk to. I see the resemblance to her mother."

Edward simply shrugged, and the pair worked in silence for a while before Edward replied. "I don't think she particularly enjoys talking to me." He dropped his side of the final panel, placing a leg on top of a neighbouring tree stump and resting his arm on his raised knee to survey the area. "That's the bulk of it. The ATV has some rope on it. If you drag all this over to the far gate, we can bring the truck down with the new wood and take this up to the barn for burning at some point."

"Sounds like a good plan." Andrzej wiped his brow with the back of his hand. "And if I can speak plainly?" He threw Edward a questioning look.

"Of course," Edward replied.

"Maybe the lady likes to be spoken to in a gentler way. Perhaps then she will be more talkative." Andrzej shrugged, holding Edward's gaze.

Edward's mouth formed a thin line at the comment, but he nodded. "Perhaps she will, Andrzej."

The two men looked at the wood in silence for a while before Edward straightened and turned back towards the hill. "Let's walk back up. You can bring the ATV down then."

"Yes, sir."

When they arrived back at the top of the hill, Edward threw the keys to Andrzej.

"Let me know if you need any help," Edward told him, avoiding the groundsman's interested gaze.

Andrzej caught the keys with one hand and nodded

as Edward watched the entrance into the woods.

After a moment's hesitation, Edward stepped back over the fence and headed towards the waterfall, Andrzej's quiet chuckle trailing after him.

CHAPTER 9

It was only after her feet began aching that Scarlett realised she'd been stomping. Not exactly what she'd had in mind when she set off for a relaxing, leisurely nature walk.

What is his problem?

She didn't mind the awkward meetings or his social ineptness, but the whole surly Scottish thing was infuriating.

He made her feel like an incompetent and weak little girl, though she was neither, and she would not put up with it, even if he was her boss, all tall and aloof and frustratingly hot, and despite the latter, she was really starting to dislike him.

By the time she reached the gushing waterfall, which she couldn't fault as being anything less than stunning, she was too annoyed to appreciate the medicinal properties of her surroundings. Forest bathing was all very well when one didn't have Edward Cameron-Reid invading their thoughts.

The only saving grace was that, in her distraction, Jason hadn't crossed her mind once since awakening that morning. But when she realised this, a pang of guilt stabbed her in the chest.

How was she already discarding thoughts of her husband in such a brief space of time?

It made her wonder if she'd perhaps known something was amiss long before Angelica came on the scene. She found it unsettling. That, along with the creeping realisation that something else had been missing between them and probably had been for a good number of years.

But there was nothing for her to feel guilty or bad about.

It wasn't Scarlett who'd thrown away thirteen years of marriage – Jason was the one who'd been able to do that with apparent ease and little conscience, had it not been for getting caught out, of course.

"What a douchebag!" she said to a robin perched in a tree nearby.

"Have to admit, I've been called much worse," a voice replied from behind her, making Scarlett spin around.

Seriously, people had to stop sneaking up on her around here.

She was about to say as much but stalled when she properly took in the sight of the man standing in front of her – it was basically Edward, just a few years younger and with thicker hair.

Her surprised reaction made the man laugh.

"I know. It freaks most people out. I'm Leonard, Edward's younger brother; arguably the better version." He drew closer and held out his hand, not breaking eye contact.

Scarlett shook his hand, which felt firm yet soft against her skin; a privileged hand, much like Jason's.

She briefly wondered what Edward's hands would feel like. Were his a little coarser because of the manual work he did on the estate? What would they feel like on her ...

"And you are?" Leonard was still looking at her, keeping hold of her hand, his expression showing mild amusement.

"Sorry, I'm Scarlett. June's daughter." Scarlett felt hot under his gaze and worried her hand would become sweaty in his grip. His eyes, she noted, were the same deep blue as Edward's, with the *exact* same intense pull.

Jesus, two men like this in the same house is a bit much.

She laughed nervously, but regained her composure and smiled politely, releasing her hand from his.

"I'm just staying here for a while, you know, giving Mrs Wilson a hand. I was just heading back to the house after getting a bit of fresh air." She nodded her head towards the main house.

"I'll join you," he said, still smiling. "If that's okay with you?"

"Of course, please do." Scarlett looked away, feeling her cheeks flush.

What is it with these Cameron-Reid men?

"Thanks. Have you been here long then?" Leonard threw her another easy smile.

"No, just a couple of days." Scarlett stopped and looked up at him. "You're early, though. I thought you wouldn't be here until Saturday. We were planning to get everything ready for you before you arrived."

Leonard laughed. "I imagine he's trying to get me holed up in the east wing?"

This made Scarlett smile. He clearly wasn't an idiot.

"It might have been mentioned."

"I like to keep Edward on his toes. I mean, someone has to." He winked at Scarlett when she glanced across at him.

"I see." Scarlett smiled again.

"So, how long will you be staying, Scarlett?" he asked, still watching her.

"Not sure yet. A while, I imagine." She really didn't want to get into this with him.

"It seems a strange place for someone like you to be holed up, out here in the middle of nowhere." He stretched out his arm to allow Scarlett to pass in front when the path narrowed.

Scarlett smiled her thanks.

"It's beautiful here." She shrugged. "Truth be told, I feel quite privileged to be allowed to stay."

"Christ, you sound like my brother." Leonard's smile slipped for a moment, but he quickly retrieved it again. "Talking of which, I heard he went off in this direction. Have you seen him?"

Scarlett felt uncomfortable telling him where he'd gone, for reasons she was unsure of, but not wanting to lie, she told him, "He left with Andrzej to fix some fencing."

Leonard groaned and then smiled again. "I'm especially glad I bumped into you instead, then. Otherwise I might have got dragged into some tedious fence-mending expedition."

Scarlett couldn't stop stealing glances at him. "It really is uncanny, you know." She slowly shook her head, a curl springing free from behind her ear, which she tucked back again. "You could literally be twins were it not for the age gap."

Leonard let out a good-humoured laugh. "Yes, some say we're carbon copies of our grandfather, apparently." He looked at Scarlett again. She felt like he was drinking her in. It made her feel heady. "I possess a bit more charm, though; the whole grumpy laird thing never appealed to me. He's more our dad in that department."

"Whereas you are?" Scarlett cocked her head at him, pausing briefly so they were walking in step with each other now the path had widened again.

"My sweet Scarlett, I can be whoever you want me to be." He smiled widely and winked.

Scarlett laughed. She realised that probably wasn't the reaction he was looking for, but it was such a well-rehearsed line, she couldn't take it seriously. "Does that usually work?"

Leonard had the good grace to smile, looking at her with a sidewards glance. "As it happens, yes, I'd say it has a 99.9% success rate."

She laughed again. "Seems to me it's becoming a tad stale."

"You're a tough crowd."

The pair laughed and continued their walk back towards the house.

Their conversation turned to his journey to Scotland, about which he had a few amusing anecdotes, and Scarlett laughed at them with ease. She wouldn't yet call him the better brother, but he was much easier to talk to than the other one.

Yet, despite the effortless chat, it was still the older brother her thoughts kept pulling her towards, pausing on the idea of him lifting panels of heavy wood – she imagined that would be a pleasant thing to watch.

No sooner had she mused on the image of Edward flexing his biceps than she took a sharp intake of breath, her heart leaping to her throat as she looked up to see him watching their approach.

She knew she had done nothing wrong, but a sense of disloyalty tugged at her gut, especially when she saw his lips tighten in a thin disapproving line, his hands deep in his pockets.

He had a talent for seeming both authoritative and vulnerable at the same time. He was an enigma and fast becoming her very own version of catnip.

Edward's icy stare, however, made her shudder, and she was relieved when a grin appeared on Leonard's face and he moved away from her to greet his older brother.

CHAPTER 10

ON HIS WAY to seek out Scarlett, Edward's thoughts had been scattered, not having a clue what to say to her. What was going to be his excuse for coming to find her? Surely it was just to check she was okay – after all, the incline down to the rock pool was steep, and she hadn't been in the best shape yesterday morning. It was the right thing to do; he had a duty of care to all his employees.

However, as he turned the corner, he could once again hear the muffled sound of laughter coming towards him, and his heart sank as he saw who was accompanying Scarlett.

"Brother!" Leonard called out. "There you are."

Edward didn't respond, coming to a standstill and placing his hands deep in his pockets as he awaited their approach.

He noticed Scarlett was smiling, her cheeks flushed, and she appeared energised by her walk and the fresh air – and no doubt his brother's company.

"I came looking for you and found this delightful creature instead." Leonard threw Scarlett a radiant smile. "I can't say I was disappointed."

"You're early." Edward didn't smile.

"Thank you. It's good to be back." Leonard threw his arm over his brother's shoulder, turning him towards the house. The gesture made Edward stiffen. "Much to discuss, brother."

Edward could sense Scarlett falling back, allowing

them space and privacy, no doubt out of politeness, not realising it was the last thing he wanted.

"The place is looking great, as always," Leonard continued, despite Edward's lack of response. "Mother sends her regards and apologises for not accompanying me. She told me to tell you to call her. She's not heard from you in a few weeks."

"I spoke to her on Sunday," Edward replied, shaking his head with a note of disdain in his voice.

Leonard shrugged off the comment.

"So, no doubt you're dying to hear my news!" Leonard beamed at him.

"Is it that obvious?"

Leonard laughed and squeezed Edward's shoulder before releasing him. "You hide your enthusiasm well."

Edward still didn't respond, painfully aware Scarlett was still behind them and wishing she wasn't, or more, that Leonard wasn't beside him.

"Appreciate you don't keep abreast of big news from across the pond—"

"Try my best not to," Edward said honestly.

He wanted to send his brother back to the house, alone, so he could fall back and talk to Scarlett. Maybe even apologise for his prickly behaviour towards her earlier.

"Well, I'm finally doing the deed." Leonard smiled, ignoring the interruption. "I'm getting married."

Edward finally looked at his brother. This was genuinely not the news he was expecting.

"Who's stupid enough to do that with you?" Edward was genuinely stunned.

Leonard laughed, clapping his brother on the back. "Knew you'd be happy for me."

Edward glanced behind him to see Scarlett was heading away from them towards the loch.

"I mean," Edward said, trying to refocus on the

conversation, "congratulations. Who is the lucky lady finally capturing the notorious bachelor from the deep south?"

"You don't know her. Her name is Anaïse. Great girl. Daddy is filthy rich, like off the scale type of shit." Leonard looked extremely pleased with himself.

Edward rolled his eyes. "Wouldn't expect anything less."

"And here's where you come in." Leonard beamed again.

"Jesus Christ, why do I need to be involved?" Edward was not interested in playing any part in any wedding.

"She's a bit of a romantic and has her heart set on a winter wedding at her fiancé's ancestral home in the Scottish Highlands."

"For fuck's sake," Edward muttered.

"I told her you'd be over the moon about it. She's sending out the save the dates as we speak. The week before Christmas. It'll be the event of the decade! Although I've told her I can't promise snow, but we can buy some in."

Edward laughed sarcastically. "We'll buy in the snow?"

"Absolutely! Mother is obviously bitching about the cold, but we'll buy her some new ethically sourced furs to keep her sweet."

"Right, because there is such a thing." Edward rolled his eyes at the absurdity of this entire conversation.

"Come on." Leonard nudged his brother playfully. "Who doesn't love a wedding?"

Edward raised an eyebrow, making Leonard laugh.

"Also ..." Leonard pulled on Edward's arm, bringing them both to a standstill.

He became serious, looking at Edward with unnerving sincerity.

"Who on this sweet earth is the hot redhead?"

Edward flinched and continued walking back to the house. His brother's presence on the estate was already annoying him.

※

MATTERS HADN'T IMPROVED by the following evening.

The brothers sat across from each other in the large oak-panelled dining room, both eating a thick red wine venison stew that had been filling the house with its rich smell since that morning.

Edward watched Leonard's interaction with Mrs Wilson, who had been their housemaid and cook since they were boys and who was now enjoying fussing over him as if he was still the charming, albeit wayward, young man he'd always been before he left to live in the States.

"Thank you so much, Mrs Wilson." Leonard flashed a smile at her before she left them alone to eat.

It seemed his brother's high energy and light humour permeated the entire house, infecting everyone in it.

Edward knew he was being unreasonable, but it felt like every time he entered a room or rounded a corner, Leonard was there laughing and joking with one member of the staff or another. Then there was Lily.

His usually surly daughter had arrived as soon as she heard of her uncle's arrival, more animated than he'd seen her in months and ecstatic to hear about Leonard's inappropriate adventures over in the States.

This was all irritating enough, but what annoyed

him most was how often he saw Leonard hanging around Scarlett like a bad fucking smell.

He'd seen them earlier that day talking and laughing in the corridors, and again later, in a room someone was to redecorate or freshen up for the big event.

Each time, it would make his mood sour even further.

"So, I spent a bit of time with Scarlett today," Leonard said now, as if reading his mind, simultaneously shoving a bit of fresh bread soaked in gravy into his mouth.

"I've noticed." Edward was moving food around on his plate, not hiding his lack of enthusiasm for the company or this particular line of conversation.

Ignoring Edward's tone, Leonard continued in his usual upbeat fashion.

"She's a gem, you know, not sure what she's doing playing housemaid here in the sticks. She's been quite reticent on that front. But she has some great ideas on how to get the house in order. I've put her in touch with Anaïse."

"Great."

"I'm assuming you're okay with that?" Leonard looked across the table at his brother, seemingly trying to suss out his mood. "You seem a bit shirty. I won't lie."

"Do what you need to do. I only hired Scarlett as a favour, so I'm pleased to hear she's useful to you."

"A favour?"

"To her mother."

"Ahh, the lovely June." Leonard smiled, a lascivious twinkle in his eye. "I would, you know."

"Your inappropriateness knows no bounds." Edward put his fork down; his appetite was gone. "As for Scarlett, if you feel she'll be of use, please, by all means, utilise her talents."

"Ohh, I would." Leonard smiled again. "But, you know, I'm soon to be married and all that."

"God help Anaïse, hopefully she knows what she's getting into." Edward shook his head.

"I'm a changed man, Edward." Leonard wiped his mouth with his napkin, his plate empty, and sat back, taking a long sip of his wine. "What about you then? Still the most eligible laird in the county, or is there anyone in line to be the next Lady Cameron-Reid?"

Edward also sat back, watching his brother and feeling a distinct lack of anything that could be construed as affection.

"Nobody else had anything to say on the matter, either." Leonard surveyed the room, absentmindedly tapping his wine glass. "I've noticed you get a bit sketchy when I mention the redhead though. Is there anything I should know?"

"Now you're being ridiculous. She's an employee." Edward rolled his eyes.

Leonard nodded, a slight smile playing on his lips. "Never stopped me."

"Don't we all know. I'm pretty sure there are some kids in the surrounding villages who bear an uncanny resemblance to you."

"Fallacies and lies, brother. I was always meticulously careful in that department." Leonard winked at him.

Edward scoffed and took out his phone, noticing a couple of new notifications.

"Anaïse will be coming out next week to do a bit of a recce. We might stay on until the wedding. Hope that's okay with you?" Leonard asked, his tone becoming bored.

"Sure, whatever you need." Edward was also losing interest in the conversation and distracted himself by composing a polite yet noncommittal message to one of his *acquaintances*.

Edward: *Sorry, been busy with the estate. Hope all is well.*

He hit send and copied and pasted it into another message, pressing send again. He didn't want to be rude and hoped that was enough to show he currently wasn't interested in meeting up.

"She may have a bit of an entourage. Hopefully that won't be a problem. Scarlett is confident she can get the rooms ready in time, so Mrs Wilson can get on with the rest of the preparations."

"How many is an entourage?" Edward wasn't keen on the idea of the house filling up with a group of eccentric rich kids.

"Just her maid of honour, Miranda – a bit of a handful, but she's okay. And Anaïse's spiritual guide, some Buddhist monk from LA. Oh, and perhaps a wedding planner called Andre – not sure if he's going to make it." Another smile crept onto his face. "Also can't work out if he's gay or not. Think he might swing both ways if I'm honest." Leonard smiled. "Not that it matters. I've experimented a bit in my time, too."

"Jesus, Leonard." Edward rubbed his eyebrows and closed his eyes.

"The problem with you, Edward, is you're too strait-laced." Leonard narrowed his eyes and shook his head.

"Being straight is a problem now?" Edward responded, his gaze cold.

"Not necessarily, but you're so fucking straight I could use you in a geometry class!" Leonard shook his head again and took a deep drink from his glass.

"Still don't see the problem." Edward simply shrugged, enjoying the fact he was getting under his brother's skin.

"You're so stuck in your ways with your head wrapped up in this place, you're not even vanilla, you're just cream at this point."

"I quite like cream," Edward said, a smile tugging at the corner of his mouth.

"Fucking magnolia more like, and to be clear, that's not a compliment."

Edward paused and watched Leonard. He could see the wine was clouding his younger brother's cool exterior, and he was becoming visibly irritated.

"I know it may be difficult for you to get your head around this, Leonard, but I don't live my life for your or anyone else's approval. And if you want to fuck your way through every county, or country for that matter, with any individual on the rainbow spectrum, that's entirely your prerogative, but don't get the arse because that's not what I choose to do with my life." Edward drained his own glass of wine. "And that doesn't make me homophobic or bigoted. I just don't feel the need to expand my experiences beyond whatever I'm comfortable with."

Leonard released a bitter laugh. "You're slightly bigoted. Let's be honest."

"I'm a traditional man with traditional values. That doesn't make me bigoted," Edward shot back.

"Whatever helps you sleep at night, brother." Leonard scanned the room as though looking for another bottle of wine. Finding none, he settled his gaze back on his brother.

The pair stared at each other, the alcohol bringing their thinly masked contempt closer to the surface.

"Do you know what helps me sleep at night?" Edward finally said.

"What's that?" Leonard raised an eyebrow, his tone sarcastic.

"When you're five and a half thousand miles away

across the pond." Edward scraped back his chair and stood up. "Get your fiancée and her Buddhist monk over, sort out your wedding, and then all of you fuck off back there, okay?" Edward didn't wait for a response and left the room.

He knew regret would set in soon enough.

For starters, he rarely allowed his feelings to be aired openly and, although he cared little for Leonard, he was still his brother. Albeit his half-brother.

It was something none of them ever spoke of, but the reality sat between them as wide and deep as the Yosemite Valley.

They shared the same father, but their mother was only Leonard's by birth. Edward was less than a year old when his own died, and his father remarried a year later.

Verity had been a wonderful mother to Edward, and whether he was truly her son was never in question, but the truth placed a large wedge between the brothers – especially because of their father's will and the guardianship of the estate being given solely to Edward.

Their mother hadn't cared – her money and estate, which the boys would have equal shares of after her death, far outweighed what Haddon House was worth – but the principle grated on Leonard to the point of obsession. It was something that Edward was aware of but did his best to ignore.

As Edward readied himself for bed, he knew he'd have to make peace in the morning. He wouldn't apologise, but he would improve his tone, at least briefly, and take a more active interest in wedding planning. He would swallow the bitter pill and show an element of familial affection. It was the right thing to do and would make Lily and his mother happy.

Edward went to the window and paused when he

saw the lights from the stables. The Hope women were still awake. He could see that both bedrooms were lit as they had a sideways view over the gardens themselves.

He leaned against the wall and wondered what Scarlett was doing.

Was she a keen reader like her mother? Or was she on her phone, scrolling through social media, or talking to someone? Was she still in contact with her ex?

He didn't like the idea of that and pulled the blinds closed.

Removing and kicking his boxers into the corner of the room, he got into bed, his thoughts drifting back to the first moment Scarlett set eyes on him.

The memory of their first meeting was seldom far from his thoughts, and feelings of embarrassment were now surpassed by fantasies of how it may have been different in another situation, or life, for that matter.

Frequent and unwelcome thoughts of her in bed with him had plagued him since her arrival, which had barely been a week ago.

Jesus, man. Pull yourself together.

He shook his head. He must be going soft. Or mad. Or potentially both.

But he couldn't help himself, especially in moments like this when left alone, imagining what it would be like to have her in his bed with the freedom and time to explore her body with his hands and mouth, wondering what she'd feel and taste like.

He groaned, wishing Scarlett, and his brother for that matter, would both fuck off and leave him in peace.

Neither were helping him sleep at night, and to make matters worse, thoughts of Scarlett's curves and naked skin under his touch caused a strain beneath his sheets that he would need to deal with if he was to have any chance of sleeping.

Tonight, he would allow himself a little more time to indulge in thoughts of Scarlett, but he promised himself he would banish them for good by the next morning.

CHAPTER 11

THE FOLLOWING MORNING, the house was full of energy and Mrs Wilson was beaming when Scarlett found her in the kitchen.

"Good morning, Scarlett," she almost sang. "Lots to do."

Scarlett couldn't help smiling at the small woman whose glasses were steaming up from the various pots and pans bubbling and frying on the huge Aga.

"There is. But it'll be fine." Scarlett took the toast handed to her.

"Indeed! It's going to be a busy household, that's for sure. A wedding! Offt, what a treat!"

Scarlett merely nodded, taking a bite of her buttery toast, wondering if Leonard's bride-to-be was aware of his outrageously flirty nature.

"Aye, lots to do. Lady Cameron-Reid will no doubt be coming over, not on this trip, mind, but certainly for the wedding. And a week before Christmas! It's all very romantic."

"Yes, very," Scarlett agreed. "So, I'm thinking I'll carry on getting the rooms in the east wing ready. Will that be best?"

"That would be magic – I'm certainly grateful to have you here at the moment." Mrs Wilson beamed another smile at her.

"No problem at all. I'll head up now." Scarlett shoved the last bit of toast into her mouth.

"Thanks, oh, and Lily is home again, too. It's been

a fair while since she's seen her uncle, so she'll be wanting to spend lots of time with him."

Scarlett smiled and nodded. "Busy day ahead then."

"Certainly is. Now, don't you be doing too much on your own, though. Ask for help when you need it."

"Don't worry, I'll be just fine."

Scarlett let out an enormous sigh of relief when she exited the kitchen. The heat from the cooking and Mrs Wilson's enthusiasm were overwhelming.

Great, a wedding – just love those.

Deep in thought, she rounded the corner towards the main stairwell, walking straight into the broad hard chest of Edward.

"Ohh, I'm sorry," they said in unison.

Edward's hands were holding the tops of her arms, whether to steady her or himself she wasn't sure, but his touch created a rush of heat that seared through her.

She looked up into his eyes and, for a moment, the crazy idea he might kiss her entered her thoughts, which, even more disturbingly, didn't appal her in the slightest.

Realising she wasn't breathing, she exhaled and looked down.

"Sorry again, I wasn't looking where I was going," she said.

"Me neither, my fault, really." He quickly removed his hands from her arms, making her skin cry for their return.

Seriously, what is wrong with me?

"How are you?" he asked.

She could feel the heat of his gaze on her, making her lift her eyes back up to his.

They were still standing too close, making Scarlett feel self-conscious – worried he might actually hear her heart pounding, the sound thudding loudly in her ears.

A NEW *Hope* IN THE HIGHLANDS

"Much better, thanks. You were right, some rest and fresh air did me the world of good." She took a small step back.

"Glad to hear it." He placed his hands in his pockets, pausing before glancing back at her. "I hear you've been helping with the wedding plans – for my brother."

Scarlett smiled. "Yes, Mrs Wilson is so excited. She's close to bursting, I think."

Edward smiled too – she liked it when he did.

"Aye, she seems to have a bit of a bounce to her step this morning."

The pair locked eyes again, neither seeming to be able to look away this time.

"I hear your daughter is here, too. Sounds like it's going to be a full house for a while?"

Edward nodded. "Seems like it. Which reminds me, Leonard was looking for you to talk about the preparations for the bride-to-be arriving. I imagine he'll come and find you to discuss things in more detail at some point today."

Scarlett noticed a slight annoyance creep into his voice.

"That's no problem. I'll be happy to help."

"Tad serendipitous you being here, considering your background. Didn't realise you were so experienced in the whole event organising thing, but I suppose it makes sense with your ... with being involved in book launches and what have you." Edward frowned and looked at his feet.

"Yes, I suppose it is." She watched him with curiosity as he began looking around, clearly searching for an escape route. "How did you know all that about me?"

"Your mum – mostly," he said with a shrug, and she could almost swear there was a slight blush to his neck and cheeks. "Great, well, I'll let you get on." He nodded.

Has he been googling me?

"Yep, you can get on too." Scarlett cringed as soon as the words were out.

You can get on too? What am I even talking about?

"See you later." He nodded again and walked away towards his office.

Right, enough of this idiocy.

She shook her head.

Edward was beyond her reach. She knew this and shouldn't even be entertaining the idea.

Besides, she wasn't actually interested, not really. He was just an annoying distraction that she would not spend any more time thinking about.

Enough was enough.

She would keep her head down and work hard. She would do her best to avoid seeing Edward and focus on helping Leonard with his ambitious wedding plans. Although, it wasn't exactly helping that her dreams weren't offering any kind of escape.

Since her arrival, Scarlett had found herself waking several times throughout the night, often with a start, wondering where she was and feeling as if the heat of Edward's body was seeping across the mattress towards her.

Last night, she'd woken again from a dream in which his deep blue eyes had been watching her, leaving her feeling hot and breathless. As she grappled with reality, for a moment she even thought she saw his sleeping silhouette snoring softly beside her.

Realising she'd been dreaming, she attempted to drift back off to sleep, although she'd felt a residual ache in her body as if she was missing him in places he'd clearly never been.

What was wrong with her?

The man was literally haunting her to the point that when she now woke up every morning at six am – *on the dot* – she would be reluctant to fall back asleep in case he was still waiting for her, ready to consume every part of her, leaving her frustrated and undeniably horny.

The insanity is real!

She groaned with frustration. She really was done for.

CHAPTER 12

EDWARD CHECKED HIS phone. It was six am.

His body was so attuned to waking up at this time, he didn't need an alarm clock anymore, but this morning he was hesitant to get up.

The day that lay ahead was uncertain except for the fact that he would need to make the necessary move away from his fixation on Scarlett.

But it was easier said than done. Especially when every thought that entered his head was of her. It didn't help that despite the promise he made to himself that the *last time* would be the *final time* he'd indulge in thoughts of Scarlett – *particularly at night* – she was already in his thoughts, stirring awake his currently overactive imagination and subsequent hard-on.

He raised his hands to his face and rubbed his eyes before dragging them through his messy hair.

Christ, man, get a grip.

With a groan, he swiftly sat up, placed his hands on his knees, and shook his head.

"No more of this shite," he said out loud, standing up and walking naked into the bathroom to have a cold shower.

He was resolute that things were going to be different from hereon in.

There was work to be done, let alone the preparations for the impending wedding.

He cringed; it was all going to be a complete nightmare. The wedding party would be here for weeks to make the preliminary preparations, and it was all already encroaching on his routine and his patience.

He and Leonard were back on speaking terms. Barely. But Edward wouldn't be disappointed when they all buggered back off to the States.

With any luck, Scarlett would also realise that she could better use her talents elsewhere, and his life could return to some semblance of normality.

She wouldn't be in his house, or thoughts, potentially not even in the same country, and the more distance between them, the better at this stage.

He didn't feel the need to upend his entire life with unnecessary emotions or drama. In fact, he'd respond to the messages awaiting his attention on his phone. An evening with Evelyn should do the trick. She was usually footloose and fancy free, and always keen for an evening with him, and, in her words, her *favourite plaything*.

She was a nice enough woman. Her husband worked away, and they had an arrangement in place allowing them the security and comfort of marriage with the freedom to enjoy discretional extracurricular activities.

They'd met a couple of years ago at a charity ball that his mother supported, and who, on that occasion, made the trip over, which meant Edward had to make a public appearance. He rarely enjoyed such outings, but Evelyn had sat next to him and made it no secret that she wanted his company elsewhere. She was persistent, getting his number from a mutual friend, and one thing led to another. He succumbed to a meal, which led to drinks, then sex, and a reunion every couple of months.

It seemed to suit them both.

"Eddie, your talents never fail to surpass my expectations," Evelyn told him after their last meeting. She'd watched him in the reflection of the large mirror as she fixed her hair at the dressing table – in their usual eye-wateringly expensive penthouse suite, which she always insisted upon.

He hadn't responded, observing her cosmetic ritual and perfect composure.

"It's quite sizeable, you know." She'd smiled, enjoying his discomfort.

"Thank you very much," he'd replied, picking up his phone to signal the conversation was over.

"How about dinner next week?"

"I'm busy, I'm afraid." Edward hadn't looked up, feeling her expectant gaze on him.

She tried again. "The week after then?"

"I'll let you know." He finally looked up and offered a tight smile.

Evelyn huffed loudly.

Her theatrics had irritated him and even though the sex was okay, and she was fun company, the next morning he always felt deflated and hollow.

He didn't enjoy emotionless sex, but equally, he didn't want a relationship, which was the precise reason women like Evelyn worked for him.

It was just unfortunate that the aftermath always left him feeling a bit shite – about his own lack of feeling more than anything else.

That was the last time he'd seen or spoken to her, but perhaps an easy dinner somewhere at a discreet hotel, a couple of bottles of red and some uncomplicated sex, was the precise antidote he needed to get Scarlett out of his head.

Because the fiery redhead, as his brother liked to refer to her, was just *too much*.

He knew enough about women to spot the ones who would want more, who needed the level of affection and emotional validation that he wasn't comfortable giving, nor had the time for.

Not anymore.

He saw how his mother had left his father broken.

Christ, even his own marriage had fallen apart because of Natasha's affair, and he didn't even want to think about his last serious relationship.

A toxic shipwreck was an understatement.

No, passion and romance weren't for him, and Scarlett, he could tell, was all fire, full of life and love. It would be all-consuming, and for him, that would be too much.

She would be too much.

Besides, she was also staff. And, more importantly, June's daughter. It was all shades of wrong and he was a man of values. He wasn't his brother.

June had worked here for years, his father's employee and friend from what he'd seen of their interactions before he'd passed away.

Edward just couldn't do it.

But no sooner was his resolve set than it was completely blown out of the water.

Leonard was on his way to the airport to pick up his soon-to-be blushing bride and Edward decided it would be a good token gesture to do a last walk around the east wing before their arrival.

He wanted to ensure that everything was as it should be, and part of this he knew was selfish; it would limit the need to interact with the couple and their entourage if everything that should be ready was all set and prepared for them.

On his way around the rooms, which all seemed clean, aired, and smelling of polish and fresh linen, he heard the loud scraping of furniture, followed by language he seldom heard coming out of the mouth of a woman.

He winced, recognising the English accent immediately, and silently cursed his quickening pulse, his body already betraying his hardened decision without a second thought.

Fuck's sake, woman.

As he rounded the corner, he could still hear Scarlett muttering and swearing, "Stupid fucking bed, move!"

Edward slowed to peer into the room where Scarlett, facing away from him, was leaning over trying to move a huge oak bed, each effort only budging it a half centimetre at a time, at best.

He tried to ignore the sight of her tight jeans hugging her perfectly rounded behind, making him stir in places he was desperate to keep under some semblance of control.

Looking away, he cleared his throat to announce his presence, making her spin around with her eyes wide, cheeks flushed, and hair, as usual, fighting for freedom from its ponytail.

It took all his self-control not to stride across the space between them and take her in his arms *or* throw her onto the bed behind her – possibly both, whether the bed was in the right position or not.

Instead, sanity prevailing, he said, "Hello."

"Hi," she replied, out of breath. "You all really need to stop creeping up on me like that. Is it a family trait?"

Edward bristled at the thought of Leonard sneaking up on her.

"You could turn the air blue with that language, you know."

He saw her cheeks and throat redden even further. "I'm sorry. I didn't know anyone was around. Apologies for being inappropriate."

The formality made Edward smile. "I've heard worse."

Scarlett smiled in response and shrugged her shoulders. "It's not my best trait. I'm embarrassed. Sorry again."

The way she looked up at him through her long dark lashes was making him melt and, for a long moment, the two just stood looking at each other.

"Can I help?" he finally offered.

Scarlett looked back at the bed and laughed. "Actually, that would be really great. I moved it a little to the left to centre it, and since then it's barely moved an inch. The thing weighs an absolute tonne."

Edward smiled. "Yeah, solid wood has a habit of doing that. Where's it going?"

"Just a couple of inches towards the window, to the edge of the rug."

He walked towards the bed where Scarlett stood.

She didn't move, and the closeness of her was disarming.

He smelled the faint scent of shampoo and face cream, but not a trace of the potent, expensive perfume he usually detected on the women he was intimate with.

He wanted to inhale her to the point it was driving him mad, and it wasn't helping that she wasn't taking her eyes off him.

"It's okay, I've got it." Edward bent at the knees and, with a loud scrape, pushed the bed across until he could feel the resistance of the rug. "That do it?"

He straightened to face her again.

She nodded, not looking at the bed, her eyes still stuck on his.

Edward looked down and rubbed his hands to remove the remnants of wood polish before looking back at her.

"You're not making this very easy for me."

Scarlett creased her forehead in genuine confusion. "What do you mean?"

"I mean." Edward sighed, looking away, not trusting himself. "You're just very ..." He trailed off.

"Very what?" Her lips tightened, and she narrowed her eyes at him.

He looked at her again. "Just very *you.*"

"And that's a bad thing?"

He couldn't help smiling at her annoyed expression. "No, it's not a bad thing. It's the total opposite, which I suppose is bad."

"I don't understand." Her face told him she really didn't, and he marvelled at the fact she was so oblivious to the effect she had on him.

"You're just incredibly—" He stopped, searching for some recognition or permission in those eyes that seemed to look into his core every time he was in her company.

Then, for reasons he couldn't explain, he saw something in her look change, instantly making him disregard his freshly imposed resolution to steer clear of her. Maybe it was the way she wetted her lips. Or the way her gaze rested on his. He wasn't sure.

"I find you very distracting, truth be told," he finally said, heat rising to his neck and cheeks.

"Distracting how?" Her head tilted a little to the side.

Edward wondered if she was being deliberately obtuse.

"I think you know exactly how." His voice resembled a growl.

"I'm not so sure I do, though." The way she bit the smile forming on her lips almost finished him.

"Stop doing that with your lip," he said, fighting the urge to bite it himself.

"Or what?" Her eyes were laughing at him, silently goading him.

They stood staring at each other for what seemed like an age before he lost all semblance of sense and control.

"Fuck it," he said, pulling her towards him, making her catch her breath.

He hesitated for a moment to see if she was going to resist, but he needn't have worried as she responded by reaching up and pulling his head down closer to hers, their lips finding each other with a hunger he'd not experienced in a long time.

His hands wrapped around her waist, pulling her in even closer, her hands in his hair, neither coming up for breath.

The chemistry he'd felt between them wasn't a figment of his imagination after all, and as her body reacted to each movement of his mouth and touch, he knew the feeling was mutual.

He picked her up in one swift motion, one hand scooping her bum and the other tight around her waist, and she wrapped her legs around him.

He didn't know where the overwhelming urge was coming from, but he needed to have her. Everything about her disarmed him and easily bulldozed through his carefully constructed wall. The one he had, until now, kept firmly in place to avoid anything as careless as this ever happening. But he couldn't wait another moment and lowered her onto the bed.

All common sense and restraint were gone.

Their hands tugged and loosened each other's clothing, searching for bare skin to touch.

"You feel insanely good," he growled again.

The woman is turning me into a possessed fucking animal!

Scarlett pulled his head up so she could look into his eyes before kissing him again.

He felt out of control, greedy, wanting to touch every part of her.

Edward groaned with pleasure as his hand reached down underneath Scarlett's loose jeans and underwear, discovering her wetness. Everything about her was irresistible, especially the way she responded as his fingers found their way deeper inside her, making her gasp.

He was busy imagining how good it would feel to have more than just his fingers buried deep inside her when a sudden sound from further down the hall stopped Edward in his tracks.

There were definite footsteps approaching.

"You've got to be kidding me!" Edward rested his head on Scarlett's chest for a moment before gathering his wits. "Down here, quick!"

He gently released his hand, pulled Scarlett across the bed and onto the floor next to the window, and checked for visible clothing before ducking his head down to face Scarlett's flushed face and laughing eyes.

The closeness of her body was too much, and he was conscious of his hardness straining against her, the feel of her breasts firmly pressed against his chest not helping the situation one iota. The unfairness of being so close yet miles away from being able to do what his body was silently roaring for made his cock strain and twitch further.

He closed his eyes and held his breath, waiting for the footsteps to pass by, screwing up his face when they paused at the doorway.

Please, no.

He silently begged a god he didn't believe in.

CHAPTER 13

Scarlett covered her mouth with her hand as a laugh began bubbling up her throat. Edward's bright red face, eyes shut tight, wasn't helping. Seconds felt like hours, but Mrs Wilson closed the door and continued her walk down the corridor with a singsong hum.

"Thank Christ." Edward shook his head before raising himself to a kneeling position. "I'm so sorry. This should never have happened."

For a moment, Scarlett felt numb until foolishness quickly washed over her instead.

"No, I don't suppose it should have, sorry." She wriggled out from underneath him and turned towards the wall to fix her clothes. When she turned around to face Edward, he was standing, clothes straightened, and no one would know anything had happened except for his hair, which was dishevelled, prompting her to fix her own.

"I don't really know what to say." His hands were back in his pockets, eyes darting around like a startled deer looking for its escape route, finally resting on the door before returning to look at Scarlett.

Scarlett sighed, shaking her head. "I don't imagine there's much *to* say. We're all grown-ups here."

"Just not sure this is a good idea. I've overstepped the mark. Sorry."

"Don't mention it. It won't happen again." Scarlett wanted – no, *needed* – to get out of the room. What on earth was she thinking?

Fuck.

"It feels awkward now. I'm sorry." He still wasn't able to look at her, making Scarlett's mortification increase twofold.

"Seriously, it's all good. I've been knocked back in worse ways than this."

"Ach, it's not that at all. I do like you, I'm just ..." He paused.

"No need to say any more. Let's just pretend this never happened." Scarlett gave him a thin smile before nodding and leaving the room, closing the door behind her.

Kill me now.

Feeling suitably humiliated, she made her way outside and despite the thin drizzle of rain that had recently become a permanent fixture above the house and surrounding area the last few days, Scarlett could breathe again.

The drops of water against her hot face was a relief and she willed it to wash away any suggestion of Edward, but she could still smell and feel him on her skin as if he'd burned invisible markings everywhere that his fingers and lips had touched her – she could liken it to torture were it not for how delicious the memory of it was.

What was I thinking?

Scarlett closed her eyes and lifted her face to the sky before releasing a shaky breath and opening them again.

She saw her mother in the distance walking towards the entrance of the root cellar below the house, briefly lifting her spirits. But when June disappeared, loneliness overcame her. She knew it wasn't all because of Edward, although he certainly wasn't helping; this feeling had been chasing her for days now.

All the talk of weddings and new beginnings was grating on her, with lurking thoughts of Jason trying to break through, urging her to face up to the inevitable truth that she really was alone now.

Scarlett had no intention of dwelling on it.

Looking around briefly, she glanced up at the darkened windows of the big old house. This wasn't why she was here. He wasn't why she was here. She had to remember that.

Scarlett needed to stay busy and distracted so she decided she would help her mother for a while. It wasn't something she would openly admit, but she was craving comfort. This wasn't something she would have previously associated with her mother, but she was doing a lot of things she hadn't previously done.

"Hi, Mum." Scarlett tried to sound light and cheerful as she walked down the stone steps. "Thought I'd come and give you a hand."

"Hello, Scarlett," her mum called back. "Andrzej is here too, but we're always glad for the help."

"Hi, Scarlett," Andrzej called up to her. "The more the merrier."

When Scarlett arrived in the cellar, June and Andrzej were working side by side, sorting vegetables into groups, surrounded by wooden pallets and straw.

There was an air of relaxed companionship between them that made her heart ache, but she pushed the thought away and ignored the tightening feeling in her chest, instead donning her best smile.

"Hi. So, what can I do?"

June smiled at her and nodded to a pallet on the worktop. "You can start lining the pallet with straw and layering the potatoes. Just brush off the excess dirt and leave a bit of space between them before covering them and layering on more."

Scarlett began the task and looked up at her mother

to check she was doing it correctly.

June nodded. "That's right. Good job."

The trio worked in silence for a while, lost in their own thoughts.

"Much going on at the house at the moment?" Andrzej asked Scarlett.

"It's the quiet before the storm, I think." She shrugged. "Leonard is picking up his fiancée and her friends from the airport."

"Exciting times for everyone." A smile that was difficult to decipher played on June's lips. "Funny to think he's getting married – I still see him as a young man."

"Yeah, I can see why." Scarlett rubbed her nose with her sleeve to ease away an itch.

"Are your allergies flaring up again? I had Mrs Wilson pick you up some antihistamines yesterday when she went into town. I put them on your bedside table this morning."

Scarlett lifted her eyebrows in surprise. "Oh, really. Thanks."

"No problem." June moved away briefly to pick up another box of vegetables, but Andrzej got there before her.

"Please, allow me." The pair exchanged a smile, which, if Scarlett didn't know better, could have been construed as flirting.

But as quickly as the thought occurred, she disregarded it; she wasn't sure why, but her mother's celibacy was as assured as that of the Pope's.

Scarlett always found June's opposition to men as romantic partners strangely contradictory, given her love of historical romance novels. Perhaps it was the fact that a romance such as Darcy and Elizabeth's was so far beyond anything attainable, her mother preferred to not even try. Despite various attempts during her childhood and adolescence to pry more information out of her mother on the subject, the only thing Scarlett ever found out was that June was not and never had been on the market for love.

End of.

So, no matter how appealing she thought Andrzej may be to the general population of women who liked the wholesome, rugged, gardening type, she felt confident her mother wouldn't be seeing it. Scarlett pictured June preferring a more gentrified type, maybe a chauffeur. Not that there was one around here, but that's who Scarlett thought would most likely win her mother over. But really, who knew what sort of man would catch June's eye.

"How are you enjoying it now then, Scarlett?" Andrzej pulled her head back into the room.

"Good – the wedding has been a fun project to get stuck into. I've enjoyed getting the rooms ready and helping Leonard find suitable suppliers, stuff like that. It's only a few weeks away, but I like the pressure of a quick deadline."

"You enjoy this type of work?" he asked, glancing up at her.

"Yeah, I'm good at it, and I enjoy watching it all come together in the end." Scarlett shrugged. "It's satisfying."

"Makes sense. It's a bit like watching the bulbs awakening in the spring and sprouting up through the ground and flowering," Andrzej said.

Scarlett smiled at the poetic analogy. "Exactly like that."

"I get that." June nodded. "It's nice to have purpose. We all need it, I think."

They all nodded and continued with their tasks, remaining that way for a good hour, before they cleared up and Scarlett said her goodbyes, feeling noticeably more relaxed.

Edward would not hold this kind of power over her, dictating her mood or feelings with his nonchalant and changeable attitude towards her. She'd spent enough years allowing Jason to do just that, and she wasn't about to let another man do the exact same thing again.

Scarlett was resolute.

She would keep her head up and pretend their moment of madness never happened – and no matter how delicious it had been, she would not repeat it under any circumstances. *Ever.*

With any luck, he'd be hiding away in his rooms somewhere to avoid seeing his incoming guests. Who should, she realised, be arriving within the hour, but Scarlett was feeling hungry. She hadn't eaten since early that morning, and it was already approaching mid-afternoon. She'd need to be quick if she was going to grab a bite before the madness ensued.

"Hello, Scarlett," Mrs Wilson sang as Scarlett entered the kitchen. Her glasses had steamed up from the various pots bubbling on the large stove. "Grab yourself a bowl of this soup here. You must be starving. I've not seen you since this morning!"

"Thank you." Scarlett grabbed a bowl from the table and took a ladleful of the thick broth.

"There's a nice bit of mutton in there. It'll keep you going until supper, that's for sure – and there's a hunk of bread and butter on the side there. Just help yourself. I've got a couple of lads arriving soon to help, so you're best sitting before it gets busy in here."

The smell of the soup, meat, and whatever else was being prepared made Scarlett's stomach growl. "Thank you. It all smells incredible."

Mrs Wilson glanced at her, a look Scarlett couldn't decipher crossing her features.

"Get yourself sat and fed, hen. As soon as the troops arrive, you'll no doubt be busy again."

Scarlett made a noise of agreement, a spoonful of soup already in her mouth whilst she was busy slathering a thick layer of butter on some pre-sliced bread. It dripped into her soup as she dunked it and quickly swooped it up, closing her eyes in appreciation of the silky, salty flavours combining in her mouth.

She'd demolished the entire bowl in minutes, and as she took her last mouthful, Scarlett glimpsed a tall figure in the doorway.

It was Edward, of course, who filled the entire space, leaning against the doorframe and watching her with intent.

"You seem to have a bit of something there." He pointed to a corner of his mouth to show where he meant, and Scarlett quickly wiped away a smear of melted butter with the side of her hand, looking down and away from his intense gaze.

"Thanks," Scarlett muttered in response.

"Oh, hello," Mrs Wilson chirped, realising the laird was present. "Have they arrived?"

"Not yet, no, just thought I'd check in to see if everything was going to plan."

"Yes, everything is in hand. Scarlett has been busy all morning preparing the rooms." Mrs Wilson paused for a second before continuing. "Boys are arriving soon, and there will be a variety of light dishes available for the weary guests, in case they're hungry on arrival. Young Leonard instructed us to serve dinner at eight thirty pm. Hope that's all okay with you too?"

"You've both done a grand job. Thank you for being so accommodating. It's noted and much appreciated." Edward's eyes still rested on Scarlett's mouth, and she wiped it again to check there was nothing else there. "I shall join them for dinner but have some work to finish, so I'll leave the welcoming of our guests in your capable hands."

"Of course, no problem at all. Scarlett is just finishing her meal and she'll be off to get changed so she can be on hand as well." Mrs Wilson smiled at Scarlett, which Scarlett took to mean she should probably get a move on.

"Just heading now. Thanks again for the soup. It was delicious."

"Aye, not a problem. Come back here once you've changed and we'll be ready for them arriving, eh?"

Scarlett stood and moved towards the doorway, which Edward blocked, still looking at her far longer than was necessary, and he took a second before realising he needed to let her pass.

"Sorry, excuse me – after you." He moved aside and, nodding his leave to Mrs Wilson, followed Scarlett out. "Scarlett, wait."

Scarlett turned on her heel to face him. Realising they were way too close to each other, she took a couple of steps back, waiting for him to speak.

"I hope we can, you know, move past this?" Again with the hands in his pockets.

"Ancient history already." Scarlett forced what she hoped was a convincing smile.

"I just don't want things to become awkward between us. You're a great worker, and your mum is obviously a much-respected employee, and well—"

"Am I not respected?" Scarlett regretted the words as soon as they left her mouth.

She was being purposefully petulant.

Edward looked appalled.

"I'm sorry, that was unnecessary. I didn't mean that," Scarlett quickly added.

"I absolutely respect you. Christ, I hope you don't think I don't respect you or don't think the world of you, I just ..." Edward pulled a hand out of his pocket and held it against his mouth as if to stop any more words coming out. "I'm no good with things like this."

What a grown-up conversation! And what does he mean, "think the world" of me? We've known each other for all of five fucking minutes!

Instead of voicing her wayward thoughts, Scarlett sighed. "Edward, it's all fine. We're good. It was a crazy, heated moment. Neither of us was thinking straight and let's be honest, nothing really happened."

"But it could have." He was searching her eyes and face.

For what? She had no idea.

"But it didn't, and it won't happen again, like, *ever*." Scarlett forced herself to be strong and convincing.

More for her own benefit than his.

"Right, yes, of course."

The two stood staring at each other. She felt like more needed to be said, but she couldn't find the words, and neither, it seemed, could he.

Scarlett was the first to break the spell. "So, are we good?"

Edward nodded. "Of course. I'll let you get ready for the guests arriving."

"Thanks, I'll see you later then."

Edward nodded again and Scarlett managed another smile before turning away. She could feel him watching her back until she walked around the corner.

CHAPTER 14

EDWARD WAS NOT used to feeling out of control of his emotions, but it was becoming a genuine struggle to keep a handle on them when it came to Scarlett.

Watching her walk away tugged at him, and he didn't like it.

Her words, "never again," bothered him.

It even reminded him of a Taylor Swift song, something he disliked even more – especially as Lily had tortured him with it on repeat for several weeks.

He pulled out his phone and checked for messages. Evelyn, as expected, had responded to his previous message quickly, confirming her husband was currently away for several weeks and she would be happy to meet at their usual place if he fancied it.

He could see she'd sent another:

Evelyn: *It's rude to leave a lady waiting, Eddie.*

Despite knowing and being better, he left her on read, trying to determine if meeting her was actually a good idea.

She was an attractive woman, and it was of no importance she was married because of the arrangement she had with her husband.

The beauty of the entire situation was that there were no expectations or emotions involved, but all that aside, it niggled at his conscience and still felt wrong.

A NEW *Hope* IN THE HIGHLANDS

He just wasn't sure why, as it had never been a problem before now.

Although he could hazard a guess that the fiery auburn-haired woman that plagued his thoughts every day of his current existence probably had something to do with it.

Edward was still standing lost in thought, staring at the now empty corridor, oblivious to the sound of the front door opening until he heard a cacophony of voices fill the entrance hall.

"Edward, what a lovely surprise, you decided to welcome us – Anaïse, sweetheart, meet my brother, the laird of the castle."

"Oh my God, Edward, so nice to meet you, and Lennie wasn't lying. The place is divine. It's even more beautiful than he described – it's like something out of a picture book." Anaïse enveloped Edward in an awkward hug and kissed both his cheeks.

"Lennie?" Edward raised his eyebrow in Leonard's direction. His brother shrugged with a smile in return.

"Journey from the airport was the smoothest it's ever been – took no time at all." Leonard ushered the other two wide-eyed, open-mouthed guests into the house, closing the huge oak-panelled door behind them. "Welcome, welcome, come on in, get warm."

A throng surrounded Edward, showering him with handshakes, air kisses, and unwelcome hugs.

"A real laird, huh? Now that's a kick." A bald man in a deep red robe with bare feet stood before Edward, beaming and bowing his head. "Namaste."

Edward nodded and stared at his bare feet. It was freezing outside.

"Leonard, you're back! Oh my, welcome, welcome, everyone."

Edward sighed with relief at the familiar sound of Mrs Wilson's voice approaching them all.

"Ahh, Mrs Wilson." Leonard ushered Anaïse in her direction, and the other two, like eager sheep, followed suit. "This is my lovely fiancée, Anaïse."

"Oh, hello, my dear, such a pleasure. We're so pleased to have you all here. Goodness, you must all be exhausted. Scarlett will be along any minute now to help, but let's get you all up to your rooms." Mrs Wilson guided them towards the stairway.

The group responded with various noises of appreciation at their surroundings.

"You can leave your heavy bags – Andrzej and the lads will bring them all up for you. Oh, such a lovely thing to have you all here. Come along, this way."

Edward didn't need a second opportunity and silently drifted away towards his rooms and office. His mood was bleak – it was going to be far worse than even he had expected.

As he approached his office door, he heard the group become even more animated as Scarlett's unmissable English accent floated above them, unsettling him further.

The woman had the most frustrating and bewildering effect on him and it was making him feel as if he was literally going mad.

Walking into the office, he closed the door firmly behind him, wishing he could shut Scarlett, his brother, and all his American guests out for good.

Edward's recent existence up to this point had been uneventful at best, but it was peaceful with a routine, and although monotonous and not particularly exciting, it brought him peace.

He did *not* currently feel peaceful.

Looking around his office, which usually filled him with a sense of calm and organised purpose, he wanted to pull all the carefully categorised books from the shelves and rip the pictures off the walls.

He sighed and settled for a less violent approach. Instead, he pulled his phone out of his pocket and opened his messaging app to view the messages.

Evelyn was still there glaring up at him, still left on read.

Fuck it.

Edward: *Hi. Sorry, it's been busy here.*

As he expected, with her phone constantly in her hand, the three dots appeared in an instant, showing she was typing a response.

Evelyn: *Well, that took a while longer than usual. I hear Leonard is home?*

Edward: *Yes, along with his entire American entourage!*

Evelyn: *Sounds suitably painful – imagine the idea of coming to see me is even more appealing now.*

Edward: *Something like that.*

Evelyn: *Make it happen then, Eddie.*

Edward paused, beginning to regret starting the ball rolling on this.

Evelyn was a *nice* woman and although their emotionally devoid agreement was mutually beneficial, his motives felt off.

This was a blatant distraction from Scarlett, and he was using Evelyn, as opposed to just arranging an enjoyable evening with her.

He flinched as the realisation dawned on him; he shared more traits with his brother than he cared to admit – at least Leonard wore his narcissism on his sleeve. He didn't hide behind false stoic values and principles.

His phone vibrated, bringing his attention back to the room.

Evelyn: *Just know I won't wait forever x*

Edward didn't reply.

Locking his phone, he flung the offending object into a drawer in his desk – he felt now more than ever that technology was more trouble than it was worth.

Instant access to people wasn't always a good thing, and he'd now made himself, and potentially Evelyn, feel far worse than either of them had felt five minutes earlier.

Using Evelyn to distract himself from Scarlett was a low move, and not something he was remotely comfortable with.

He'd find other ways.

Besides, it wasn't as if he didn't have other people or things to focus on – he literally had an entire house full of exactly that. Which reminded him: Lily was on her way over.

The thought of her driving made him feel slightly sick. Who deemed it okay for an eighteen-year-old to be put in charge of a two-tonne killing machine?

The idea seemed obscene.

He checked his pockets to find his phone before remembering it was in the drawer, and he sighed again. He did that a lot at the moment. He took the phone back out, unlocked it, and scrolled through his recent calls until Lily's name appeared on the screen.

It only rang once before she answered. "Hi, Dad."

"Hello, just wondering what time you're planning on leaving."

"About an hour, just waiting on the tumble dryer. Have they arrived yet?"

"Aye, it's like the circus has arrived." Edward opened his laptop, deciding to do some work.

"Try not to alienate them on the first day." Lily huffed down the phone at him.

He rolled his eyes. "I've not seen them enough to work my magic yet."

"Did you at least welcome them when they arrived?" He could hear the frustration in her voice, and he almost laughed at the irony of taking lessons in politeness from an obnoxious teenager.

"Aye and then passed them over to Mrs Wilson."

"She's a gem."

"Have you filled up with fuel? And have you done your checks? Windscreen wash, oil, tyre pressure, like I showed you?"

"Yes, Dad. I'll be fine. Mum says you need to calm yourself. Frankie monitors all that for me."

"That's great for *Frankie*. You need to know and be doing it yourself, not relying on other people."

"Right, my clothes will be done. I'm going to finish getting my stuff together. I'll see you all tonight." He could hear Lily's patience wearing thin.

"Okay, drive sensibly."

"In a bit." The line went dead.

"Love you too." Edward leaned back in his chair, drumming his fingers on the desk and twirling the phone in his other hand.

Too agitated to be productive, he wondered which room Scarlett was currently in. Was she where he'd found her earlier? Were thoughts of him also plaguing her – or was he already eradicated, written off as a moment of madness?

He closed his eyes and pinched the top of his nose with his forefinger and thumb, shaking his head.

His phone vibrated again in his hand, and after a moment's hesitation he looked down at the notification – it was Briege, his ex-girlfriend.

No fucking chance.

They dated for two years not long after his split from Lily's mum, and the rumour mill recently informed him she was not long separated and asking after his current circumstances, to which he'd responded, "I'm not in the market for another toxic relationship, thanks very much."

Edward stood and placed his phone back in the drawer again.

"Nope," he said aloud.

He stood and left the office, shutting the door and the prospect of Briege firmly behind him.

Fresh air was the best thing for him. He walked into the now empty hallway and listened to the unusual sound of high-spirited voices and footsteps in the corridors and rooms above him.

For a moment he considered the thought that it was a pleasant and almost comforting sound, until a shriek of laughter pierced through his reverie, making him shudder and make a quick beeline for the back door, careful to avoid Mrs Wilson who was humming in the kitchen.

Opening the heavy door to the side of the house, a cool draught entered the room, making him stop and reach for his wax coat. His hand paused as his attention was caught by the collar and lead hanging next to it. Unable to resist its pull, he touched the red collar with the name Bruce embroidered on it in a thick, dark blue thread. The colour had faded but the memory of his trusted black labrador and the pain of losing him were still fresh.

Edward wasn't an outwardly emotional man, but losing Bruce three years ago had hit hard, and he remembered it being more painful than his divorce – even now he had to blink away a tear.

The idea of replacing him seemed appalling, but maybe it was time. The estate needed a dog and perhaps so did he.

He took his coat off its peg and shrugged it on,

pushing away his melancholy, which was irritating him.
If it's not women or my family, it's a fucking dog.
Taking a last glance at Bruce's collar, he sighed deeply and closed the door behind him.

He'd take a walk down to the loch and check all was well.

Edward knew Andrzej had it all under control and was busy repairing some of the damage to the east bank, but it had been a couple of weeks since he'd last gone down to look; besides, it was a good excuse to clear his head.

To his left, he saw June and Andrzej in the near distance, their hands full of produce from the kitchen garden. He noticed how the pair always appeared easy and content in each other's company, exchanging affectionate smiles and softly spoken words, to the point that if he didn't know any better, he might think something was going on.

But he dismissed the idea as ridiculous; neither of them seemed to have any romantic ambitions, much like himself. It's what made them so amiable and easy to manage as employees, and he found comfort in that. Perhaps needing a romantic partner was becoming outdated.

It certainly made his own life easier. Usually.

Edward shut down his train of thought and instead welcomed the drizzle of rain on his face. The summer had stretched into the autumn months, which was pleasant, but it did little good for the ecosystem of the estate and the surrounding land.

Lost in thought, he didn't hear the footsteps approaching and froze, his mouth unable to form words, when Anaïse's monk rounded the corner – naked.

The monk's serene expression remained unchanged; only a soft smile formed.

"My laird." He bowed his head. "The water and its

aura are nothing short of magnificent here."

Edward remained speechless, his eyes wide and mouth open as if he wanted to speak but couldn't.

"I will reconnect with the others. I'm so looking forward to continuing on this journey with you all in this beautiful place. I feel blessed." He bowed his head again and walked back towards the house.

Edward, astonished and dumbfounded, turned and watched the naked man walk away, noticing June and Andrzej stop what they were doing, also visibly baffled at the sight.

Andrzej had his hands raised to his head and June raised her own to cover her mouth. They looked like two of the wise monkeys – he wondered if that made him the third.

"Christ all fucking mighty," he finally said.

As the monk disappeared into the house, Edward saw Andrzej laugh and shrug, shaking his head.

He mirrored the action and averted his attention to look up at the house.

What on earth had Leonard unleashed upon them all?

A chill ran through him, but he remained where he was, looking up at the four floors of the house. Lamps were being turned on as the light outside faded.

On the second floor, he swore he could make out Scarlett's form moving across the window of his mother's old room, holding up some kind of garment. She was probably helping Anaïse unpack, or maybe dress.

Edward immediately regretted his thoughts as an image of undressing Scarlett flooded his mind, making him groan out loud.

He really needed to be free of her.

Maybe sleeping with her would be the best remedy after all – sex, even when it was good, put an end to most things. Especially when it was carnal, which was all this was – some inexplicable chemistry, nothing more.

Maybe he just needed to feel and taste her, possess her body for a short amount of time, and then be free of her and the effect she was having on him.

If only he could push past the fact she was June's daughter and now his employee living on the estate. Not to mention the niggling worry that once wouldn't be nearly enough.

CHAPTER 15

SCARLETT KNOCKED GENTLY on the open door, where she could see Anaïse pulling garments out from suitcases strewn across the bed.

She wasn't big on fashion or keeping up with the latest trends, but she could recognise money and style, which Anaïse seemed to possess by the bucketful.

"Would you like some help?" Scarlett scanned the chaos in the room – makeup bags emptied over the sideboard, shoes scattered across the floor, and several coats and dresses hanging over the freestanding bath and across the velvet-upholstered chair in the corner.

"Millie would have packed my silk scarf, I'm sure of it, but I can't find it anywhere." Anaïse turned to look at Scarlett, who could have sworn a brief salacious smile played on her lips as she looked Scarlett up and down.

Scarlett dismissed it as Anaïse returned to the mess in front of her, where she'd also thrown dresses and blouses out of another case and onto the bed.

"Happy to put things away for you, if that would help?" Scarlett approached the other side of the bed to get a better view and picked up the most beautiful gown she'd ever laid eyes on.

Anaïse smiled, watching her.

"You like it?" She seemed pleased with Scarlett's reaction.

Scarlett nodded, admiring the soft material.

"It's a Christopher John Rogers piece." Anaïse's

A NEW *Hope* IN THE HIGHLANDS

tone was nonchalant.

Scarlett's confusion about who that was must have been obvious as Anaïse rolled her eyes.

"Oh, well – I suppose I can live without the scarf." Anaïse refocused her attention to the bed. "Leonard has a Pornstar Martini ready for me downstairs, which I'm reluctant to leave waiting."

Her Southern drawl made Scarlett smile. It reminded her of years of listening to the background noise of June's favourite movies as a child.

She wondered if the whole situation she'd found herself in recently wasn't becoming increasingly surreal and like something from June's vast book collection.

"It's no problem. I'll sort it and if I see the scarf, I'll leave it out for you on the dresser."

"You're a doll, thank you." And with a wide smile and a dismissive wave, Anaïse left the room to join the others downstairs.

Scarlett marvelled at the disarray created by a single person, but seeing no point in wasting time thinking on the mysterious inner workings of Anaïse, she began moving between the bed and the large oak wardrobe and drawers, which she'd aired and waxed back to life the day before.

She began hanging and folding garments more expensive than her entire worldly possessions, which, granted, weren't much.

The thought brought Jason to mind. She wondered what he was doing and what his thoughts on her recent line of work would be – namely the sorting of clothes belonging to some Southern belle probably wealthier than half the royal family combined.

It wasn't exactly her dream job, and although wealth always impressed Jason, it left her feeling indifferent and *other*.

Scarlett paused in front of the mirror and held the

dark green silk dress she'd admired earlier against her figure, enjoying the feel of the fabric and imagining herself wearing it whilst sipping on a Pornstar Martini.

She laughed at the idea and her reflection. When would she now have cause to wear a dress like this?

Still smiling, she hung the dress in the wardrobe, shaking her head – she didn't even like dresses.

Usually.

As she made her way back to the bed, her phone vibrated in the back pocket of her jeans.

Not recognising the number, she tentatively answered.

"Hello?"

"It's so good to hear your voice, darling."

The voice on the other end of the line made Scarlett's stomach clench, and panic flooded her senses.

She couldn't speak.

"Scarlett, babe? Talk to me, please. I've missed you. This is all such an unbelievable mess. Where are you? Are you okay?"

Jason's delayed concern irritated her, and words found her again.

"I've been gone for almost two weeks and you're only now wondering how I am?"

"Sweetheart, I'm so sorry. My head just hasn't been right. I've not been able to think straight." His voice croaked with emotion.

Despite her annoyance, the familiarity of him filled her with a warmth that she knew she should instantly rebuff, but just for a moment she wanted to bask in its comfort. The sense that she belonged somewhere, with someone – that she wasn't alone in the world after all. But the feeling was fleeting, as thoughts of Angelica quickly flooded her mind.

Young, sweet, funny, and now *very* pregnant Angelica.

A NEW *Hope* IN THE HIGHLANDS

No, she scolded herself. She didn't belong there anymore, and *he* was no longer her home.

"How are Angelica and the baby?" Scarlett asked, closing her eyes and, despite her resolve, involuntary tears spilled as soon as the words left her mouth.

The silence on the phone hung heavy with pain and regret.

Finally, after what seemed like an age, Jason sighed.

"They're fine. We had a scan last week – it's a boy."

My God, how far along is she?

Scarlett tried to push away thoughts of how long they'd been fucking behind her back. It would do no good.

"I see. Well, congratulations, I guess. You must all be delighted."

"Scarlett—"

"Please don't placate me, Jason. Was there a reason for your call?" she snapped at him.

"I just needed to hear your voice." His voice cracked.

For fuck's sake.

"Right, okay." Scarlett scanned the cases behind her. "I'm actually quite busy, if I'm honest."

"Where are you?" Jason asked.

"With my mum. She found me some work." She waited for the penny to drop.

There was a long pause as he registered the information.

"In Scotland?" he finally asked.

"Yes." Scarlett sighed.

She really didn't want to be having this conversation.

"Doing what?"

"Various bits and pieces – I'm helping organise a wedding at the moment." Scarlett winced, wondering what his reaction would be.

"That's very random," he said with a hint of annoyance.

"It's actually been good ... and fun."

"Fun?" He scoffed.

"Yes, I'd forgotten what that was like. Although, you've always been good at finding that, haven't you?" She grimaced, regretting letting him know how affected she was – Christ alive, of course she was bloody affected!

Regardless, Scarlett needed this to be over now.

"Don't be like that," Jason said, his tone clipped.

"Like what, Jason? What is it you want?" Scarlett held her head in her hand, her patience wearing thin.

"I want you – I need you here."

She laughed, the bitter edge of it biting at the already painful tension hanging between them.

"For what? To look after the house? Your diary? Feed you? Babysit? Surely it'd be easier just to hire a PA or a cleaner – or a nanny, even."

"You're my wife. I need my wife." He was being serious.

It was her turn to scoff, particularly at the sincerity in his voice. "You didn't seem to need me when you fucked that child."

"Don't be so lewd, you know perfectly well she's twenty-one."

"Well, that's alright then. Coming to think of it, I wasn't much older, was I? At least you've stayed true to type." Scarlett cringed as the truth of that fact hit her in the gut.

"It wasn't – it's not like that." He sighed.

"Tell me then, Jason, what was it like? Was she fascinated by your titillating conversational skills, or your impressive *oeuvre*? Or, let's be frank, was it simply the size of your cock?"

"Scarlett, that is enough!" His patience with her was dwindling.

Good.

"I'm not a child, Jason. I'll say whatever the fuck I like."

"That language has never suited you and look, it was wrong. I was wrong, and if I could go back and change things, I would, in an instant." He took a deep inhale of breath to keep his calm, but she could tell she was riling him.

"But you can't, can you?" Scarlett's voice held a slight quiver.

"No, I can't – but I wish I could."

Another pause.

Finally, Scarlett spoke. "This is a ridiculous conversation to be having. I need to get on."

"Scarlett—"

"I genuinely hope everything goes well with the pregnancy and I wish you both luck, and at some point, I guess we'll talk about solicitors and stuff."

"We're not getting a divorce—"

"I'll also text you my address. I'd appreciate it if you could send me my personal things and clothes," she continued, ignoring his interruption.

"Scarlett, let me be very clear. We are not getting a divorce. I want you to come home." He was using his serious businesslike tone with her. He often used it whenever something she said, did, or wanted disappointed him. Which was often.

Fuck you, Jason! Fuck you very, very much.

Scarlett closed her eyes again, hugging herself, doubling over – her heart and stomach physically hurt. "I need to go, Jason. Goodbye."

She ended the call and wanted to weep from the deceit and humiliation of it all. The raw emotions felt violent and relentless, coursing through her body, stopping abruptly at her chest.

But despite the pain, the only release was a couple of renegade tears, which she quickly brushed away with the back of her hand.

Taking a deep breath, she stood, straightening her clothes and wiping away the remaining dampness from her face.

It was done.

It was over, whether Jason wanted it to be or not, and she would not sit around mourning a sham marriage – which is exactly what it was.

How many others had there been?

All those delayed trips.

The overtly sentimental behaviour when he returned home, most likely guilty displays of affection.

She felt sick.

Had it all really been a complete lie?

"No more," she told herself with a firmness that came from a place she didn't know existed within her, but she liked it.

Grabbing a couple of dresses, she walked to the wardrobe and got back to what she was doing, albeit with a little less enthusiasm than before.

Scarlett didn't need him. She had a new, purposeful life with new people, even if it was temporary, and there was no room for all this unhappiness and melancholy.

Life had to move on and there was no space for Jason in it anymore.

The truth of it was, it was beginning to feel an awful lot like relief, making her wonder if she'd even been *living* up to this point – or was it more of an existence, and a crappy one at that, constantly being at Jason's and Tara's beck and call?

Go here, Scarlett. Do that, Scarlett. No, Scarlett, not that way!

A NEW *Hope* IN THE HIGHLANDS

Yes, she was hurt, but relief was definitely winning.

It was a good hour and a half before Scarlett finished unpacking Anaïse's vast wardrobe, giving her further perspective on how little she actually owned herself. She hoped that, at a bare minimum, Jason would send on some of her clothes.

Not that she owned that many. She was a basic trouser or jeans and top kind of girl, which often irritated Jason, leading to one of his many mild tantrums.

"Could you at least make a bit of an effort?" he would say, the disapproval clear across his face.

His frustration would aggravate her.

Perhaps years of marriage would do that, but it also made her more stubborn.

"There's nothing wrong with what I'm wearing!" Scarlett would glance at her reflection in the oversized ornate mirror leaning against the wall of their bedroom.

On this particular occasion, she'd braided her hair into a bun and wore black, wide-legged trousers, a fitted white t-shirt, a black blazer, and white and cream trainers. It wasn't a dress, but in her opinion, she looked suitably smart, presentable, and, more importantly, she was comfortable – just the idea of heels would tempt a blister to appear – and she was even wearing makeup.

"You do own dresses." Jason towered over her reflection in the mirror, smoothing his blonde hair, looking smart and handsome as always. "Could you not have worn one of those?"

"Christ, Jason." Scarlett had rolled her eyes and walked out of the room, calling behind her, "It's just your mother coming for dinner, not the fucking Queen."

Scarlett considered if that's where it perhaps all

went wrong.

She simply hadn't been *Tara* enough for him.

She certainly didn't miss that aspect of their relationship.

Her overpowering mother-in-law was a bully, and Scarlett felt satisfied she had finally confronted her. The prospect of never again facing her left Scarlett feeling giddy. Life was hard enough without having someone like that dictating everything down to her wardrobe selection.

Scarlett switched on the Mackintosh-style lamps on each side of the huge bed, casting a soft warm glow across the room, and taking a final glance around, satisfied all was as it should be, she turned off the main light and closed the door behind her.

Despite the questionable event with Edward earlier in the day and the rude uninvited interruption from Jason, Scarlett found a sense of satisfaction in all she'd achieved and all the work in the run-up to it.

Sure, it wasn't brain surgery, but making houses feel like a home was something she excelled at – and although Haddon House was a huge project, Scarlett and the rest of the staff had already brought half of the east wing back to life, ready for its visitors.

It left her feeling full of pride – and hunger, according to the loud growl from her stomach; hours had passed since she'd eaten Mrs Wilson's soup.

She smiled.

Scarlett liked the older woman, whose endless capacity for kindness and cooking pleased her. The woman's genuine delight in Scarlett's efforts brought her more satisfaction than even pleasing the laird himself.

She silently scolded herself for letting him back in her head again, simultaneously pausing at a closed door further down the hall, reaching out to trace the detail of

A NEW *Hope* IN THE HIGHLANDS

the vines engraved into the wooden frame.

A lot of the doorways had similar frames – each design was unique, adding a certain charm and personality to the house.

The room was now allocated to Haddon House's monk in residence, but Scarlett wasn't thinking about anyone in the wedding party. No, her unruly thoughts were already racing back to what had occurred beyond the door before the Americans' arrival.

Before she could stop herself, the memory of Edward's hands on her bare skin, fingers hungry and searching, hitched Scarlett's breath.

Embarrassed by her thoughts and feeling ashamed that she was getting so distracted by Edward whilst fresh out of a messy marriage, Scarlett hurried along the hallway and down the stairs.

Rounding the corner to flee the house and its intoxicating inhabitants, Scarlett ran straight into a hard chest attached to two powerful arms that quickly enveloped and steadied her.

"Oh fuck, sorry." The words escaped from her mouth before she could filter them.

Leonard's lopsided smile unnerved her. "Easy now."

Every time the man spoke, it seemed like he was privy to some private joke she was unaware of.

"I'm so sorry, I wasn't paying attention …" Scarlett trailed off, suddenly feeling unsure of herself and not knowing what was and wasn't an appropriate way to talk to these people anymore.

Leonard seemed immune to any such feelings, as his hands were still holding on to her arms.

"Don't worry, I'm paying plenty." His gaze was unwavering and slightly hypnotic. "Where are you rushing off to in such a hurry?"

"My mum will have dinner ready," Scarlett said,

her attention still focused on his hands, which were now caressing her arms – or was she imagining it?

As if reading her mind, he stroked the top of her arms with more weight and purpose, as if checking she was still in one piece, and appeared reluctant to let go of her, although he finally did.

"How is it being in the studio?"

"Great, yeah." Scarlett felt she could breathe and talk normally now his hands were no longer on her. "It's beautiful."

"Yeah? That's good. I spent many misspent evenings there when I was younger whenever my mum was off on her travels. Girls would go crazy for the artwork; it was always a surefire way of getting laid."

Scarlett couldn't help laughing. "Yes, I can imagine the whole *I own an estate* didn't hurt your chances, either."

Leonard had the humility to laugh before he shrugged and nodded.

"Lennie … my glass is still empty!" Anaïse's voice shrilled from further down the corridor.

He didn't flinch, though, his eyes searching Scarlett's – for what, she didn't know – before he sighed and rolled his own.

"Anaïse waits for no man."

"Or a drink, it would seem."

The pair laughed and finally he looked away.

"Enjoy your dinner, Scarlett." He turned to walk away, but stopped and grabbed hold of her hand, stroking it gently. "You've done an incredible job with the house already, in just a couple of days. We're all in awe – the wedding is going to be spectacular."

"Lennie!" the voice called again.

He laughed, a genuine and good-natured laugh. "I'm clearly needed. Goodnight, Scarlett."

"Goodnight, Leonard." Scarlett watched him leave,

then took her coat from a hook at the back door, as was her original plan.

Firmly closing the door behind her, she shook her head.

What the very fuck was that?

Scarlett pulled her coat around her and trudged up the path towards the stables, deciding it was best to dismiss any thoughts of Jason *and* the Cameron-Reid boys. No good would come of it – no matter how attractive or charming they were.

She ran the last short distance to the big red door, where the smell of stew welcomed her.

CHAPTER 16

EDWARD COULD TURN it on when it was required, or when it suited him, oozing the quintessential Scottish charm tourists seemed to love, potentially only matched by the Irish – something spoke to their Gaelic roots on a subliminal level, perhaps.

The watchful eye of Lily, who sat immediately to his left, was also doing its part to keep him in check. To his right sat the shoeless monk, Michael. Next to him, Anaïse sat across from her best friend, Miranda, and Leonard's seat faced him from the bottom of the table. All in all, a seating arrangement his mother would be proud of. The thought made Edward almost roll his eyes.

"What kept you, darlin'?" Anaïse pouted and raised her arm in the air, reaching out her hand impatiently. "Where have you been? Edward has been regaling us with tales from when you were boys – it's been delightful."

Leonard took his bride-to-be's hand and kissed it.

"Forgive me, my love. I ran into Scarlett on my travels." As he spoke the words, he looked across the table at his brother and smiled, his intention producing the desired effect.

Edward's jaw twitched, but refusing to engage, he moved the remaining vegetables around his plate, refusing to give Leonard the satisfaction.

"Such a charming creature, isn't she? She reminds me of Merida from *Brave*. You know the movie? All wild red curls and feistiness. Just what I imagined Scottish *lassies* to be like." Anaïse beamed.

"Scarlett is actually English." Lily smiled politely.

Anaïse dismissed the correction with her hand. "Same thing, I guess." She handed her glass to Leonard. "Darlin', would you please?"

"Not really." Lily ignored Anaïse's transparent attempt to move on from the faux pas.

Despite their differences, a smile played on both brothers' lips at Lily's polite but obvious defiance – she was a true Scot at heart, which made them proud.

Anaïse was oblivious, or refusing to play the game, and instead turned her attention to Leonard, who was attending to her drink.

Edward observed the dynamics between them with interest. There was no question of her wealth, beauty, and impeccable upbringing, but the air of arrogance and entitlement soured the package for Edward.

Apparently, Lily was feeling the same, judging by the way she was watching Leonard's uncharacteristic pampering of Anaïse and his bizarre inner channelling of a golden retriever with subtle disapproval.

In a way, Edward felt disappointed for her, as Lily had been beyond excited to come and spend time with her uncle and his fiancée's dazzling entourage – only to face the cringeworthy farce taking place in their dining room.

Anaïse brought him back to the conversation with a jolt. "Edward?"

"Yes, sorry?" He looked across at Anaïse, who narrowed her eyes at him.

"It's insane how similar you and Lennie look sometimes. It's uncanny." She looked between the two, slowly shaking her head. "Anyway, I said, where did you find her?"

"Who?" Edward said, having lost track of the

mundane dinner chat.

"Your maid, Scarlett, of course."

Edward struggled to keep the smile from his face this time. "She's not a maid, per se."

"Oh, whatever you call them here then – servants, the help, you know what I mean."

The others in the room also seemed genuinely stumped by what to say in response, but Leonard, clearly the most experienced of the group at dealing with his fiancée's social bumbling, stepped in.

"She's the daughter of our gardener, June." He handed Anaïse her refilled glass, sitting back beside her as if ready to hold court. "It's an interesting story, actually. You'll like this."

Anaïse clapped her hands in delight, making Edward and Lily widen their eyes simultaneously.

Leonard clocked them, raised an eyebrow in a warning to rein in their judgemental looks, but then smiled, taking a long sip of his wine before continuing.

"So, June is an avid reader, quite the collection of books she has up there in the stables." Leonard glanced at Edward who was now glaring at him with contempt. The idea of Leonard visiting the stables, and the Hope women, made his knuckles whiten as his hand gripped the arm of his chair.

The reaction made Leonard smile, his charm turning up a notch further.

"She loves nineteenth and early twentieth century fiction. Guess what her favourite book is?"

The monk, who had been sitting in contemplative silence for most of the meal, lifted his head with a big grin on his face. "*Gone with the Wind*!"

Leonard applauded with a good-natured laugh. "There you have it. She named her daughter after Scarlett O'Hara."

"Such an epic movie." The monk was still smiling.

"A classic, for sure."

"You're so good with people, Lennie, the way you take the time to speak to them. I just love that about you." Anaïse turned her attention to Miranda, her maid of honour, who was successfully drinking herself into a silent stupor. "Maybe we should think about getting you to bed. You look a bit pale, darlin'." She reached across and placed her hand on Miranda's.

"Don't you be getting all bossy with me, Annie St. Clare!" Miranda waved her away. "You are not the boss of me."

The childish outburst sent Anaïse into a tinkling fit of laughter, and Miranda, the monk, and Leonard joined in.

Edward and Lily exchanged bemused looks.

"Told you." Edward lowered his voice so his words were only audible to Lily. "Fucking circus act."

"Dad, don't be so judgy!" Lily scolded him, but it lacked the weight of her usual contempt for his old-school dad ways, and despite the reprimand, she gave him a conspiratorial smile. "They are a bit mad, though."

Edward silently thanked the universe that he hadn't completely lost his daughter, and, even more importantly, that she could see through the ridiculous facade and pretentious nonsense at their dining table.

Mrs Wilson provided a welcome distraction when she entered the room.

"So wonderful to hear the house full of laughter," she almost sang, ushering in the two kitchen hands she'd recently hired from the neighbouring village – two lads, no older than twenty, who began lifting and clearing away plates and dishes from the long table.

Edward noticed Lily tense and blush as the eldest of the two grazed her hand as he took away her plate, softly offering his apology and hurrying back off to the kitchen.

"It was requested there be no sweets or puddings for our esteemed guests, so instead I've prepared some coffee and brandy in the drawing room whenever you're ready to go through."

Edward placed his napkin on the table and stood up.

"Thank you, Mrs Wilson. We'll get out of the way to allow the room to be cleared. Then you and the rest of the staff can finish up for the evening. We'll be able to look after ourselves for the rest of the night."

He moved around to the back of Lily's chair, moving it away as she stood – the idea of her being anywhere near the boy, judging by the palpable chemistry between them, made him uncomfortable, at best.

The rest of the party began scraping their chairs back, rising to leave as instructed by their host, Miranda finding it more challenging than the others.

"Mrs Wilson, dinner was perfect, as always." With a slight bow and a twinkling smile, Leonard escorted Anaïse and Miranda out of the room, the two women laughing and hanging over him like two drunks on a hen do.

Mrs Wilson smiled politely and nodded her head in response.

The monk passed her too, offering a polite nod of thanks, with Lily in tow, who seemed keen not to miss the rest of the Anaïse and Miranda show.

"Was everything to your liking?" Mrs Wilson smiled at Edward, who was still hovering near the doorway, contemplating his next move, or more accurately, his escape.

"Yes, as my brother rightly said, dinner was perfect, thank you." He watched as the two young men cleared the table and straightened the chairs. "Good job getting some help in so quickly."

"They're good workers." Mrs Wilson re-straightened a chair after they left the room, arms full of plates. "Alfred McNeil's boys."

"The butcher?"

"That's right," she said, continuing to busy herself at the table.

"They don't work with their father then?"

"Mark does. He's saving for his travels, so working in the evenings as well suits him."

"And the other one?" Edward was attempting to remain nonchalant, but he recognised the knowing look etched across Mrs Wilson's face. She never missed a beat.

"James?"

Edward nodded, avoiding her gaze, instead taking a vested interest in the mahogany dresser next to the door, which still bore the deep scratch Leonard had imprinted into the lacquer as a small boy, with the help of a small red matchbox car.

"He's vegan." Mrs Wilson shrugged as if that explained everything.

Edward couldn't help but smile. "Tricky in that line of business."

"Indeed." Mrs Wilson chuckled, gathering the last of the small plates. "Helps me with ideas for the vegan gentleman in Leonard's party, though." She smiled and looked up at Edward. "Is there anything else I can get for you this evening?"

A healthy serving of Scarlett would be nice.

The thought was entirely involuntary and wildly inappropriate to the extent a slight blush appeared on his neck.

He had to get over this ridiculous infatuation and grow the fuck up.

Neither Evelyn, nor Briege, was the answer. Women, he had thought for several years now, did little for his peace of mind – and with the exception of his daughter, who brought her own set of challenges, they were best kept at arm's length to be loved and admired from a distance.

This was something he'd managed successfully until Scarlett, with her curves, doe-like green eyes, and hair he wanted so badly to smell again – maybe even take a hold of and tug back, giving him full access to the lips he couldn't get out of his mind.

Despite his earlier vow to leave well alone, the taste of her skin was haunting him, and he literally ached to have access to it again; this time without interruption or clothing – there had been far too much clothing for him to fully appreciate her. And despite the vivid memory of his hands travelling under her shirt and over her bra, and the sweet moment his fingers sought her under her jeans and underwear, it wasn't enough.

He needed more, so much more, and the idea of her standing naked in front of him, confident and feisty, yet vulnerable at the same time, was driving him mad – what he wouldn't do to have access to her. To have her waiting in his rooms now.

Fuck's sake.

"No, thank you," he said finally, giving himself a mental shake. "Goodnight, Mrs Wilson."

Mrs Wilson observed him with obvious interest, clearly wondering what on earth had been taking hold of him recently, but she nodded her head politely.

"Goodnight, sir."

Edward quickly left the dining room, briefly considering joining the others, but the high-energy commotion and hilarity coming from their direction solidified his resolve to retreat towards his private rooms.

He would catch up on some overdue accounts for the tenanted cottages on the outskirts of the estate. That should provide enough of a distraction and a valid excuse not to join in with the festivities.

From the clinking of glasses and enthusiastic rising voices, each grappling to overpower the other, he wouldn't be missed. He shook his head and entered his office, shutting the door behind him. That was enough for one day.

CHAPTER 17

Upon entering the apartment, it wasn't just the comforting heat and delicious aroma of the red wine and beef stew that washed over her, there was also the warm presence of soft laughter and gentle voices coming from the kitchen – they had a guest.

"Sorry I'm late," Scarlett called to June from the hallway, leaning against the wall to untie the laces of her Converse trainers. "Got held up by the gods."

"Hello, don't worry, it's keeping warm." June popped her head around the doorway. "Andrzej's here for dinner too. Hope you don't mind?"

"Of course not." Scarlett smiled. "More the merrier. I'm just going to change quickly, if I've got time?"

"We've just opened a bottle of Malbec. I'll pour you a glass."

"Thanks, Mum." Scarlett was still smiling as she walked into her bedroom, not oblivious to the fact that the word *mum* was also beginning to feel more natural to her.

Something felt as if it was shifting, and it wasn't just with June – although that in itself was significant.

She felt lighter, especially after her call with Jason earlier, and despite the tears and gut-wrenching pain he caused her, which still ached somewhere deep in her stomach and chest, a sense of peace was settling over her – further boosted by the prospect of spending an evening in the company of June and Andrzej.

For the first time in as long as she could remember,

Scarlett felt as if she was *home*, and she sat on her bed for a moment to register this.

She let out a contented sigh, and choosing not to overanalyse, as was usually her way, she began pulling off her jeans and top, throwing them both near the washing basket in the corner – into which nothing ever quite made it.

Opening her drawer, she took out a comfy pair of thick purple socks, wide-legged yoga pants, and the green hole-riddled jumper she'd first arrived wearing that she still loved. Dressing herself quickly, she left the room to join the impromptu gathering in the kitchen.

"Oh, my days," Scarlett exclaimed, walking in. "I can't tell you how ready I am for this!"

"Scarlett." Andrzej welcomed her with a big grin and handed her an enormous glass of wine. "I was starting to think you'd never arrive, and I'd be left to starve."

Scarlett offered a sheepish smile as an apology. "It's nuts over there at the moment. In fact, they're all pretty nuts, if I'm honest."

"Yes, the guests are certainly settling in." He stood and pulled out a chair so Scarlett could join them at the table. "Please." He gestured for her to sit. "Happy to see you even more than usual, so we can finally eat this feast your mother has prepared."

Andrzej returned to his own seat and Scarlett observed the spread on the dining room table. He wasn't joking. On display was a steaming cast-iron pot full of the rich stew she could smell on entering the apartment, with swollen golden dumplings on its surface.

Sat beside the pot was a hunk of Mrs Wilson's homemade bread, sliced with thickly spread butter and piled high on a plate, all complemented with a dish full of vibrant greens on the side for good measure – no doubt from the garden.

"This all looks amazing, thank you." Scarlett felt a little overwhelmed and must've looked it, as her mother gently touched her hand.

"Let's eat." June smiled at Scarlett and Andrzej in turn. "Before it all gets cold."

Except for some appreciative murmurings, the trio ate in companionable silence, tired from a long day.

When they were all finished, Scarlett stopped June and Andrzej from getting up to clear the table. "Please, let me." Scarlett gave Andrzej a warning look as he tried to resist. "I mean it. You've both been busy working outside all day, so let me do this as a thank you."

Andrzej raised his hands in defeat. "Okay, if you insist."

Scarlett smiled and, within a handful of trips, cleared the table of its dirty plates and dishes and finally closed the kitchen door behind her, leaving June and Andrzej talking quietly about their plans for the next day.

She was now firmly of the belief there was more than just friendly working camaraderie between the two, even if they themselves weren't aware of it yet. There was nothing overtly obvious either of them had said or done, but the two shared a connection and understanding that felt far beyond a platonic work relationship – even that of a close friendship.

In all her years of marriage to Jason, the synergy between them was nothing like this, and although Scarlett wasn't spiritual, she thought it was a bit like watching two twin flames meeting and merging into a magical dance. The chemistry felt tangible and the romance of it took her breath away.

She and June didn't have the intimate friendship that some mothers and daughters shared, and there was no way she'd be able to find the words to say anything to her, but Scarlett hoped that her mother might consider the idea that there was someone for her out there after all, and if anyone was perfect for her, it was most definitely Andrzej.

Scarlett sighed, putting away the cast-iron pot, part of a set which her mother had owned since the beginning of time – or at least the beginning of Scarlett's.

She hung up the damp tea towel and listened out for June and Andrzej's voices, which were low but still animated. Smiling, Scarlett closed the cutlery drawer and the cupboard below it and opened the adjoining door to the living room, noticing the pair had settled on the sofa with the TV on in the background.

Neither seemed to be watching whatever drama adaptation was showing and Scarlett bit back her usual sarcasm, resisting the urge to point out that June had probably watched it a hundred times over. Instead, she cleared her throat, drawing their attention to her.

"That's me finished – I'm done in and ready for bed. I'll leave you to it."

Andrzej's smile was broad, but his grey-blue eyes appeared heavy from a long day working outside and most likely the two or three glasses of red wine he'd consumed with June this evening.

"I shall head off shortly too. Thank you for your company this evening. Sleep well."

Scarlett smiled at them both and nodded in response, taking a step towards her bedroom before turning back and peering around the doorway.

"And thanks for the lovely dinner. It was fab."

Scarlett cringed at herself.

Fab?

What was it about living with her mother again that made her feel, act, and talk like a teenager?

"You're very welcome, Scarlett. Goodnight." June

smiled in response, looking a little flushed from the wine and no doubt her amiable companion.

They really did suit each other.

In her bedroom, the door closed quietly behind her, Scarlett removed and discarded her clothes on the floor, realising too late she hadn't yet closed the shutters of her window, potentially flaunting herself to anyone looking in.

Not that she imagined anyone would be, and even if they were still up, it would be unlikely they'd be paying any attention to the stables. All the excitement would be taking place inside the main house, especially if the recent amount of alcohol was anything to go by.

Feeling full, tired, and content, she padded into the bathroom and turned on the shower. The steam enveloped her in a warm hug as she stepped in, and she felt instant comfort from the rainfall showerhead above her, washing away any remnants of negativity or doubts that had been clinging to her these past few days and weeks.

For the first time in an age, she felt relief and an overwhelming sense of peace and wellbeing surged through her. She felt safe and at home. The idea of leaving and finding somewhere to live was never far from her thoughts. But at this exact moment in time, she was content and enjoying what she was doing and where she was.

Haddon House and its inhabitants were far from perfect, but they were doing a good job in keeping her here, and despite having bigger, more independent plans, Scarlett couldn't deny it felt good.

The feeling stayed with her through the night and despite the following morning being a Sunday, and potentially the only lie-in she'd get that week, Scarlett was wide awake.

She wanted to seize the moment and make full use

of it; her head was spinning with ideas for the wedding, the bedrooms to accommodate all the guests, and the positioning of the gazebo on the grounds.

There were so many questions still unanswered and although she'd been repeatedly told by Leonard that money was *absolutely* no object, some idea of a budget would better equip her to plan, especially with the wedding being less than two months away. The big day would be on the twenty-first of December, just days before Christmas, so they could have plenty of time to get settled in and celebrate Christmas in the Alps for their honeymoon.

She knew who she had to speak to – the only person qualified and grounded enough to sign off on her ideas, and, hopefully, who could offer some insight into a realistic budget.

Edward.

Scarlett hadn't seen him since their last encounter and somewhat brusque exchange after the *incident*, but the thought of speaking to him didn't fill her with the angst she felt yesterday – in fact, if she was being completely honest with herself, she wanted to see him.

Throwing back the covers, she got out of bed, walked to her drawers, and surveyed her sparse but clean selection of clothes, making a mental note to thank her mother for washing and putting them away. Scarlett never asked June to do this, but she always appreciated it when she did.

Impatient to get moving, she removed a pair of jeans, a t-shirt, and a jumper and quickly dressed. Walking into the bathroom, she ran her fingers through her hair, tugging some knots loose. She huffed and scrunched her nose up at her reflection in the mirror and lost her patience, instead bunching her hair up into a messy bun, curls springing loose from every angle. Scarlett shrugged. She wasn't dressing to impress. Just eager to get started with the day.

After brushing her teeth and giving her face a quick wash, she grabbed a rolled-up towel from the side to dry herself off, her face looking fresh from the cold water.

Scarlett paused, recognising something resembling a sparkle returning to her eyes, which made her smile, and then laugh. If anyone saw her, they would think she had gone mad, but smiling and being kind to herself felt like the most refreshing and sane thing she had done for herself in a while.

Today, life felt good. She felt good. And she wasn't ashamed to enjoy it.

CHAPTER 18

THE HOUSE WAS still, as if it and the people within were softly breathing and sleeping in unison.

Releasing a satisfied sigh, Edward, already up for an hour, made his way to the drawing room. When he opened the door, briefly hesitating at the thought of what he would find, he was surprised and relieved to see everything was in order, the blazing crackling fire sufficiently masking any remnants of the stale stench of alcohol.

Mrs Wilson must have arrived at the crack of dawn to clear up the mess from the previous evening's festivities, which Edward imagined had gone long into the early hours of the morning.

He surveyed for any damage but found none, and within seconds, Mrs Wilson appeared with a tray of freshly made coffee, which Edward welcomed with a smile.

"You really are a godsend, Mrs Wilson. I'm not sure what any of us would do without you."

Mrs Wilson chuckled as she sat the tray down on the small mahogany side table beside Edward's chair facing the fireplace. "You'd most likely all starve and be drinking instant coffee, for starters."

Edward smiled and nodded. "You're probably not wrong."

"Was a good night had by all?" Mrs Wilson placed another log on the fire. "I imagine they'll all be sleeping in past noon today if the empty bottles this morning were anything to go by."

"Couldn't tell you. I didn't join them." Edward poured himself some coffee into his china cup, plopping in a singular sugar cube. The cup was part of an antique Satsuma-ware collection his mother had acquired from Japan – no doubt through one of her overpriced art dealers in Asia.

There were several items such as these scattered around the house; in fact, she'd left all her collections behind when she headed back to Louisiana, not wanting to be reminded of anything to do with her life with George, Edward and Leonard's father.

This hadn't bothered Edward that much, and although not overly pretentious or fussy when it came to designers and labels, he admitted to enjoying drinking his morning coffee from this particular set.

"I've left the morning papers by your chair. Would you like some breakfast this morning?"

"Just a couple of boiled eggs in an hour, and just one slice …" Edward paused as the door opened and a damp-haired, fresh-faced Scarlett appeared, slightly breathless.

"Good morning – so sorry to interrupt," she said, her voice raspy.

"Good morning, Scarlett." Edward returned his focus to Mrs Wilson, who surveyed Scarlett with a questioning look. "Just one slice of toast, please."

Looking back at Scarlett, he softened. "You have wet hair; come sit by the fire," he said.

Scarlett visibly hesitated, avoiding eye contact with Mrs Wilson, who Edward knew would disapprove of both her haphazard entrance and sitting down with the laird of Haddon House whilst he was taking his morning coffee, especially looking the way she did.

"Scarlett, sit down," Edward repeated. "Please?"

Mrs Wilson nodded at them both and quietly left

the room.

"You'll get ill if you don't dry off."

Scarlett sat down in the chair in front of the fire and observed the china cup. "That's beautiful."

"Thank you. Here, let me pour you a cup. That one has sugar in it." He took an identical-looking cup from the dresser and began pouring coffee from the pot.

"How do you know I don't take sugar?" Scarlett asked.

"I don't – do you?" His hand hovered over her cup.

"No." Scarlett smiled at him, her eyes sparkling, and in that moment, he felt as if he might melt.

With a mental shake, he handed her the steaming cup and sat down in the chair opposite her, nursing his own cup of coffee.

"Thank you," she said, taking a careful sip. "So, I've been thinking about the wedding, and I have so many ideas, but—"

"What are you doing later?" he interrupted.

"Pardon?"

"Later today, do you have any plans?" he asked, his face neutral.

"Err, nothing set in stone, but to be honest, I really wanted to talk through some ideas I've had and—"

"That's all fine. We can do that." Edward hadn't taken his eyes off her and he could see it was putting Scarlett on edge, so he looked away. "I have a few errands to run in Edinburgh. You could come along, and we can talk over whatever you need."

"Edinburgh? Right, okay – I mean, I can't see why not, I guess." He watched her again as several emotions crossed her face all at once.

"Good, that's settled then. It's a couple of hours' drive. Will that be enough time to talk through your plans?"

"Yes, more than enough." It was Scarlett's turn to

look at him, and it made him feel like she was trying to search into his soul, dark and twisted as it was. "What's in Edinburgh?"

A smile twitched at the corner of his mouth. "Lots of things, really."

"You know what I mean. What do you need to do there?" Scarlett relaxed into the chair, taking another sip of her coffee.

Her mouth distracted him, and it took a long moment for him to answer. "We have property there. The tenant has just left, and I need to check it over. Also, my solicitor is close by, and I need to drop some papers off to him."

"He works on a Sunday?"

"Isn't that what you're doing?" He smiled at her.

"Well, I suppose – although it doesn't feel like work, and besides, we're on a short deadline with the wedding coming up so soon." Scarlett shrugged.

"It doesn't feel like work?" Edward watched intently as Scarlett squirmed at his question.

"It's just not a nine-to-five kind of situation, is it?"

He remained silent for a long moment, still looking at her. "It's difficult to put a description to the situation, to be honest."

Scarlett cocked her head to the side. "What do you mean?"

Edward rubbed his face with one hand. Even he wasn't really sure what he meant. Or what, for that matter, he was doing, inviting her along to Edinburgh with him. All he knew was he wanted to have her close to him, to know her, and to hell with the consequences.

"Finish your coffee and be ready in half an hour – and make sure you bring a coat. It's cold and wet out." Edward stood, nodded, and left the room without another word.

Within the hour, they were on the A9 heading towards Perth, and the passing forest, its trees ablaze with shades of orange and red, clearly captivated Scarlett. He always enjoyed this time of year for that precise reason, and it filled him with a sense of pride to see Scarlett enjoying it.

"It's all so beautiful," she finally said after several minutes of neither of them saying anything.

"Yes, it's pretty stunning. Although this is unusual – the leaves don't usually hang on for this long. But it's been quite mild, and we've had no storms yet." He glanced across at her to see a sad smile on her lips as she absentmindedly twirled her rings around her finger. "Do you miss home?"

Scarlett shook her head. "No, not really."

"Do you miss him?" He cringed inwardly at his forwardness.

Scarlett snapped her head from the view to look at him. "Who? My ex?"

Edward nodded.

"God, no. I mean, not him as he is now." She shook her head. "I don't think I really knew him, to be honest."

The two sat in silence for a moment before Scarlett spoke again. "I think I was missing what I thought it all stood for, but not him. Or more that I was missing *me* – if that makes any sense."

Edward nodded. "It does."

"It just doesn't feel very good being made a fool of, you know?" There was a slight quiver in her voice.

"Sorry, I didn't mean to pry." He offered her a smile as an apology.

Scarlett looked across at him. "Didn't you?"

Edward didn't look at her but could still feel her smile. "Yeah, alright, I was being a right nosy bastard."

They both laughed.

"He sounds like a bit of a prick, to be honest."

Scarlett nodded. "A massive one."

"Talking about pricks, I know you want to talk about the wedding, but do you think we could have one day where I don't have to think or talk about my brother's upcoming nuptials?"

"I thought that's why you wanted me to come along – to kill two birds with one stone?"

Edward remained quiet.

"Not that I mind the drive," Scarlett continued. "It's nice to get off the estate. It feels surreal coming back into the real world."

"Yeah, I know what you mean. I'm the same now that Lily is driving. Weeks sometimes pass without me venturing anywhere else."

"It's like its own little micro-universe. There's something magical about that, though, isn't there?"

Edward smiled. He liked that she felt that way because it was exactly how he felt about his home and land. "Aye, I'd agree with that. But it's also good to get out, stretch our wings a bit."

Scarlett went back to looking out the window and within minutes, she fell asleep.

Edward struggled to keep his eyes on the road for the rest of the journey and it wasn't until they arrived in Edinburgh that Scarlett woke up. Sleepy and dazed, her eyes widened at the scenery. Edward wasn't immune to the visual charms of this part of Edinburgh, nor it would seem were the tourists that saturated the streets and paths, angling their phones for the perfect selfie.

"What is this place?" Scarlett asked, craning her neck to see the medieval buildings surrounding them.

"Dean Village. Do you like it?"

Scarlett's wide-eyed expression made him laugh.

"I'll take that as a yes."

Edward signalled the car right, driving slowly into a

A NEW *Hope* IN THE HIGHLANDS

small tunnel where discreet gates opened to unveil a small courtyard big enough for two or three cars. He pulled up and parked outside a tall and impressive stone house, designed in the same vein as the buildings Scarlett had just been gawking at.

"This is one of our Edinburgh residences. I've got one in the centre I use for business now, and there's a house in the West End that we rent out. We only let this one out to known acquaintances these days, but my dad used to pawn it out to visiting dignitaries, all part of the boys' club." Edward rolled his eyes. "Not really my scene, to be honest."

Scarlett was still sitting in silent awe.

"Come on, let's see what state they've left the place in."

"Okay," Scarlett managed as a response, and he smiled, still not immune to the aesthetics of the place either.

Edward unlocked the door and allowed Scarlett to pass, and she marvelled at the high cornice ceilings and luxurious furnishings and made a beeline for the wide floor-to-ceiling windows looking over the water.

"It's called the Water of Leith," Edward told her, standing behind her, close enough to smell her hair.

"It's breathtakingly beautiful."

Edward murmured an "aye" in response, too distracted by her close proximity to form a proper sentence.

He didn't know what he was expecting. He had very little self-control, even in a busy household, when it came to Scarlett, let alone in this kind of intimate setting.

Something shifted in Scarlett, too. Her shoulders tensed, then slowly relaxed, and she turned to look up at him.

"Edward, why did you bring me here?" Her eyes

were full of questions. Questions he didn't know the answers to.

He sighed and shrugged. "Honestly, I hadn't actually thought any of this through. I just wanted to spend time with you. I didn't think about how it would pan out when we actually got here. I mean, I genuinely need to check all is in order." He looked around as if to make a point. "And I also have to hand Gerard the papers I have in the car, but ..." His voice trailed off.

"But what?"

"But I'd be lying if I didn't say I think about you a lot and now that we're here ..." He was struggling to find the words to explain any more than that.

Scarlett looked at him, her head slightly cocked, as if trying to see through his words and intentions.

"What do you think about?" There was an undeniable sparkle of mischief in her eyes as she continued to look up at him.

Edward's eyes raised to the ceiling as he tried to gather some sense and strength. "You know very well what I think about."

"No, I don't. Tell me," Scarlett insisted.

"Christ." Edward groaned and closed his eyes.

Maybe if he willed it, this would all stop, and he wouldn't do what every cell in his body was aching to do.

His eyes sprung open when he felt Scarlett's hands take hold of his.

CHAPTER 19

"Do you think of this?" she asked, pulling his hands towards her and placing them under her jumper. His eyes didn't leave hers. "Or this?"

Scarlett left his hands on her bare waist, placing her own on his chest, feeling his heart racing. He was holding back, she could tell, so she drifted them to the back of his neck, whilst stretching up onto her toes, pulling him towards her until their lips met.

She didn't think about where this newfound confidence came from, but she wanted him. She wanted him more than anything she'd wanted in a very long time. Kissing him softly, almost hesitantly, she fought against her feelings of vulnerability, and there was something in that which made Edward groan and snap from his hesitant state.

He wrapped his arms tightly around her, drawing her close to him, their kiss turning into something hungrier and more visceral with each passing moment. Every cell in her body was screaming to have him close to her, on her, inside her. To hell with decorum and socially accepted timeframes on how long a woman should wait until she slept with another man. She would not wait another minute.

Evidently, Edward had similar feelings, as his mouth travelled down her neck, his hands now hungrily exploring the bare skin beneath her jumper, pulling down the fabric of her bra to caress and softly squeeze one of her nipples.

Scarlett gasped at the contact, pulling at his hair and arching her body harder against him. Taking her reaction as permission, he briefly pulled away, taking hold of her jumper and removing it in one smooth movement, leaving her half naked and dishevelled, with her bra straps halfway down her arms and one breast exposed.

"Fucking hell," was all he managed to say before cupping both breasts and taking the uncovered nipple in his mouth, teasing it with his tongue and gently nibbling it with his teeth, making Scarlett cry out.

Everything inside her sparked into life, screaming out to be touched, kissed, and explored. Moving his hands to her back, he unclipped her bra and moaned in appreciation as his hands took the full weight of her breasts, his mouth unrelenting in its sweet assault on her nipples.

Edward released an animalistic groan as he took a step back to take a better look at her, swiftly bringing her right back into the moment.

She wasn't used to being observed, and it certainly hadn't been something she felt comfortable doing with Jason anymore – but the hungry and appreciative look of lust in Edward's eyes fuelled her confidence, and she felt unashamedly sexy.

Even more so as he kneeled before her and undid the buttons on her jeans, kissing her abdomen along the top seam of her knickers, slowly tugging both down and briefly placing his hot mouth against her wetness. Scarlett moaned at the sensation of his tongue pushing inside her, and were it not for Edward's hands holding her steady, she would've lost her balance.

Her reaction made him look up and smile.

"Please don't stop," she begged him.

Kissing her clit gently, he pulled away and focused on untying her trainers. "You couldn't have worn something easier?"

Scarlett laughed, holding his head for balance as he removed one shoe, then immediately started on the other. "I might've done if I'd known this was the planned activity for the afternoon!"

Edward pulled off the second shoe and removed her jeans and underwear before raising himself back up to standing. "But where would have been the fun in that?"

"I feel a little underdressed at this point." Scarlett moved her arms across her chest to cover her top half.

"Nuh-uh." Edward shook his head. "No covering up. I want to enjoy every minute of this. Are you cold?"

Scarlett shook her head. "Just very naked."

Edward smiled and kissed her. "Just the way I like you."

He scooped her up, wrapping her legs around him, and carried her to the large cream sofa behind them. Pulling down a soft chenille blanket hanging over the back, he lowered Scarlett onto it, his eyes drinking in the view of her lying beneath him.

Kneeling over her, he quickly pulled his jumper over his head, revealing the toned chest that was imprinted into her memory from the very first time she'd seen him.

Scarlett's hands drifted over his abdomen, following the trail of hair towards the enticing V shape revealed by his low-sitting jeans. She wasted no time in unbuttoning them, pulling both his jeans and boxers down to his knees, then using her feet to slide them down his legs until he could kick them off, leaving them both entirely naked.

"That's a neat little trick." Edward nodded in appreciation.

Scarlett lost her train of thought, and her eyes widened as she looked down, instantly distracted by the sight of Edward's eager, straining cock.

"So that's what you were hiding under the sheets." She smiled at Edward, blushing, and before he could look away, she pulled him down to kiss her again. "You're rather delicious, you know."

"You're not bad yourself." He kissed her neck and caressed her breasts, gently tweaking her nipples and groaning as her body reacted to every part that he made contact with.

"Which reminds me ..." His voice trailed off as he made his way from her neck to her breasts, licking, sucking, and nibbling every inch of her until he parted her legs, making Scarlett cry out as his mouth continued its previous exploration. At a pace that was slow and leisurely, almost unbearably so, his tongue explored every soft layer of her, seeking to taste and savour her essence, applying pressure at her most sensitive core, whilst his fingers sunk deep inside her, releasing her at the exact right moment, each time enveloping her in waves of delicious arousal.

His refusal to rush turned her on even more and every time she came close, her heart racing and blood rushing to her ears, she could feel him keeping a watchful eye, bringing her back down, steadying her, only to start all over again.

She lost count of how many times he pushed her towards the edge, until finally she reached the point of no return, aching for release, unable to hold back any longer – and as if he was able to read her body like a book, Edward's hands firmly gripped her hips to still her, and taking full control of her, he brought her to a climax that shattered her being into a million stardust particles. The world around her dissolved, and even as she slowly came back to her body, wave after wave of pure, uninhibited pleasure washed over her, insistent and all-consuming.

It felt like an age before she slowly returned to

herself fully – panting, shuddering, and clinging to his hair, as if letting go meant she might never return in one piece.

Eventually, Scarlett released him, worried about hurting him, but he didn't seem to care, still lost in her pleasure, kissing around her now raw and sensitive clit, careful to avoid direct contact and any discomfort.

"Edward, that wasn't normal," she finally said. "I think you've broken me."

She could feel his smile as he kissed the inside of her thigh before bringing himself up to look into her eyes.

"Scarlett, I've not even started." His smirk was full of mischief as he manoeuvred himself to pull his wallet out of his jeans.

She watched him as he tore the packet of a condom open with his teeth, his eyes not leaving hers, and as he pulled the condom over his now impatient-looking cock, she wasn't sure she'd ever seen anything sexier.

"You okay?" he asked her, positioning himself above her.

She nodded eagerly.

"I'm more than okay, Edward, I—"

He obviously didn't need to be asked twice, as he slid himself inside her, making her cry out.

He moaned loudly, his face now lost in her hair, his whole body shuddering with each thrust. Still sensitive from her orgasm, Scarlett was immersed in a feeling of utter bliss, arching her hips towards him and encouraging his cock deeper inside her, which seemed to make contact with every nerve the further he pushed.

"Fuck, Scarlett – why do you feel so good?" He groaned loudly.

She couldn't speak. It all felt too good. He felt too good, and words simply weren't forming properly in her head. So, instead, she pulled him back to her and answered with her lips against his, her tongue teasing his mouth open so she could explore him.

He grunted with pleasure, returning her kiss with a force that took her breath away, but slowing his pace until he stilled, finally tearing himself away from her kiss and shaking his head with his eyes tightly shut.

"Christ, I'm not sure how long I can last. This feels too good." He leaned his forehead against hers, his eyes still closed.

Scarlett took his face gently in her hands and stroked his cheekbones, dusted with stubble, waiting patiently until he opened them. She kissed him softly and then pulled away slightly to look at him again.

"This doesn't have to be a one-time event, you know. You don't need to hold back." Something clouded across his face, a passing thought perhaps, but Scarlett dismissed it. Pushing her hips towards him, the feeling of his cock deep inside her made *her* gasp and *him* groan. She pulled his face to her again, kissing him deeply before whispering, "I want you to come for me."

Her words had the desired effect, as his body tensed with newfound purpose, and a spark of hunger flashed in his eyes. Moving her hands above her head, he held them firmly in place, the fingers of his other hand entangled in her hair, making Scarlett cry out in pain and pleasure as he began thrusting at pace, unapologetically.

The combination of the pressure of his hand keeping hold of hers, the tingling pain of her hair being tugged, and the sensation of his cock pounding in and out of her was exquisite; to the point that, within minutes, another orgasm took her by surprise as it surged and rippled through her.

Her eyes sprang open to see him watching her, tentatively, at which point he closed his own, releasing an almost animalistic groan that echoed through the house as he climaxed inside her.

CHAPTER 20

He wasn't sure how long they'd been there, tangled limbs and interlaced fingers, the smell of sex lingering on them both. Equally, he didn't want to move or speak, not wanting the moment to dissipate and worried he'd never again feel a peace such as this.

She was right; it wasn't normal.

He'd never experienced sex like it, and he didn't want it to be a one-time event, even though every logical bone in his body knew it absolutely should be. But she was exquisite in every way. He wanted to inhale her and keep her within him for the rest of time, which he knew was a ridiculous thought, but so was the idea of letting her go.

He noticed her breathing become heavy and slow – she was asleep, which further made the idea of breaking the moment feel like a crime. Eventually, he must've fallen asleep too, as when he opened his eyes it was dark outside, and the lights of the surrounding buildings were reflecting into the darkened room from the water.

Scarlett shifted beside him and rolled over to her side, her back facing him. The softness of her curves woke him further and, casting any of his previous thoughts aside, he began caressing her soft skin, making her arch and murmur in response.

His cock stirred, and like she was a beacon guiding him home, he moved closer to her, finding the apex of her thighs damp, warm, and welcoming. He wanted to slide back inside her again, to return the world to an even keel, and he sighed a moan of relief as Scarlett, responding sleepily, reached behind her, taking hold of and stroking his cock.

Edward groaned with pleasure and gently bit her shoulder before reaching down to the floor and taking another condom out of his wallet, which he'd strategically left in easy reaching distance. Within seconds, it was on and he was back inside her, making her call out his name as he built his pace up slowly, caressing her breasts and nuzzling into her neck.

"You feel incredible," he moaned softly into her hair.

Scarlett reached behind her again, this time pulling him closer to her, and he could feel her become increasingly wet.

"Fuck's sake, woman," he growled. "I cannot get enough of you."

"Good," Scarlett replied, her voice hoarse. "Because I can't get enough of you either."

Edward let out another animalistic groan, pulling out and turning Scarlett onto her front, pushing her knees up so she was on all fours. She gasped at the quickness of it, making her spasm around his cock as he thrust himself inside her again. This time, he wasn't going to come in a rush. He wanted to enjoy her in every way. He reached his hands around, taking her full breasts in his hands.

"I love the way you react to me," he said, his breath ragged and his cock throbbing, eager to orgasm inside her for the second time. But he was nowhere near finished yet.

He wanted to make her climax again – today, tomorrow, the day after that – in fact, he wanted to fuck her forever and beyond. Taking hold of her hips, he groaned again. The way their bodies connected snapped something in him and he lost all sense of everything – everything except the delicious sensation of being buried deep inside her.

Watching her back arch as he entered her, followed by her low cries of pleasure, made him want to possess her even more, but he was under the distinct impression it was her doing the possessing at this point.

"Turn around," he told her as he pulled out – which, to his delight, she did immediately on his command, her huge eyes full of sleepy lust, turning him on almost to the point of no return.

Taking her by surprise, he pushed her onto her back, making her laugh.

"You're just a tad too sexy when you get all domineering, you know. I like it." She smiled up at him.

Scarlett's hair was wild, framing her face, and making her look like a mermaid or a siren. He wasn't actually sure there was a difference, perhaps it was both. And it was in that moment he realised he was completely and utterly done for.

Her eyes sparkled as she reached down to stroke his cock, guiding him back inside her. It was then he stopped fucking her. Instead, and what he'd later reflect on, it was the moment he began making love to her.

But he told himself it was just physical. Infatuation at best. It was the chemicals in his body doing insane things to his brain. Nothing more.

Yet the feeling was overwhelming and all-fucking-encompassing, and he wasn't sure how long they continued that way, intense and trancelike, but eventually Scarlett's eyes closed, her back arched, and as she moaned loudly, free and beautifully uninhibited, he felt her tighten around his cock, a slow orgasm taking hold of her – it was truly something to behold.

But before another thought could cross his mind to appreciate it for longer, he lost complete control of his own as it built at a force he couldn't hold back, and he surrendered to a slow, intense climax, the pair clinging to each other, caught in combined spasms of exhausting pleasure.

For a long moment, they stayed that way until Edward finally pulled out of her and they each lay on their backs until their breathing returned to normal. Neither was tired, despite their bodies feeling spent.

"I'm thirsty, and hungry, and I need the toilet." Scarlett turned her head to face him.

Edward laughed. "Aye, I think we could both probably do with all the above, and maybe add a shower to the mix. Come on." He stood up and smiled, pulling her up to sitting with her hand. "I'll show you where the bathroom is, and then I'll give you a delayed tour of the house."

He briefly turned away and, taking a tissue from the somewhat conveniently located box on top of the table, he removed and deposited the condom inside of it, shoving it in his jeans pocket.

Scarlett scrunched up her nose and laughed.

Edward shrugged and smiled, suddenly feeling like a teenager.

"Shower sounds like a solid idea," she said, still smiling.

Edward then pulled his jeans on, and Scarlett wrapped the blanket around her.

"This way," Edward said, holding his hand out to her, which she took, seeming suddenly shy. "You okay?"

Scarlett nodded. "Yeah, just a bit out of my comfort zone, I think."

"How so?" Edward pulled her around to face him full on.

He disliked the uncertainty and self-doubt replacing Scarlett's usual directness, especially if he was the cause. However, she seemed to shake herself out of whatever was worrying her, and a smile crept over her face.

"You're just new to me – I'm used to the surly Scot, as opposed to this weirdly salacious and attentive version I'm dealing with today. Not sure if I should relax into it or be prepared for the inevitable fight."

He cupped her face and kissed her. "We don't fight." He laughed then. "And I don't think I've ever been called surly and salacious before, especially not in the same sentence." He paused for dramatic effect. "To be fair, I have been called plenty of other things, though."

Scarlett relaxed under his touch, and in turn, so did he.

"Show me this bathroom, then. I'm dying here!"

Edward placed a kiss on her forehead before leading her to the curved stone staircase. "You'll be pleased to hear the cleaners have been in already, so a clean bathroom and fresh towels await."

"Oooh, you do know how to treat a girl," Scarlett teased.

Edward laughed again. "There may be some whose opinions differ."

"I can't believe that!" Scarlett feigned surprise, to which he rolled his eyes.

Still holding her hand, which he wasn't wanting to let go of, despite not being the most naturally affectionate of men, he guided her upstairs and after bypassing the first couple of bedrooms, he stopped and opened the door to the master suite.

Scarlett took a sharp intake of breath as he turned on the light, revealing the enormous room, with its super-king-sized bed, all elaborately furnished in cream and gold and reminiscent of a huge, very expensive, high-end hotel suite.

"This place is ridiculous, Edward!" she said, not hiding her awe.

"It's certainly something, isn't it? Not entirely to my taste, but it has the wow-factor, I guess." He smiled at her stunned face. "Right, missus, the bathroom is through there on the right. Have a bath, shower, whatever takes your fancy. I'm going to jump in the shower down the hall and I'll see about ordering some food – hopefully there will be a bottle of something downstairs too." He drew her close and kissed her again. "Come find me when you're done. There should be some clean robes and slippers in there. Just take whatever you need." He gave her a final kiss and left her to her own devices, softly closing the door behind him.

Edward sighed. This wasn't what he'd planned. In fact, his plan to stay away from Scarlett had been the most sensible one by far. But it didn't seem that was going to work out for him.

Best laid plans and all that.

CHAPTER 21

SCARLETT RELEASED A deep breath and made her way into the bathroom. Her head was filled with delicious flashbacks of the last few hours.

She felt content.

Sex with Jason hadn't been terrible. In fact, at the start of their relationship and marriage, it had been good, but with Edward it was on another level. She couldn't stop the smile from spreading across her face – she was feeling all the feels. And, suddenly, incredibly thirsty.

She found a tumbler and drank two full glasses of cool water from the tap before looking around the bathroom, which was fitted out in the same lavish, no-expense-spared style as the rest of the house.

The idea of soaking in the enormous roll-top bath was tempting, but hunger won, and she decided on a quick shower instead. Turning on the water, she twisted her hair into a messy bun on top of her head with one of the assorted hairbands she always had on her left wrist, and stepped into the open floor-to-ceiling shower area.

Nodding appreciatively at the variety of expensive and aesthetically displayed organic products, she lathered on a generous helping of shower gel, filling the bathroom with the rich scent of orange blossom.

Lost in thought and in the middle of lathering on a second helping of the orange stuff – just because it smelled so damn good – a soft knock on the door startled her.

"Hello?" Edward appeared slightly damp with a towel around his waist and another in his hand, rubbing his hair dry, and she wondered if she'd ever tire of looking at him – it didn't seem likely.

"Just wanted to check you had everything you needed," he said, instantly distracted, watching Scarlett absentmindedly wash herself.

Scarlett smiled. "My back could probably do with a scrub."

She was joking and expected him to decline, already fresh and mostly dried off after his own shower, but without need of further encouragement, he dropped the towels on the floor and stepped in to join her, making her laugh.

"You didn't want to think about it then?" Scarlett couldn't help but admire the sight of him naked.

"Absolutely not – turn around," he told her.

"Well, if you insist. You should've just come in here in the first place."

"Ach, I thought to give you some peace as it's becoming quickly apparent I'm struggling to keep my hands off you."

Scarlett smiled again, relaxing her head forward as he softly massaged the back of her neck. "Luckily, I don't mind too much."

His hands moved from her neck, down her back, caressing her waist, until reaching around to lather her breasts. He sighed as he released them, instead wrapping his arms around her waist and pulling her tightly against him.

"You're too fucking sexy for your own good, woman!" He nuzzled into her hair. "I need to give you some rest."

Scarlett slipped out of his hold and turned to face him. "What if I don't want any?"

He looked at her for a long moment before kissing her and pulling her tight against him, and she could feel his hardness straining against her abdomen.

"I need to feed you." He laughed. "With more than just that." He nodded down towards his cock. "You're incredible," he said, leaning back to take hold of her chin so she had to look at him. "I'm not kidding."

She smiled and kissed him. "I'll take that."

"Right." He untangled himself from her, holding her away at arm's length. "I need to go order food. What do you fancy? Thai? Indian? Greek?"

Scarlett grinned.

"Insatiable woman, enough!" Edward stepped out of the shower, and Scarlett chuckled to herself, turning off the running water.

"Could you please pass me a towel?" She pointed to a pile of thick white towels rolled up on the dresser behind him. Edward grabbed one and passed it to her, taking another to dry himself.

"I'll order in some Thai. I know a decent place that delivers."

"Sounds perfect."

"Good, right, I'll get that sorted. Do you need anything else?"

Scarlett shook her head. "Nah, I'm all good. I'll finish up here and come down." Edward gave her a chaste kiss, giving her a last look up and down, then shaking his head, he left the bathroom.

Scarlett dried off and put on the oversized robe and slippers, making her feel as if she was on a spa holiday. She quickly checked her reflection in the mirror. This time she didn't do the usual turning up of her nose, as the woman staring back beamed, looking invigorated and alive. It made a pleasant change, liking who was looking back at her.

Smiling and shaking her head at herself, she left the

bathroom to join Edward downstairs. She found him standing by the window, shirtless, wearing only his jeans and lit up by his phone screen and the blazing wood burner, which took up a huge portion of the wall. She paused on the stairs to admire his form, irresistibly tall, toned, and slender, his face serious and concentrating, unaware he was being watched. There was something vulnerable and boyish about him, which she found wildly attractive.

As if feeling her presence, he looked in her direction, a smile forming on his face. "Hello, you."

"Did you manage to order something?"

He slid his phone into his back pocket. "I did. It'll be here within the hour. There's a bottle of white in the fridge. Do you want a glass?"

Scarlett descended the rest of the stairs and nodded. "Yes, please, that'd be lovely."

Edward disappeared into the kitchen, and Scarlett sat on the sofa, seeing her earlier discarded clothes neatly folded with care and placed on the chair in the corner.

She cringed, wondering how he'd react to the usual treatment of her clothes, which she knew were currently strewn all over her bed and floor at home.

Edward appeared with two glasses, handing her one before sitting next to her. "Cheers."

"Cheers." She smiled, gently clinking his glass.

The wine was delicious, its crisp acidity feeling like a burst of sunshine in her mouth. "This is lovely, thank you."

Edward took a long drink, nodding in agreement, then placed the glass on the table and turned to face her, his dark blue eyes intense. "I'm assuming you're okay spending the night here with me?"

Scarlett nodded to the wineglass. "It being a zero-tolerance country and all that."

Edward laughed. "Aye, exactly." He looked away, some of his familiar awkwardness returning, before he met her eyes again. "I'm not ready to give you back yet."

Scarlett put her own glass on the table and turned to face him. "Who exactly are you planning on giving me back to?"

"Nobody, if I have my way." He glanced down at her left hand. "Why are you still wearing them?"

Scarlett followed his gaze and wriggled her fingers, the precious metals and stones suddenly feeling heavy and uncomfortable.

"Honestly, I'm not sure. Initially, I couldn't get them off. Then, when I could, I was worried about losing the engagement ring. It was his grandmother's, and expensive. His mum was furious when he gave it to me."

"Looks pricey. Can I see?" Scarlett gave him her left hand to inspect. "Have you had it valued?"

"Hancocks in London priced it at around £95,000 when Jason had to update the insurance on it."

"I think it's probably worth another £30,000, at least."

"Really? How do you know?"

Edward released her left hand, taking hold of her right one instead, kissing her palm and wrist, which she found wildly sexy.

"My mother. She's a bit of an antique nut – jewellery, art, furnishings, most things, to be honest. She had a particular liking for the 1930s. I think that's the period it's from."

"Very knowledgeable of you, Mr – oh, sorry, my error, *my laird*." Scarlett winked at him.

"How do you make even my title sound erotic?"

Scarlett laughed and rolled her eyes. "It's one of my few gifts."

Edward didn't laugh. His face was serious, almost stern. "Don't do that."

"Do what?"

"Be so self-deprecating."

"I was only messing around, but really, it's not as if I've got that much currently going for me, either." She squirmed in her seat at Edward's unwavering seriousness. "Not in a bad way, just, apart from this stupid ring, I don't actually have anything to my name. No career. Kids. I mean ..." She sighed, no longer enjoying the direction the conversation was going in. "I just feel a bit lost. As in, what happens next, that's all."

"What do you want to do?" he asked, running his hand up and down her forearm, making it difficult for her to focus on the conversation.

"What do you mean?" she asked.

"What do you want to happen next?" He stopped stroking her arm and looked at her, his face sincere and questioning.

Scarlett felt embarrassed and unsure if she wanted to let him into her plans. They seemed so small compared to everything he had and the life she had with Jason.

"I just want a divorce. He can have the stupid ring back and give it to Angelica, for all I care—"

"Who's Angelica?" he interrupted her.

Scarlett took a deep breath and shrugged. "Our twenty-one-year-old tenant he got pregnant."

Edward sucked in his breath, and his face softened. "Fuck, I'm sorry, I didn't know."

"Please don't do the whole pity thing. I don't want it." She swallowed down the emotion that was annoyingly threatening to bubble up.

Edward looked away, as if worried about what his eyes would convey, making Scarlett look at the fire and shrink away from him.

He sighed. "I'm not, I mean, I wasn't – but it's all very recent. I feel like I'm taking a bit of advantage—"

"It's all fine." It was her turn to interrupt him before he said anything ridiculous about taking advantage of her. "I mean, clearly it wasn't *fine*, but I am now. And I know the leaving part is recent, but we've not been okay for years – we haven't had … we've not been intimate for months now, probably closer to a year. And honestly, I want no part in it all." She released a heavy sigh. "I just want out, maybe buy a little Airbnb business – I wasn't bad at getting the hotels and B&Bs up and running in Bath. It'd obviously be on a much smaller scale, but I think I could do it, do something …" Her voice trailed off. She felt ridiculous talking about a small business to someone who owned and ran half a sodding county.

"Scarlett." He took hold of her chin again to make her look at him. "He's a massive prick, as we've previously agreed, and a fucking idiot of a man." He kissed her. "And you are exceptionally good at a lot of things, trust me." He kissed her again and she couldn't help laughing.

"What?" He narrowed his eyes at her.

"Making beds and fucking?" She smiled teasingly.

Edward pushed her back onto the sofa and kissed her again.

"You know that's not what I meant." He untied her robe, exposing her to him, and her body melted as his hungry eyes drank in the sight of her lying there. "You've got a great deal of business and commercial acumen." He slowly pulled her arms free from the robe, so she was now fully naked beneath him. "You're great with people. Everyone from the kitchen staff to the eccentric bourgeois guests we currently have invading the house all love you."

She laughed at first, but then released a soft moan

and lowered her gaze to watch him slide his hands over her ribs and kiss her abdomen, one hand travelling further down to between her legs, making her back arch as his fingers found what they were looking for.

"And last," he said, kissing each breast before bringing his face up to hers, kissing her deeply on the lips. "I don't particularly like *fucking* you."

He raised himself above her and smiled at the incredulous look on Scarlett's face, unbuttoning his jeans at the same time to free himself.

"It's not what I would call this," he said.

Scarlett's breath hitched as she felt him gently pressing his hardness against her entrance before bringing himself up to kneeling and taking a condom from the table.

She hadn't noticed them when she'd sat down.

"How many of those have you got stashed away?"

She laughed when he smirked, full of mischief.

"I might have found a box in one of the bathrooms upstairs." He shrugged as he pulled the condom over his cock.

"How very convenient." Scarlett narrowed her eyes at him. "So what were you saying about *not* fucking me?"

"It feels like more than just fucking." His eyes darkened, sending a shiver of anticipation through her. "And I particularly enjoy how wet you get for me."

He stroked his cock against her clit, making her take a sharp intake of breath and clutch at his arms.

"Are you okay?" He stopped and looked at her with concern.

She nodded. "Yes, just a little delicate."

"Do you want me to stop?"

She noticed the genuine concern in his voice and eyes, which made her insides melt for him. She shook her head, offended by the mere suggestion of it.

A NEW *Hope* IN THE HIGHLANDS

Edward smiled. "We'll go slow."

Their eyes locked as he slid deep inside her, rippling waves of pleasure overwhelming them both.

"Fuck, that's good!" he growled.

She smiled. "I like it when you do that."

He slowed further and looked at her with a raised eyebrow and a lopsided smile. "Do what?"

"That whole animal growl thing you have going on there."

He grinned, his eyes darkening further, full of want, as he pushed even deeper inside her, making Scarlett cry out his name.

"I love the sound of my name coming out of your mouth." He pulled out slowly before plunging himself back in, deep and hard.

"Fuck!" She closed her eyes and arched her back at the impact.

"Say it again," he told her.

"What?" Scarlett was struggling to produce a cohesive thought, let alone a full sentence, as he was thrusting in and out of her, the feeling more intense each time.

"My name. Say it." He pulled out, leaving only the tip of his cock inside her.

Her eyes flung open at the absence of him to see him towering over her, a wicked smile on his face.

"Edward," she breathed, needing him back inside. "Please ..."

His smile widened. "Please what?"

"You're driving me wild!" Scarlett raised her head and bit his shoulder, making him cry out and laugh.

"Alright, wildcat – only because you asked so nicely." He pushed his cock slowly back inside her, making her moan loudly with relief, the pressure of him against her clit bringing another orgasm close to the surface.

The man was a walking climax!

It was slow and torturous. Their earlier exertions had made them both sensitive, on the verge of being painful, but deliciously so, and lowering himself and nuzzling into her damp hair, he whispered, "You are perfect."

CHAPTER 22

WHEN HE WOKE up the next morning, Edward felt confused and it took him a moment to remember where he was, but he quickly relaxed as the events of the previous day and night flooded back.

He glanced over to look at Scarlett, who was still fast asleep, and couldn't remember the last time he'd had so much sex in such a short space of time, let alone sex that good.

After their food arrived and they'd eaten, they were both exhausted, and as soon as her head hit the pillow, she'd fallen asleep; it was impressive. He'd watched her sleep for a little while but must have dozed off soon after.

Not wanting to wake her, he snuck out of the bed, grabbed his clothes he'd strategically placed on the chair by the door, and made his way downstairs. After relieving himself in the downstairs bathroom, he made himself a coffee and settled into the reclining chair overlooking the water.

Pulling out his phone, he sighed, knowing the world would require him to leave the oasis of pleasure they'd created since the day before. He tapped the screen to bring it to life.

There were four messages waiting for him: Lily, Briege, Leonard, and Andrzej. He pressed on Andrzej's first.

Andrzej: *Sir, sorry to trouble you, but June is concerned about Scarlett. She hasn't heard from her, and she didn't return home last night. Her car is still here, but I see yours isn't. Apologies for the intrusion, but are you aware of her whereabouts?*

Fuck

It hadn't occurred to either of them that people would wonder where they were. Oblivious and immersed in their own world, they'd failed to think about the fact their absence might seem strange and concerning in the real one.

Edward: *Scarlett accompanied me to Edinburgh yesterday to run some errands. We were delayed. Please apologise to June for any concern caused.*

Edward rubbed his face and groaned inwardly as he hit send, then pressed on the message from Lily.

Lily: *Err, Dad, have you kidnapped Scarlett?*
Lily: *Dad?*
Lily: *Like, seriously, people are actually freaking out.*

Fuck.

Edward: *No, caught up in Edinburgh for work.*

He hesitated before pressing on Leonard's message.

Leonard: *Oh, how the mighty fall. You surprise me, oh brother, holier than thou.*
Edward: *Fuck off.*

Finally, he hovered above Briege's.
For the love of God, why will this woman not get out of my life?

Briege: *Darling Eddie. I am absolutely buzzing. Can't wait to see you, my love. It's been way too long xxx*

What the fuck?
Edward reread the message several times before responding.

Edward: *What are you talking about?*

Deciding he wasn't overly keen on engaging with the real world any further, he got up, shoving the phone back in his pocket, and went to make Scarlett a coffee.

As he entered the room, he watched her stir, reach across the bed, and open her eyes, realising he wasn't there. The gesture made him smile.

"I made you coffee."

Scarlett relaxed and closed her eyes again. "That's very sweet of you."

He placed the cup and saucer on her bedside table and walked around the other side, lying down next to her.

"What time is it?" she asked, her voice croaky and full of sleep.

"Still early, but we should, unfortunately, probably think about getting up soon. I still need to get those papers to Gerard," he said as Scarlett opened her eyes to scowl at him, making him smile again. "I don't think it deserves that look."

He stroked her naked back down to where the duvet just about covered her backside, and not being able to resist, he pushed the covers down further, fully exposing her. He wanted to slap and bite where his fingers dragged along her soft curves, but he worried where it would lead, knowing full well he'd want to do much more than just bite and slap – and they both needed some time to recover.

"I never want to leave. I think we should stay here forever, eating Thai and having sex." She paused and shook her head. "Maybe not only Thai, but we could also expand our palate to some Greek, too."

"I like Greek." He smiled, his hand stroking the cleft just above her bum cheeks.

"I bet you do." She laughed, her voice still laced with sleep.

"As much as that idea is more than just a little appealing ..." He kissed her shoulder and then her neck. "All of it!" he said, gently kissing the sensitive skin behind her ear. "The world awaits."

She turned around from her front to face him, inviting him to come closer with her arms. He cupped both her breasts, kissing each nipple before nuzzling into her embrace. She felt so good it was verging on dangerous – he was losing all sense of anything remotely sensible.

"We really do need to get moving." He moaned into her neck. She stroked his hair and wrestled herself free from the duvet, wrapping her legs around him and pressing her naked body against him. "You're going to be the death of me, woman."

"But what a way to go, right?" She kissed his neck as he prised himself away, the sight of her making him stir again.

"No, that's enough. Come on."

Scarlett's eyes smiled at his weak attempt to regain his former sternness towards her, especially when his eyes diverted down to between her legs, which he wanted badly to touch and taste again, just briefly.

This is impossible.

He groaned, looking at the moist and glistening skin at the top of her thighs and shook his head before untangling himself and getting off the bed. "Come on, get dressed! We need to make a move."

Scarlett sighed. "Fine. You're so boring when you get all serious."

"Up," he said. Taking one last glance at her naked body, he shook his head again and left the room to clean up downstairs.

WITHIN A COUPLE of hours they'd washed, cleaned up after themselves, dropped off the papers to his solicitor, and were back on the road again, both of them quiet, each lost in their own thoughts. It wasn't until they were about twenty minutes away from Haddon House that he sensed Scarlett turning to face him.

"What happens now?"

He glanced at her before turning back to look at the road. "What do you mean?"

"When we get back, I don't know what happens."

He hadn't thought about it. Actually, that was a lie. He hadn't really wanted to.

What was he supposed to say?

They each had their own roles to play, and they couldn't exactly turn up holding hands and play happy couples. She was still his employee. June's daughter. And more than anything, he didn't *want* a relationship. He wasn't equipped for them, emotionally or otherwise.

And she deserved so much more – he wasn't lying when he'd called her perfect. She really was. And after what her ex had done to her, he knew he'd also only ever be a disappointment and let her down. He knew he would – it's what he always ended up doing.

Fuck's sake, this is all impossible. She is impossible.

"I don't know," he said, almost inaudibly.

"I mean, I'm not sure how I'm supposed to behave?" Scarlett's voice was an octave higher than usual.

"Like normal, I guess." He knew she was becoming upset, but he didn't know what else to say.

"Normal like before, or normal like this morning? What's supposed to be normal, Edward?"

He was beginning to feel annoyed. Not necessarily at her, but at the entire situation. This was why he avoided situations like this. The reason he tried to stay away from her. From relationships in general.

He could never find the right thing to say or do and it always, inevitably, turned to shit.

"Are you pissed off with me?" Scarlett pushed.

"No," he snapped. "Of course not."

"You sound pretty pissed."

"Fuck's sake, Scarlett, what do you want from me?" He could feel her fiery glare without even looking at her.

"Absolutely nothing, as it turns out." In his peripheral vision, he could see her turn away from him to stare out the window.

He sighed, disliking himself and the coolness of his tone towards her, but he pushed the thought away, returning his focus to the road as the heavens opened.

Despite moving the windscreen wipers to their highest setting, the visibility was crap, and he assured himself his efforts were better spent focusing on the road; they could probably both do without him crashing the car.

"I'm sorry," he finally said, turning into the drive leading to the house.

"Don't bother."

"Scarlett—"

"I can't switch this on and off like you." Her voice quivered with emotion, and he instantly hated himself for making her upset. This wasn't how he wanted this to go.

"I'm not switching anything off," he said, doing his best to soften his voice.

"Yes, you are. You're doing your whole awkward aloof thing again." She wouldn't even look at him now.

"My what?" He glanced across at her.

"That thing you do whenever anything gets a bit uncomfortable for you."

"I don't know what you're going on about," he said, trying to think how he could bring the situation back to a more amicable level.

"Fine, whatever you say." She turned her body towards her window.

"Scarlett—"

"What?" she almost growled at him.

"I don't know what you want me to say." He really didn't. How could he make all this go back to the way it was before they left Edinburgh?

"Don't bother saying anything, Edward." Her voice cracked, and he didn't know if it was because she was mad or crying.

Fuck's sake!

He slowed the car to a halt outside the main house and, wasting no time, Scarlett opened the door and jumped out, slamming the door behind her.

He watched her whilst clutching the wheel, his knuckles whitening, as she fled around the side of the house towards the stables, no doubt getting drenched from the rain that was now falling in biblical proportions.

"Fuuuuuck," he shouted, thumping both hands against the steering wheel several times, finally leaning back against the headrest. "Fuck."

After several moments, he switched off the engine and got out of the car. The rain hadn't eased up, but he didn't care and was in no rush to face whatever was waiting for him indoors.

Hesitating briefly, he opened the front door, carefully listening for any form of life in the house, but all he could hear was the huge oak grandfather clock on the east-facing wall of the hallway and the muffled sounds of Mrs Wilson from the direction of the kitchen.

He released a deep sigh, closing the front door behind him, intent on getting out of his wet clothes and potentially having an enormous glass, if not the entire bottle, of Janneau Armagnac he had stashed away in his office.

He began sloping off towards his rooms, but his false sense of security was quickly shattered when the library door opened and Leonard and Briege stepped out, directly blocking his path.

"Ah, and here he is." Leonard made no attempt to suppress his mocking smile.

"Eddie, baby!" Briege moved forward to embrace Edward, but thought better of it when she noticed the water dripping from him. "Christ, what happened to you? You're drenched."

Edward wondered how he didn't spot her car outside and kicked himself for being so absentminded. He couldn't, however, not notice that she still looked svelte, glamorous, and polished, not a hair out of place, but Edward didn't feel an ounce of attraction or affection towards her.

What he felt was a great deal of annoyance and contempt towards both of them – Leonard in particular, who was still grinning.

"What are you doing here, Briege?" Edward muttered, making no attempt at civility.

Briege bunched up her freckle-spattered nose, which he recalled he'd once found sexy and endearing, something that was definitely no longer the case.

She playfully slapped Leonard on the arm. "Leonard, you told me he knew!"

Leonard smiled and put his hands in his pockets, shrugging sheepishly and rolling his eyes for further dramatic effect. "I was going to, but my dear brother disappeared with the help."

Edward didn't respond, not trusting the words that would come out of his mouth if he did.

Briege's smile faltered for a moment but she brushed off whatever she might've thought Leonard was inferring. "Well, come on then, tell him." She nudged him.

"Briege has agreed to take charge of all the catering for the wedding – she's pulled together a whole team, despite it only being weeks away."

Edward still didn't speak, so Leonard continued, "Obviously couldn't have done it without Scarlett's pre-planning – talking of which, where is our delightful firecracker this morning?"

It took everything within Edward not to launch himself at his brother and pummel his face beyond recognition. Instead, remembering he was a grown man and no longer ten years old and fighting to regain his pride after their mother took his little brother's side in an argument yet again, Edward pushed past Leonard and headed for his rooms.

Briege gasped. "Ed ... Edward! Where are you going?"

"Don't worry about him. He'll come around," he heard Leonard reassure her. "Let's go see Anaïse, she's dying to meet you."

Edward rounded the corner and once out of sight, he stopped and leaned against the wall, closing his eyes.

Fuck.

CHAPTER 23

BY THE TIME Scarlett reached the sanctuary of the stables, the torrential rain had soaked her to her underwear.

Kicking off her trainers outside the front door, she rushed through to her bathroom, stripping off and getting in the shower to warm up.

Scottish fucking weather and Scottish fucking men!

She closed her eyes, furious with herself more than she was with the weather, or even with Edward.

Sex was all that either of them had wanted. He was never meant for her. How could he be?

He was a wealthy laird, and she was a penniless divorcee-to-be who worked for him. It wasn't like they were dating or ever going to be anything more than what they'd always been.

It was just meaningless sex between two people who found each other attractive and now that was out of the way, they could both continue with their lives.

She'd finish helping with the wedding, as originally planned, and then she would make her own arrangements and leave, set out on her own, *exactly* as she'd planned. He was never part of that – it was just a bit of escapist fun, that's all, and now they would go back to normal.

Normal.

She'd never hated a word so much.

Out of the shower, hair dried and dressed again, Scarlett wasn't sure how long she'd been sat on her bed staring into space, hours could have passed, but the sound of the front door opening and closing snapped her back to reality, even more so when June stormed into her room without knocking, her face flushed and angry, her eyes almost bulging out of their sockets.

"Where in God's name have you been?"

The force of her mother's tone took Scarlett by surprise.

"Excuse me?" Scarlett narrowed her eyes at June.

"Where have you been? I was worried sick! You couldn't call or send a message? I was beside myself with worry."

It was all a bit much, but Scarlett silently reprimanded herself for her careless actions. She hadn't even considered calling home when she was in Edinburgh and, of course, that's exactly what she should have done, but *still*.

June continued, "Eventually Andrzej had to go to the main house and speak to Mrs Wilson and then young Leonard. It was all horribly embarrassing, but we didn't know what else to do! How could you be so thoughtless?"

Scarlett could feel her own face and neck redden.

"It was embarrassing? So, you weren't worried about me at all. You were worried about how it all reflected on you?"

"Of course it was embarrassing. This is where I live and work. Andrzej is my boss!" June raised her hands to her chest for emphasis.

Scarlett scoffed. "Sure, okay."

"And what is that supposed to mean?"

"Oh, why does it even matter? So Andrzej went to the house. Big deal. And yes, you're right, I absolutely should have called, but I forgot! I'm sorry."

"That's it? You forgot?" June spat the words at Scarlett.

"Yes, I forgot. We were busy and got distracted, and then it was too late to head back, and I don't know what else to tell you. We forgot."

"*We?* What were you even doing with Edward in the first place?"

Scarlett did not and could not get into this with her mother.

"We were meeting with a supplier, then he had to run some errands. He was delayed. Then the weather turned, it got late, so we stayed at one of their houses."

June was evidently trying to process it all, but Scarlett could see the anger was overruling any logic. "Running off and not letting anyone know is just plain reckless, Scarlett!"

"Mother, I am not a sixteen-year-old girl who passed her curfew! I'm a thirty-five-year-old woman who left the estate with her employer and got delayed. Yes, I should have let you know, but it doesn't warrant this tirade. And besides ..." Scarlett considered quitting whilst she was ahead but couldn't help herself and continued, "You are the very last person to lecture me on running off and not letting anyone know!"

June appeared as if she'd had the wind taken out of her, and Scarlett immediately regretted her words.

She didn't want to hurt her. But she had. She could see it in her mother's eyes, right before she lowered them and left the room and the apartment.

"Shit, shit, shit!" Scarlett fell back onto her mattress and grabbed her pillow, hugging it tightly.

This was fast becoming a momentously crap day. She groaned when her phone vibrated on her bedside table, as if taunting her it wasn't over yet. Despite thinking better of it, Scarlett moved onto her side to reach for it.

Edward: *I meant what I said. I'm sorry.*

Scarlett stared at the words on the screen.

Dazed and perplexed, she continued to stare at the message, paralysed by what she wasn't sure – fear, anxiety, a sense of self-preservation? Eventually, she sighed and typed out her response.

Scarlett: *It's fine.*

His response was immediate.

Edward: *Don't be like that.*

Scarlett: *Like what?*

Edward: *Cold.*

Scarlett: *I'm not. I mean it, it's fine.*

Edward: *It's not fine. I don't want it to be 'just fine'.*

Scarlett: *This is ridiculous. I don't even know what's going on. What do you want, other than it's fine?*

Edward: *You.*

Scarlett: *In what capacity?*

Edward: *In every capacity.*

Scarlett: *You and I both know this won't work. We're back to 'normal' now, remember?*

Edward: *Come and see me.*

Scarlett: *Are you drunk?*

Edward: *May have had a couple, but that's not the point.*

Scarlett: *I was joking – are you, actually?*

Edward: *Not drunk, no.*

Scarlett: *I can't, I've just had a huge row with June.*

Edward: *Can't be good if you're calling her by her first name. What happened?*

Scarlett: *I didn't call.*

Edward: *I'm sorry, that's my fault.*

Scarlett: *It was on me. But I think she forgets I'm an actual adult.*

Edward: *Aye, but we should've called.*

Scarlett: *I know.*

Edward: *Are you coming over?*

Scarlett: *No.*

Edward: *Please.*

Scarlett: *No.*

Edward: *We need to talk about this.*

Scarlett: *There's nothing to talk about.*

Edward: *You're being stubborn.*

Scarlett: *Sensible.*

Edward: *If you don't come to me, I'll come to you.*

Scarlett: *Do NOT come here!*

Edward: *I'm in my office.*

Scarlett: *Ffs.*

Edward: *The others are getting ready for dinner. No one will see you.*

Scarlett: *Edward!*

Edward: *Scarlett!*

Scarlett: *…*

Edward: *I mean it, if you're not here in ten minutes I will come over and I don't care if your mother is there or not.*

Scarlett: *This is stupid!*

Edward: *Tick tock.*

Scarlett: *You're a cock!*

Edward: *See you in five.*

Scarlett: *Aaggh!! I'm coming.*

A NEW *Hope* IN THE HIGHLANDS

Scarlett snuck along the corridor towards Edward's rooms like a paranoid ninja – the fear of being caught by the likes of Mrs Wilson was real and had her pulse throbbing in her ears.

She could hear the muffled sound of voices upstairs, with footsteps walking across the corridor and doors opening and closing. There was something comforting about more life being injected into the vast house and she was very much of the opinion that a house, after all, deserved to be lived in.

Sounds from the kitchen reassured her that Mrs Wilson was also busy cooking, so she prayed that nobody would find her skulking about and heading in the general direction of the private rooms of the laird. Thoughts of the last time she entered his bedroom quickened her pulse even further.

Stay composed! This needs to end!

She needed to leave it all well alone. No good was going to come of it. Jason was only just out of the picture, and she needed time to gather her thoughts and feelings, and, more importantly, sort the divorce.

Hopefully she could trade the ring back to Jason's family for a reasonable settlement, just enough so she could buy her own place and business. She could then pack up her stuff, leave her mother and Haddon House to themselves, and start over on her own terms.

Scarlett no longer wanted to rely on anyone, especially not a man, even if the man in question was unequivocally hot and eligible and appealing, *and* utterly unattainable, regardless of the fact she'd been summoned through blackmail and her body was already betraying her.

"Be still, oh treacherous heart!" she muttered under her breath as she approached the office door. She hovered for a while, not knowing what to do.

Do I knock? Just enter? Use morse code?

Eventually, she used a combination of a soft knock and trying of the doorknob, which opened with ease.

Taking a final glance over her shoulder, Scarlett entered the room. Closing the door behind her, she scanned the office for its owner, quickly spotting him on the antique oxblood Chesterfield sofa facing the open fireplace, which was lit and crackling, giving the room an inviting smell and glow.

He was nursing a glass of something alcoholic; she could tell by his eyes and the half-empty bottle sat in front of him that he'd probably had a few.

On the way over to the house, she'd decided this would be quick, in and out, right after delivering her monologue, which went something like:

> *Edward, I had the best time with you, truly. But honestly, it's only going to end in heartache, probably mostly mine, and I'm not equipped to deal with that at the moment. I'm just getting my head straight, I want to get on my own feet, not become embroiled in some sordid secret affair – although who we're cheating on, I'm not exactly sure, but that aside, this can't and won't work and ...*

... and then he was upon her, pressing her against the door, his forehead leaning against hers, the tang of expensive liquor on his breath – something she'd usually find mildly offensive, but coming from him, it was more on a level with being intoxicating.

What is wrong with me?

She closed her eyes as he took hold of her hands and placed them above her head. Words escaped her.

"You're lucky you came or I would've come to find you." He softly bit her ear, trailing kisses down her neck, making her catch her breath.

"Edward ..." She tried to speak, but her body was already ignoring her and arching towards him, wanting him more than oxygen. "We shouldn't ..."

"Why not?" He continued his soft assault on her skin, his lips leaving a trail of heat which left her feeling breathless.

"Because ..." The man was just *too* good. Felt *too* good.

He grabbed both her wrists with one hand, the other moving under her jumper, finding her breasts, and she moaned as he tweaked one of her nipples, and the now all too familiar ache inside her roared back to life.

Despite all the sex they'd recently had, she wanted and needed him again.

Holy fuck! How am I ever staying away from him?

"Edward," she finally whispered.

"Hmmm?"

"I'm here to talk."

Edward sighed, slowly removing his hand from under her jumper and finally letting go of her wrists, but he instantly changed his mind, instead placing a hand at the base of her neck and kissing her for a long moment before breaking away.

Her knees almost buckled, and her body let out a silent scream, bereft at the loss of his touch, as he moved aside and beckoned Scarlett over to the sofa, pulling a hand over his face to straighten himself out.

"Okay, come and sit. We'll talk." As she sat down, he pointed to the bottle, which she could now see was Armagnac. "Would you like to join me?"

Scarlett shook her head – she needed to keep it clear.

"No, thank you," she said with resolve.

He sat beside her, his posture commanding even when relaxed, which she found immensely sexy and distracting.

She leaned against the side of the sofa to create a bit of distance and see him more clearly. He stared at her intently with his dark blue eyes; his hair was unkempt, and the top buttons of his shirt undone, showing the neck she had playfully licked and nibbled only a few hours earlier.

Looking at him, she knew she wasn't leaving the room without having him again, at least once more. They moved towards each other at the same time, hands and lips fervent and searching, as if it wasn't just a few hours that had passed since they'd last touched and felt each other's skin.

Scarlett pushed him back and straddled him, her hands framing his face as she kissed him, then drew away just enough to meet his eyes.

"You're impossible!" she told him, meaning it.

CHAPTER 24

As THEY LAY on the sofa, limbs tangled, breathless, covered in a blanket Edward sourced from the Indian trunk-turned-coffee-table in the centre of the room, it still didn't feel *finished*. If anything, it felt endless.

He stroked the curve of her spine, and Scarlett let out a contented sigh.

"That's nice."

"Just nice?" he asked.

"It's *just fine*."

He could feel her smile against his chest, to which he responded with a swift slap on her arse, making her yelp.

"That was mean." She nipped his chest with her teeth in response, making him cry out.

"Fucking wildcat with your little sharp teeth!" He rubbed where she'd bit him, but she nudged his hand away with her head, kissing the spot gently.

"If I'm a cat, that must make you a weird form of catnip."

He laughed. "That's definitely another first."

"Cat kryptonite. It's a fancy new term of endearment. All the kids are using it these days."

"Really?"

It was Scarlett's turn to laugh. "No. That was my attempt at being nice." She shrugged and then rested her head on his chest. "Better than being an old, mean, and surly Scot."

"Less of the old, thank you very much! And trust me, I could be so much meaner," he said, half joking, more than a little aware that he did indeed have a bit of a mean streak and was, in fact, renowned for it.

But not towards her. Never to her. At least not intentionally.

Scarlett leaned up on one elbow to look at him, suddenly serious, as if she'd read his thoughts.

"So, this talk …"

Edward groaned and tried to pull her back to his chest, but she resisted, and he knew he couldn't avoid it any longer.

"Okay, let's talk." He closed his eyes, awaiting the *talk*.

"It's not a Scarlett talks *at* Edward session, it's a two-way adults discussing adult stuff type of situation."

He opened one eye to look at her, quickly noticing the annoyance on her face taking form. He didn't want another fight, so he opened both eyes and focused on being engaged.

"Let's do this then," he told her.

Scarlett took a deep breath before starting. "What do you want from this?"

"I thought I'd been pretty clear on that front." He shrugged playfully, but her eyes told him she wasn't playing.

He let out a deep sigh. "I want this, I want to, you know, date you, get to know you, spend time with you … I just don't know how we do *this* without everyone and his horse having an opinion. Or making things awkward. I want us to have a bit of space and time to enjoy each other like normal people. But it's hard when …" His voice trailed off.

"When it's *the help* that you're fucking?"

"That's not it. I mean, there's a bit of that, but not how you think."

"Go on," she said, and he could see she was doing her best not to let her temper get the better of her.

He leaned forward to kiss her. "I will not tell you to calm down, as my balls are quite close to that elbow there, but just let me try to explain, okay?"

A smile played on her lips, and he felt her relax. "Go on," she said again.

"Leonard has been *fucking*, as you politely put it, members of staff, their daughters, wives, cousins, nieces, and best friends, pretty much since his balls dropped at the age of fourteen."

Scarlett laughed and shut her eyes tightly. "Great visual there, thanks!"

"It's true." He laughed. "The boy was an absolute liability. The number of scraps and questionable situations that my dad, and later I, had to get him out of are nothing short of ridiculous. A local farmer once turned up with a shotgun looking for him, accusing him of taking advantage of his daughter when she worked here one summer." Edward shook his head at the memory. "That was the last straw, so we sent him kicking and screaming to uni, which he didn't want to do. After six months, he dropped out to live in the States." Edward paused. "Anyway, point of the story, I don't want people to think the same of me. We may look similar, but I'm not like that. I'm nothing like him, and vice versa."

Scarlett was no longer looking at him, instead focused on the small patch of hair on his sternum, which she was absentmindedly playing with. "I know that," she eventually said.

"Which is why I'm finding this entire situation difficult."

"So, maybe we just take a pause." Scarlett lifted her head to look at him. "Get the wedding out of the way. Let me sort out my divorce, buy my own place, and then we can see how things are."

It seemed like a sensible approach, but the idea didn't sit well with him, and he struggled to keep the annoyance from his voice. "Where are you thinking of buying? In *England* I presume?"

She looked down again. "Not necessarily, no. I just want a bit of independence, that's all. Something that's mine, that nobody can come along and swipe from underneath me."

His annoyance dissipated. She was scared, and rightfully so. Her ex had done the unspeakable.

How was she now supposed to let her guard down to trust anyone after that?

But he didn't want her to go. The thought made him feel uneasy, which was alien and disorientating, and not something he was even remotely comfortable with.

"That could take months. I'm not going to be able to stay away from you for *months*." He immediately cringed, usually being the cool, collected, and aloof one in his romantic dealings with women.

She smiled up at him. "And I'm the impatient one?"

"When it comes to moving furniture and wanting answers, abso-fucking-lutely!" He pulled her close to him and this time she didn't resist.

Her hair smelled clean and fruity, and the feel of her naked body pressing against him felt too good. He didn't want her to leave the room, let alone the estate, never mind the sodding country.

He needed to keep her here, he just wasn't sure how to do it yet, even though the idea of her staying scared the living shite out of him too.

How could two things feel so true at the same time?

"Edward?"

"Yes?" His voice was gravelly from too much brandy and tiredness, thanks to all the physical exertion in the last twenty-four hours.

"This all scares me a bit."

"Me too," he whispered, stroking and kissing her head. "But maybe we just need to stop overthinking it."

"I don't know how to act in front of you and other people now."

"We don't need to act like anything, really. Just behave like—"

"Do not use the word *normal* again!"

He laughed. "Okay, how about we just behave like us, but leave the PDA for behind closed doors? Would that work?"

She was quiet for a while before nodding. "I can work with that."

"Good." He sighed, grateful they'd found a way to relieve the tension and anxiety that had built up between them since their return to Haddon. "Do you need to go home?"

"I don't know, probably. I've upset my mum, so yeah, I should maybe attempt to smooth things over."

He stroked her back and nuzzled his face into her hair. "At least you're not calling her by her first name anymore."

They both laughed.

"And you could come back after dinner? Stay the night."

"She'd know if I don't sleep there." Scarlett sighed.

There seemed to have been a lot of those these past few days – on both sides.

"I suppose," Edward conceded half-heartedly.

"We should probably both get some rest, anyway. I'm going to end up with an infection at this point."

"We've been careful – and I am clean!" he said with a tad too much force.

Scarlett laughed before straightening her face at his incredulous look. "I didn't say a STI!"

"What's the difference?"

"A bladder infection, UTI, whatever you want to call it – you get it from too much sex!"

"Oh. Ouch." He didn't fully understand, but at least he wasn't being accused of spreading diseases.

"Exactly."

"But I am clean and always careful." His voice was firm.

Scarlett nodded. "I know, I can see that. Plus, I'm also on the pill."

"Well, there we go – all bases covered. But I still want you to come back and sleep here."

"Not tonight, oh demanding one," Scarlett told him, patting him on his chest.

Edward sighed and then groaned, disliking his sudden need to have her in his bed, but also knowing that a night away wouldn't kill him and would probably do them both some good.

And for fuck's sake, we've known each other for barely a fortnight. Get a grip!

Lost in his thoughts, Scarlett brought him back to the room when she kissed him before untangling herself and standing up – she really was nothing short of magnificent.

He studied her full breasts, her curves, and the glistening remnants of their sex at the top of her thighs as she bent down to find her clothes and began dressing in front of him – her eyes locked on his. It was erotic as fuck.

"What time is your dinner?" she asked, breaking the spell.

He groaned again, rolling onto his back and covering his face with his hands. "I don't want to!"

"You'll be fine. Jump in a cold shower, wake yourself up a bit, and put on a smile."

"Leonard is being a particular fuckwit at the moment, not to mention he went and employed ..." Edward wasn't sure he wanted to drop this particular bombshell at the moment, but he'd started so had to finish. "He's brought someone in to sort the catering for the wedding."

Scarlett's face brightened. "That's great news! We were worrying about the short timeframe Mrs Wilson had to sort it all."

He knew the brightness would fade when he told her, but she needed to know. "The woman he's brought in, well, she's my ex."

"Lily's mum?"

"No, someone I was with for a couple of years after the divorce. Her name is Briege."

He watched Scarlett's face and demeanour change as she processed the information.

"I see," she finally said, some of her self-assuredness fading.

"There's nothing between us anymore. We haven't spoken in an age, and I have zero interest in her."

"How come she's doing the catering?" Scarlett took a sudden keen interest in her feet.

Edward sighed. "Because Leonard is an arse."

"So he knows her well, too?" She looked back up at him and he hated Leonard even more than before, if that was even possible, for putting those clouds of doubt in her eyes.

"Kind of. They're not exactly friends, more like acquaintances."

"Because of you?" she asked.

"Our families know each other." He winced, knowing how this must all seem to her.

"Right, okay." Scarlett sat on the chair positioned away from him to put on her trainers.

"Scarlett ..." He didn't like the way she was closing herself off to him again. "There's nothing to worry about here." He sat up, suddenly feeling underdressed with nothing but a blanket covering his bottom half.

Scarlett sighed and then met his eyes again, offering a half-smile and a shrug. "I'm actually not usually this insecure."

Edward stood, letting the blanket fall to the floor, and strode over to her, pulling her up to standing.

The mischievous sparkle he was becoming increasingly fond of returned to Scarlett's eyes as she looked down at his cock.

"Focus," he said sternly, which made her look up with a genuine smile. "Briege, and Leonard for that matter, are colossal pains in the arse, but," he kissed her, "neither is anything for you to worry about. Okay?"

Scarlett's eyes bore into his for a long moment before she spoke. "Okay."

"So, is that still a no to coming back later?"

Scarlett laughed. "It's still a no. I'll catch up with you tomorrow."

"Alright, as you wish."

"Enjoy your dinner." She smiled and went on her tiptoes to kiss him. "See you tomorrow."

He reluctantly let her go so she could make her way to the door.

"Goodnight," she said, and blew him a kiss before closing the door behind her.

Realising he was standing in the middle of his office naked, he went in search of his clothes.

He really wasn't looking forward to sitting through another meal with them all again. Lily was already back in Perth. She'd texted him earlier, questioning him further on his whereabouts the night before, which he swerved by avoiding giving her a direct answer, to which she'd responded by telling him he was boring and she was off home.

It would therefore be a dinner with the undesirables.

Great.

And as for the whole Briege debacle, he'd simply swerve her too.

He genuinely didn't have any concern on that front. As long as they all stayed away from Scarlett and left them both alone, everything would be *just fine*.

Edward shook his head. This whole wedding farce would be done and dusted in a matter of weeks, and life on the estate could then return to some semblance of normality.

Not that he was entirely sure what that looked like anymore. The pre-Scarlett era was quickly becoming vague and unmemorable, despite her short time with them. And although he was sure he didn't want her going anywhere else, he wasn't entirely sure how he felt about her staying, either.

Scarlett offered many things, but peace and quiet certainly wasn't one of them, and wasn't that what he wanted from life?

Had he not sworn off women and the effect they could have on his inner and outer peace?

But Scarlett wasn't just any woman and that, if nothing else, was something he was absolutely certain of.

CHAPTER 25

SCARLETT TOOK A deep breath as she shut the back door behind her, but instead of the fresh air she was expecting, she inhaled a cloud of cigarette smoke.

Coughing, she wrinkled her nose in poorly masked disgust and turned to see Leonard standing against the wall. For a brief moment, she could see the wayward boy that he once was – and potentially remained to be – just with a few more years on him.

"Hello." He winked at her. "Been busy?"

There's that look again.

Scarlett shrugged. "Usual stuff. How's things?"

Leonard gave her a coy smile. "All the better for seeing you in the flesh again."

Not knowing or particularly interested in what he meant, she nodded at the cigarette in his hand. "Awful habit, that."

"Yeah, it is. Sorry." He threw it on the ground, stubbed it out with his foot, and turned to face her, one shoulder still leaning against the wall. "So …"

Scarlett thrust her hands in her coat pockets, not really sure what to do with herself. "So." She smiled, nodding.

"I hear you and my brother were out meeting suppliers yesterday. Was it a success?"

Scarlett's heart sank.

What did he know?

"I think so, yes."

"That's good. I'm pleased."

Scarlett simply nodded her response. She could feel her nerves getting the better of her and she didn't want her voice to give anything away.

"I had some success myself, actually." Leonard reached out and touched the lapel of her coat, as if removing something. "I managed to get the catering sorted."

Irritation quickly overshadowed her nerves.

What game is he playing?

"A friend of the family. I reached out, and she's been able to pull some strings with a business they finance, so catering is all sorted."

"That's fantastic news." Scarlett beamed the most genuine smile she could muster. "That's a tremendous help, and Mrs Wilson will be relieved, bless her."

"Indeed, she will." Leonard was still touching her coat, which was making Scarlett feel increasingly uncomfortable.

"I need to get on, but that really is great. I bet Anaïse is pleased, too?" Scarlett hoped that a reminder of his fiancée might pull him back into some kind of order.

It worked. He retracted his hand and smiled at her. "Very much so. It all seems to be coming together. Not long until the big day now. Although still lots to do." He paused, continuing to look at her for a long, uncomfortable moment. "But I'll let you get going for now. Always a pleasure, Scarlett."

At that moment she spotted Andrzej in the distance, making his way to the greenhouse, and she felt a rush of relief wash over her – she almost felt like running to him, getting as far away as possible from Leonard's intense gaze and vague innuendos.

"Thanks, I'll catch you later." Producing a curt smile, she left Leonard standing at the wall and made a beeline for the greenhouse, hearing him light another cigarette behind her.

Edward was right. There was absolutely no similarity between them other than their looks. Edward *was* surly, awkward, and stubborn, no doubt about it, but what you see is what you get. At least he was honest. Whereas Leonard's warmth came from a place of superficial charm and something else that she couldn't quite put her finger on – whatever it was, she didn't trust it.

She squinted as she walked on. The sun was setting, throwing its final golden glow across the back lawns and shimmering across the loch at the bottom of the hill. That, and the bronzed trees on the edge of the woods to her left, all made for a perfect picture.

Away from Leonard's toxic smoke, she took another deep breath and welcomed the damp freshness of her surroundings. The tranquillity of the gardens was always a tonic, but there was something visceral and magic about its stillness and beauty that evening that tugged at her heart.

It felt a lot like perfection.

She smiled to herself and continued on her way to the greenhouse, where she could see Andrzej putting some small tools away.

He looked up and smiled as she approached.

"Hey, Scarlett, nice to see you." Any worries she had about seeing him after his visit to the main house, because of her disappearing act, dissipated. He was, to her relief, his usual warm and friendly self.

"Hi, Andrzej, nice to see you too." Scarlett returned his smile, glancing back towards the house. Leonard had returned inside, making her relax further. "I just wanted to apologise for last night. It was thoughtless of me not to call or message."

Andrzej dismissed the comment away with his hand.

A NEW *Hope* IN THE HIGHLANDS

"We're all good and you're safe, which is the main thing." He continued packing away a handful of clean forks and trowels. "The weather is turning wet and cold, so need to make sure all the tools are clean and stored away." He paused for a moment before continuing, "It's harder to sort them once the rust sets in. Best to prevent than fix, huh?"

Andrzej looked up at her and she wondered if they were still talking about gardening paraphernalia.

It didn't take long for the penny to drop, though, and Scarlett nodded, understanding that she needed to go home.

"I'm always around, though, for the fixing part, if you need me." His amiable smile made her heart swell by a centimetre or two.

"Thanks, Andrzej." Scarlett turned to leave but then paused. "Will we be seeing you for dinner later?"

Andrzej shook his head gently. "Not tonight."

Scarlett nodded again. "Okay, see you tomorrow?"

"Absolutely, it's lentil soup night." He smiled again.

"See you, then." Scarlett gave him a small wave and left him to it.

It was time to head *home*.

The idea of it being that still felt alien, yet the word was becoming easier to say each day.

As she approached the front door, her phone vibrated in her pocket. She'd reply quickly and then deal with whatever was waiting for her beyond the threshold.

She'd thought it would be Edward, but a message from Jason glared up at her.

> **Jason:** *Thanks for sending me the address to ship up your things. I won't be sending them, though. I've decided to come and see you. Of course I'll still bring your belongings,*

but don't think for a moment that I've given up on you coming home. And I'm not and will not be considering anything as terminal as a divorce anytime soon. I believe there's still a way for us to move past this. A marriage is more than just a mistake, and it was a mistake! We can talk more when I see you and I hate to say it, but there is the small matter of my grandmother's ring. Mother has requested that it be kept in Bath for safekeeping until you come home. Like I said, though, we'll talk more when I'm there.

A fucking mistake? You're having a baby with another woman, you absolute prick.

Scarlett took a steadying breath.

He wasn't getting anywhere near the sodding ring. She would put it in Edward's safe if she had to, but it was about the only bargaining chip she had left at this stage.

Her dislike for Jason, his mother, and everything they represented was growing bigger and uglier by the day.

And what is he thinking threatening to come here?

Scarlett shook her head. There was no way he'd drive all the way up here. He'd get a nosebleed if he was further than five miles away from his mother.

But why all the theatrics? Scarlett groaned inwardly.

This could wait until morning. She had to speak to her own mother first.

Whether Scarlett liked it or not, she was in the wrong, despite June's earlier reaction. And she had to make things right – no matter how uncomfortable it felt, which it did, in no small measure.

Scarlett slid her phone back into her pocket. She prepared herself to *literally* face the music as Carole King was singing at the top of her lungs through

Alexa – probably consoling her mother on some deep and profound level.

As she entered the living room, she spotted June on the sofa, staring into the wood burner with a glass of red wine in her hand; the usual smell of something cooking was absent, so she'd clearly opted for skipping food and diving straight into the bottle.

Scarlett walked over and sat beside her. June didn't turn to look at her.

"Alexa, quieter please," Scarlett said loudly over Carole King crooning over some heartache or other. Compliant as ever, Alexa reduced the volume enough for conversation to be possible.

"I'm sorry, Mum." There, she said it. Properly.

June sighed. "I know," she replied, looking at Scarlett. "I'm sorry too."

"I should have called or messaged – I should have known you'd be worried. I just wasn't thinking, and it's no excuse. It was careless. You were right."

"I'm not talking about that. I probably overreacted to be fair, it all just felt very out of control, but Andrzej told me you were more than likely with Edward, and it made sense, I just wasn't listening to reason." June paused for a long moment. "I'm sorry for running out on you. I should never have done it that way – it was unforgiveable."

Scarlett's mouth opened to speak, but no words came out.

This wasn't how she expected this conversation to go. At all.

Her mother was a woman of few words, especially when it came to anything painful from the past, including her youth and Scarlett's parentage. June had never talked about her leaving Bath without so much as a phone call.

"I can't actually tell you what made me do it. I was

at work, nothing out of the ordinary, you'd been at uni, close to graduating, and something just came over me. I felt like I was suffocating, as if the world was shrinking around me with every breath I took. It felt like your Aunt Maggie, who was busy with her shop and her own life, was all that was keeping me from disappearing into my own shadow, and I couldn't take it anymore, I just felt like I needed to get out of there, somewhere out in the open, just so I could breathe again. I'd been given an open invite to work here years before, and the idea just dawned on me, and it became the only glimmer of light I could see. I packed a small bag, scribbled you and Maggie a letter, and just left. I didn't hesitate and I didn't look back."

June paused again, taking a moment to collect her thoughts, but Scarlett still couldn't speak, so June continued. "After I settled here, I was too ashamed to visit you, especially because I couldn't find the words to even begin to explain my reasoning. Maggie then told me about you meeting a fancy author and being swept up in a wild romance and running off to get married. She told me about your beautiful life and then ... well, too much time passed, and I didn't know if I would ever fit into that ... *your* new world. I didn't feel I deserved to."

June and Scarlett looked at each other for a long time, neither speaking, and it was June who broke the silence again. "I tried to write, and I obviously did send the odd card or message, but the words always felt empty, and I realised I'd been absent long before I even left. In fact, I don't think I've ever really been *there*. And I can't even begin to tell you how very sorry I am. I know it's too little and much too late, but you coming here, being here, it's felt like I finally have a chance to be *some* kind of mother to you, even though it doesn't even begin to make up for ... well, everything." June finally fell silent, looking back into her glass.

Scarlett released her breath, which she must have been holding for longer than she realised, trying desperately to process the information and emotions that were batting around her like the ball inside a pinball machine. She was still unable to say anything, so instead she took her mother's free hand and squeezed gently.

Sometimes, maybe words weren't needed.

CHAPTER 26

THE FOLLOWING MORNING, Edward was up even earlier than usual.

Dinner the night before was the usual affair, which he'd sat through without incident, but even though Scarlett told him she wouldn't be back over, he was disappointed to sleep without her. Frustrated and very awake, he was up and dressed, and having skipped his usual morning coffee, now stood at the back of the house looking up at the stables.

There was a small light on in the smaller bedroom and he wondered if she was also awake, or if she'd left it on and fallen asleep.

Was she struggling to sleep too?

He took out his phone.

Edward: *You awake?*

The familiar dots quickly appeared, showing she was typing a response.

Scarlett: *Good morning 😊 x*
Edward: *Look out your window.*
Scarlett: *???*

He watched as the blinds pulled up halfway and a silhouette with a head of curls appeared.

A NEW Hope IN THE HIGHLANDS

Scarlett: Stalking much ... what are you doing?

Edward: Come for a walk with me – and make sure you put on your boots and coat.

Scarlett: Edward, it's still dark!

Edward: Let's call it our second date.

Scarlett: You're mad!

Edward: A bit, aye.

Scarlett: Where are we going?

Edward: I'm going to pop back into the house and grab some bits and a torch. I'll meet you downstairs in 10.

Scarlett: You're such a weirdo ... but ok.

A smile played on his lips as the day made sense to him again, perhaps not in a logical way, but the pent-up energy that was fizzing inside him settled down.

She was basically acting as an antacid at this stage, and he wasn't sure if that was a good or bad thing, especially considering it was probably *her* that caused the fizzing in the first place. Taking a last glance up at the window, he saw the blinds come down again, and he went back inside.

He walked into the boot room, which was clean, but the smell of muddied wellington boots, dog paraphernalia, and old wax coats was ever present. He grabbed the torch sat on top of the old and chipped tallboy leaning against the wall, placing it in his pocket, then unhooked the dark-brown leather satchel hanging on a brass hook and stuffed in a soft throw and a plastic-backed picnic blanket from the drawers.

Grabbing the battery-powered lantern from a shelf, he checked it had some power and packed that in, too. There was just about room for a flask, which he'd get filled with some coffee from the kitchen.

Mrs Wilson was busying herself with breakfast

prep, James working at her side in companionable silence. The smell of coffee and freshly baked bread made his stomach rumble, but he wasn't interested in getting food.

"Good morning," he said, hoping not to startle them.

James looked up, taken aback by his presence. "Good morning, sir."

Edward nodded and turned his attention to Mrs Wilson, who was already cleaning her hands on her apron. "Apologies, sir, I didn't hear you come down. I'll bring your coffee through now. It's all ready for you."

"No need, thank you. If you wouldn't mind filling this flask with it, though, that would be much appreciated."

"Of course, no problem at all." She walked over to take the flask from him.

Edward knew it would be good form to make some sort of polite conversation but was eager to get out of the house and didn't want to be asked where he was heading.

James and Mrs Wilson seemed to sense that was the case, as James returned to his prep work and Mrs Wilson quickly filled the flask for him and then hesitated before asking, "Would you like any sugar in there, sir?"

Edward shook his head. "That won't be necessary, thank you."

Mrs Wilson raised an eyebrow but made no comment and simply dried off the closed flask before handing it back to him. "Let me know if you require anything else this morning."

"Thank you, will do." He nodded a goodbye and left the room. There was something to be said for his usual *surliness*, as Scarlett liked to call it. It meant that

A NEW *Hope* IN THE HIGHLANDS

people rarely made any unnecessary conversation with him.

He returned to the boot room and put the flask in the satchel, closing it over, and hurried out of the house. They couldn't be too long. He knew Scarlett had lots to do, and so, in fairness, did he, but he wanted to spend a bit of time with her before they got pulled into the fray of the rest of the household.

As he turned the corner, he could see Scarlett's figure in the doorway.

"Ah, there you are," she said in a hushed voice. "Was beginning to think you'd stood me up!"

He placed the satchel by his feet and pulled her in to kiss her.

"Never."

She smiled into his lips. "I suppose that's something."

Edward steadied her back on the step and picked up the satchel, taking out his torch and switching it on. "Let's roll."

Scarlett laughed at his casual tone, stepped down, and sped up to walk next to him. "Where exactly are we going?"

"Someplace special." He felt heat rush to his cheeks and shrugged. "To me, anyway."

It was dark, but the sky was lightening, so when he turned to face her, he could see Scarlett eye him with suspicion. "At this hour, in the dark?"

"Granted, my timing may be a bit off, but this is me being spontaneous. Doesn't happen often, so I'd enjoy it whilst it lasts."

"Fair enough," she laughed softly.

"Besides, the day will spiral out of control as soon as the hordes are awake, so now is perfect. Hardly anyone will even know we're gone."

"I told my mum," she said, a smidge of uncertainty

in her voice. "You know, especially after last time."

"That's okay." He didn't want her to feel bad for talking to June, but equally, he didn't particularly want his longstanding employee to know *everything* either. The boundaries were blurring, which made him uncomfortable.

Scarlett clearly sensed something was off and stopped.

"I know we're being discreet, but if this is supposed to be some state secret, you need to let me know."

Edward turned to her again, almost blinding her with the torch.

"Sorry." He pointed it to the ground. "No, it's not a secret and of course I don't have a problem with you telling your mum ... I mean, up to a point. What did you tell her?"

"Just that I was heading off to meet you. She didn't ask why or anything, but she might've raised an eyebrow." He could hear the anxiety rising in her voice and he didn't want to spoil the morning.

"It's all good. Now come on, before it gets too late." He turned back in the direction they were heading.

"What do you mean late? It's the crack of fucking dawn!" she said, breathless from the pace they were now walking.

"Mouth, woman!"

"Mouth?"

He grabbed her hand and pulled her towards the woods. "Watch it before I put something in it!"

Scarlett laughed. "Ohhh, it's that kind of outing!"

Edward shook his head. "Insatiable woman. Come on, before it gets too light."

It didn't take them long to reach the waterfall he'd directed her to shortly after she first arrived at Haddon House, which seemed like an age ago. The rain had been heavy during the night, making the water hitting the rocks more thunderous and dramatic than usual.

He looked across at Scarlett, who appeared engrossed in the view.

Some light was filtering through the trees now, so he turned off the torch and placed it back in his pocket, freeing up his hand.

"This way – just watch your footing here. It might get slippery."

Scarlett nodded and followed him, both of them carefully skirting around the wall of rocks to their right, edging towards an opening behind the curtain of water gushing over the cliff above them.

He hadn't been here for a while and noticed the moss had built up, making the area trickier than usual to navigate, so he kept Scarlett under careful watch as she followed him through to the opening.

"I mean, this *is* pretty special." Scarlett smiled up at him. "But, Edward, it's fucking freezing!"

"I'll warm us up! And I'm glad you think so." He gave her a quick kiss before pulling away and removing the satchel from over his shoulder. After laying the picnic blanket on the floor, he switched on the lantern and emptied the contents of his bag. "Also brought some coffee."

"You've obviously thought of everything!" She laughed.

"If you're lucky, some of the firewood at the back there may be dry enough to light a fire." He walked towards the back of the cave and thankfully he'd stored a lot of the wood on top of a plastic pallet and covered it with tarpaulin, which meant some of the wood, at least, had remained dry and unaffected by mould or decay – the fact they'd had a dry summer and autumn also played a part.

Pulling out suitable branches, he watched Scarlett

make herself comfortable on the blanket, kicking off her boots so as not to muddy the blanket. He smiled seeing her thick oddly matched socks.

"How's it looking? Can man make fire?"

He nodded. "Aye, I think so."

And after a couple of false starts, he managed it.

"I'm suitably impressed ... The fire, the setting, even the coffee – it's all a *very* nice touch. Anyone would think you're trying to seduce me, my *laird*."

Edward laughed. "Again, how is it you can make that sound smutty?"

"Told you before, it's a talent." Scarlett shrugged and made room for him to sit beside her. He untied and kicked off his own boots and joined her on the blanket, grabbing the flask and pouring a cup of coffee for them to share.

"I blame the accent. No sugar, of course." He passed her the coffee, winking.

"Like I said, thought of everything. Thanks." She took a sip and passed it back to him. She went silent for a moment before continuing. "So, what's the deal with your brother?"

Edward's jaw tightened.

Why did it always end up back on his brother?

"What's he done now?"

"Nothing in particular, at least not anything I can put my finger on ... He just behaves strangely sometimes."

Edward frowned. Irritation at his brother was never far away, but the fact it was affecting Scarlett raised the scale to more than mere annoyance. "What's he said?"

"Nothing, really, it's just his mannerisms and innuendos. I never quite know what he means. He's perfectly pleasant, don't get me wrong. Charming, really. I just sometimes get the feeling he's saying more than the words he uses ... if that even makes sense?"

Edward picked up the stick beside him to stoke the fire, which was now giving off a surprising amount of heat.

He put the stick and coffee down and pulled off his cable-knit jumper, tugging the t-shirt back down over his abdomen.

"Gives off more heat than you think." He nodded his head towards the fire in response to Scarlett's coy look.

"Of course." She smiled. "Don't mind me. I'm just admiring the view."

"And it does make sense. He's usually up to one thing or another. Has he been making you feel uncomfortable?"

He thought there was a moment of hesitation, but she smiled again. "No, he's harmless enough."

"Hmm, I wouldn't be so sure. I want you to tell me if he ever steps out of line, okay?"

Scarlett shook her head. "He won't, but let's not spend whatever time we have left talking about your brother. Can't say I've ever had sex behind a waterfall before …"

"I didn't just bring you here to do that," he said, watching her as she shrugged off her coat. "But if you're going to get undressed, I can't promise I won't."

She laughed as he pulled her over to sit on top of him. "I'm kinda hoping you will!"

"Then who am I to rob a lady of her wish," he said before kissing her again, something he was becoming very comfortable doing.

CHAPTER 27

By the time Scarlett made it to the main house, its residents were already filling the corridors and rooms with noise levels she was fast becoming used to.

Mrs Wilson's new recruits, although looking dapper, both appeared flushed as they left the dining room.

"Is everything alright? Do you need help with anything?" Scarlett caught James's eye.

He shook his head and smiled. "No, thank you – just the usual level of carnage going on. My brother foolishly put an egg in front of the maid of honour." He laughed at Scarlett's look of confusion. "She has a chicken phobia." A wide grin spread across his face as he shrugged and continued to the kitchen with his hands full of plates.

Scarlett shook her head – their guests really were something.

Silently wishing James and Mark good luck, she left before someone else spotted her. She wanted to be productive this morning, starting with the orangery, a huge sunroom where the ceremony was to take place.

Anaïse was leaving most of the preparations, such as the flowers, for Scarlett to organise, with only one stipulation: "Absolutely no pinecones! Authentic is all well and good, but it's my wedding, not a craft fair, okay?" Anaïse had mentioned a few days ago, looking intently at Scarlett, who was doing her best to keep a straight face.

No trips to Hobbycraft for me then.

"Message received. No pinecone will make it over the threshold," Scarlet had reassured her.

"Wonderful, such a relief to have staff who actually listen and take on board what I say. At home, Millie just rolls her eyes these days and does what she damn well pleases. Talks about changing my diapers, as if that means she can't take any direction from me." She rolled her own eyes in dismay. "And they say I'm the brat in the house."

Scarlett couldn't think of a response that wouldn't comprise at least a slight element of sarcasm, so she chose a comforting smile and nod instead.

"I like your idea of the burgundy and white winter roses, though, with the pearl and crystal accents – I want them to be real, mind you. People will notice. The snow berries on the centrepieces sound nice too – and the ivy and white roses mixed through and draped over the arches ... and what were the other flowers?"

"Hellebores, they're known as Christmas roses, and the camellias will give a soft romantic winter feel. They're actually grown here on the estate."

"Fantastic, yes, you seem to have it all under control then. Just make sure it all screams winter luxury and, like you said, romance. Lots of lights. And the orangery, it's still quite crowded with furniture?"

"We'll be making a start on that soon. First, we're deep cleaning and airing it out fully, then the furniture will be moved out before the weekend so we can get everything ready. The seating and covers you chose will arrive a couple of weeks ahead of the day to make sure you're happy and to give us time to set it all out just how you want."

"Well, nothing more to be done for me then. We're off to some spa today. It's been an exhausting week, so it's much needed." Anaïse smiled at Scarlett. "We're not all cut out to be so ... active and lively."

Scarlett wasn't entirely sure if that was meant as a compliment or an insult, or merely a point of fact, so she'd simply disregarded it altogether. Really, what was even the point? They were from such different worlds, the communicational void between them was the least of her concerns.

She was there to do a job, which she wanted to do well, and her client's lack of social or communication skills weren't remotely her problem. Scarlett realised it probably wasn't due to an actual lack of kindness. She'd been around women like Anaïse before, and there was rarely malice in any of their behaviour; simply put, sometimes status and wealth stood people so far apart, they may as well be trying to reach each other via the moon.

Now, taking out her notepad, Scarlett checked through her to-do list. She'd provide Edward with action points and the associated schedule later, so he could ensure there were enough hands on deck to move the heavy furniture the next day. That meant the deep clean could be done, and she could then make a start on the arrangement of the room and the decorations.

June and Andrzej had been a godsend and were incredibly helpful in planning the flower and plant arrangements; and Anaïse and Leonard were delighted with the sketches Scarlett provided for both the orangery and the outside marquee.

Scarlett was pleased. She had done nothing like this before, especially on this scale, but the trust and autonomy she received made her feel good about herself. The sky felt limitless; she was so much more than someone's wife and the family's general dogsbody, where her efforts had never been recognised or valued. But at Haddon House, she was at least her own person and people respected what she was capable of.

The sound of someone clearing their throat brought

her back into the room and she turned to find a rather attractive and polished brunette standing in the doorway.

"Hi." Scarlett smiled politely. "Can I help you?"

The brunette smiled a perfect white-toothed smile, delicately tucking a loose strand of hair behind her ear. "No, thank you – it's just been a while since I've been in here, so I thought I'd take a quick look." Her accent was Scottish, but softer and more subtle than the locals she was used to hearing.

Scarlett cocked her head slightly to the side. "Sorry, I don't think we've met?"

"Briege, close family friend – and you are?"

"I'm Scarlett. Nice to meet you." Scarlett moved closer and held out her hand, which Briege hesitantly took, her shake limp and reluctant. "I'm helping organise the wedding."

Briege nodded slowly. "I see – one of the women living in the stables." She half smiled, looking away to gaze around the room. "I considered marrying in here, but I wanted a more intimate beach wedding with Edward. Less work, but also less stuffy, you know? This is all very novel and Brontë-esque for the Americans, but not really my style."

She glanced at Scarlett as though to check she was paying attention. Scarlett took an instant dislike to the woman. Briege continued, "Growing up on these types of estates takes the novelty away, really. No doubt we'll revisit our plans at some point, though. Talking of which, I'll go announce myself properly. Can't keep the laird waiting, can I?" She winked at Scarlett and left, her shiny dark hair glistening under the lights Scarlett had just turned on to check all the bulbs were working. She watched Briege turn and leave, noticing how her tight pencil skirt and heels accentuated her slim hips and taut calves.

Scarlett disliked her even more. Not just because of the endless legs and perfect ... well, everything! No, it was because she had the malicious vibe that most of the girls at her secondary school had possessed – pointless nastiness that was usually overlooked because of their good looks, charm, and academic or sporty talents. Scarlett, in contrast, was short, awkward, and lacked the coordination skills that most sports required, being more of an endearing Shetland pony than an impressive gazelle.

And what was she talking about marrying Edward? He'd never mentioned how serious their relationship had been, let alone the minor fact he was meeting her today. A sinking feeling settled in her stomach. Was he being genuine with her? Or was that entire speech about worrying what people might think of him being with *the help* because of Leonard a complete load of bollocks? Were they in fact as bad and entitled as each other? Maybe she *was* just a game or convenient stop gap until the main event could strut back in, as if she'd just returned from a photo shoot in Milan. Maybe this was what Leonard knew and why he was always smirking at her. Maybe this was what all marriages and relationships were like – disloyal, dishonest, and full of disappointment. She was hardly the expert.

Scarlett had only had one boyfriend before Jason, an awkward and standoffish guy in her Colonial Literature module at uni. Geoffrey had been and probably still was a very nice guy, but despite being on the same English Lit course, they shared nothing in common and the sex had been beyond terrible. Potentially it could've been better if he'd been able to recognise the fact that it took more than some brief penetration to help a woman reach orgasm.

Although, it probably had more to do with the fact that much later, she'd discovered he was now happily married to an Irish man called Lawrence. Scarlett cringed at the memory. No, she was definitely not qualified as a relationship expert by any stretch of the imagination.

But perhaps Jason wasn't the anomaly. Maybe it was the norm. Christ, was Tara right about her, after all? Did she just not know how to keep a man happy? Was this whole thing with Edward some ridiculous fantasy, and he was just slumming it until his proper girlfriend came back?

Oh my God! I'm officially a fluffer girlfriend!

She had read about it in *The Guardian* a few months previously and thought how dreadful that must be, to invest in someone emotionally and in every other way, knowing they weren't ready yet, so waiting patiently, only for them to leave and fully commit to someone else. Scarlett stared at the empty doorway. Is that what Briege was? The *proper* girlfriend? If she was, could Scarlett still stay? Should she reconsider Jason's offer? Was this really it? Should she just go home? The thoughts and doubts were running wild in her head, and she had to close her eyes, taking a few deep breaths.

Eventually, she shook her head.

Don't be so bloody paranoid, woman!

Until she knew the complete story, she wouldn't be jumping to conclusions. She took another deep breath in and out, refocusing on her to-do list. But the sick feeling in her stomach remained.

CHAPTER 28

Fresh out of a shower, Edward had just buttoned up his jeans when his bedroom door opened to reveal Briege standing there, looking more than just a little amused.

"Ohh, rather great timing on my part!" She smiled, her eyes drinking him in. "Don't dress on my account."

Edward grabbed his t-shirt from the bed but remembered it stank of smoke from earlier that morning. Huffing, he turned away from her to pull a fresh one from his wardrobe.

I really need to start locking that fucking door!

"Are you lost?" He turned to face her, feeling better now he was no longer half naked.

"What is your problem with me at the moment?" Briege came into the room, ceremoniously sitting – no, more like lounging – on his bed. "I'm getting some very hostile vibes from you at the moment."

Edward crossed his arms across his chest, his look purposefully stern. "Briege, what do you want?"

"I want us to be friends, babe." She smiled again, leaning back so her long hair hung seductively behind her. Granted, he used to love twisting it around his fingers to tug it whilst ... No, he wouldn't go there. "Don't you miss us, even a little?" she purred.

"It was a fucking car crash. Why would I miss that?"

"Ohh, come on. We had a lot of fun." She paused and focused her attention on his crotch area. "And some great fucking sex."

The woman is insane.

"I think you'd best leave."

"Is there someone else?" A dark look passed over her eyes. He used to call it the psychotic look, as it was always there right before she would lose the plot entirely. No, he definitely didn't miss *it*, *her*, *them* – any of it.

"Leonard seems to think you've got something going on with the wedding planner." She sniffed, her distaste evident as she turned up her nose.

The wedding planner? God, I hate him.

"Briege, whether I'm seeing someone or not is none of your or my brother's business. I've got work to do so if you wouldn't mind ... Actually, I don't care if you mind, you need to leave. Now. Go do whatever you're here to do for the wedding and let's both do each other a favour and stay out of each other's way."

For a moment, with her eyes dark and wild, he thought she was going to fly into a rage and launch herself at him, something that was common practice during their volatile relationship, but not today. Instead, a little smile crept onto her face.

"I'll give you some more time, then." She stood, straightened her skirt, and slowly walked towards him, her big brown eyes full of mischief and lust. He bristled as she stopped in front of him and he caught her hand as it reached up to touch his cheek, making her laugh.

"Oh, Eddie, you're so uptight. Don't you remember how good I was at making you relax?" And she was so quick, he had no time to react to her hand grabbing his crotch area, enough to make his cock twitch. His reaction made her smile.

"He certainly does," she said, kissing the side of his mouth and giving his cock a slight squeeze through the denim.

"It's not something that appeals anymore, Briege." He took hold of her hand and pinned it to her side. "And believe me when I say, just because my cock reacts, doesn't mean I intend to."

Another storm brewed in her eyes, but after a brief hesitation, she blinked it away and smirked.

"We'll see, babe." She straightened her back, and, as if nothing at all had happened, left the room.

Edward closed his eyes and released a breath. At one point, he'd enjoyed her forwardness and sexual mischief, but it was now a tired and overplayed act. She *was* right, though. They had physically enjoyed each other, a lot – and if he was honest with himself, if it wasn't now for Scarlett, he may well have even contemplated the idea of one more trip down memory lane, no matter how much she pissed him off.

But the thought made him grimace. He was better than that. And despite still finding her physically attractive, and clearly his cock did too, it was no longer something he wanted. At one point, he even believed he loved her, and since they had similar upbringings, it had made sense.

It had been different with Lily's mum, who he'd met at uni and who was from a *nice* middle-class background. They'd both been incredibly young; he was doing his finals, and she was barely a year out of graduation when she'd fallen pregnant with Lily. The idea of being a lady captivated Natasha; but the estate, Edward's commitment to it, the inescapable class system, and all its associated traditions annoyed her so much that she eventually left him for a solicitor from Aberdeen. Frankie.

Having watched his parents' marriage crumble and failing miserably himself twice before – once with Natasha and then with Briege – Edward had been determined to not get emotionally involved with another woman. The idea of upending his life only for it to all fall apart again was not something he'd been remotely interested in doing. That was until Scarlett.

But wasn't she simply a combination of his exes? Although, he mused, she wasn't anything like either of them.

Scarlett was full of life and love, even, it seemed, for the estate and all its inhabitants, not to mention how her enthusiasm for bringing the house back to its former glory in preparation for the wedding – it was contagious and intoxicating. She also excited him, in more ways than one, and for the first time, possibly in his life, he felt a sense of peace – which seemed like a contradiction, but he was learning that two things could in fact be true at the same time.

Another stark truth was that he needed to keep Briege away from Scarlett. Briege was toxic, and Edward was more than a little aware that Scarlett's recent experience with her husband had left her feeling vulnerable and cautious, something he was familiar with from his own experiences.

The exchange with Briege had left him feeling agitated and worse, *horny*. The truth of it made his insides boil and his head roar. He didn't want Briege, of course he didn't, but more than that, he didn't want Briege to get even a whiff of his relationship with Scarlett – to do that he had to keep the two as far away from each other as possible.

He also needed to talk to his brother. A discussion about behaviour, boundaries, and maintaining distance was necessary. He didn't like that Leonard was sniffing around Scarlett, even more so that it was making her feel uncomfortable; and despite her telling him the opposite was true, he knew Leonard well enough to know he was up to no good.

Edward found his brother with his feet up, absorbed in his laptop, alone in the drawing room.

"Good morning. We missed you at breakfast." Leonard glanced up at Edward before looking back at his screen.

Edward walked past him to the French doors overlooking the rear gardens. "I doubt that."

Leonard let out a huffed laugh. "In good humour as always, I see."

Edward put his hands in his pockets and sighed. "It's difficult to find humour when you're up to your usual shite."

"Do tell, what game is afoot that I'm responsible for now?" Leonard closed his laptop and looked over at Edward.

"Why have you brought Briege here?" Edward finally turned to face his brother.

Leonard shrugged and smiled. "I told you – she's sorted the catering for us."

"There's at least a handful of other companies that could have done that." Edward narrowed his eyes at Leonard.

"Potentially none that could turn it around in such a short amount of time and to the standard we want. What's wrong with Briege, anyway?"

Edward marvelled at how Leonard could keep such a straight face.

"You're being a complete prick," Edward muttered, shaking his head.

"Look, I'm sorry if it puts you in a situation, but as far as I was aware, it's been over for years. I didn't think it would be an issue. She's a family friend, after all." Leonard shrugged again and folded his arms across his chest, a glint in his eye.

"She's a fucking car crash waiting to happen – as well you know, and you've done it to piss me off. The only question is why?" Edward's tone was sharper than he intended, but he was quickly losing patience.

Leonard's mouth twitched. "Why would I want to piss you off, brother?" He smiled and looked around the room. "Suppose it's nice to have the estate all to yourself, usually. Appreciate it's a big change to have so many people around you at the moment."

"What's that supposed to mean?"

"Just saying, maybe the pressure of all the social interactions is making you see things that aren't actually there. Like my alleged intention to piss you off." Leonard looked past Edward out onto the lawn, a smile playing at the side of his mouth.

Edward caught Leonard's gaze and held it steady. "What have you been saying to Scarlett?"

Leonard couldn't stop the grin that spread across his face and Edward knew he'd lost this one. "The sumptuous Scarlett. What wouldn't I say, or, more to the point, do? Wouldn't you?" He watched Edward's fists clench before he quickly released them.

"Stay away from her, Leonard. I'm not playing. And keep Briege out of my way too. Understood?" Edward walked to the doorway.

"Yes, my laird. Understood," Leonard responded, his tone laced with sarcasm.

Edward left the room, his breathing ragged and his temper rising. He was in danger of losing it with his younger brother on a level that wouldn't do either of them any good.

He needed to see Scarlett, just to bring some inner calm back so he could get his ever-growing list of jobs for the day done. He knew she was making plans for the orangery so made a beeline for the side of the house.

On his approach, he could hear her humming. She probably had her earphones in, and he smiled at the memory of the first time he came across her – properly that is – after their first meeting, cleaning the staircase and bopping along to her music.

Scarlett was standing with her back to him, hunched over a table at the top of the room, softly swaying her head and hips to whatever she was listening to. His cock twitched and the urge to be inside her overwhelmed him.

Ah, fuck it.

He locked the door behind him and checked outside. It was grey, miserable, and raining, the contrast of temperatures steaming up the windows, briefly reminding him they needed to sort out the ventilation before dampness became a problem again.

Andrzej and June were in the village getting supplies, and no one else would be outside in the gardens. Approaching Scarlett from behind, he circled his arms around her, making her jump and squeal. He turned her around to face him and, taking her face in his hands, he kissed her.

"You scared the fucking life out of me!" She thumped his chest as his mouth travelled down her throat. "What are you doing? What happened to subtle?"

"The door's locked." He pulled her baggy jumper down one side to expose a bare shoulder, his other hand pulling it loose from her jeans so he could feel her skin underneath.

"Edward, everyone is up and about. This is insane!" She wriggled out of his hold and kept him at arm's length. "What's going on with you?"

He wanted to tell Scarlett everything – about Briege, Leonard, his worries about this turning into *something*, the fear of losing the opportunity for it to do so, or worse, hurting her – but the words weren't reachable and the visceral need to feel her and have his cock inside her was making it impossible for him to gather any thoughts or words resembling any semblance of clarity.

"Nothing, I just need you," he replied, his voice hoarse.

Her eyes searched his for longer than was comfortable, but when he saw them soften, felt her hands fidget with the bottom of his t-shirt, he wasted no time in pulling her close again. This time she was as hungry as he was, her hands tugging at his hair as he undid her jeans and pushed them and her knickers down her legs. Not wanting to waste time removing her trainers, he turned her around to lean over the table, simultaneously undoing his jeans and releasing himself.

Edward was so hard and sensitive it was almost painful as he pulled a condom from his back pocket, tearing it open and hurriedly sheathing it over his cock. The relief when he pressed the tip against her made him groan, teasing her until she became moist and ready for him.

Holding on to her shoulder with one hand, he used the other to guide himself closer to her entrance, making her moan loudly when he pushed hard and deep inside her.

He closed his eyes as her silky wetness welcomed him, eradicating everything outside of the room in an instant. The way her body reacted to his touch and the sensation of his cock inside her drove him wild. He couldn't imagine not having access to this – to her.

His hands reached around to massage her breasts. But he needed more and pulled down her bra so he could feel her hardened nipples, the impact making her moan and tighten around him. His name on her lips made him push even deeper inside her.

Fuck, this is too good.

His pace was fast and unforgiving, but he wanted to make her come, despite knowing she'd still be sensitive from their recent lovemaking. He slowed, moving his hand down to her clit. His fingers were tentative at first, carefully judging how much pressure she could handle. She didn't flinch as he pressed the flat of his finger against her, so he increased the pressure ever so slightly, waiting to see how she responded, which she did by moving her own hand against his. Her wetness made his cock ache and he had to thrust deep inside her to relieve it, making her cry out.

He could feel her orgasm building up around him, her hand pressed hard against his, to the point she was hurting him, but he could take the pain for the prize of her climaxing over his cock. He needed her to.

"Fuck, Edward, I ..." Her words trailed off as she moaned loudly.

"I want you to come for me," he told her, now firmly rolling his fingers over her clit. "Don't hold back, come for me now," he growled, and he had to move his free hand to cover her mouth as she fell back against his chest, crying out and coming apart around him, her orgasm contracting and releasing around his length.

Wave after wave, her body bucking against him, her back beautifully arched until finally she stilled and relaxed, releasing his hand and panting, supporting herself with both hands on the table.

"I fucking love it when you come like that!" he groaned, grabbing her hips with both hands, pushing deeper inside her again, his pace almost frenzied, each thrust making her cry out and quiver until finally he couldn't hold back any longer and cried out himself as his orgasm, fierce and all-consuming, released inside her.

The two of them collapsed against the table, their collective breathing uneven and shaky. He pulled away, kneeling behind her and careful not to hurt her as she remained pressed against the table. He kissed her buttocks, pulled up her underwear and jeans, and turned her to face him.

Her face was flushed, and her hair was loose and wild, making him smile – she really was his own personal brand of siren. He carefully did up the buttons of her jeans, her eyes locked on his as he did so.

"That was rather hot and bothered!" Her voice was still raspy.

"In a bad way?" he asked, adjusting himself and fixing his own jeans.

"No, definitely not bad." But she paused and looked at him carefully. "Just, I don't know – there was something a little reckless and angry about it."

"I'm not angry with you." Edward didn't like where this was going.

"I get that." She began fixing her hair before continuing, "But … oh, I don't know."

"Did you not want to?" His voice cracked as the realisation he had potentially hurt her dawned on him.

"Of course I did – I'm not saying I didn't want to, or it wasn't good, clearly!" Scarlett sighed. "It just felt as if you were needing to get something out of your system, as opposed to wanting to have sex with me."

"I don't know what you're talking about." Edward recognised an edge of hostility in his response but couldn't stop himself.

Scarlett looked taken aback. "I'm sorry, I'm – although I'm not sure what I'm apologising for, to be honest. I'm just voicing how it felt."

"Noted. I'll try to be more restrained in future—"

"Edward, don't be like that! I was just—"

"Appreciate you're busy. I've got a fair bit to do myself, so I'll catch you later."

"Edward?"

Edward knew he should stay. He knew he needed

to reassure her that he was okay – that *they* were okay. He also knew that she was right. But he didn't know how to explain what was going on in his head, or that she absolutely had a point and that his need for her was something deeper than just fucking her. He needed her to make him feel calm and at peace, and—

Oh, for fuck's sake, man, get a fucking grip.

Making his way to the boot room, he grabbed his coat and walked out into the rain, which was now falling out of the sky in solid sheets. He didn't care. He'd check on the stock of firewood that was running low with all the fires currently burning in the house.

Fucking visitors. Fucking family. Fucking everything.

CHAPTER 29

SCARLETT FELT WEAK in the knees.
What the very fuck was all that about?

She felt the remnants of their ... she wasn't actually sure what that had been; it hadn't just been sex, but it wasn't like the other times either. Sure, he'd been considerate and even tender, especially when he'd redressed her, but there was an undercurrent of something else that she was struggling to name or even describe.

It'd seemed so emotionally charged but simultaneously distant, and it made her uneasy, and that he'd left like that made her feel hurt and used – not something she wanted to experience again. No matter how much she liked him.

Scarlett also didn't like how her knickers felt damp and uncomfortable, and she sighed, irritated that she'd have to head back to the flat again to wash and change.

She was also feeling an uncomfortable ache in her lower abdomen, which she recognised as the first sign of something she hadn't experienced in a long time but was difficult to forget. She'd been prone to UTIs from when she and Jason were much more sexually active than they had been in recent years, and the symptoms were never pleasant.

Fucking great.

The rest of the day, thankfully, passed without further incident or much interaction with anyone in the house. She had some brief chats with people in passing, but everyone seemed very much preoccupied with their own tasks and affairs, leaving Scarlett able to complete her to-do list in relative peace.

On a couple of occasions, she'd spotted Edward leaving or entering the house, his own personal thunderstorm hanging over his head, no match even for the unrelenting rain that had descended on the house.

What on earth is the matter with him today?

She paused to watch him from the third-floor corridor, where she was working in the guest rooms. There were twelve on that floor, and another eight above that she might or might not get to in time for the wedding. She still had several to clean and prepare before the guests arrived. Much to be done.

Most of the rooms hadn't been used in decades, and although Mrs Wilson had them cleaned periodically, each had to be aired, deep-cleaned, checked for faults with electrics, water, and furniture, and all the bedding stripped and replaced.

Scarlett had felt in control of the schedule up to this point, but with the constant distraction of Edward, she was feeling increasingly behind. But despite that being the case, she still couldn't make herself move from the window, watching as his slightly stooped figure walked towards the woods.

There was such a vulnerability to him that reminded her of a little boy, which was ridiculous as she'd never come across such a capable and commanding man in her life; yet it didn't stop her from wanting to envelop him in love and kindness. He was absolutely impossible in every way, which was making her frustrated as hell.

"Scarlett, there you are!" An American accent floated down the corridor towards her.

She turned to see Anaïse, her golden hair bunched on top of her head in a messy bun.

A NEW *Hope* IN THE HIGHLANDS

"Hello, how are you?" Scarlett said, watching the approaching woman with interest. She thought there was an air of sadness surrounding Anaïse, which she usually masked well, but judging by the purple under her eyes, it seemed today she was struggling to keep it entirely under wraps.

"Fine, thanks," she replied, joining Scarlett to look out the window. "Although I really don't understand how y'all cope with all this rain. It doesn't stop."

"Hmm, I'm not used to it either. It's not even like this where I live ... lived in England."

"It's no wonder their mother moved back home. I wouldn't cope either. I don't know how she did for so long!"

Scarlett simply nodded in agreement, distracted again by the sight of Edward walking further on in the pouring rain.

"Verity had her art, I suppose." Anaïse shrugged.

Scarlett hummed in noncommittal agreement, although she made a mental note of Edward's mother's name.

Anaïse continued, "And I think she travelled a lot, especially to Asia. She built up that massive collection of antiques that are randomly spread all over this crazy house that Mrs Wilson enjoys explaining to me in the greatest of detail." She paused and briefly glanced at Scarlett before looking back out the window. "He's very different from Leonard, you know."

Scarlett shook herself from her own thoughts, feeling caught out. "Who is?"

Anaïse smiled, but it wasn't mocking and held an element of warmth.

"Edward, he skulks around this place like some tragically wounded animal – all hot air and grump, but I see a lot of their mother in him. The softness."

She now had Scarlett's full attention. "You think so?"

"A hundred percent, which is ironic, as she's not even Edward's biological mother." Anaïse continued, despite Scarlett's raised eyebrows. "She's pretty formidable, but she's a good woman, albeit a bit out there." Anaïse threw Scarlett a conspiratorial smile. "Although, in my opinion, all the best ones are."

Here reference to *Alice in Wonderland* made her smile and the two women stood in silence for a while, both watching Edward disappear into the woods.

"Leonard isn't all bad either. He's just a bit angry and lost. Funny how families can mess us all up, ain't it?"

Scarlett nodded. "Yes, it is."

"Did you have a good upbringing?"

Slightly taken aback by the quick change and candid nature of the conversation, Scarlett paused for a moment, wondering if she should trust it. Realising she had nothing to hide, she responded, "It wasn't bad. It was just lonely – single working mother, and when she was there in person, her mind was usually elsewhere."

"Your mother works here, doesn't she? The lady gardener?"

Scarlett smiled at Anaïse's description. "Yes, that's her. We've started making our peace since I've been here."

This time, it was Anaïse's turn to pause. "Lost in books of faraway places and times. Could be a response to pain, you know."

Ignoring the psych diagnosis, Scarlett asked, "How do you know about the books?"

"Leonard – he knows everything about everyone. It's one of his charms, until it gets a tad tiresome and annoying." Anaïse laughed, but Scarlett noticed an edge of bitterness to it. "Like I said, he's not all bad." She looked across at Scarlett. "But you need to watch out for him. He's a bit of a fox, in every sense. Don't be

A NEW *Hope* IN THE HIGHLANDS

caught unawares, okay?"

Scarlett was confused but nodded. "Okay."

"Anyway, there's a reason I came to find you. I feel completely overwhelmed by the amount of clothing in my bedroom – not sure why we brought so much, truth be told – and Mrs Wilson said there are enough rooms still available on my floor where we could either rehouse some of them or potentially give them away."

Scarlett nodded and replied, "Okay."

"I have zero interest in selling them, even though I hear it's all the rage, so I'd like to go through what I don't want and then you can take what you like and do with the rest whatever you see fit... Although, you don't look well. Are you alright?" Anaïse was scanning Scarlett's face.

Scarlett was definitely *not* alright and feeling definitively *off*. The ache in her lower abdomen was worsening, and it felt like a chill was making a home there too. She desperately needed a hot bath, a hot water bottle, and potentially some antibiotics.

"Come on, let's get you downstairs. I'll get Mrs Wilson."

"Please don't. I know what it is, and it's embarrassing and probably very much self-inflicted." Scarlett was whining, but she didn't care – Mrs Wilson was not an option right now.

Anaïse looked at Scarlett with genuine concern. "What is it? What's wrong?"

Scarlett closed her eyes as the pain worsened, accompanied by the urgent need to pee. "I'm pretty sure I've got a bout of cystitis." Scarlett cringed as the words left her mouth.

"Oh, you poor dear." Anaïse was genuinely sympathetic. "Do you know they used to actually call it the honeymoon disease? Fucking delightful, huh?"

Scarlett went to laugh, but the pain was becoming unbearable.

"Right, let's get you down to my room. I'll get this sorted." Scarlett found the idea of Anaïse sorting anything out for herself, let alone anyone else, slightly bizarre, but she had very little fight in her.

Avoiding anyone on their way, Anaïse ushered Scarlett into her ensuite toilet. "I'm going to run you a bath—"

"Not in your room!" The idea horrified Scarlett.

Anaïse's room was like something you'd expect in a boutique hotel, with a freestanding Victoria and Albert chrome bath with claw feet, installed by Edward's mother during her time there. It was too much, though. Mrs Wilson would fly through the roof. Besides, it was fucking weird.

"Really, it's fine. Let me use the toilet and I'll go home," Scarlett said, trying to breathe through the pain.

"Hush now, and do what you're told. Don't start being like Millie on me now!" Anaïse closed the bathroom door behind her and whilst Scarlett relieved herself, doubled over, she could hear Anaïse running the bath and calling Miranda into her room.

"Fuck's sake!" Scarlett muttered under her breath; this was the last thing she needed. But the pain was crippling, and she closed her eyes tightly, no longer interested in trying to make out what the hushed voices on the other side of the door were saying.

She eventually heard the bedroom door closing and the water of the bath being turned off.

"Sweetheart, you'll feel better coming off that toilet and getting in this bath for a while. I've put some Epsom salts in there." Anaïse's tone was warm and full of empathy. But Scarlett couldn't speak. A mixture of pain and humiliation had dried up her vocal cords.

"Listen, I know how this feels. I had bouts of these to a chronic degree for years. Miranda has gone to make Leonard take her to the store to get some of those cranberry sachets and juice. Not that crappy sugary stuff, though." Anaïse sighed. "She's a doll, really. She's telling him it's for me, and she's going to have a real quiet word with your mom – as we all know how she reacts when you go AWOL ... although, at least this time you're still on the grounds and haven't absconded with her boss!"

Scarlett appreciated Anaïse's attempt at humour and managed a smile.

"Come on now, I've locked the bedroom door. It's just us."

Scarlett sorted herself, wincing at the effort, but she relented and opened the bathroom door to face Anaïse, who was all smiles and genuine warmth. She briefly wondered if aliens had come down and possessed her, but realised this side of Anaïse had probably always been there.

Despite Scarlett's weak attempts not to, she'd been dismissive and prejudiced against Anaïse and her friends, for no justified reason, and Scarlett disliked herself for it.

Looking over at the bath, she felt an immense amount of gratitude towards her unlikely friend, if she could call her that, and in that moment couldn't think of anywhere else she'd rather be or who she'd rather be with. Scarlett felt cold to her core, and the chilled ache was now pulsating and clawing at her insides.

"Come on, let's get you in there. I promise I won't let anyone else in, okay?" Anaïse offered a warm smile.

Scarlett nodded and undressed, no longer caring that Anaïse was about to see her naked, and as soon as she sunk her body into the bath, a feeling of relief washed over her.

The heat soothed her, and she closed her eyes, completely submerging herself underneath the water. When she came up, Anaïse was kneeling beside her with a small towel.

"May sound silly but get this wet – the weight of this on your lower stomach will make you feel a little better. When you're out, we'll replace it with a hot water bottle, which should make its way to us shortly, courtesy of Mrs Wilson – she's a dream, isn't she? I want to take her home with me. Although, I think Edward may take that shotgun of his and gun me down before I even got to the end of the drive! Not to mention if I got her home, Millie would probably do the same before we made it even halfway up mine!" Anaïse laughed at her own joke, making Scarlett smile. "You know, us girls, we need to stick together; if we don't have each other's back, what have we got?"

Scarlett again spotted that hint of sadness in her eyes, which Anaïse quickly blinked away.

"Right, you relax. I have to respond to some messages." Anaïse waved her mobile. "The world awaits, and while I have service, I need to make the most of it." She stood and made her way to the chair by the window, now more talking to herself than directly at Scarlett. "Like, seriously, there's no rhyme or reason to it. One day the Wi-Fi works just fine, and the next, you could hang out the attic window and you're lucky if you can even get 3G!"

Scarlett smiled to herself. Anaïse's incessant chat relaxed and comforted her. She'd always imagined what it would be like to have a sister and wondered if it would feel a little like this.

CHAPTER 30

For the rest of the day, Edward avoided every living soul, except for a couple of deer and a fox he'd disturbed whilst he'd been cutting and stacking enough firewood to last a good couple of weeks. The work was hard, and his muscles ached with exhaustion, but it was exactly what he needed to clear his mind and unwind his frustrations.

He knew he'd have to clear things up with Scarlett. He'd behaved like an absolute dick and hurt her for no justified reason. It was the last thing he wanted to do, but words and emotions, especially words about emotions, rarely came easy to him.

As he showered and dressed, he rehearsed various speeches in his head, but none felt like a sufficient apology, and then the realisation dawned on him – what if she didn't forgive him? What if this time he'd gone too far? The idea made him feel nauseous.

Food was also on his mind. Dried and dressed by six, he knew dinner wasn't until eight, but he figured Mrs Wilson would have a snack for him. After that, he'd have to find Scarlett, even if it meant going to the stables. He no longer cared what anyone else thought, but he cared what Scarlett was thinking *and* feeling.

God, I wish I was better at this.

He walked into the kitchen, relieved the boys hadn't arrived for their shifts yet. He couldn't be arsed facing more people than was absolutely necessary at this point.

"Evening, Mrs Wilson," he said, doing his usual lingering in the doorway.

Mrs Wilson turned and smiled at him. "Good evening, sir. How are you?"

"Hungry. Is there anything I could grab and head out with?" Edward asked, looking around the kitchen for options.

"Of course. How about some soup?" Mrs Wilson offered. "Or I could quickly rustle up a ham and tomato sandwich."

"A sandwich would be good, thanks." Edward nodded.

"Would you like me to bring it to you?"

Edward thought for a moment. "I'll wait and take it with me."

Mrs Wilson nodded and opened the fridge, bringing out a large ham joint and placing it on the worktop. Edward briefly considered just taking that with him to gnaw on and the image of him chomping on it like a caveman almost made him smile.

"Do you know where Scarlett is? Has she finished for the day?" he asked in the most nonchalant way he could muster.

Mrs Wilson looked up and paused her slicing of the ham.

"Oh, were you not aware? Ms Hope took ill earlier today. I believe she headed home around two-ish."

"What's wrong with her?" Edward dismissed the weird use of Scarlett's surname and did his best to keep his voice level.

"Couldn't tell you, I'm afraid," Mrs Wilson replied, continuing with the sandwich. "Miss Anaïse's friend, her name keeps slipping my mind—"

"Miranda?" He didn't care a jot about Anaïse's companion, but he cared about what was wrong with Scarlett.

"Aye, of course – Miranda. She informed me that Scarlett had become unwell and requested a hot water bottle for Miss Anaïse, who also seems to be under the weather. I hope they're not all coming down with something." Mrs Wilson shook her head, continuing to busy herself. "And then they went off to the shops. Miranda and young Leonard, that is."

Edward took the sandwich on a plate offered by Mrs Wilson. "Thank you."

"You're welcome. Do you want anything else?"

Edward shook his head. "No, thanks."

He left the kitchen, unsure of his next move. He'd take his sandwich to his office and message Scarlett, or should he phone her? She'd seemed fine earlier, healthwise anyway. Was it because of what had happened? He really hoped not. Shutting his office door behind him, he took out his mobile. He saw another message from Briege.

Fucking relentless.

Ignoring Briege, he typed a message to Scarlett instead.

> **Edward:** *I'm really sorry about earlier.*

He saw Scarlett come online and watched the two ticks turn blue, but even after several seconds passed, she didn't reply and then disappeared.

Fuck.

His stomach growled. He needed to eat. Then he would call her. Or find her. Maybe he'd just go find her.

After he'd finished his sandwich, he looked at his phone again. Still no reply.

Fuck's sake.

He stood and brushed the crumbs from his jeans; to the stables he would go then.

He hoped June wouldn't interfere, but she was Scarlett's mother first, his employee second, and he'd need to be prepared for a potential pushback; he had no idea what Scarlett had told her. Probably that he was an absolute arse, which was a perfectly fair summary of him at present.

The house was still quiet, and he made it outside and all the way to the entrance of the stables with no interruption. He trudged up the stairs to the big red door at the top, somewhere he hadn't been for a long while, and certainly not since Scarlett had arrived at Haddon House. He paused for a long while without knocking, still not sure what to do or what to say once he did.

Christ, this is awkward.

His brow began to sweat and the confidence he thought he had was dissipating fast. Then, without warning, the door swung open, revealing Andrzej with nothing but a towel around his waist, looking ripped, his skin damp from a shower.

"Sir?" Andrzej's face flushed with embarrassment and confusion. "I thought I heard something, but – we weren't expecting anyone ... or you. Is everything okay?"

Edward pulled his hand over his face, not knowing how to explain himself. There was too much to process and nothing was connecting for him. To make matters worse, June came into the hallway drying her hands on a tea towel, shock and surprise in her eyes.

"Sir?" Her voice was an octave higher than usual.

"I was looking for Scarlett." Edward finally formed a coherent sentence. "I heard she was unwell today?"

June and Andrzej looked at each other. Eventually, June sighed, taking control of the situation.

Thank God.

"You'll catch your death here, Andrzej. Go get

dressed. Dinner is almost ready."

Andrzej smiled sheepishly at Edward and shrugged his shoulders. "I will do as I'm told."

Edward nodded, still unsure what to make of the entire situation.

"Would you like to come in?" June asked him, stepping aside, making it difficult for him to refuse without seeming rude. He nodded again, taking in the aesthetically pleasing decor and the general warmth of the place. June had made it a lovely home, and the food smelled amazing. He glanced through the doorway of the spare bedroom, which was dark, the bed empty.

Where is she?

Edward walked into the lounge and June signalled for him to sit on the sofa, which he did.

"Sorry, I don't mean to intrude," Edward told her, rubbing the back of his neck.

"That's okay." June sat in the chair across from him. "As you can see, she's not here."

Edward looked at her. A thousand questions were swimming around his head. Had she left? Was she coming back? And why was Andrzej there, showering and half naked, getting ready for dinner?

"She's at the main house," she told him, but he could tell there was more.

"Mrs Wilson told me she'd gone home ill … Is she better then?"

June seemed to be trying to find the right words before she finally took a deep breath and spoke again. "No, she is not. Miranda came by earlier to advise that Scarlett was unwell, and Anaïse was taking care of her and keeping her at the main house. It's nothing serious, but she felt it was best for her not to come back to the stables this evening." June watched Edward closely.

Nothing was making any sense, though. Wasn't Anaïse the one who was sick, too? And why on earth would she, of all God's creatures, be taking care of Scarlett? And why had Miranda and Leonard gone to the shops?

What the fuck is going on?

"I'm sorry to have disturbed you, I'll go and—"

June raised her hand. "Maybe just leave her for now."

"What do you mean?" Edward snapped, immediately regretting his tone.

She raised her eyebrow as only a mother knew how. "Just give her some space, Edward."

A mother first and foremost.

His shoulders slumped, and he nodded, feeling reprimanded and dejected.

"She'll be fine, she just needs a minute, okay?"

Edward stood suddenly, making June startle. "Sorry again. Enjoy your dinner."

He didn't wait for June to see him out and rushed out of the apartment, down the stairs, and into the damp evening air, where he felt he could breathe again. He appreciated June meant well, but he needed answers, and he needed them now.

Storming back into the house, Edward launched himself up the stairs, two steps at a time, until he stood outside his mother's old room, which he knew Anaïse was occupying. He still wasn't sure why she wasn't sharing a room with Leonard, but put it down to her virtue and traditions, as opposed to those of his brother.

Now standing outside, he didn't actually know what to do, much like how he felt standing outside the Hope residence, so without overthinking it, he simply knocked on the door with more force than he intended.

Edward could hear muffled voices through the door, followed by footsteps approaching. The door opened and Anaïse stood before him, looking quite well.

"Sorry for the intrusion. I heard Scarlett is unwell, and you've been *caring* for her." Edward tried to see behind her into the room.

"Is there a question in there somewhere, Edward?" Anaïse straightened, blocking his view, as he continued to steal glances behind her.

"I'd like to see her ... please." Edward noticed for the first time how tall she was; she was level with him, if not a little taller.

"Still not much of a question, darlin'."

"Anaïse, don't play games with me. Is she there – in the bathroom?" He was losing his patience. "I want to know she's okay."

"She's with me. She's not feeling her best, but all is well. There, you happy?"

Edward could feel the heat of his temper rising to his temples. "No, I am not happy, Anaïse. I would like to speak to her – I want to know what's wrong."

Anaïse briefly frowned, and he wasn't sure if it was in sympathy for him or pity, but as quickly as it appeared, a smile took its place, infuriating him even further.

"She's okay, Edward. Just give her a little space. I'll tell her you called for her," she told him, her saccharine Southern drawl stronger than usual. She then gave him a nod as a goodbye and closed the door firmly in his face. He heard the lock turn.

He wanted to tear the door, its frame, and the entire house down around them.

What the fuck!

Edward knew he needed to calm down, but not as much as he needed to see and talk to Scarlett. He couldn't find any rational reason why everyone was being so secretive, and it was driving him insane. He growled and banged his fist against the door in frustration before storming back downstairs to his

rooms, slamming and locking the door behind him.
Fuck them all. I'm going to bed.
After grabbing his almost empty bottle of Armagnac, that was exactly what he did.

CHAPTER 31

Some random nostalgic song was playing on the stereo in Scarlett's mother's old car.

"Andrzej gave me this CD. Cigarettes After Sex, I think they're called. An odd name for a band, don't you think?"

"I've heard of them. I didn't realise this was them."

"The songs are a bit sad, but I sort of like it."

Scarlett nodded. "Yeah, they are."

"Who would've guessed I'd be down with the kids, huh?" June winked at Scarlett, making her smile. "How you feeling?"

"The painkillers have helped." Scarlett turned away and looked out her window. It was difficult to see where the grey drizzle in the sky ended and the land began. It was the long Scottish winter, so she'd been told, and the damp grey skies echoed it to be true.

If it wasn't this depressing, it could almost be beautiful.

"Well, I'm just happy we got you in to see the GP so quickly. It's good that the Cameron-Reids have always provided private health to all their employees, don't you think?"

"Hmm, very thoughtful." Scarlett didn't mean to sound ungrateful, so she added, "Thank you for taking me."

"Of course." June briefly glanced across at Scarlett. "Do you want to talk about it?"

"It's just a urine infection. There's nothing to talk

about."

June nodded and, for the remaining half an hour, hummed along to her CD.

When they arrived back at the stables, June switched off the ignition and looked across at Scarlett. "He came looking for you last night."

"Who?"

"You know who." June rolled her eyes.

Scarlett nodded, avoiding looking at her mother.

"He obviously cares."

Scarlett nodded again, still unable to find a suitable response.

"Right, well, why don't you rest? I've got some work to be getting on with. Do you need anything before I shoot off?"

Scarlett shook her head. "Thanks again for taking me. I'll see you later."

They both got out of the car and Scarlett headed straight up to the flat whilst her mother headed towards the garden workshop on the other side of the building.

What a fucking shit show.

She knew she had to find him and talk to him, but it could wait another couple of hours – just a little more time to allow her to gather her thoughts, which were still running riot in her head. She also knew she should've at least messaged him, but she was so angry, upset, and in pain; all she'd wanted to do was curl up and try to sleep, which was exactly what she'd done.

Anaïse had insisted Scarlett stay in her room, and after ensuring she had taken the painkillers and had enough to drink, she left to have dinner and spent the rest of the night in Miranda's room. But Scarlett still should have messaged Edward, and she felt rotten for not doing so. He'd also not called or messaged after being turned away by Anaïse the evening before, and she felt sick at the idea of him potentially never speaking to her again. But she still felt humiliated and angry with him.

It could all wait, though. She had to prioritise herself. But she was in the flat for all of five minutes before a thunderous knock on the door frightened her half to death.

Her bath was running, and she was already half undressed, in just a t-shirt and knickers, so she grabbed the thick cream bathrobe her mother had bought her during her last trip to Aberdeen with Andrzej. It still had that newish smell and felt like a hug. Another impatient knock struck at the door, and she knew it was Edward. No one else on the estate had the gall or temperament to knock like that.

Reluctantly, she opened the door and almost laughed at the sight of him, nostrils flaring and fists clenched, readying himself to knock again.

"Edward," Scarlett said, her voice steady as she folded her arms around herself.

"What's the matter?" he barked at her. "And why have you been avoiding me?"

Scarlett closed her eyes. She didn't have the energy to deal with tantrums, so she turned around and headed to the bathroom. "Come in and shut the door. I'm cold!"

She could hear him sigh behind her, but he came in and shut the door.

"And take your shoes off!" Scarlett added, struggling to hide her frustration.

He sighed again, loudly this time, but when she turned around to check, he was doing as she asked, still not taking his eyes off her.

Those eyes.

Even when she was furious with him, and his eyes looked as if there were a violent storm brewing in them, she could still get lost there. She shook her head, suddenly remembering the water was still running – they could probably do without the bath flooding on top of everything else. Turning off the taps, she tested the water – much warmer than she'd usually like, but she wanted to chase the cold out of her.

Scarlett was grateful for more private surroundings than the night before, but hearing Edward padding through her bedroom towards her, it seemed like bathing solo wasn't something she was doing anytime soon. She stripped off and got into the bath, wincing as her skin became accustomed to the heat. Her eyes glanced across the room towards Edward standing in the doorway, all tall, delicious, and awkward as usual. He really was her own brand of catnip. Everything about him was alluring to her, even as she noted his discomfort and the way his restless hands now sank deep into his pockets.

Despite being massively pissed off with him, she still wanted to be close to him, to feel him, inhale him, even when he was being a complete arse and, evidently, in an almighty strop.

"What's wrong, Scarlett?" His voice was softer now, but his face still appeared caught between empathy and anger.

"I've got a urine infection."

"Huh? What even is that?" His voice hitched, rising an octave.

She rolled her eyes at his reaction.

"A UTI. Cystitis, whatever you want to call it. We've already spoken about this."

"Ohh ..." His brow furrowed. "Because of me?"

"No, Edward, you didn't *do* this. We've just been having a lot of sex, and to be honest, I've always been prone to it." She sank deeper into the bath, too tired and sore to be embarrassed by the frank conversation they were having.

They fell into silence and Scarlett watched him as his eyes darted around the room, unable to meet hers. She could see he was struggling with talking about stuff like this. "Edward!"

"What?" he snapped, but she could tell he immediately regretted it as he pulled his hand across his face. "I was ready to kill people last night."

"Why?" *This man, honestly.*

"Everyone was being weird and keeping me away. Why didn't you just speak to me? Or message me?" Edward closed his eyes and leaned his head against the doorframe.

"Because you acted like a complete wanker yesterday and then I felt like shit!" Scarlett scowled at him.

He sighed. "I'm sorry."

"What is going on?" She shook her head. "What's got into you?"

He looked at her and sighed. *Again.* "I don't know. My head is all over the fucking place."

"Why?" She watched him straighten and then begin to take his clothes off. "We are not having sex!"

"Shut up, I know that." He rolled his eyes at her and within seconds he was naked. "Move forward and let me sit behind you."

It was Scarlett's turn to huff and sigh, but she reluctantly obeyed, unable to stop herself from stealing a quick glance at his cock. The slight smirk playing on his mouth told her he noticed.

Luckily, the bath was enormous, but she leaned forward and let some of the water out so it didn't overflow.

"Fuck! How hot is it in here? Fucking hell," he groaned.

She half laughed. "It's my bath. You don't have to be in here."

He grunted and then slid in behind her and she put the plug back in, staying sitting upright until he pulled her back to lie against him. The hairs on his legs and the small patch on his chest softly grazed her skin. She liked the feel of it and as she adjusted herself, she could feel him harden. "Ignore him. He'll settle down," he grumbled.

Scarlett grabbed the towel she'd placed on the side of the bath and laid it across the bottom of her stomach. Edward placed his hands on top of it and she closed her eyes as comfort washed over her.

"I'm sorry you're not well, and I – *we* didn't take it easier. And I'm sorry I was a complete prick."

Scarlett placed her hands on top of his. "It's becoming a habit I'm not particularly keen on."

"I'm sorry," he told her, his voice small.

"I know." She squeezed his hand.

They stayed silent for a long moment.

"Seriously, though, what was that about with Anaïse? How did all that come about?" he asked, freeing a hand to move some of her hair from her neck and placing a kiss in its place.

A laugh bubbled out of Scarlett. She wasn't sure she could adequately put into words how it went from weird to the most logical and natural turn of events. "She was just there ... I was in a lot of pain, and she took control. It was odd and then – well, then it wasn't."

"Women are strange. I don't get it." Edward continued to trace his fingers across her neck and shoulders.

Scarlett released a contented sigh. "I'm not sure you're supposed to."

"If she was a man, I would've put her through that door. I was raging." His tone was matter-of-fact.

"I heard." She shook her head, remembering how

his reaction had made her cringe with embarrassment.

"Wish you'd just talked to me." He spoke softly against her ear and she melted.

"Sorry," she said, closing her eyes, leaning into him and into the moment, which she knew would spoil if she were to voice the words, thoughts, and doubts still swimming around in her head.

Just a little while longer.

He took the sponge from the shelf hanging on the wall and filled it with warm water, gently washing her neck, arms, and collarbone. His tenderness was such a stark contrast to his usual stormy nature that it made her dizzy.

"Appreciate I'm not the easiest of people, but I never want to hurt you," he said, his voice now almost a whisper as he kissed the side of her head.

Scarlett wondered how much of that was true. She didn't doubt he'd never want to physically hurt her, but what about her heart? Did he feel as protective over that? She wasn't sure he did. And what about …

"I can't wait until this wedding is over and done with and we can get back to normal," he said, pulling her from her thoughts.

"What will normal look like?" Scarlett said, squeezing her eyes shut and wincing as the words came out – they just couldn't stay inside her, they needed oxygen, whether that meant everything exploded or not.

"What do you mean?" She could feel him tense. Any time she mentioned anything about the future, he tensed. Was that because he knew deep down that she wouldn't feature in it? Was his future tied up with a certain brunette who still had their beach wedding planned out in a Filofax somewhere? She seemed the kind to still have something like a Filofax … that or a human form of one – a PA that nervously followed her around, manically taking notes about important state appointments and Brazilian blowouts.

"Exactly that. What are we doing?" She knew it was foolish of her to push further, but she needed to know. As much as she hated her insecurities and however desperate she might seem, she needed some reassurance before her emotions ran away with themselves – more than they had already in the *very* brief time they'd known each other.

"Having a bath." She felt his shoulders shrug, and she felt like *accidentally* digging her elbow into his balls, which were innocently buoyed behind her.

"Don't be flippant, Edward."

"We've talked about this." The motion of his shoulders shrugging made her bristle.

"Yeah, but that was before …" She didn't want to continue that sentence. Saying it out loud made it seem final.

"Before what?" His voice was strained, and Scarlett could tell frustration was lacing the outer edges of his patience.

"What is the whole thing with Briege? It all feels very loaded and weird." There, she said it.

His body slumped behind her, and in that instant, she knew her gut was right about everything. Scarlett couldn't take it; she refused to put herself through all this again, especially not with him. It had been bad enough with Jason, someone she was doubting was ever right for her. But Edward was something else. He was different and had the ability to not just break her heart, but destroy her completely.

In such a short time, she could feel herself falling for him on a frightening level, and she couldn't – no, she *wouldn't* – allow this to happen to her again. He wouldn't get the chance to.

Her breath caught in her throat and for an awful moment, she thought she was going to sob, but somehow she caught it and swallowed it down. She felt shaky, but she didn't care and wrangled herself free from Edward's arms and legs, getting out of the bath. Edward watched her, apparently still struggling to find words and looking like a deer caught in headlights.

Scarlett wrapped a bath towel around her, which was as big as a sheet. "You actually have nothing to say?"

"It's not – fuck's sake." Edward stood up in the bath, splashing water everywhere, and she struggled not to look at him, but she had to stop being sidetracked by how attracted she was to him. This was too important. She had to protect herself from him and whatever *this* was, as it wasn't the safe place she thought and hoped it was.

"Pass me a towel, please," he asked her.

Scarlett pulled one from the towel shelf, passed it to him, and left the bathroom to get dressed. The painkillers were working, the antibiotics would soon, and she was no longer cold. She had work to do, and she needed to think without him being all naked and beautiful around her.

As if on cue, he walked out of the bathroom dressed, his hair messy and damp. "It's not what you think, okay?"

"And what is it I'm thinking?" Scarlett asked, pulling a jumper over her head.

"That there's something going on you don't know about. Well, there probably is but—"

"You don't owe me anything, Edward. I mean, we've barely known each other two weeks. It's ridiculous and we're not exactly teenagers. So, we *fucked* a few times, but really, this was never going to go anywhere, was it? Not really."

"If that's the case, why are you so upset?" He made a move towards her, but she stopped him in his tracks by raising a hand.

"I'm not upset!" she snapped.

"You *very* clearly are." He pushed his hands in his pockets and shrugged. "I've not actually done anything wrong here."

Scarlett looked up at him before focusing back on her feet and putting her socks on, which, as usual, were odd. "You didn't warn me about her, not really, and now I feel ridiculous."

"Why? I don't understand." Edward was losing patience, she could tell.

"You were getting married!" Her voice cracked as the words burst from her lips.

"Fuck's sake – it was years ago! Scarlett—"

"I thought you were different." She no longer cared what she looked or sounded like. It was all becoming too much.

"Different to what? Who?" He was struggling to suppress the annoyance in his voice, but she couldn't stop herself.

"Everyone, okay! I thought you were someone I could trust, that you weren't going to hurt me or just fuck off and …" Her voice quivered, and she couldn't allow the tears that were dangerously close to falling to spill from her eyes.

"I have done nothing wrong or gone anywhere, Scarlett. I'm standing right here, aren't I?" His eyes were wide and the storm within them stirred all manner of feelings inside her, but she pushed them away.

This is just too much.

She couldn't hear him anymore. All she could think of was Briege. Perfect Briege. Perfect Angelica. They were both *perfect* and there was always going to be someone else more perfect than her to take away what she foolishly thought was hers.

Fuck, what am I even doing here?

"Scarlett ..." Edward made to move towards her again.

"What?!" she snapped at him, making him think better of it.

"There is nothing going on between me and Briege. She's my ex and Leonard is a knob for bringing her in when he knows perfectly well she's a toxic parasite that I sent packing out of my life a long time ago. I have absolutely zero interest in the woman. She could be on fire, and I literally wouldn't—"

"I don't want this," she interrupted him. "Any of it. I don't want you or for me to feel this way. I want to finish the job, get paid, and leave this godforsaken place out here in the middle of nowhere and start my life again. I just want to be left alone, okay?" She couldn't look at him, but the way he sucked in his breath, she could tell that her words had landed where she'd wanted them to and she immediately regretted them, wanting nothing more than to take them back. Take it all back. Be back in the bath, their limbs tangled, as he gently washed her, kissing the side of her head and ...

"Right, I'll get out of your way then," he said with a finality that crushed her.

And just like that, he was gone.

CHAPTER 32

EDWARD WAS NOT the type of man to cry. He couldn't remember the last time he did, but the unmistakable hot burning feeling behind his eyes was there, reminding him that this was exactly why he'd done his best to avoid this type of nonsense for all these years. The drama. The pain. It was all pointless and a waste of time and energy.

He and the estate were better off alone. He knew this, he'd always known this, but Scarlett had somehow penetrated through his logic and resolve, and for a moment, a very brief moment, he'd believed that he might share it with someone after all. With her.

But she was right. They barely knew each other and, more importantly, she obviously had other plans. It would have always happened, Briege or not; Scarlett would have eventually left, maybe even gone back to her husband and their easier, more comfortable life in Bath – and maybe that's where she should go back to. Not that he particularly liked the idea – in fact, he hated it. But at least she would be cared for, secure, and hopefully happy.

He didn't have the inner resources to make her happy, no matter how hard he tried. Past experiences had taught him that so he'd stopped trying a long time ago. Although, how easy it'd been with Scarlett, it was effortless – almost.

Her *usually* easy manner and smile made it a natural reaction to want to please her and be with her, to want to make her feel good. The way she'd so easily made him feel good, too. She'd made him feel like a whole person, even though he didn't believe in people completing each other – he thought a person should do that by themselves, and he still thought that, but equally, there wasn't any doubt in his mind that she *did* make him want to be a better version of himself, and as he began shutting down his emotions, a hidden part inside him silently wept at the sadness of it all.

Edward, however, preferred to harness the one reliable emotion that had always served him well and he held on to it tightly. Anger. And it was predominantly aimed at one person: his brother.

He wouldn't be violent, it wasn't his style, but Leonard was going to hear exactly what he thought about him and his careless, dickish actions. Enough was enough. If he didn't sort his behaviour out, Edward had no qualms calling the whole thing off and they could all fuck off back to the States much sooner than expected, unmarried and unhappy. He just didn't care anymore.

As he turned towards the house, the sky darkened, and he noticed two figures standing by the side entrance to the kitchen. If he didn't know better, he could've sworn he caught a brief glimpse of Lily's salmon pink raincoat, but she wasn't due back until the weekend and was currently interviewing for medical school in Edinburgh with her mother. He shook his head and headed for the boot room. He had enough to be getting on with to distract himself from the entire Scarlett situation, but not before he found Leonard. And then he would move on.

Once inside, he spotted Mrs Wilson sorting the flower arrangement in the grand hall. She looked up when she heard him approach.

"My brother, have you seen him?" He couldn't subdue the gruffness in his voice.

Mrs Wilson peered over her small glasses to observe him. "The last time I saw him, he was in the lounge with—"

"Thanks," Edward cut her off and walked away. He didn't care who he was in there with, but much to his disappointment, Leonard was nowhere to be seen. However, as he stepped further into the otherwise empty room, a tearful Briege turned to face him.

"Oh, Eddie, I've just had the most awful news." She rushed over to him. "Dad has just passed away."

Edward stood still. He hated her, but not enough to not have *any* sympathy. He knew how close she was to her father. "I'm sorry," he told her, lifting his arms in a loose embrace and patting her back. "What happened?"

"He was at his place in Geneva." She circled her arms tightly around his neck, which he tried to gently prise away, but she started crying. "Heart attack and he was just gone."

Edward patted her arms, hoping someone would come in and take over. He didn't want to be unkind but equally wanted to be as far away from her as humanly possible.

"Oh," Briege suddenly said, slowly pulling away, staying close to him and taking hold of his upper arm. He looked down at her and, behind the tears, he recognised the familiar look of smugness in her eyes as she focused on whoever was behind him.

His stomach twisted in knots as he knew without turning that Scarlett was there. He could sense her.

Edward turned slowly and, sure enough, there she stood, hurt and anger etched across her face. He closed his eyes.

She'd probably rushed after him to make things right between them. He wished with all his might this moment could be erased. That he'd stayed in her bedroom, forced her to see sense, taken her in his arms, and lain with her on her bed until she fell asleep, just like in Edinburgh that night. But he couldn't erase it, and to make matters worse, Leonard now stood behind her, placing a comforting arm around her shoulder to protect her from whatever it looked like was going on.

"Not even if she was on fire, huh?" Scarlett said as she turned to leave, but not before he saw the tears spill down her cheeks.

"Scarlett ..."

"Leave her be," Leonard said, turning to follow her.

Briege still clung to his arm and wrapped herself around him again. "It was so awful, baby," she continued. "The maid found him. I don't even know where to start with it all. It's not like I've got siblings to help. Oh, Eddie, what am I going to do?"

Enough.

He firmly took hold of her wrists and peeled her from him, pushing her away to arm's length.

"Briege, I'm very sorry for your loss. Genuinely, I am, but I am no longer the person who can help you deal with this. There is no more *us* and there never will be. I'm very sorry, but there isn't. You're the most toxic person I have ever known and I don't want you anywhere near me, my family, or my house ever again, okay?"

Briege's mouth opened and closed, but no words came out. For once, she was too shocked to speak.

"Look, wait here for my brother or call one of your *many* friends. And then get off my property, okay?" He looked at her one last time before letting her go and leaving the room, thinking for a moment to rush after Scarlett, but something stopped him.

What on earth could he say to her at this point? It was now truly and properly fucked. Briege had made sure of that and there was nothing he could say to make Scarlett trust him again.

Maybe this was all for the best. She'd soon realise that he wasn't good enough for her, that this wasn't the place for her, and perhaps that husband of hers would come to his senses and beg her to return home, where he could spend the rest of his life making up for the mess he'd made.

But then there was now a baby coming into the mix, and really it had nothing to do with Edward, and maybe she was better off without either of them. She wanted to start her life over, buy that bed-and-breakfast or Airbnb she'd talked about, and be independent and free, far away from him and Haddon House. And be happy. That, he decided, was all he wanted for her, even if that meant she wasn't with him. The idea made his heart sink into his stomach, but he believed to his core it was the right thing to do.

Forgetting all about Leonard and his anger towards him, Edward retreated to his office, firmly locking the door behind him. He didn't want to eat or sleep, so he would work – that's where he was most useful. He understood his purpose there, somewhere he couldn't hurt anyone and vice versa, and where he could remain undisturbed and alone in peace.

CHAPTER 33

THE FOLLOWING WEEKS passed by in a blur without so much as a word from him. It was done. They were done. And to fill the void, Scarlett had thrown herself into the wedding with a frightening force, to the point people's looks and carefully chosen words highlighted their concerns – something she paid little notice of. There was a wedding to plan.

With the wedding taking place just four days before Christmas and the date fast approaching, the place was swarming with tradespeople coming to the end of their shifts for the evening.

The guest floor bedrooms were finally finished, and some had needed much more than just a deep clean. Several required fresh plaster and paint in addition to new taps and curtain poles in the ensuite bathrooms.

Finding enough workers was initially difficult, but with Scarlett's bottomless budget and the approaching Christmas season providing a whole host of people seeking temporary employment, James and his brother mobilised local businesses and, working constantly, finished the job.

The chairs arrived for the orangery and Anaïse was pleased with them and their covers, along with the seating arrangements for the ceremony and the dining room.

The marquee company Scarlett got on board on short notice had finished setting up, and the couple's close family would arrive in a few days – although Lady

Cameron-Reid's decision to arrive on the actual day was making everyone nervous and stressed. All was going exactly to plan, yet Scarlett struggled to find joy in her accomplishments.

She noticed how Edward remained out of sight by either leaving the house early or, according to the gossip from the kitchen, staying cooped up and locked behind his door.

He no longer dined with his brother or their American guests, even when Lily was visiting, which was almost constant these days. Mrs Wilson's eyebrow raised as she shared that particular nugget of information. She did the same when she casually mentioned that Miss Briege was now in Switzerland and would be for the foreseeable future.

Scarlett tried not to react and would leave the kitchen whenever talk such as this came up, politely excusing herself. She didn't want to think about Edward. It was over. It needed to be over, and his absence showed he felt the same. Yet, she worried about him and her mind would regularly betray her with thoughts of him and their brief time together, moments when everything had felt so right.

Enough already!

She couldn't keep torturing herself about it all. She had to focus on herself and her future. Jason was visiting in a week or so and promised they would talk and come to a financial arrangement, even though he was still refusing to discuss the option of a divorce, and she was refusing to entertain his calls, even though, as he kept messaging, he had important news to share with her. She didn't care about his news – she just wanted to be free from them all.

Of course, she knew she would miss people here – even the Americans, she realised with surprise, but they would soon leave too. It was all coming to a natural end.

She would really miss June and Andrzej, more than she'd like to admit, and even toyed with staying in Scotland. She doubted she would revisit Haddon House, but they could visit her if she didn't choose somewhere too far away. The money she'd earned from arranging the wedding was generous and would be enough for a deposit and the first couple of months' rent for a little flat somewhere, at least until she found a job or the money from Jason came through, whichever happened first. She didn't imagine it would take long, as Tara wanted her ring back and Jason was constantly texting her about it, making it clear to Scarlett that it was her only remaining leverage with them.

Something else was bothering her though and the memory regularly caught her off-guard when she least expected it. After the whole Briege debacle in the lounge, feeling humiliated and rejected, she'd let Leonard comfort her, and the events that had unfolded had left her feeling shaky and violated. Despite doing her best not to mull over it, she still felt annoyed and upset, wondering how it had even occurred in the first place or gone as far as it did.

After seeing Edward and Briege's embrace, tears blurring her vision, Leonard had caught up with her in the hallway, taking hold of her shoulders and guiding her into the empty dining room, clicking the door shut behind them. He took her gently in his arms, where she'd sobbed for what felt like an age.

"It's okay, you're okay," he told her, stroking her hair as she burrowed her face into his chest. She felt raw and vulnerable, and there was a comforting familiarity to his body that offered relief. It wasn't Edward, but he felt close to it.

"I've got you," he whispered into her ear.

Scarlett wasn't sure how long they stayed that way,

but he remained silent and let her cry until she had no tears left.

"Oh God, I'm so sorry." She felt mortified and extremely snotty, bringing up the sleeve of her hoody to clean herself up.

Leonard released her, squeezing her arms. He opened a drawer in the dresser beside them, on which she noticed a deep scratch, and pulled out a napkin. Lowering her arms away from her face, he looked at her tentatively, lifting her chin towards him, and gently dabbed her face dry.

She could see the tenderness in his eyes, so similar to his brother's. It was much deeper under the surface than with Edward, but it was still there. She wondered how two boys from the same family could be so different in so many ways yet share so many similarities.

"I'm a mess. I'm sorry. You shouldn't have to be doing this." She tried to turn her face away, but he kept a firm hold of her chin.

"He doesn't deserve you – you should know that." His eyes darkened. "He thinks he can have everything and doesn't care who gets in his way to get it. You deserve better, Scarlett."

She didn't like the turn the conversation was taking. It made her uncomfortable, as did their proximity, and the way his thumb was now brushing near her bottom lip. Anaïse's words echoed somewhere in the back of her mind.

Watch out for him. He's a bit of a fox, in every sense.

"I should really get going. I'm sorry for all this. I'm embarrassed." She tried to smile and move away, but his arm circled around her, and he pulled her closer to him, trapping her against the wall behind her.

Her eyes widened in horror as she felt him stir in his

trousers. She panicked but remained frozen where she stood, unable to speak or move.

"How does he do it, hmm?" His eyes glazed over as if he was looking through her, and Scarlett's stomach contracted with fear. "Lily's mum, Briege, now you ... Let's not even get started on the estate and our father." He stroked the hair away from Scarlett's forehead and kissed her cheek, then moved closer to nuzzle into her neck. He hardened further against her and a single tear fell down her cheek.

"You are exceptionally beautiful, though, Scarlett. I'm not surprised he's been so distracted by you. I'd be lying if I said I haven't caught the odd glimpse of you too, especially when you haven't noticed anyone is looking." He smiled that lopsided cheeky smile, which she'd grown accustomed to in much less intimidating circumstances. But not like this. Never like this.

"What do you—" Scarlett began.

He interrupted her. "You do really need to draw those curtains before you undress." He shrugged as Scarlett's eyes widened in shock. "You can't blame a guy for looking up when he's smoking a cigarette at night."

He winked at her, ignoring the fact Scarlett wasn't seeing the humour in the situation. At all.

"Leonard, I'd like to go now," she whispered, struggling to find her voice.

His eyes darkened again, and his jaw twitched.

"And honestly, Briege isn't a patch on you. Trust me, I know, I've been there. Looks fantastic, but she's bleak and empty inside. But you ... fuck, what I wouldn't do to you." He pushed her legs apart with his knee and pressed his cock against her.

"Leonard, please," she tried to say with more force, but he pressed his greedy mouth against hers. He tasted like cigarettes and alcohol.

He moved his lips to her neck.

"Shhh, now, it's okay. Everyone is busy. No one will come in and I've locked the door. It's okay, I've got you," he whispered into her ear, his hand travelling up her jumper towards her breasts. "Don't fight it. I promise it won't take long, and it'll be good. Just let me have a taste of what he's been getting." He undid his trousers, his fingers hurrying to the opening of her jeans. "I've wanted to do this from the moment I saw you in the woods and then ... up at your window, getting undressed, thinking you weren't seen. God, I'm so fucking horny for you." He groaned as his hand slid towards her most intimate parts.

A surge of rage flooded through her.

No, this isn't happening.

Some vague memory of a long-ago self-defence class came back to her and, using the wall as leverage, she twisted and turned with force, escaping from his hold. Breathless and wild, she held her arms out towards him as a warning. "Leonard, no!"

His eyes were dark and dangerous, and for a moment she worried he might continue – and if so she wouldn't be able to fight him off for long – but a flicker of sense resurfaced, taking hold of him, and he took a deep breath, looking down and straightening his clothes.

"I'm really sorry, Scarlett. I don't know what just happened. I – look, I'm sorry. Please forgive me." He looked back up at her and the sincerity in his eyes seemed genuine, but it was nowhere near enough for Scarlett to feel safe in his presence. A fox was an understatement. The man was a wolf.

Scarlett took a deep breath to steady herself. "I don't know what that was or what gave you the impression I wanted it, but you have got it very, very wrong." She began fixing her own clothes.

"Scarlett, I—"

"Don't ever do that again, do you understand?" Scarlett's voice was still shaky.

He looked like a reprimanded kid, but Scarlett had no sympathy. There were clear boundaries of decency and consent, and he had completely crossed both.

"You talk of Edward taking whatever he pleases, but he has never taken anything not freely given, and I never implied that you could have or take me. What the fuck was that?" Rage was now fuelling the sudden calm descending on her.

Leonard pulled his hand across his face in the exact same way Edward did, but this man was not Edward, and in all his days would not even come close to being the man his brother was. Leonard, she was quickly realising, was a spoilt entitled boy with a chip on his shoulder because he probably knew he could never be like Edward, or even compete, and instead of forging his own way in life, was hell-bent on taking from his brother what would never really be his. She had no plans to be one of those things.

"Scarlett, I'm genuinely sorry. I read the room wrong, okay?" Now it was him who was clearly panicked.

"You didn't read the room at all!" Scarlett could feel her face redden with heat.

How fucking dare he!

"I-I'm sorry," he spluttered, his hand covering his mouth.

"I mean it – don't you ever do that again. Not to me, or anyone else for that matter. What is wrong with you? Not to mention you're about to get married!"

Leonard scoffed at Scarlett's comment. "As if that means anything."

"What does that even mean?" Scarlett shook her head in confusion.

"It's a scam marriage, Scarlett. Smoke and mirrors." He grimaced. "Forget it, okay? But you're right, I've behaved appallingly and have no excuse. I'm not usually such an idiot. I genuinely don't know what came over me. Are you okay?"

"No, Leonard, I am not fucking okay."

"I – fuck, I don't know. I don't have any reasonable excuse for how I just behaved, and I promise it won't happen again, but please know I never intended to hurt you. I understand I crossed the line." He lowered and shook his head.

"You crossed all the fucking lines." Scarlett still felt full of indignant rage, but took another breath to calm herself. "I'm going to leave now, and we will not speak of this again – ever. Understood?"

Leonard nodded.

Scarlett cautiously moved towards the door, where Leonard remained, and, suddenly understanding, he put his hands up and moved away. Turning the lock, Scarlett opened the door, and relief washed over her as she entered the airy hallway.

Not a soul was around and the realisation of what could have just happened dawned on her and she shuddered. She wanted to believe that he would've stopped himself, but she honestly wasn't sure. The thought made her feel sick but empowered at the same time. She wasn't a victim, nor would she ever be. Her body and her life were hers and would not be *taken* by anyone against her will, especially not a sad, desperate manchild like Leonard Cameron-Reid.

CHAPTER 34

EDWARD KNEW HE should be relieved that the day of the wedding was almost upon them and the circus would soon be leaving town. But that also meant *she* would soon be leaving too.

The idea made him feel sick. Rarely a moment passed that Scarlett didn't cross his thoughts – a turn of phrase, a memory of her smile, something he'd see or hear that made him think, *Would Scarlett like that?* Or *Would she find that funny?* Or *What would Scarlett think about this?* On and on it went.

Considering how little time they had spent together, his visceral reaction to the situation, to her, made little sense to him. It made him angry with his past, the world, and himself in particular. So, he did what he did best and leaned into everyone's least favourite characteristic of his: his pig-headed stubbornness.

He'd bat each thought away like a midge, and during the day it was a relatively easy feat as he would be up before five am, filling the hours with various tasks, particularly anything that took him outside. His current favourite pastime was taking a more active interest in forestry and game management.

As a child, he'd always found game hunting barbaric and that hadn't changed as he became an adult. He hadn't allowed any hunts on his land to take place after his father's death. Instead, he tirelessly researched more effective and ethical ways to manage the ecosystem of the estate, and trudging through the woods, he once again mulled over the idea of introducing a couple of lynxes.

Maybe this would be the year to do it. It was a more unorthodox way of doing things, but they were adaptable and able to make their new environment their home without much hassle. They also shied away from humans, could share the estate with other species, and were a good natural predator. He was enthusiastic about the idea, but Andrzej wasn't sure how their neighbours would feel. Edward decided he would have a conversation about it at the next meeting.

Besides, he had enough to get on with. So far, he'd done an inventory to ensure the woodlands were in good health, including checking that they'd planted enough vegetation that year, monitoring water sources, and overlooking the various animal habitats they'd installed over the summer. Andrzej had put up numerous bird and bat boxes and Edward had created more log piles in the past couple of days, too. There was plenty to do to keep him occupied and away from the house.

He was always on hand to carry out duties on the estate and had a detailed overview, but he was visibly more active than usual. However, he avoided any direct contact with Andrzej, who he knew could read his mood well enough and, much like the rest of the household, was giving him a wide berth. Besides, he still wasn't sure what he'd seen in June's apartment.

Was Andrzej having boiler issues, so June invited him over to take a hot shower? Was she treating him to a meal, and he spilled something on himself? Or was there something else going on? He didn't like it – everything was out of sync with his usual rhythm and although he didn't begrudge his staff having personal lives, he expected to be kept in the dark about it. Although wasn't it he who had intruded on them, not

A NEW *Hope* IN THE HIGHLANDS

vice versa? Again, he swatted the thoughts away. They weren't welcome.

He could see through the dense canopy of the trees above him that the sky was darkening; a chill was taking hold of him. He was tiring, yet he didn't particularly look forward to the evening. As was usually the case, when the house fell silent and he tried to sleep, feeling his most vulnerable, particularly when the usual respite of unconsciousness evaded him, thoughts of Scarlett returned, and even when he finally drifted off, there she was, waiting for him in his dreams.

Everything in him ached for her. It was like a whole new level of torture, which left him feeling physically and mentally exhausted. Upon entering the house via the boot room, he strained his ears for any activity. Save for the usual kitchen noises, he didn't hear anyone so quietly made his way towards his rooms.

His shoulders slumped when the library door opened and Anaïse appeared, beaming a smile in his direction.

"Finally, Edward! Please join me for a moment," she said, taking hold of his arm and leading him inside.

He contemplated pulling his arm loose and walking back out, but he was cold and tired, and the warmth of the crackling fire was too much to resist.

"What is it?" he asked, as she signalled for him to take the armchair across from the one she'd been sitting in, judging by the blanket discarded over the arm.

"This port you have is divine – here, I've got a glass ready for you. Sit."

Edward raised his eyebrow, suspicious of what was coming next, but he took the glass and sat down, briefly closing his eyes.

Fuck, he was tired.

"We need to have a little talk, Edward," Anaïse

said as she sat back in her chair, pulling the blanket over her curled-up legs.

"We do?" Edward looked at her steadily.

"Y'all have that steely look running through your family, but it doesn't have any effect on me. You should know that." Anaïse shrugged. "Besides, I've just invited you to sit and have a drink with your future sister-in-law. Nothing to get your back up about."

Edward didn't respond or change his facial expression, making Anaïse roll her eyes.

Always with the theatre, he thought.

"First, I wanted to say thank you. You have been immensely generous and gracious, letting us all invade your home and allowing us to have the wedding here. I don't know you very well. You've kinda made sure of that." She winked to show she was being good-natured, making Edward shrug and nod in concession.

She continued, "But I realise that this hasn't been easy for you to accommodate and I wanted to personally make sure you know how grateful I am – we are – that you've allowed it."

Edward hadn't been expecting this, and his face must have softened, because Anaïse smiled at him, seemingly pleased it had the desired effect. She then sat back, taking a drink from her glass, looking into the fire.

Edward did the same. "The house hasn't had this much life in it for a while. It's good for it to be in use," he finally said.

"None of us fare well alone and abandoned," Anaïse responded.

Edward looked across at her and noticed she was talking to herself more than him, and for the first time since meeting her, he saw past the blonde mass of hair, high-pitched laughter, and obscene demands.

He realised there was a sadness he couldn't quite

put his finger on and a depth of feeling she seemed to keep hidden behind her childlike attitude to everything, and he wondered why she did that.

"No, I don't suppose we do," he replied, moving his attention back to the fire. "You're welcome, by the way, and you know, I'm not quite the miserable old bastard I make myself out to be, or that others might tell you I am."

Anaïse laughed quietly. "You give off that impression quite well all by yourself, Edward."

Edward smiled. "That's fair."

"I don't think that's an accurate depiction of who you *really* are, though, and you hide behind it. Safer that way, I guess. But it must get lonely after a while." She raised an eyebrow at him.

"No different to hiding behind superficial conversations, high-pitched giggles, and copious amounts of alcohol." A smile tugged at the corner of his mouth.

"Oooh, touché." Anaïse laughed. "And he bites."

"And no doubt she stings." It was his turn to raise an eyebrow at her.

"I can, but I don't tend to waste my energy on that anymore. Life is too short." She waved the idea away with her hand.

"So, you're now diverting your energy into marriage instead?" Edward returned his gaze to her, suddenly curious about the woman he was soon to consider family.

Anaïse's smile faded, just a little. "Something like that, yeah."

"Whatever floats your boat, I suppose."

Anaïse looked down into her glass for a moment before brightening up again. "Oh well, it's something to do, I guess."

"Indeed." Edward watched Anaïse's eyes glaze over. That was the honest exchange over, and it was obvious she was relapsing back into the status quo. "Well, if that's all, I need to get showered and changed."

"Will you be joining us for dinner, then?" Anaïse's face lightened.

Edward drained his glass, placed it on the small table between them, and shook his head. "No, I have work to do."

Anaïse nodded slowly. "Very well."

"I'll say goodnight, then." He stood and gave her a curt smile.

"Edward?" Anaïse said as he reached the door.

"Yes?" He looked back and saw her staring at him.

"We don't get many chances at *real* happiness, you know. And I'm a firm believer that we only get presented with a limited number of opportunities to find it in people, maybe once or potentially twice – if we're really lucky."

"Right, okay." Edward furrowed his brow, turning to leave again.

"You'd be a real fool to let yours pass you by," she added.

Edward paused for a moment, his hand hovering over the doorknob.

"Goodnight, Edward," Anaïse said, turning back to look at the fire, which was now crackling angrily.

"Goodnight," he said again, his voice small and barely audible. But Anaïse wasn't listening anymore, her thoughts clearly absorbed by the burning embers in front of her.

Edward walked towards his rooms, slightly dazed with a diminished sense of purpose and determination. Anaïse's words had shifted something inside him. Was that what Scarlett was – his last chance at happiness?

When Lily was born, he'd felt it, but his wedding and subsequent marriage hadn't been a happy one, and although some of his past relationships and trysts had brought him elements of enjoyment in various forms, happiness was not something he'd attributed to any of them.

For a long time, Edward had concluded that happiness was overrated, superfluous, and temporary – there for only brief moments in time. But that way of thinking was beginning to feel a bit like a lie – one he'd been feeding himself over the years to defend his personal choices and protect himself from making poor ones.

This approach kept him inside the carefully constructed bubble he'd created around himself and the estate; he'd handpicked the people inside, like actors in a play, and this was fine, as long as everyone followed the script.

However, Edward saw his players were now improvising – Andrzej and June's situation was a perfect example of this – and that was probably because his script was feeling old and outdated, and he was potentially the last stubborn player in the cast to realise it. Or even worse, he'd had very little control over it all in the first place. He may well see himself as the director of all he surveyed and the people around him, but he wasn't God.

CHAPTER 35

THE NERVOUS ENERGY in Anaïse's bedroom was palpable to the point that Scarlett felt like she was walking through an anxiety-fuelled force field. The usually spacious room felt uncomfortable and warm from all the bodies swarming around Anaïse, who was positioned on a stool close to the floor-to-ceiling mirror leaning against the wall in the far corner. Flashes of white lace and tulle were evidence that she was being pruned and primed to an inch of her existence.

The previous days had passed in a flurry of activity, with decorations, lights, flowers, and people arriving in what felt like droves. As Scarlett paused, taking in the mania in front of her, she took a deep breath to calm her nerves. Everything was perfectly in place; all that was required now was a bride and a groom. Simple.

They were still a few hours away from the ceremony, but Anaïse's mother was adamant that Anaïse should be dressed and ready in plenty of time. The idea of the bride being late had appalled her. Early that morning she'd requested Mrs Wilson gather the staff, including Scarlett, making Mrs Wilson flutter around like a nervous bird as she tried to find everyone, who, because of their varied duties, were scattered all over the house and grounds.

"There will be no delays or theatrics today of any kind, do y'all hear?" Eva Marsden-Beasley, standing tall and formidable in swaths of navy and plum velvet at the top of the staircase, her light blonde hair militantly contained in a complicated baroque-style updo, had addressed her group of subjects like a grand old mistress.

The irony of Eva's opening statement was not lost on Scarlett, who covered her mouth with her hand to hide her smile. Mrs Wilson cast her a reprimanding look.

"None," she'd continued – this time looking at Anaïse, who stood behind her mother, eyes cast downwards with her shoulders slumped. Her usual spark was absent, replaced by an eerie and vacuous version of her former self.

There was something pointedly off about the whole situation, but Anaïse had shared nothing with Scarlett, nor was it expected that she should.

Despite their rather intimate evening together when Scarlett was ill, Scarlett was still staff or *the help*, as she often heard herself being referred to. They weren't friends. It was a professional relationship, and Scarlett understood the clear boundaries – yet she still felt a warmth towards Anaïse and wished she knew what troubled her, even if all she could do was offer some comfort and support.

Now, Scarlett scanned the bodies surrounding Anaïse and relaxed when she saw Eva was not amongst the throng. Miranda wasn't present either, which Scarlett thought strange. It wasn't often that Anaïse's best friend and maid of honour wasn't by her side or somewhere nearby.

"I can't breathe!" Anaïse's voice travelled across to the doorway where Scarlett stood, yet nobody seemed to hear, too occupied with their individual tasks to create the vision that Eva no doubt had put the fear of God into them to produce. "Please ..." Anaïse's voice was small and weak.

Scarlett clapped her hands loudly. "Everyone take

five, please!" Several surprised heads turned to look in her direction, followed by various protests and complaints about time scales and clocks ticking. "Out, all of you. In fact, come back in fifteen minutes."

Despite being surprised at her own assertiveness, Scarlett was pleased the others seemed to buy into it. Although they all appeared reluctant, they put down their curling tongs, combs, and brushes and left the room. Scarlett closed the door firmly behind them and turned the key in the lock in case any of them changed their minds and returned sooner than instructed.

Anaïse's bottom lip quivered, and her eyes filled with tears. "Fuck, my makeup!"

Scarlett rushed over, pulled out a tissue from the box on the dressing table, and handed it to Anaïse.

"Thanks," Anaïse said in a cracked voice. "I just got a little overwhelmed."

Scarlett handed her another tissue, which Anaïse took, looking up at the ceiling and dabbing under her eyes.

"It's all a bit of a mess." Anaïse sniffed.

"Here, let me." Scarlett took another tissue and removed some of the mascara that had smudged next to Anaïse's left eye.

"My mother, if you haven't already noticed, is a real bitch." Anaïse let out a broken laugh.

Scarlett smiled. "She's certainly a force to be reckoned with. I'll say that much."

"This whole match is a farce." Anaïse shook her head, and Scarlett stepped back to give her some space. "This wedding isn't the real deal, Scarlett."

Scarlett frowned, and Leonard's words repeated in her mind.

Smoke and mirrors.

"Leonard and I are a business deal to keep up appearances – it's basically a publicity stunt."

"I don't understand." Scarlett frowned. "What deal?"

"My personal choices were putting the family name at risk, so a deal was struck between Leonard and my father. Have you had the pleasure of meeting him yet?" Anaïse gave herself a small shake and straightened herself.

Scarlett shook her head. The various people who had arrived were a haze of faces and luggage – mostly luggage, really.

"You think my mother is a piece of work? Well, my dad is a real *delight*, let me tell you. Banker and Republican to the core, conservatism runs through his veins. It was bad enough that he never got that son he wanted, but then to have a ... well, that was a real kick in the nuts for him. So, here we all are ..." Anaïse's voice trailed off, and she released a weak laugh.

Several things occurred to Scarlett at that moment: the separate sleeping arrangements, the alcohol-induced hilarity, the hidden sadness, the sudden descent on Haddon House. Not to mention the superficial and forced affection between her and Leonard, and the more subtle and intimate looks and touches between her and Miranda.

Anaïse Marsden-Beasley, an only daughter of a public and conservative ancestral family, was not a heterosexual woman. Something that Leonard Cameron-Reid was ruthlessly capitalising on. Scarlett felt sick.

"I'm so sorry, Anaïse," was all Scarlett could think to say.

Anaïse smiled kindly. "Sweet Scarlett, don't look so devastated for me. It's not ideal, but this is my choice. I'm choosing my lifestyle and money over love and personal preference, that's all." She sniffed, stood, and straightened further, looking at her reflection. "Not bad, huh?"

Scarlett frowned at the sudden shift in attitude, but then nodded. "You look incredible."

"Exactly, and that's what money can buy." Anaïse turned slightly to see the back of her dress. "Today is just another day playing dress-up, smiling sweetly, and tomorrow, life will return to what it's always been. Whatever I want it to be, within reason, of course." She laughed, more heartily this time, and then shrugged. "It's not even like I have to sleep with him all the time, just a couple of times a month to get pregnant, and then the deal is done. So to speak."

Scarlett's jaw dropped, making Anaïse laugh again.

"Don't be so naïve, Scarlett. You think marriage is anything more than a contractual agreement? People in my circle have very little choice in the matter – you think we always get to marry for *love*?" She shook her head for emphasis. "Nope, if it happens, it's over time. Unless you're extremely lucky, which is rare. Look at my parents, living comfortably together but apart. Freedom looks different to everyone."

Scarlett still had no words. It was like watching a Brontë novel play out and she didn't feel well-read or qualified enough to comment, let alone pass judgement; nineteenth-century fiction was more June's bag.

"Anyway, enough of this. Before I let the torture sisters back in, open that wardrobe. I have a present for you."

"For me?" Scarlett was still reeling from Anaïse's confession.

"Yes, for you, now hurry up," Anaïse told her.

Scarlett opened the large oak wardrobe and the dark green dress she had admired when Anaïse first arrived hung inside on its own, the rest of Anaïse's clothes already packed and ready for when she and Leonard left in the morning.

"Mrs Wilson and your mother helped with the

alterations, so it should fit like a glove. It's to say thank you. You've been a good sport and quite frankly I'm not sure this wedding would be to the standard it is if it wasn't for you."

"Oh, God, I can't accept this," Scarlett said, her fingers gently tracing the soft silk material and detailed stitching of the deep neckline. "How did you even know?"

"Don't be stupid. You can, and you will. Especially after all the trouble I've gone to." Anaïse glanced at the dress and then at Scarlett. "A girl can see the spark of love at first sight. I knew as soon as you first saw it lying on my bed, and I wasn't all that keen on it, anyway."

Scarlett knew she was lying. "I'll never have occasion to wear it. It's such a waste."

"How about the wedding you're attending today? Did you think you'd be wearing those old jeans and Converse trainers?" Anaïse raised an eyebrow.

Scarlett laughed. "Obviously not, but I'll only be in the background making sure everything goes okay."

"You will not." Anaïse snorted, walking over and pulling out the dress along with a box from the shelf above the railing. "Here are your shoes, too. You'll be attending as a guest. Now, off you get, everything is done. Go have a bath and get ready. I'll need you here for support later." Anaïse paused and smiled at Scarlett. "You're worth much more than you think, Scarlett. I mean, you are literally named after a Southern hellraiser, for God's sake!" Anaïse turned away from her to check her makeup in the mirror. "Go on now, let them back in before my mother notices and has all our heads."

Anaïse winked at Scarlett in the mirror, who sighed, still feeling reluctant to take the dress and shoes, but she knew she was beaten. So she followed Anaïse's instructions and left the room. The awaiting women and men urgently bustled past her to get back to their jobs, no doubt fearing the wrath of Eva if their efforts weren't up to her high standards.

Scarlett paused outside in the corridor, suddenly feeling overwhelmed by the whole affair. Whatever happened to a quiet life?

This place and its inhabitants were so far removed from her previous existence that she wondered if she would ever readjust to the real world, where normal people like her existed in delicious ignorance of how the other half *really* lived.

Feeling the presence of someone else, Scarlett looked up and noticed Miranda standing against her bedroom doorway. She never smiled at Scarlett or spoke to her – her vacant, almost hostile expression often made Scarlett feel uncomfortable, but she now realised where it came from. It was pain.

Miranda was, after all, the ultimate jilted lover. Scarlett couldn't help but feel sorry for her – playing the part of a lifelong best friend at the wedding must be an emotional torture Scarlett couldn't even imagine – so she smiled and nodded before turning to head back to the stables.

"You take care now," Miranda called to her.

There was a sharpness to Miranda's voice that told Scarlett it wasn't coming from a place of kindness or concern, so without turning she continued walking and called back, "You too."

CHAPTER 36

Edward was almost there. It was almost over. The wedding. The guests. Not to mention the longest family visit known to man. Normality was once again within his grasp and as soon as it was, he would have the house and *her* back to himself, and he could make things right. At least he hoped he could, that it would be enough, and that he wasn't too late.

He'd been a stubborn fool. Even without Anaïse's prompt, he knew Scarlett was his shot at real happiness; he could feel it in his bones and probably would've known sooner if his head didn't constantly get in the way of forming a singular clear thought about it all. Something he could do with ease when it came to other matters, but when it came to her, nothing was clear other than his apparent need for her in every way.

A positive to all this was that his sense of purpose had returned, and although there was little he was looking forward to about the wedding itself, except for maybe the end, his spirits lifted slightly as he adjusted the belt on his kilt and checked his reflection in the mirror.

The Sgian-Dubh, a small ceremonial knife tucked neatly into his sock, and his crisp white shirt and formal jacket, adorned with silver buttons and clan insignia, completed the ensemble. A sense of pride filled his chest.

The outfit was all performance, of course, but it still

echoed generations of his ancestry and the blood that flowed through his veins – something his father had been fiercely proud of and which seeped from every fabric within the house and its surrounding lands, down to each creature and blade of grass across the estate.

Haddon House and the Cameron-Reid lineage were hundreds of years old and, ultimately, ended with them, and it was down to him to ensure its protection and endurance. No matter how little he cared for his younger brother, they shared a bloodline that no amount of animosity could diminish, and if a wedding meant its continuation, he would do whatever was needed for that purpose.

Satisfied with his appearance, Edward left his room to ensure everything was in order. The guests, he knew, were in the excellent hands of his staff, and although there were several external factors involved, he knew Scarlett was managing them well. The only remaining matter to take care of was his brother. He would push their differences aside and put on the act of best man.

Their mother was yet to arrive, having refused to take an earlier flight, so he knew Leonard would be feeling nervous – probably more concerned about how it would appear to others if she didn't make it, but Edward felt obliged to at least try to calm the waters.

Walking towards the main hall, he could hear the distinct English accent his ears had become accustomed to. However, this one belonged to a much older woman, accompanied by a man.

"I don't have an invitation, no, and quite frankly, I don't give a flying hoot if there's a wedding taking place today. I demand to see my daughter-in-law. Right this instant!" The woman's voice boomed through the hall as Mrs Wilson stood there helplessly.

"Mummy, please—" a feeble voice pleaded.

"Jason, I will handle this," *Mummy* instructed.

"Excuse me," Edward interjected, his voice raised but controlled. Panic crumpled Mrs Wilson's face, and sweat had formed on her brow, making her blink more than usual.

"Sir, I'm so sorry, this lady and gentleman …" Mrs Wilson's voice trailed off as Edward gently touched her shoulder.

"Mrs Wilson, I'm sure you have plenty to be getting on with. Thank you." Edward looked towards the kitchen as a sign for her to leave.

He could see her nerves were in tatters as she bustled away and out of sight.

The two uninvited guests were now focused on Edward, whilst he was watching the Englishman in front of him with interest.

"And who are you?" Tara asked, her voice laced with contempt.

"I'm Laird Cameron-Reid and this is my home. Who are you?" Edward asked, though he already knew.

"You're the laird?" Jason almost spat.

A smile twitched at the corner of Edward's mouth. "Were you expecting someone else?"

The woman cleared her throat loudly. "I am looking for Scarlett Shrewsbury, my daughter-in-law."

"There's no one here with the name Shrewsbury," Edward replied, folding his arms across his chest.

The man sighed, clearly finding this game tiresome. "Scarlett Hope – she works here."

Edward didn't respond.

"I'm Jason Shrewsbury. Scarlett is my wife. This is my mother, Tara Shrewsbury." Jason's jaw tightened as he continued to size up Edward.

Edward's eyes narrowed, and he pushed away the urge to clench his fists.

Jason straightened to his full height, still falling short of Edward's, and although his confidence was faltering under Edward's glare, he maintained eye contact. "I would like to see my wife." He swallowed. "Please."

Tara offered no pleasantries. "We are adequately informed that the Hopes are both living here at Haddon House. And I warn you, I will cause unmatched mayhem if I am not directed to where I may find her. I will not—"

"Now then, folks, what do we have here?" The deep Southern drawl of Anaïse's father boomed from the stairwell as the large man approached them. "Some more guests!"

"We're not guests," Tara responded, a little shakily.

Thomas Marsden-Beasley was an impressive man, even though he was well into his seventies. Even taller than Edward, with movie-star looks and a glint in his eye, he was more than a match for anyone, even the likes of Tara Shrewsbury. Edward disliked him immensely.

"They are not guests." Edward repeated Tara's words.

"Come on, now. Today is a great cause for celebration. My daughter is getting married!" Thomas beamed down at Tara, taking her hand and kissing it, making her whimper or giggle – Edward wasn't sure. "And a fine-standing Englishwoman such as yourself is more than welcome to join this happy occasion," he said, holding out his arm. "In fact, please let me show you to the drawing room so I can get you a drink. Edward will arrange whatever or whoever you're looking for. Isn't that right, son?"

Edward bristled at being called *son* but could see what the old man was doing. There would, after all, be no drama at Anaïse Marsden-Beasley-Cameron-Reid's wedding. Edward looked to the ceiling as if pleading with the gods to grant him patience. "Yes, of course."

"Great then, now that's sorted, let's get you that welcome drink. What do you say? And what did you say your name was again?" Thomas beamed another winning smile at Tara.

"Well, I mean – I-I'm Tara Shrewsbury." A violent blush formed on her cheeks.

"Beautiful name. And what part of England is lucky enough to have you call it home?" he asked with genuine interest.

"Bath, actually." Tara tilted her chin with an obvious sense of pride.

"That sounds delightful." Thomas guided her through to the drawing room, where the hubbub of the other guests was spilling into the hallway.

As they disappeared inside, Edward could still hear Thomas talking.

"Now then, ma'am, let's get you comfortable and you can tell me all about you and your beautiful country, and I can tell you all about mine."

Edward refocused on Jason, who had beads of sweat forming at his temples. Edward conceded he was a good-looking man; a bit twee and professor-like, and much older than Scarlett, even older than him, which instantly reminded him of her ex-husband's inclination towards much younger women.

Jason cleared his throat. "Are you aware you're openly snarling at me?"

Edward remained silent for a long moment. He wanted to do far more than snarl at the man standing before him – for all the hurt he'd caused Scarlett, for making it so hard for her to trust someone new, and especially for having the gall to come here and refer to her as his *wife*. But Edward kept his face void of emotion and simply shrugged. "I wasn't aware, no, but that's probably because I don't like you."

"Right, well, now that we have the pleasantries over and done with, could you please point me in the direction of my wife?" Jason's eyes widened in question.

Edward didn't move. "She doesn't stay in the main house, and to be honest, I'm not comfortable with you traipsing around my property." He signalled with his head towards the drawing room. "You can join your mother and the other guests through there. I'll let Ms Hope know you're here."

"She's still married, you know. It's *still* Shrewsbury," Jason grumbled.

Edward ignored him and walked away.

She's no Shrewsbury. Not anymore.

Reaching the back of the house, he opened the door and took a deep breath of fresh air to calm his nerves and temper. He saw people busily preparing the marquee to his right; generators were now in place, and the toilets, which looked more like a spa retreat, were installed around the back.

He noted the covered pathway was now lined with flowers and fairy lights, which had been weaved into perfectly pruned hedges to light the way once it got dark. But, expensive tents and toilet facilities aside, he conceded that the lawn, marquee, and the entire house looked incredible. In the short timeframe given, Scarlett had done an impressive job.

The sound system was being tested and he could hear music playing, which was when he saw her – her auburn curls piled on top of her head, with unruly strands escaping down her neck and back. She wore a low-cut green dress that hugged and accentuated every curve as she walked into the marquee.

Edward had no idea what he was going to say to her, but she was like a magnet he couldn't resist as he followed in her direction. However, he paused as he entered the vast twinkling space where she stood in the centre of the dance floor, directing one of the young workers to adjust some tables and chairs to her left.

He knew he could have called out to her, but he quietly approached her instead. The eyes of the workers alerted her to his presence, and as she turned, she came into direct contact with his chest. He placed his hands on her waist to steady her.

"Edward," she said, in almost a whisper.

He hadn't been this close to her in weeks, and the feeling of silk against her skin made it hard for him to focus.

"Hi," he finally managed.

She was searching his eyes for some understanding, but her frown told him she found none.

Fuck's sake. Why is this so bloody hard!

"Is everything okay?" she asked him. He didn't want to let go of her, and she wasn't moving away either.

"Excuse me," someone called from the side of the stage. "Would you mind staying there for a moment so I can adjust the lighting for the first dance?"

"Sure," Edward responded, taking hold of Scarlett's left hand and pulling her closer to him.

"So now we're dancing?" Her eyes sparkled with mischief.

"Aye." Edward nodded. "We're dancing."

Scarlett appeared to be doing her best to stay serious, but she couldn't stop the smile from forming and placed her forehead on his chest in an attempt to hide it. Dancing certainly hadn't been part of his plan, but it was doing a better job than his words could at that point.

She finally looked up at him as they were slowly moving to the music. "What is happening right now?"

"Isn't it obvious?" He shrugged.

God, she feels so fucking good.

"No?" She narrowed her eyes at him, and he had to fight off the urge to kiss her. To block out the last few weeks and especially block out her arse of an ex waiting for her at the house.

Still, he couldn't bring himself to speak the words to break the magic of the moment. "I don't actually know what we're dancing to. Who is this?"

"Lusaint," Scarlett offered.

Tell her. You need to tell her that her ex-husband and his wretched mother are basically wedding crashers, with the latter currently fawning all over the father of the bride.

Instead, he said, "I recognise the lyrics."

"It's a cover," she told him, blissfully unaware that her world was going to be disrupted on a day she'd been militantly working towards for weeks.

"Of what?" he asked.

For fuck's sake, man. Tell her!

"En Vogue," Scarlett replied, now eyeing him suspiciously, knowing damn well this wasn't his kind of music. "'More Than Friends.'"

Damn her and her uncanny ability to see straight through me.

Still, he didn't tell her. Instead, he said, "I see. Think I prefer this one."

She nodded. "Me too."

They continued to dance, both now listening to the lyrics, which seemed to be written personally for them.

He held her closer and breathed in the scent of her hair, making his insides ache. He needed to make this work; the idea of her leaving Haddon was not something he could accept. She needed to stay. She belonged here, with him, and he'd do whatever he could to convince her of that fact. There was no alternative as

A NEW Hope IN THE HIGHLANDS

far as he was concerned.

The song finished sooner than he wanted, and they slowed to a stop, looking at each other.

Now.

He had to tell her now.

"Scarlett, I—" he began before he was cut off.

"You found her then?" Jason's voice went through Edward like nails on a chalkboard, and he felt Scarlett stiffen in his arms. "Glad to see there was some urgency."

Edward noticed Scarlett's breathing becoming uneven as she looked searchingly up at him, confused and hurt.

"I was going to tell you he was here, and then—"

"The music must've made you forget, clearly," Jason interjected, approaching them.

Scarlett still didn't speak, but she moved out of Edward's hold.

"Scarlett—" Edward began.

"What are you doing here?" She was looking at Jason, the little vein at her temple becoming dark and angry.

"I told you I was coming to see you." Jason made to move closer but thought better of it.

She was trembling. "Not today, you didn't. I told you not for another week or so after Christmas!"

"You told him to come here?" Edward snapped.

"Yes, to bring my things and so we could sort the divorce. I asked him to send everything, but he refused, and he wants that stupid ring." Scarlett's cheeks flushed with anger.

"What ring?" Edward knew exactly *what* ring.

"My mother's ring. It's a family heirloom." Jason straightened his shoulders and raised his chin in the air. "It's very expensive."

"We could have sent it by courier." Edward moved

closer to Scarlett, who moved even further away from him.

Jason raised his eyebrow. "We?"

"Shut up, Jason." Scarlett closed her eyes and rubbed at her temples.

"There's no need to speak to me like that, Scarlett. I've come to talk," Jason told her, matter-of-fact.

"About the ring?" Edward asked.

Jason scowled at Edward before focusing his attention back on Scarlett. "Look, I want to talk to you before my mother comes looking for me and without *him*."

"You brought your fucking mother?" Scarlett spat at him.

"She was quite persistent, actually." Jason's voice was small.

"Holy mother of fuck, Jason, I think you've just reached an epic level of ... I don't even know!" Scarlett's voice crept up an octave.

Edward's stomach clenched when he heard a shrill voice. "Jason, darling! There you are! Oh, there she is as well ... Scarlett."

"Is she drunk?" Scarlett's eyes widened at the sight of her mother-in-law approaching them, still accompanied by Thomas.

Edward no longer knew what to do, but despite Scarlett already being visibly pissed at him, he wasn't leaving her alone with this lot.

"Have you told her yet?" Tara called across the room.

"Told me what?" Scarlett snapped her head towards Jason.

Jason groaned. "I didn't want this to go this way."

"What were you expecting, a fucking welcome party?" Edward asked, sarcasm dripping from every word.

"Angelica, the baby ..." Jason looked like he was about to cry. "He's not mine."

The room was suddenly silent. Thomas was looking around at the stunned faces surrounding him with absolutely no idea what was going on. Edward almost felt sorry for him. Finally, the silence broke with Scarlett's laughter, which continued uncontrollably to the point Edward worried she was verging on hysteria.

"There she goes." Tara rolled her eyes. "Can't manage a shred of decorum, even in the most inappropriate moments."

Scarlett was still laughing, but tears were now falling down her cheeks.

"Scarlett, are you okay?" Edward tried to touch her arm.

"No!" She suddenly stopped laughing and snatched her arm away. "So, what, you thought you'd come here and try to get me to come home with you ... and your mother?"

Jason cast his eyes down and shrugged. "That was the plan, yes."

Scarlett raised her hands to her head. "You are all absolutely fucking crazy!"

Tara gasped at Scarlett's outburst, to which Thomas patted her hand in a show of comfort.

"Scarlett, mouth, really." Jason gave her a reprimanding look, which Edward wanted to punch from his face.

"Ohhhhh, wonderful, and here comes the mother. Honestly, it's turning into an episode of *Eastenders* at this point." Tara rolled her eyes again.

"What on earth is going on?" June walked into the marquee, with Andrzej following close behind her.

Edward noted how remarkably well they both cleaned up, but quickly returned his focus to Scarlett, who he was convinced was about to blow up, and he wasn't sure everyone was leaving the tent unscathed. Even the workers had stopped what they were doing as the drama continued to amplify and more people entered the ring.

"A wedding! That is what's going on." Scarlett's voice was even and controlled. "There is a wedding taking place in about an hour, actually. Currently, about fifty guests are milling around in the drawing room and hall for drinks before they make their way to their seats in the orangery. The bride is expecting me, so that's where I am now going. You should leave." She looked at Jason. "With your mother."

"Now, let's not be rash. I'm sure this can all be settled amicably." Thomas was still comforting Tara. "You're my guests, please, come with me. Let the young ones settle their differences. Shall we?"

Tara looked at Scarlett with disdain. "Very well, Thomas, thank you. You've been so kind, and it was such a long drive. I mean, we stopped over, but still."

"I can only imagine," Thomas said, leading her away.

"As you wish," Scarlett replied, shaking her head, and then shrugged. "I've got places to be."

"Scarlett?" Edward tried again to reach out for her, but she evaded him.

"Not now, Edward." Scarlett shook her head again, not looking at him, and in an instant, she was gone. June and Andrzej quickly followed her, leaving him standing alone with Jason.

Fuck.

CHAPTER 37

"SCARLETT?" JUNE CALLED after her. "Are you okay?"

Scarlett didn't stop her march back to the main house. "I'm fine. I'll see you later."

It was clear she was far from *fine*.

A million thoughts were racing through her mind, none particularly cohesive, but there was little point in trying to make sense of them now. She had a job to complete, and neither the Shrewsburys nor Edward would distract her from it. The wedding was the priority, and time was no longer on her side.

Walking in through the French doors of the main hall, she was pleased to see that the guests were oblivious to the events happening in the background, milling around in small groups, making pleasant conversation, and sipping their bellinis. Skirting around the outskirts of the room, she thought she was safe when a very well-groomed woman stepped into her path, looking down at her.

"Excuse me, dear." Scarlett couldn't place the accent – potentially Scottish, but she couldn't be sure.

"Yes?" Scarlett smiled politely.

"Could you be a sweetheart and let the laird know Evelyn has arrived and is waiting for him. In fact, even better, could you point me in his general direction?"

Scarlett looked the woman up and down and realised she was almost a carbon copy, if not a bit older, of Briege, immediately making her blood boil.

He clearly has a type!

Deciding violence wasn't the answer, Scarlett leaned closer to Evelyn and lowered her voice so only she could hear. "I've just told him to go to hell, so maybe go look for him there."

Evelyn moved away as if an electric shock had jolted her, her mouth gaping open at Scarlett's comment.

Scarlett smiled again, nodding politely, and made a beeline for the stairwell, heading straight up to Anaïse's room.

The horde of makeup and hair artists, their assistants, and all the paraphernalia that went with them were nowhere to be seen. Anaïse stood in the centre of the room and looked exquisite. Even Eva, who was inspecting the stunning off-white Vera Wang gown, looked on with appreciation.

Scarlett spotted Miranda sitting in the chair in the corner, with the usual expression of contempt on her face, but Scarlett, and seemingly everyone else in the room, chose to ignore it.

"Scarlett, there you are!" Anaïse's face brightened. "I was beginning to think you weren't going to show. The dress looks incredible on you!"

"Thanks, and apologies, some last-minute hiccups." Scarlett saw Eva raise an eyebrow, so quickly added, "Nothing to worry about though."

"Are the guests all arrived and looked after?" Eva asked, moving to the mirror to check her own makeup and hair. The old woman was clearly itching to go downstairs, but something told Scarlett she was worried her daughter was a flight risk and would stay to physically force her down the aisle if needed.

"Yes, except Lady Cameron-Reid. I checked and her flight landed on time, so I expect she should be here any minute now."

Eva pursed her lips. "I can't abide a lack of punctuality."

And don't we all know it!

"Can I get anybody anything in the meantime?" Scarlett plastered on her best winning smile.

"We're all fine, Scarlett, thank you." Anaïse sighed. "I'll be glad when it's all over."

"That is not the attitude, Anaïse." Eva narrowed her eyes at her daughter. "You will remember who you are here to represent today – you will carry yourself in the right manner and frame of mind, you hear me?"

"Yes, ma'am," Anaïse responded, quickly dipping her head, possibly to hide the depth of resentment in her eyes.

"Hurry along, Scarlett. Do whatever is necessary to make sure the *great* Lady Cameron-Reid has everything she needs when she arrives. I want no more delays." Eva waved her hand to dismiss Scarlett.

"Of course, just call if you need anything, and good luck – not that you'll need it." Scarlett smiled at Anaïse, who smiled warmly in return.

"Run along then," Eva snipped.

Scarlett nodded and left the room.

These people, honestly.

Lady Cameron-Reid's rooms were ready for her arrival. A small team waited to help her with hair, makeup, and everything else; everyone was prepared and knew they had less than half an hour to work their magic once she arrived.

To keep herself busy, Scarlett went to the orangery to check the harpist was hydrated and not becoming overly restless because of the delay. Upon entering the room, she stopped, surprised to see Edward and Leonard already there.

Michael, the monk, was sitting cross-legged at the altar in meditation, no doubt readying himself to do the service.

"Hello." She offered them a thin smile. "Just checking in on everything."

"Thorough as always." Leonard beamed at her.

She hadn't been alone in the same room as him since the *incident*, and she was grateful that Edward was there now, even though she was still massively pissed off with him. She felt safer with him there.

Scarlett noted Leonard had returned to his earlier smarmy self as he held her gaze, his lopsided smile playing on his lips.

"Needed to see Faye has everything she needs," Scarlett said, looking over at the harpist, who appeared uninterested and bored.

Faye was to play just before the guests were guided through, but seeing it was only Scarlett, the young harpist went back to scrolling on her phone.

Scarlett didn't want to stand making awkward conversation with the two brothers and turned to leave the room again.

"I'm surprised you took it so well, brother," she heard Leonard say, making her stop at the doorway. The tone in Leonard's voice told her he was up to no good, and she was right.

Why can't he leave well enough alone?

"Took what well?" Edward's tone was clipped, tiring of his brother and his obvious games.

Scarlett looked over her shoulder to see Leonard's smug smile as he slowly looked her up and down. She glanced across to Edward, whose jaw was twitching.

Please God, no. Don't do this.

"She obviously told you." Leonard rolled his eyes.

"Told me what?" Edward's voice was calm to the point of being terrifying.

Something in Leonard shifted then. Had he realised his error? Was it nervousness?

Scarlett felt nauseous.

"Leonard, don't be an arse," she said, her voice shaky.

"Tell me what?" Edward turned to face his brother full on.

"You didn't tell him?" She saw Leonard swallow, a mixture of emotions washing across his face. "I genuinely thought you would have?"

Scarlett shook her head slowly, unable to form words as she saw a flash of panic in Leonard's eyes.

"It was a misunderstanding of sorts, that's all." Leonard shrugged, looking down at Edward's fists, which Scarlett also noticed were now clenched. "She was upset, I consoled her, and then one thing led to another—"

"Scarlett, there you are. I've been looking for you. What …" June's voice trailed off as she took in the scene. "Is everything alright?"

Words still escaped Scarlett, but June read the room fairly quickly.

"Boys?" June spoke calmly.

Edward ignored her.

"What did you do?" His words were slow and laced with icy rage.

Leonard stepped back, but Edward grabbed the lapel of his jacket, making Scarlett, June, and the harpist gasp in unison.

"Edward." Scarlett found her voice. "Don't!"

"Someone better tell me what the fuck happened, or this will not end well!" Edward's nostrils flared, his forehead almost touching Leonard's.

The three women froze, afraid to act or speak and make things worse.

A voice from behind them startled Scarlett.

"Jeez." Miranda half laughed. "Y'all like keeping it in the family, huh?"

Scarlett could smell alcohol on Miranda, who gave

Scarlett a side-eye before concentrating on the two men.

"What are you talking about?" Edward growled.

"I mean, I honestly can't see what all the fuss is about." Miranda looked Scarlett up and down. "But you're all getting a little heated about her, and the whole thing is a bit *ick*, don't you think?" She looked at Leonard. "Especially as *you're* already aware it's a possibility. But you should both really know that sleeping with your half-sister, I mean, isn't that illegal or something?"

Edward loosened his grip on Leonard, who pushed Edward away.

"Miranda, shut the fuck up," Leonard told her sharply.

Scarlett noticed the harpist was watching the scene with interest as Miranda's words slowly sank into her conscience. She looked across at her mother, who was slowly shaking her head.

Miranda leaned against the doorway, enjoying the catastrophic bombshell she'd so carelessly dropped. Scarlett stepped further into the room, away from Miranda's stench. The woman's eyelids were heavy as she swayed slightly.

Leonard tried to move too, but Edward was too quick for him to react. He grabbed his younger brother by the throat and pushed him hard against the wall.

"Talk," Edward said, the words barely audible through his anger. "Fast."

"She found letters – Ed, I can't actually breathe." Leonard tried to pull Edward's hands off his throat, but Edward was too strong. Too angry.

"Talk," he said again.

"She found some letters between Dad and June. They've known each other for years – before Scarlett – and were still seeing each other a couple of years after you were born."

"Edward!" another voice from the doorway called out. "Put your brother down. Now."

Edward looked across the room, and his face lost some of its fierceness.

"Now, I said." A woman in her early seventies paused beside Scarlett and her mother. "June," the woman said in acknowledgement as she walked past. Scarlett looked at her mother for answers, but June looked away.

"Mother, I—" Leonard began speaking, but she raised her hand to quiet him.

She approached Edward and kissed him on the cheek, using both her hands to unclench his fists. Edward reluctantly relaxed a little. She walked across to where Leonard stood and straightened his shirt and jacket before kissing him.

"You know." She looked over at the three women before continuing. "They've always been like this. Squabbling and fighting over toys, bikes, girls. It never stops. It's exhausting." She looked at the two men again before settling her gaze on Scarlett. "So, this is Scarlett, I take it?"

Lady Cameron-Reid assessed Scarlett, not unkindly. "I see what all the fuss is about, but Leonard, it's your wedding day, for Christ's sake."

"This isn't my fault." Leonard's voice was almost childlike. "It was ages ago that I kissed her and—"

"I will end you!" Edward made to move towards Leonard, but their mother stepped between them and raised her hand.

He didn't push past her.

"Your sister! You kissed your sister? Does this not bother anyone else here?" Miranda piped up again.

"Whose sister, now?" Thomas Marsden-Beasley walked into the room with Tara close behind him. "Ah, Verity, you've made it! Thank God for that. Eva is just about ready to have kittens." He chuckled loudly. "So, what's happening here. What's all the commotion? Guests are getting restless. Young lady over there with the instrument. How about you play some tunes? Settle these folk down a little. Now, what's this about someone's sister?"

The harpist looked at Scarlett, puzzled by the events in the room. Scarlett nodded at her to go ahead, feeling numb.

Nothing felt real anymore.

But she looked around the room, which she realised was perfect. The sun had now set outside and the lights of the marquee and the pathway up to it twinkled invitingly. It all looked like something from a glitzy wedding magazine. The flowers and subtle lighting from the chunky candles and lanterns provided a gorgeous atmosphere, and with music from the harp now filling the room, Scarlett saw she had done her job well.

As the voices in the room all meshed into inaudible tones, she came to the sudden realisation that her services were no longer needed and she was, in fact, free to leave. She didn't want to know what Miranda was referring to, but whatever it was she must be wrong, or confused, or misinformed – there was no way on this earth her mother would have allowed her to continue with Edward if, if – *Oh, God, what if it's true?*

It couldn't be. It mustn't be.

But Scarlett had no intention of hanging around to find out. She needed air. Needed to leave. Had to get as far away as possible from all these people. It was all too much. She couldn't breathe.

CHAPTER 38

"THAT IS ENOUGH!" Edward's mother silenced the mania in the room. "June, dear, won't you enlighten the curious people in this room regarding the parentage of your daughter?"

All eyes fell on June, who clenched and unclenched her fists, evidently uncomfortable with the attention.

"Well, I – I'm not sure I'm best placed ..." June's voice trailed off.

"It's okay." Andrzej appeared beside her – from where Edward wasn't sure, but he was struggling to keep up with all the fresh faces entering the room. "We can go if you wish?" Andrzej's voice was kind and gentle.

June shook her head. "No, it's fine. It's important people know."

"If you are sure?" Andrzej squeezed her hand and Edward no longer felt resentful about their situation, whatever it was. But he needed to hear the truth.

All of it.

"Scarlett isn't related to either of you boys," June finally said, and Edward exhaled loudly. The relief was immense, and his mother reached over and squeezed his hand.

"Pull the other one, lady. I read the letters!" Miranda waggled her finger at June.

"You may well have read the letters, *young lady*, but I can assure you, neither Laird Cameron-Reid, nor his younger brother, Murray, was Scarlett's father."

"What does Uncle Murray have to do with it?" Leonard asked.

Edward saw his mother and June exchange a look, which he couldn't place.

June continued, "The Cameron-Reids used to visit Bournemouth once a year. They had a house belonging to a distant relative, and your grandmother," she said, looking at Edward, "enjoyed staying there in the summer. I met George and Murray when we were very young. My grandfather used to look after the gardens and grounds, and we used to play together as kids." June paused for breath, grappling for the right words. "During the last couple of summers that Murray visited, your father, George, was already married and had you, Edward. I'd always liked Murray. Truth be told, I'd been in love with him for years." Edward watched as Andrzej circled his arm around June's waist for support. "That last summer, I was sixteen, he was seventeen, it was only us two, and we became lovers. He promised me the world." She laughed and looked at the ceiling. "Needless to say, he went back home to Scotland, and I never heard from him again."

"Sounds like Murray, alright." Verity's voice was laced with contempt, which Edward found strange but dismissed it, still eager to hear the end of June's story.

June tucked a strand of hair behind her ear, just like Scarlett often did. It prompted him to look around for her but he couldn't see her. But he stayed put, needing to hear what June had to say.

"Anyway, I was heartbroken, and later on that winter, there was a lad I knew from school who took pity on me, and we spent a bit of time together. When he found out I was pregnant with Scarlett and he was the father, he couldn't handle it and disappeared. George, bless his heart, tracked him down a few years later. He'd moved to Manchester and started another family, but he'd died in a horrible car crash. He used to race cars, you see. Anyway, he left a widow and two young children behind. All very sad. And such a waste."

"That doesn't explain the letters?" Leonard didn't sound convinced.

June looked across at Edward's mother and the women shared a moment that no one else in the room could interpret.

"This doesn't make any sense," Miranda piped up again.

"Who is this girl that has so much to say?" Verity asked Edward.

"Nobody important." Edward shook his head. "But why were you writing to each other?" Edward looked across at June.

"Your father came down to sell the house after your grandmother passed. He had no use for it. It was sheer chance we bumped into each other. I'd just been offered a job and was about to move us to Bath. Scarlett was still very little, and George jumped to the same conclusion as some of you – that Murray was her father. He sprang into hero mode because of Murray's history of ... Well, that's not my place to talk about. Of course, I put him straight and refused any financial help, but we stayed in touch and became pen pals – friends, really. He used to write about his troubles, and then, after your Uncle Murray's death, we supported each other. But friendship was all it ever was." June looked at Verity, who cast her eyes down to the floor. "He then offered me a job and a home, should I ever need it, and when a time came that I did, he kept his promise."

"Piece of work that Murray was, the old bugger." Leonard chuckled, the only one who found any of this remotely funny. "He was always a bit of a player but a good sport."

Edward noticed his mother look across at Leonard with a pained expression.

"Ohhhh, this all makes sense now!" Miranda clapped her hands, walking further into the room. Thomas took hold of her as she stumbled.

"Good grief, child," he muttered under his breath. "When will you ever learn?"

"Hush, me and you ain't friends." Miranda pulled away from him. "Leonard, baby, the joke is on you!"

Everyone looked on, confused. Everyone except June and Verity – who frowned, concern etched across both faces.

"There was a passage that I didn't get. I get it now!" Miranda was still swaying, although evidently enjoying herself. "What was it now? It was addressed to *her*." Miranda pointed at June. "Although he obviously didn't send it. What was it … '*He did it once. You can't blame me for thinking he did it again. Leaving others to pick up the pieces to look after his lovechild. I know better than anyone.*' Or something like that and then he—"

"Missy, you watch what you say now. Some things cannot be unsaid." Verity's face was rigid and stern.

"I know you, ma'am – I know what you've done." Miranda straightened herself and addressed Leonard. "The question we should all have *really* been asking is, Lennie, who was your daddy?"

At that moment, even with the harpist playing a beautiful rendition of Bach's *Wachet Auf*, you still could have heard a pin drop.

Verity's shoulders slumped, and June watched the scene unfold with sympathetic eyes. Leonard initially looked confused, but Edward saw realisation dawn in his eyes as they both reached the same conclusion.

This was why George Cameron-Reid had left none

of the estate to his youngest son and why only if there should be no heirs from Edward would Leonard come into ownership.

It was the part of the will that had confused Edward, and the only explanation he came up with was that Leonard had settled in America and was enjoying their mother's fortune.

Leonard had never shown any interest in Haddon House other than to sell it to rich investors. But it ran so much deeper than that. The deception and humiliation his father must have shouldered, and yet he had still taken responsibility for Leonard. That both sons looked so much like his younger brother must have been a daily torment.

Edward now understood why his father was so distant and reticent, and why their mother had returned to live in the States, away from her husband and sons. That was, of course, until Leonard moved there himself. But the rift between their parents must have been too wide to repair.

"Well." An English voice spoke up. "To think I thought I was the one with all the problems. I only came to collect my ring and daughter-in-law." Tara shook her head.

"I can only apologise for this somewhat embarrassing scene, Mrs Shrewsbury." Thomas patted her hand, which still rested on his arm. "I believe we need to pull things back into some kind of order here. There is still a wedding to take place." Thomas looked at Verity for support.

"Yes," Verity responded, straightening herself. "Boys, this will keep until later. You both pull yourselves together, you hear?" She looked at Leonard, whose jaw was tight.

He raised his eyes from the floor to look at their mother with visible contempt and then scanned the rest of the room, his gaze settling on Thomas.

Most likely the idea of his future, particularly the financial aspect of it, brought him back to himself and he plastered a reassuring smile on his face.

"Indeed, let the wedding farce commence," he finally said.

"Now then, son." Thomas gave him a warning look and Miranda snorted with laughter.

"Miranda, that's enough." Leonard gave her a steely look. "Let's not pretend anymore, though. Yes, there will be a wedding. There will be a child or children until there is a son. We'll all be rich beyond our wildest dreams. And then, no doubt, Anaïse will carry out the rest of her days with her lesbian lover."

Everyone's jaw dropped.

Leonard continued to look at Miranda and then returned his gaze to Thomas. "But at least there will never be a question of who the father is. Now, if you'll excuse me, I'll freshen up for the big event." Leonard straightened and walked down the aisle and out of the room, leaving the others to process his words.

Edward scanned the almost comical scene in front of him. The harpist was still playing on, whilst his mother collected herself and, with a stiff nod, left the room to get ready. Tara was now comforting a seated Thomas, with Miranda hunched over in the row across from them, nursing her head. Andrzej placed an arm around June's shoulder, leading her out of the room too, but Scarlett, the only face he actually wanted to see, was nowhere to be found.

CHAPTER 39

Scarlett's eyes filled with unwelcome tears, which she rubbed away angrily with the palms of her hands between pulling out the little clothing she had from her drawers and cupboards.

Unlike Anaïse, she didn't own an array of colour-coded Gucci suitcases, so instead she stomped into the kitchen and grabbed a roll of black bin bags out from under the sink. Not exactly classy, but they would do the trick.

The sight of two mugs beside the sink, probably from earlier this morning before June and Andrzej left the apartment for the day, made her pause. He was here most nights now to the point it was weird when he wasn't, but the sight of the used mugs created an uncomfortable swelling of emotion in her chest, ambushing her with a whole new onslaught of tears.

She didn't want to go. For all her musings and determined planning to do so after the wedding, the very idea of leaving the flat, her mother, Andrzej, Mrs Wilson, the house, and its grounds ... *Edward* ... all made her struggle to catch her breath.

This is my home.

Scarlett leaned over the sink, unsure if she was going to sob, faint, or puke. The effort to stay upright was overwhelming. She couldn't understand how emotions could physically hurt like this, and she'd felt plenty of pain and disappointment before. This was a whole new level.

She considered she might be having a panic attack, but as she steadied her breathing, she gathered her thoughts and realised it was just the result of her heart shattering into a thousand tiny pieces.

It sounded ridiculous when she'd read about it in the past, but she began to genuinely believe that people could actually die of heartbreak because she couldn't conceive the idea that she would ever get over leaving this place.

But she had to. She couldn't stay, not anymore.

With a new sense of purpose, she returned to her bedroom, tearing a bag from the roll and haphazardly pushing in socks, knickers, and second-hand jumpers. Part of her wished she'd never tracked her mother down, never found Haddon House, and never laid eyes on either of the Cameron-Reid brothers, especially not Edward!

She would've got over Jason and built a life again, blissfully unaware that a place and life like this ever existed. But she *had* met them and, despite all her good intentions, had fallen madly and deeply in love with Haddon House and all its quirky and loveable inhabitants, not least their insufferable laird and master.

And now she would have to go through the rest of her life knowing what she was missing, which was so much worse than never having experienced it in the first place.

"Fuuuucck!" she cried out and threw the clothes in her hands against the wall, slumping down to her knees, and sobbing into the bed. It was all so horribly unfair – all of it.

The clearing of a throat made her turn with a start.

"I did knock, but the door was open so I …" Edward's voice trailed off as he took in the sight of Scarlett and the chaos surrounding her.

Scarlett groaned, covering her face with her hands,

mortified, knowing full well that her hair was wild, mascara was likely running down her face, she was surrounded by clothes and half-empty bin bags, and, worst of all, she was snotty.

"Scarlett, what's happening here?" he asked, shaking his head.

"I'm leaving!" she cried into her hands, despite now not feeling capable of doing anything, let alone packing her things and driving a car.

"No, you're not," he said simply.

"I am!" She half snorted and sobbed simultaneously. "This is not cool; we can't be related—"

Edward huffed a nervous laugh. "We're not."

"And everything is a mess—" she continued, not hearing him.

"It's really not. Except for your room. This is most definitely a mess."

"The wedding is ruined, and we've ruined everyone's lives and—"

He sighed loudly. "We really don't have that much power and influence, Scarlett. Nothing is stopping those two from getting hitched today, least of all us or a drunk maid of honour, trust me."

"Really?" She finally dared to meet his eyes.

Edward nodded and approached Scarlett, crouching down and pulling her up to standing. He smoothed her hair back from her face and wiped the tears from her cheeks with his thumbs, then pulled out the handkerchief from his jacket pocket to clean her nose.

Just great.

"Everything is going perfectly to plan down there. Trust me." He moved his thumbs near her eyes and gently wiped away the tears there too – or maybe it was her smudged mascara, she wasn't sure.

An involuntary sob escaped before she asked, "And you're really not my brother or cousin or nephew, or anything equally weird and disgusting?"

"No, I can happily confirm we are not in a live reenactment of *Game of Thrones*." He kissed her forehead.

"I've never actually watched that," she said, another faint echo of a sob escaping from her chest.

"We can do that – together. It's been a while, and it's probably one of my all-time favourite books and series." Edward smiled at her, continuing to gently stroke the dampness from her face.

"I didn't know that." She shrugged.

"There's a lot you don't know." Edward kissed both her cheeks.

The tears finally stopped. "Like what?"

Edward paused for a moment. "I don't like cornflakes, especially not with fruit, not even banana. And if I need to eat cornflakes, they have to be coated in sugar."

"Why not just have Frosties?"

He let out a soft laugh. "I don't like those either."

"Neither do I," Scarlett said, her breathing finally returning to normal.

"I'm sorry I didn't tell you about Jason being here. We were having a moment – I didn't want to ruin it or stop. It was so long since I'd had you near me and—"

"It's okay, I get it. It *was* a good moment to be fair." Scarlett looked up at him. "You should've told me though."

"I'm sorry."

"I know."

"I can't let you go. I won't, especially not with him." Edward tensed, and his face was suddenly serious.

Scarlett couldn't help but laugh. "Edward, I have no intention of going back there, you must know that?"

His frown and pained expression told her he didn't.

"Where were you going then?" He looked around at the devastation surrounding her.

Scarlett was finding it hard to concentrate with his deep blue eyes drilling into hers for answers.

"To my car." She realised how ridiculous she sounded. "Genuinely had no master plan other than that."

Edward's face relaxed. "So, you weren't planning on going back to him?"

Scarlett made a face, making Edward smile. "You've met the delightful duo. You really think I'd do that to myself?"

"No." He took a deep breath in and out before continuing, "I don't suppose you would."

"What did you mean?" she asked after a brief pause.

"What?"

"When you said you won't let me go?" Pushing, always pushing. When would she learn?

"You know what I mean." Edward's trademark awkwardness was returning as his eyes started darting around the room, but she wasn't letting him get away with it. Not this time.

"Tell me." Scarlett made to pull away, but he kept hold of her.

"You're really going to make me say it?" He groaned at being forced to say the words.

But she needed to hear them. Words held power, especially to her.

Scarlett nodded. "Yes, abso-fucking-lutely."

"I'll never tell you to watch your mouth again, just so you know." He gave her a lopsided smile.

"Don't change the subject!" Scarlett *needed* him to say it.

"Aarrgghh." Edward raised his eyes to the ceiling before looking back down at Scarlett. "I don't function properly when you're not with me. Literally, nothing makes any sense. When I'm not with you, I want to be and if I can't be, you're in every waking fucking thought. I need you."

"You need me? For what, sex?" She couldn't help herself.

He rolled his eyes at her. "No, I mean, aye, that's part of it. But it's more than that, a lot more."

"Like what, Edward?"

"Really?"

"Yes, really."

"I love you, okay? I've tried not to, but I do. It's impossible not to. Have you met you?"

Scarlett's face broke into a massive goofy grin, and she no longer cared what she looked like. "I mean, that's quite cute."

"I'm not fucking cute," he growled.

"Oh, but you are!" Scarlett pinched his arm, making him twist away from her hand.

"That's not the response I was looking for, to be honest." There was a trace of hurt in his voice.

Scarlett pulled him back to her and looked up, the smile leaving her face.

"I love you too." It felt weird for her to say the words out loud.

She'd only ever said them to Jason, and after a while, it felt like they had lost all meaning. But with Edward ... with Edward, it felt like everything.

He was *everything*.

Well, almost. She still had a lot about her future to consider.

He interrupted her thoughts. "You look beautiful, by the way."

All she could see was his smile, full of mischief – that delicious smile that made her insides go soft.

She wasn't sure she agreed with him, especially

considering the state she'd been in just moments before, but she wasn't foolish enough to check her reflection in the mirror.

"This dress is something," he said, tracing his fingers down the deep neckline, exposing the swell of her breast. She did agree with that. Its beautiful and clever design was intended to be inviting, but not so much that it looked cheap.

His fingers caressed her nipples, making her take a sharp intake of breath. "The material is insanely soft."

"It's silk, apparently," she breathed.

"Nice."

"You're pretty dashing in the whole Scottish laird get-up you've got going on too." She could feel his smile against her neck as he bent down to kiss beneath her left ear.

"Thanks. And no, it's not just the sex. But you've got to admit it's pretty damn good?" He continued to trace the sensitive skin on her neck with his mouth.

"It's not bad." Scarlett shrugged, a smile playing on her lips. "I can take it or leave it, really."

"Really?" He drew back to look at her and Scarlett laughed at his frown.

"Is it true what they say about Scots and their kilts?" Scarlett cocked her head in question.

Edward relaxed, clearly putting his ego back in check.

"Why don't you see for yourself?" Edward cupped her backside, squeezing hard enough to make Scarlett squirm against him.

With a coy smile, she reached below the front of his kilt and inhaled sharply for effect when she felt his nakedness beneath.

"Interesting," she said, watching as his mouth parted and he let out a soft groan. She moved her hand further inside to take hold of his hardness. "And always very impressive."

He closed his eyes and released another low growl. "If you want to make this wedding, you'd best stop that, or we're not leaving this room for a good couple of hours."

"I don't actually like weddings that much." Scarlett smiled and shrugged again. Edward gathered the back of her dress with his fingers, exposing her thighs, then slid his hand inside her panties to feel how wet she was.

"This never gets old for me," he breathed into her ear as her head fell back at the impact of his fingers inside her. "You drive me wild."

"I hadn't noticed ... but you do have an awful lot of clothing on ... and I won't lie, this fabric is quite itchy!"

Edward laughed. "Aye, I get what you're saying."

"May I?" Scarlett made to remove his jacket.

Edward nodded, and Scarlett proceeded to undress him.

First, she carefully removed his jacket, which she placed over the chair next to her bed. Next, she took hold of his wrists to take off his cufflinks and, after placing them on her dresser, she moved on to the buttons of his shirt.

All the while, Edward watched her intently, moving and adjusting himself to allow her to slowly remove each piece of clothing. She enjoyed taking her time, running her hand over the back of his exposed shoulders and kissing his biceps as she pulled the sleeves from his arms.

His body looked and felt so good. She marvelled at his toned torso as he stood shirtless with nothing but his kilt, socks, and shoes on. She was half tempted to leave them all on. It was all a bit *Outlander*-esque.

Instead, though, she lowered herself onto her knees, removing his belt, the sporran, and, after a few moments of fiddling around, figured out how to unravel his kilt. She leaned back to admire him as he stood proud and rigid in front of her, at which point she couldn't resist taking him in her mouth, making him draw in a sharp breath through his teeth.

"Holy fuck, Scarlett," he growled at her. "That's too good." He grabbed her head to slow her pace. "I want to make it last."

His eyes, flooded with want, locked onto hers as she looked up at him, doing her best to relax to accommodate all of him, which she could see was pushing him to the edge of his control.

"Enough!" he said sharply, pushing one last time deep inside her mouth before withdrawing. Groaning, he pulled her up to standing and kissed her deeply, pulling her close into him.

She could feel his cock straining against her through her silk dress, and she briefly wondered if it would dry-clean okay, but as his hands began moving across her breasts, finding her nipples again, she stopped caring.

"You forgot about the Sgian-Dubh." Edward smiled against her lips.

"I'm sorry, the what?"

Edward laughed loudly from his belly – a sound Scarlett delighted in.

"The knife …" he told her gently.

Scarlett looked down and laughed. "Oops, sorry! Didn't realise you were carrying!"

Edward kicked off his shoes, pulled off his socks, and wasted no time in casting the items aside.

Pulling her towards the bed, with one quick swoop, he cleared the bags and clothes from the mattress onto the floor.

"I'll help you clear that up later." He smiled, throwing Scarlett on top of the bed, and she squealed at the impact of his forcefulness. She watched him as he walked over to close and lock her bedroom door.

"I've learned the hard way. Always lock the door." He winked at her as he returned to the bed, kissing her like only he could.

He might not be everything, but he comes pretty damn close!

CHAPTER 40

Edward wanted to savour her. For the first time since their night in Edinburgh together, they weren't hiding from anyone and were in no rush to be anywhere.

His hands slid over the silk dress covering her body. Taking his time, he gathered the material and slowly pulled it over her head.

He was on his knees, towering above her, not taking his eyes from the sight of her semi-naked body as he moved on to drag her knickers down over her hips and legs, and with a slight tilt at the corner of his mouth, he carelessly threw them across the room. The curves and softness of her made him ache everywhere, and not just in his cock, which, to be fair, was straining and at this point begging to be inside her.

Lowering himself, he kissed her again, to which she responded, as she always did, everything about her so warm, open, and vulnerable.

She's so insanely fucking hot.

"I really need to be inside you," he said, his voice low and ragged. He needed her permission, despite the knowledge he already had it, but yet ... he still needed and wanted her to give it.

She smiled and reached down, slowly guiding him towards her wet entrance, using her free hand to pull his hips closer to her, until the anticipation was too much, and he pushed deep inside her, making them both cry out with relief. Edward was pretty certain that the world could have ended and he wouldn't have noticed.

AS THEY LAY with their limbs tangled and breathing uneven, Edward pulled her close to him.

"That was epically good," he whispered into her hair, kissing her head.

Scarlett nodded, still unable to speak, and he could feel her heart pounding against his ribcage. He released her for a moment to pull up the duvet gathered at the bottom of the bed and looked down at her. Her wild hair splayed out behind her, her eye makeup smudged, and her mouth slightly parted.

She was watching him, and at that moment he'd never found anyone as sexy in his entire life. Edward didn't want to ruin the moment, but he needed to know. He had to know what had happened.

"What did he do, Scarlett?"

Her gentle eyes darkened, replaced by pain, and he instantly regretted his question, somehow managing to control the anger still festering inside him towards his brother. If Leonard knew what was good for him, he would leave first thing in the morning and never darken his door again, because Edward wasn't sure he'd be able to keep control of his temper if he was to see him again and couldn't imagine that ever changing or simmering down, not even in time.

"You don't need to tell me, but I would like to know." He stroked her cheek, which was reddening and becoming hot.

Scarlett looked away, but he gently turned her face back to his. "I'm not mad at you. I know this wasn't anything you did, but I need to know what he did.

Please?" he asked her, his voice as soft as he could manage.

She sighed and swallowed. "I feel foolish ... and angry. I knew what he could be like, but I never expected him to – I was so hurt and upset, I didn't pay any attention when he led me into the room and locked the door behind us. Hadn't even noticed he had." She swallowed again. "He was just so detached, and I don't think it was even about me. It was more about him and you, and everything you had and he didn't. Then he kissed me and tried to ... For a moment I didn't think he'd stop, and I asked him to, but then ... but he *did* stop, and I told him he was out of order. He apologised and then let me leave."

A violent storm brewed in his chest, so he took a careful moment to calm himself before responding. "What do you mean he *let* you? Was he stopping you from leaving? Did he hurt you?" Edward's rage was eating him up inside, to the point he wanted to roar and unleash hell on his brother.

But he couldn't. He could see Scarlett was finding this difficult to talk about, so pulling it together and gathering all his efforts, he swallowed it down, keeping his breathing and temper under control. "Scarlett, did he force himself on you?"

Tears filled her eyes, but she shook her head. "Only for a moment. I got out of his grip and got away before he could ... Like I said, he then apologised, and I left."

He looked at her for a long moment and then kissed her. He felt tears pricking at his own eyes. "I'm so sorry. You did not deserve that. Any of it."

As if sensing his pain, she took hold of his face and kissed him back.

Barely removing her lips from his, she told him, "I took care of myself, okay, I'm not some damsel in distress. There was a moment I felt trapped and vulnerable, but your sad little brother wasn't winning whatever sick game he was playing. I made sure of that."

Edward was choking on his own emotions, but nodded, determined not to cry, or at least let her see. Instead, he rested his head on her chest whilst she stroked his hair until he pulled himself together.

"I might just stay here until they leave, or I might get done for murder."

Scarlett laughed.

"I'm serious!" He was.

"I'm aware – that was a nervous laugh!" Scarlett pulled him closer to her.

Edward kissed her before moving onto his side, positioning his arm under his head and stroking the skin between her breasts, watching them rise with her now steady breaths.

"He will never get another opportunity to get anywhere near you," he told her, in almost a whisper.

"I know," she said.

He released a sigh. "I promise."

"I know," she said again.

After a long pause, he cleared his throat with dramatic effect. "So, what happens now?" he asked, looking across at Scarlett, who barked a laugh in response.

"What?" He shrugged in feigned innocence.

She smiled in response. "Dunno, really. I should probably clear up the mess on my floor and put my stuff back in my drawers."

"And then?"

"Sleep."

"And then?"

Scarlett laughed. "And then we can maybe go on a date, like *normal* people."

He smiled at the dig. "*Normal* people, huh?"

She nodded. "You know, I'll get dressed up. You'll pick me up, looking all hot and dapper, and we'll go somewhere nice. We'll eat and talk about normal stuff. Like favourite cereal habits. Music. Holidays. You know, like *normal* people."

Edward leaned over and kissed her again. "You realise there's absolutely nothing *normal* about you?"

Scarlett smiled.

He continued, "But okay, we will *date*. Like normal people."

"I think that would be a good start. I'd like that." Her contented smile made his heart crack open.

"Then I will make it so." He pulled her on top of him, her eyes widening as she felt his hardness press against her. "In the meantime, though, before you come up with any crazy rules about first dates …"

But she was already ahead of him, taking hold of his cock and lowering herself onto him, moaning softly as she did so. "Zero crazy rules."

"I find these terms acceptable," he said, his breath ragged, pushing deeper inside her.

CHAPTER 41

Six months later

ANDRZEJ STRAIGHTENED THE canvas and took a step back to take a last look.

"I think this is good, yes?" He looked across at Scarlett, who was standing with her hands on her hips, beaming from ear to ear.

"It's perfect. It's all perfect!" Scarlett turned and hugged him tightly.

Andrzej laughed. "You're welcome, but careful you don't mess up your hair and makeup! I saw firsthand how much time was spent on that!"

Scarlett stepped back and carefully touched her updo. "Does it still look okay?"

"You look wonderful, not a strand out of place." Andrzej smiled down kindly at her. "What time do your guests arrive?"

"Not for ages, but I've sent plenty of clear directions as well as instructions for the key safe, so there won't be any issues with their check-in."

"How long are they staying for?"

"Just four days for a long weekend."

Andrzej nodded with approval. "You have done a good job here, Scarlett. You should be very proud."

Scarlett beamed again. "Thanks. Couldn't have done it without you and Mum. The garden looks spectacular!"

They stood for a moment to take in all their combined efforts. The open-plan kitchen and lounge were

A NEW Hope IN THE HIGHLANDS

compact, but with the freshly plastered walls in the lounge, white paint, and cleaned exposed brick in the kitchen, it felt light and airy. The kitchen was sleek and practical, fitted with refurbished light oak units and worktops, with antique brass knobs and handles that she and Edward had found at a clearance sale at a nearby estate being sold off for redevelopment.

The first floor contained two small double bedrooms, newly plastered and painted like the downstairs rooms, with exposed ceiling beams. The master bedroom had a beautiful brass bed they'd also sourced from the clearance sale, and she'd placed two single beds in the second bedroom. They'd also done a full refurb of the bathrooms in all three cottages, with Andrzej and Edward fitting each one with a beautiful three-piece suite, including freestanding baths.

Feeling content, Scarlett inhaled the scent of fresh herbs and flowers that she'd placed on the windowsills, gathered from the garden, and combined with the faint smell of the fresh bread she'd collected from Mrs Wilson's kitchen that morning, the whole place smelled and looked like a dreamlike country escape – which was exactly what she'd been busy marketing across social media these past few months.

When Edward had first shown her the three identical cottages on the edge of the estate, they were empty and barely habitable. Nonetheless, she'd instantly fallen in love with them, convinced that the bones were there and they were full of potential, so, with some of her divorce money, she bought them from him, converting them into three beautiful little holiday lets.

The money had taken its time to come through but as it turned out, during Jason's time at Haddon House, somewhere between being sat amongst the throngs of random wedding guests and watching his mother fawn over a rich American for an entire evening, he'd realised that he was never getting Scarlett back. Desperate to leave, he didn't even try to find her and press her for the ring, and wasting little time, he returned home, solemn and very single. A couple of weeks later, she received an email from him:

Dearest Scarlett,

There are so many things I want to say to you, but where to even start? I have acted and behaved appallingly and have spent far too many years taking you for granted. I've been selfish in chasing my dreams, expecting your constant love and support, whilst disregarding all of yours – and worse still, I betrayed you past the point of ever expecting your forgiveness. I'd love to be able to provide reasons for my infidelity, but honestly, they're all inadequate and if I were to be entirely truthful, an uncomfortable reflection of my shallow desires.

I'm ashamed to say, ultimately, I did it because I could. Fame has never and probably will never suit me, not with my ego, something I feel at my age probably won't ever change. I imagine it makes no difference to you now, but I did love you—from the first moment I saw you in that lecture hall during my visit to the uni, watching you debate gender inequality in literary fiction. That feisty redhead will live in my heart forever.

I'd be lying if I said I wasn't immensely jealous of your Scottish bloke, because you haven't looked at me the way you looked at him for several years, that's if you ever did, which I've come to realise over the last couple of weeks is entirely my own fault. I built houses and walls around you, giving you an existence, but little to no sun to flourish under.

Ha – look at me becoming all poetic and soft in my old age!

In all seriousness, though, I am deeply sorry for everything. I will, of course, take care of the divorce and my solicitor will soon be in touch with a financial proposal so you are taken care of. Judging by your current abode, your new fellow doesn't seem too strapped for cash, but it's beside the point. You've been by my side at every turn, and you deserve to be compensated appropriately so you never need to feel trapped or stuck again, especially if it doesn't happen to work out with him.

He's a bit of an intimidating character, isn't he? I can't say it was a particularly comfortable conversation after everyone else left and only us two men remained. He seems to be very protective of you though, and appears to care about you, and says he wants to look after you. Something he was quite forthright in saying I'd failed to do. Not that you need or want that, but you deserve it. And he's right, of course, I have been a total shit; I know that, but I also mean it. You deserve the world, Scarlett Hope.

There's not much more I can say about it all, other than take care, my darling, and I hope you find the happiness you deserve.

All my love, always.

Jason xx

P.S. Mother is a bit distracted by that American guy at the moment, all very scandalous. But when you get the chance, if you could courier that ring down, as per your man's suggestion, it would be greatly appreciated.

Scarlett felt little emotion reading the email, perhaps only some sadness and love for that feisty young redhead who had dreams bigger than the moon, who was dazzled and starstruck by a charming and good-looking author who whisked her away to a life full of excitement and literary promise.

She wasn't heartless, also feeling a pinch of pity for Jason. His moment of touching reflection was all very well, but she knew him well enough to realise that he would quickly snap out of his malaise when the next piece of hot ass, amazed by his authorly talent and success, fluttered her pretty eyelashes at him. Still, she wished him well, feeling no anger or bitterness towards him.

When she'd looked across at Edward on the other end of his long leather sofa, their legs tangled, she'd smiled at his scruffy hair, furrowed brow, and silently moving lips as he lay engrossed reading some tome of a book. The estate's two new labrador puppies, Daisy and Duke, slept on the floor, gently snoring beside them. In that moment, her heart felt full to bursting and she couldn't have been more content. Nothing in the world would make her miss her old life. She'd returned her attention to her laptop and briefly touched Edward's hand, which was stroking her calf. She didn't reply to Jason. There was nothing left to say.

Andrzej brought her back to the present.

"We must go now before we both get in trouble for making you late!"

"Yes, let's go! Christ, is that the time? I need to get dressed!" Scarlett screeched.

"Indeed, let's go." Andrzej left the cottage, car keys in hand.

Scarlett took one last look, smiled, and followed him, locking the door behind her.

APPROACHING THE DOORS of the small church, both women appeared hesitant, nervous energy radiating between them. It was a glorious early summer's afternoon, not a cloud to be seen, which was unusual for Scotland in Scarlett's opinion – even though she was slowly acclimatising to its moody and changeable weather; not dissimilar to Edward's disposition, she often thought.

"Right, then." June smiled at Scarlett, who was still feeling and probably looking a bit like a flight risk – she didn't do well with a crowd's attention on her, and everyone involved knew this. "Shall we get this bit over and done with, so we can get to the fun bit of alcohol and food?"

Scarlett laughed. "I suppose, when you put it like that."

June kissed her cheek. "You look beautiful."

"Thank you. So do you." Scarlett smiled and took a deep breath.

"Come on then, he'll be getting restless in there." June squeezed her daughter's hand as they linked arms and entered the church.

Scarlett couldn't focus on any of the faces that turned to look at them. Instead, she searched for, found, and locked onto the deep blue eyes of the man standing and waiting for her – eyes that now felt like home. A smile twitched at the corner of his mouth, which made her relax. He was there, and she had the comforting feeling that he always would be.

Her mother squeezed her hand again when they reached the top of the aisle and Scarlett smiled warmly at her. June mouthed the words *thank you* as she handed Scarlett her bouquet, turning her attention to Andrzej, who took June's hand and kissed it. Scarlett's heart felt full to bursting with pride and happiness for them both as she moved across to stand beside Edward, who nudged her and winked.

"Well done," he whispered, so only she could hear.

Her mother and Andrzej stood beaming at each other throughout the entire service, and Scarlett was pretty sure the two of them were oblivious to everyone else in the church, even when they all cheered as the vicar finally said, "And now you may kiss the bride." Something Andrzej wasted no time in doing.

CHAPTER 42

LILY AND JAMES had been dancing the night away, something that Edward was no longer violently opposed to. He'd been so wrapped up in his own and Leonard's drama that his daughter's romance with James had completely gone over his head. That was until the day Lily walked into his office, her chin lifted, with the air of stubbornness he was fully aware she had inherited from him.

"Dad, I have something to tell you."

Edward had looked up and put down his pen, leaning back into his chair and clasping his hands together.

"Don't try to do the whole Al Pacino Godfather look – it doesn't work on me."

"I have no idea what you're referring to. This is how I look whenever I'm working and someone barges into my office unannounced."

Steely blue eyes glared at him.

"What is it?" he finally said, bored with the stare-off.

"James and I are in a relationship."

"James who?"

"James McNeil."

"The butcher's vegan son?"

"What does veganism have to do with anything?"

"It doesn't, but you're not going out with him."

"Excuse me?"

"I don't care if he's vegan, a carnivore, or only eats sardines. You're not seeing him. And what do you mean you're in a relationship with him? You don't even know him."

"Shows how much attention you pay to my life. We've been seeing each other for months."

"Over my dead body."

"You've been breathing since it started and, as far as I can see, still are."

Edward could feel his face reddening. She was a cheeky wee shit. "Lily, you are starting uni next year. You won't have time for a relationship. And I can tell you right now, you're not giving up your education for a boy from the fucking village!"

"I'm not giving anything up, especially not him. I can have both. James is extremely supportive of me and my plans. We'll find a way to make it work."

Lily's nostrils were flaring, and her fists were clenched, ready for a fight. The sight almost made him laugh; she really was a miniature version of him.

He remained silent for a long time, watching his daughter, who he remembered appearing the exact same way when she was ten, with plaited hair, raging and pouting when he'd refused to buy her a horse.

"Fine," he finally said. "You know best, but I won't have you fucking up med school, understood?"

Lily's eyes widened in surprise. "That's it?"

"What do you mean?" Edward picked up his pen to continue with his work.

"It's fine?"

Edward shrugged. "You're eighteen, Lily, what am I going to do? Lock you in your room?"

Lily rolled her eyes.

"I expected more drama, a bit of shouting and screaming, perhaps."

"You want me to shout at you?"

"Well, not exactly."

"So, what do you want?"

Lily huffed. "Nothing, I suppose."

"Suppose you'd best start inviting him for dinner then, rather than him serving it."

"He's not worked here for ages, Dad."

"You know what I mean. Bring him tomorrow, let Mrs Wilson know. Is that everything?"

Lily was frowning, obviously still unconvinced he was making it this easy for her, but then she shrugged. "Fine."

"Fine," he repeated as she turned to leave.

"She's made you soft, old man," she said as she gave him a backwards wave.

"Cheeky little fucker!" He'd shaken his head at her disappearing figure down the hallway.

Now, looking at them laughing and dancing, he could admit he'd been wrong. It turned out that James was a good kid and genuinely only wanted good things for his daughter, even refusing to visit her when she was running late on assignments, much to her annoyance. But despite her fiery wrath, he'd stick to his guns, something Edward respected, even admired. James had even started helping around the estate. Andrzej had taken him on to work alongside him on Scarlett's cottages, and Edward was now supporting him in obtaining his carpentry and joinery qualifications at college. It was all very *keeping it in the family*, but Edward liked to reward hard work, and despite James's relationship with Lily, he was a great worker and fast learner, something he could always do with more of.

"Excuse me, I believe you still owe me a dance?" Scarlett snuck up behind him.

He turned to face her and smiled. She had meticulously pinned and tamed her hair that morning, but as the evening progressed, curls escaped. Although she'd looked stunning earlier, he preferred her natural, chaotic state.

"I believe you are correct." He leaned down to kiss her. "But I'm pretty sure I just heard the lyrics *don't embarrass me motherfucker*!"

"It's Sabrina Carpenter – *Please Please Please*."

"You don't need to beg." He winked and took hold of her, swinging her onto the dance floor and making her squeal.

Lily grinned and winked at him.

"I think my daughter approves of me being with you."

Scarlett smiled as he spun her away and pulled her back in close to him again.

"Why's that?"

Edward shrugged. "Probably because I'm less of a miserable fucker around you."

He kept her close as they danced.

"I'll take that as a compliment."

"You should." He bent down and kissed her gently. "You know, weddings are starting to grow on me."

"This one is definitely an improvement on the last one."

"You know, the house could do with a Lady. Do you know anyone you could recommend? Asking for a friend."

Scarlett laughed. "Hmm, I'll think on it and let you know."

Edward slowed to a stop, his voice serious suddenly. "I'd like you to move in with me. Properly."

Scarlett looked at him and he watched as conflicted emotions crossed her face. She stayed most nights anyway, but all her things remained in the flat she still shared with Andrzej and her mother.

"It's not like I don't have the space." He looked around the hall to make his point and was relieved when she smiled.

"What, even to store all my odd socks you hate?"

"I'll even unpair them for you if you like."

"Wow, that's some big game you're talking there!" Scarlett laughed.

He bent down and kissed her again, and she leaned into him, the way she always did, making him feel as if he was everything she'd ever want or need in this world.

"So, you want me to move in?"

"Aye."

"Into your big house?"

"Aye."

"Into your *rooms*?"

"Aye."

"And sleep in your bed – all the time?"

He nodded and this time she kissed him, deeply, with more tenderness than anyone had ever shown him before, making the rest of the world melt into the background.

Fuck, aye.

The End

The Story Begins Here ...

But it's only just getting started.

Craving more Heat, Heart, and Highland Charm?

Before there was Haddon House ... there were the early days.

Scarlett Hope wasn't looking for love when bestselling author Jason Shrewsbury walked into her final-year seminar – but his invitation to dinner sets off a chain of events she never could have predicted.

In a story of first flings, missed chances, and the friendship that changed everything, *The Salad Days* explores the choices we make at the cusp of adulthood ... and the ones we carry with us.

A spicy, emotionally charged prequel to **A New Hope in the Highlands.**

Scarlett and Edward's story continues in *Too Much to Hope For* – coming soon!

Sign up as an RDB Reader to download your free copy of *The Salad Days* – and be the first to know when *Too Much to Hope For* is on its way.

☞ www.racheldebrave.com

Rachel Debrave

Connect, chat and follow the *beautiful* chaos in all the usual places:

Facebook: @racheldebraveauthor
Instagram: @racheldebrave
Threads: @racheldebrave
BlueSky: @rdbauthor.bsky.social

Printed in Dunstable, United Kingdom